P9-BZQ-631

A DEATH IN LIVE OAK

ALSO BY JAMES GRIPPANDO

*Most Dangerous Place**
*Gone Again**
Cash Landing
Cane and Abe
*Black Horizon**
*Blood Money**
Need You Now
*Afraid of the Dark**
Money to Burn
Intent to Kill
*Born to Run**
*Last Call**
Lying with Strangers
*When Darkness Falls**
*Got the Look**
*Hear No Evil**
*Last to Die**
*Beyond Suspicion**
A King's Ransom
Under Cover of Darkness
Found Money
The Abduction
The Informant
*The Pardon**

OTHER FICTION

The Penny Jumper
Leapholes

*A JACK SWYTECK NOVEL

A DEATH IN LIVE OAK

A JACK SWYTECK NOVEL

JAMES GRIPPANDO

HARPER
An Imprint of HarperCollins*Publishers*

This is a work of fiction. Names, characters, places, and incidents are products of the author's imagination or are used fictitiously and are not to be construed as real. Any resemblance to actual events, locales, organizations, or persons, living or dead, is entirely coincidental.

HarperCollins books may be purchased for educational, business, or sales promotional use. For information, please email the Special Markets Department at SPsales@harpercollins.com.

FIRST EDITION

Library of Congress Cataloging-in-Publication Data
Grippando, James.
A death in Live Oak / James Grippando.
p. cm.
ISBN 978-0-06-265780-0
1. Swyteck, Jack (Fictitious character)—Fiction. 2. Legal stories. 3. Suspense fiction.
PS3557.R534 D43 2018
813'.54—dc23 2017022885

18 19 20 21 22 LSC 10 9 8 7 6 5 4 3 2 1

For Tiffany

A DEATH IN LIVE OAK

PROLOGUE

JANUARY 2, 1944

Nothing changed.

The first Sunday service of the new year ended in song, as always.

Let Jesus lead you
Let Him lead you
Let Jesus lead you
All the way.

Gospel music was the heart and soul of Mission Baptist Church of Live Oak. Not another house of worship in Suwannee County had a more enthusiastic choir and congregation. From opening procession to final hymn, Sunday morn at Mission Baptist was ninety minutes of inspired vocals, hand clapping, and *alleluia*s, with enough sermon and scripture to give old-timers a breather and youngsters the love of God.

All the way from
Earth to heaven
Let Jesus lead you
All the way.

Lula Howard loved to sing. Her fifteen-year-old son shared her passion, which was no surprise. Willie James was her only child.

Lula had poured herself into raising him right, even singing gospel to him in utero, starting with his first kick. He was the strongest tenor in his sophomore class—in *both* sophomore classes, some boasted; though, admittedly, neither Willie James nor anyone else at Frederick Douglass High School had ever heard the singing voice of any student across the street at the whites-only Suwannee High.

"That'll do," said Lula's husband, glancing in the rearview mirror. James Howard was behind the wheel of an old Buick that was "new" to him. Willie James was on the passenger side, seated behind his mother, where he'd been singing the same traditional gospel hymn since leaving the church parking lot.

"Oh, let the boy be," said Lula.

"Like a broken record back there," said James, grumbling. "At his age he could at least throw in a little Dixie Hummingbirds or Golden Gate Quartet every now and then."

Lula smiled and caught his eye. "He's a good boy, James. Thank the Lord for that."

There was no argument. Lula was right. Willie James had a hard-to-explain quality that, in the eyes of friends and relatives, would somehow propel him past the grim life of smothered dreams and limited opportunity. Even James had seemed to come around in the last few months and believe in the possibilities. Lula's formal education had taken her only through the sixth grade. James had even less. Twenty-plus years in Florida logging—an industry built on forced labor and peonage—had left James jaded, but suddenly the Howards were the proud parents of the only black teenager in Live Oak to land a job at the white-owned dime store. With her husband off to war, Mrs. Dott needed extra help. Not that a boy his color would have dared to step up to the counter, plop down his dime, and reach into the canisters for a fistful of Dubble Bubble, root-beer barrels, and other "penny candy." As a dutiful employee, however, Willie James had earned the manager's trust, working before and after school that autumn. Mrs. Dott made him full-time over Christmas break. Main Street shops were closed on Sundays, so Willie James had the day off. His father had no such reprieve.

"What time will you be coming home tonight, James?" asked Lula.

"Huh?"

James was a good listener, as far as husbands went, but his hearing had slipped—a hazard of working at a sawmill.

"Will you be home for supper?" Lula asked in a slightly louder voice.

"Dunno," he said. The mill was shorthanded with men off to war. Second shift on Sunday was supposed to be a half day, but a three-month timber harvest of the Mattair Springs tract had been keeping crews busy well into the evening, seven days a week.

"I'll pack you something," said Lula.

The drive continued to the outskirts of town, beyond the old railroad junction that dated back to the Civil War, where settlers and rail workers would rest in the shade of a massive oak—which, the story goes, is how Live Oak got its name. A live oak is never leafless, canopied year-round. Lula knew of no prettier sight than a centuries-old pillar of strength rising from a Florida pasture, its mighty limbs stretching out above the slash pines, palmettos, and white-sand roads.

James was alone in his thoughts, and Willie James was enjoying the breeze on his face with the window down. Lula checked her pompadour hat in the side-view mirror, and then her gaze drifted across the old crack in the windshield. It started on the passenger's side at the upper right corner, angled downward, then made a wide left turn in the shape of a "C" before dropping off sharply and disappearing into the dashboard. "Kinda like the Suwannee," Willie James had once remarked, and Lula had listened in awe as her then eleven-year-old son proceeded to explain the circuitous path of the legendary river, which originates in the Okefenokee Swamp of south-central Georgia and hooks past Live Oak on its ceaseless journey to the Gulf of Mexico. Lula had never thought that big. The river, her dreams, and everything she'd ever known began and ended in Live Oak, where she was born and raised.

"Sorry about that," said James, as the car bounced across a pothole. They'd reached the end of the highway. Pavement gave way to gravel, until finally the road became a one-lane path of white sand covered with fallen pine needles, which at least kept some of the dust down. The Howard residence was like all the others in the area, a two-bedroom frame house that predated the Great Depression. The clapboard siding needed a good whitewashing, for which Lula had been saving pennies in a jar since moving in.

James pulled up outside the gate, where the ground scrub had been flattened into a defined parking space. The engine continued to sputter even after he pulled the key from the ignition, as if the ten-year-old Buick had a mind of its own. They climbed out when the car settled, but the tailpipe emitted one last gasp as they started toward the house. North-central Florida had been dry and unseasonably warm since Christmas, and Willie James removed his suit jacket and tie before reaching the front door. James led the way inside and walked straight to the bedroom to change into his work coveralls. Lula went to the kitchen to pack her husband's lunch and, just in case, his supper.

"Bye, Mama," said Willie James. He'd snuck up behind Lula at the counter, and as soon as she turned, he planted a quick kiss on her cheek.

"Where you headed?"

"Just out back. Gonna teach Mugsy a few tricks." Mugsy was a stray mutt that had followed Willie James home from the dime store.

Lula cut an extra slice of meat loaf on the sandwich board. "Take this. He'll learn faster."

"Thanks, Mama," he said, and Willie James went quickly out the back door.

Lula woke on the couch. The radio hissed from across the living room. She'd been listening to gospel music but dozed off, and the dial had drifted between stations.

Lula switched off the radio and checked the clock on the end table: five minutes past twelve. The sun was streaking through the open window, floating dust mites aglow, as if to confirm that it was 12:05 *p.m.*, not a.m., and that Lula hadn't slept away the entire day. It would be hours before James returned from the sawmill. She sensed that she was still alone in the house, but she called her son's name nonetheless.

"Willie James?"

It was always *Willie James*—never just Willie, not even to his friends—and he always answered his mother if he was within earshot. She waited, but there was no reply.

A car door slammed outside the house, startling Lula. She walked to the window, pulled the curtain to one side, and watched. Three white men were standing beside a sedan, talking. One stepped away and started toward the house. The other two waited at the gate. The lead man came to the screen door and knocked hard—much harder than necessary. Lula collected herself and went to the door.

"Yes, sir?" she asked through the screen.

"Where is James?"

Lula had never seen his face before, but she didn't dare break Jim Crow etiquette and directly ask a white man who he was or what he was doing, even if he had just shown up on her front step unexpectedly. "James is not here."

"My name is Phillip Goff," he said with a measure of self-importance. "I need to find James."

"He's gone to work."

"Where's he working?"

"At the Bond-Howell Lumber Company."

"Where is Willie James?"

Lula hesitated, her concern growing. "I don't know."

"I think you *do* know," said Goff, his tone accusatory, if not threatening.

"I—I fell asleep after church. He was—"

Lula stopped, having heard the back door open. A call came from the kitchen.

"Mama?"

She glanced at Goff, who seemed perversely pleased to see Willie James enter the living room. A horrible feeling came over Lula, strong enough to make her wish that just this once her son had wandered off without telling his mother where he was headed—someplace no one could find him.

"I saw the car pull up," said Willie James. He went to his mother and stood beside her. "Everything all right?"

Goff yanked open the screen door, stepped inside, and grabbed Willie James by the collar. "You're coming with me, boy."

Lula shrieked. "Why? What for?"

Goff jerked Willie James forward, forcing himself between Lula and her son.

Lula could barely speak. "What's this about? What has he done?"

A pistol suddenly appeared, and Lula was staring straight down the business end of the polished barrel. "He's coming with me," Goff said.

Lula stepped back, her heart pounding with fear. Goff pulled Willie outside, forced him down the front step, and marched him down the walkway toward the gate. Lula hurried after them, pleading.

"Why are you doing this? What has Willie James done?"

Goff ignored her and pushed through the front gate to the waiting car. The other men jumped into action. One opened the rear door and the other helped shove Willie James into the back seat.

"Mama!"

"Quiet!" Goff shouted, turning the pistol on Willie James.

Lula lunged for the door, but Goff knocked her to the ground.

"Please don't do this!" she said, climbing to her knees. "Sir, I'm begging you! Sir!"

Goff slid into the back seat beside Willie James and pulled the door shut. His accomplices jumped into the front seat. The engine roared, the rear tires spun, and Lula shielded her face from a spray of dirt, sand, and pine needles. She pushed herself up and gave chase through a cloud of dust, her arms pumping and lungs burning.

"Willie James!" she cried, the tears streaming down her face. Lula ran as fast and as far as she could, but the car got away from her. It continued beyond a hummock of oaks and disappeared from sight, the trail of dust evaporating into the clear blue sky.

At the end of the sandy road she fell to her knees, sobbing as she gasped for breath, wishing that her husband hadn't gone to the sawmill that Sunday, hating the town she was born in, and calling on her Lord and Savior to watch over Willie James.

OCTOBER

Seventy-Four Years Later

CHAPTER 1

The Suwannee River winds through the forested wetlands of north-central Florida like a tea-colored ribbon, its chilly waters connecting one small town to the next. Beneath it flows the watery underworld of the Florida aquifer, a limestone labyrinth of interconnecting caves and caverns that discharges billions of gallons of spring water every day. Feeder springs near Live Oak rise up through the riverbed and flow directly into the Suwannee—crystal-clear waters stained "black" by the tannins of vegetative decay. Countless other springs serve smaller rivers across the region, which eventually flow into the great Suwannee or its tributaries. The recreational king among the feeder springs is Ichetucknee. Tubing down the Ichetucknee—a long, lazy float in an inflatable inner tube—has been a veritable rite of passage for generations of students from the University of Florida in Gainesville, to the south, and Florida State University in Tallahassee, to the west.

"*Shee-it*, this water is cold!" shouted Percy Donovan. He was waist deep in the river. His girlfriend was afloat on an inner tube, and Percy was being a gentleman, guiding her away from the launch site so the current didn't carry her straight into the brush along the riverbank.

"It's not cold," said Shawna. "The guy at the tube rental said it's seventy-two degrees all year."

They'd met at UF, but Shawna was from Chicago. Percy was born and raised in Fort Lauderdale. "Seventy-two degrees puts enough ice in my veins to dunk on LeBron," said Percy.

Shawna laughed and splashed him, which sent Percy scurrying

back to shore like a skipping stone in reverse. His friend Kelso watched from the bank, nearly falling over in laughter.

"Such a pussy!"

It struck Percy as funny that the fraternity brother calling him "pussy" was the only one in the group wearing a wet suit. Kelso, too, was a *south* Floridian.

There was nothing unusual about fraternities and sororities teaming up for a day trip down the river on a Saturday morning—even in early October, when most of the country was raking leaves but Florida was still sweating. It was the first time, however, that the black Greek-letter organizations at UF and FSU—the "Divine Nine," as they were known—had coordinated such a trip. By eleven o'clock, more than sixty men and women were adrift in the lazy current. Some had "rafted up" into groups of six or eight to share conversation and laughter on the six-mile journey. A few couples broke off for an innocent kiss and a slightly less innocent breach of the "no skinny-dipping" rule. Every now and then, a shriek could be heard, followed by group laughter, as Kelso emerged from the black depths in his wet suit, upended an inner tube, and sent another bikini-clad student into the river for an involuntary swim.

"Kelso!" shouted Shawna, as she splashed to the surface. She was his third victim.

"Ha!" said Percy. "Who's cold now?"

Shawna climbed back into her inner tube. "Cold? You ain't seen *cold* till you seen tonight, Percy."

That drew a chorus of "ooohs" from friends.

The group followed the bend past the halfway point, and Percy was beginning to wish that they'd signed up for the ninety-minute float, not three hours. His butt was cold, the sunbaked rubber singed his skin every time he moved his leg, and holding on to an extra inner tube while Kelso swam off to play Loch Ness monster was getting tiresome. Of course there were the marine science and horticulture majors who could have stayed all day and then some, pointing out every natural wonder along the river. Tall cypress trees rose from the marsh, their limbs reaching out over the river, providing ample shade for those who wanted out of the sun. Near the mouth of springs, the unstained waters were so clear that rafters appeared to float on air above the sandy riverbed. Every now and then a young woman shrieked at the sight of a motionless alligator or a turtle sunning itself on the banks. It *was* beautiful, unlike anything Percy had seen growing up in South Florida, which wasn't "the South" at all.

A shrill scream suddenly jolted Percy from his oneness with nature.

What the hell?

It was very different from the playful screams Percy had heard earlier; this wasn't just another reptile sighting or sneak attack by Kelso. A couple of sorority sisters—the lead rafters who'd rounded the bend first—were in the water. Their inner tubes were floating farther downriver without them. Their arms flailed and legs kicked against the current as they frantically struggled to swim back to the group.

"Kelso, let's go!" said Percy, as he shoved the extra tube toward his friend. Then he jumped into the river, and side by side they swam with urgency, pushing their inner tubes ahead of them. Percy had never swum that fast in his life—with the current, it felt like the wind-aided record in the hundred-yard dash he'd set at Dillard High School. Percy arrived first, and Kelso was just a few seconds behind him.

"Grab on!" shouted Percy, and each woman draped an arm over the inner tube. Percy knew one of them from UF—Tomika. He held her, and Kelso grabbed the other, making sure they didn't slip away. They'd reached a sandbar in the middle of the river, so Percy planted his feet firmly and stopped the flotilla, allowing them time to catch their breath as the water rushed past them.

Tomika gasped, but she looked more frightened than exhausted.

"What happened?" asked Percy.

Three other rafters floated alongside them and stopped at the sandbar. Tomika glanced at them and then back at Percy. The fear in her eyes remained as she turned her head toward the riverbank and pointed.

"An alligator?" asked Kelso.

She shook her head and pointed again, her hand shaking. "In the forest."

The tide was low, so the overflow along the banks had receded. The tall, trim trunks of cypress trees rose from the glassy black water—hundreds of them, nature's version of a picket fence in front of a picket fence, making it hard to see daylight between the pencil-straight trees. Percy squinted and followed her finger to the point she was indicating. Beneath the cypress limbs, a shadowy figure hovered just above the swamp line.

"I think it's . . . human," said Tomika.

Percy and Kelso exchanged a worried glance.

"Wait here," said Percy, and he started swimming toward the bank. Kelso followed. The current fought them until they reached an eddy at the bend. The river was a different place at its flooded banks, where flowing spring water gave way to the stillness of swampland. Splashes of sunlight broke through the occasional opening in the leafy canopy, brightening the Spanish moss that hung from limbs like tattered old fishing nets. With the gentle sounds of moving water behind him, Percy could discern the aural signs of wildlife in the wetlands—the croak of bullfrogs, the screech of a hungry bird in flight, perhaps a heron or an osprey. Percy breathed heavier with each stoke toward the bank. The river became shallower, and even though the black-stained water remained transparent, a rich muck had replaced the sandy bed. Percy's knee grazed the bottom, which was more than enough to stir up years of decomposition and the sulfuric odor of the marsh.

"Dude, there could be gators here," said Kelso.

Percy was undeterred but not unaware. He pulled himself up onto a fallen cypress tree, careful not to slip, as the smooth trunk had lost its bark to the river's rising and falling tides. He gazed into the forest and did a double take.

Something *was* suspended from a tree limb. And Tomika was right: it *did* appear human.

Percy took a few more steps along the fallen tree and stopped, barely able to trust his eyes. It was a man. A black man. Hanging at the end of a taut rope. With a noose around his neck.

An anger and sickness rose inside Percy, even more intense than his feelings upon seeing for the first time those chilling old photographs from the days of Jim Crow. It wasn't exactly like those black-and-white images, however, in which the bare feet of a black man hung in perfect vertical alignment with the victim's eerily elongated frame. This body was contorted, the man's ankles and wrists bound together behind his back. He'd been hog-tied.

"What the fuck?" said Kelso. He was a few steps behind Percy, having climbed onto the same fallen tree.

Percy's heart pounded. Part of him wanted to turn back, but he put one foot in front of the other, stepping deeper into the swamp, all the way to the upturned roots of the fallen cypress tree, where he froze. Percy recognized the man.

"It's Jamal Cousin."

"Who?" asked Kelso. He was right behind Percy.

"Alpha president," said Percy.

Percy and Kelso were Kappas, and the only fraternity higher in the Divine Nine pecking order was the Alpha house. Jamal had been a conspicuous "no show" for the tubing trip—but no one had suspected *this*.

"Holy shit."

"Yeah," Percy said in disbelief. A hog-tied body was definitely no suicide. "Jamal's been *lynched*."

CHAPTER 2

On that steamy Saturday afternoon at Florida Field—"the Swamp"—ninety thousand screaming fans cheered the Florida Gators to a 17–14 victory over the Rebels of Ole Miss. Fraternity Row had reason to party, even if that team from Tuscaloosa was still No. 1 in the nation.

"Chug! Chug! Chug! Chug!"

It was a chant heard all over Gainesville, as Natty Light flowed through beer bongs like chilly water through Suwannee Springs.

Around midnight the postgame celebration was popping at Theta Pi Omega, the premier fraternity on the UF campus. Theta had over a hundred active brothers, sixty of whom lived in the two-story antebellum-style house. Most were "legacies," their fathers and grandfathers having pledged before them. Not one was black.

"Party central" at the Theta house was the main, oversize room on the ground floor, which was packed with students gripping red Solo cups, a few holding one in each hand. Spotify supplied the latest hits at deafening levels. Some students danced, mostly groups of drunk girls entertaining drunker frat boys. The honor of administering the beer bong went to whoever had just turned twenty-one, so long as she looked good in a string bikini and stiletto heels. There was serious action at the beer-pong table, not to be confused with the beer bong, which in turn was nothing compared to the "bong within a bong," an ingenious device that was kept upstairs for anyone who liked to drink beer and smoke pot in one seamless, mind-blowing hit.

Mark Towson stepped away from his friends, walked around the rowdy crowd at the beer pong table, and introduced himself to the blonde who'd caught his eye from across the room.

"I'm Mark," he said, loud enough to be heard over the music.

"Lisa," she shouted back.

He signaled toward the hallway, and she followed him to a smaller room where they could hear each other talk, so long as they didn't mind the couple making out on the couch.

"Can I get you something to drink?"

"Um, sure," she said.

Mark shook his head. "Bad girl."

"Huh?"

"Never—*never*—let someone get a drink for you. Get your own drink, preferably in a can that you opened yourself."

"Uh . . . okay."

"Freshman, right?"

She seemed a bit deflated. "How'd you know?"

"Lucky guess. And I saw you ditch the bunny ears in the bushes before coming through the front door. Always double-check when an upperclassman invites you to a 'costume' party."

She smiled. "You're just a fountain of good advice, aren't you?"

"You don't get to be Theta president if you haven't seen it all."

"Ah," she said, as if her eyes had suddenly been opened. "Should I start humming 'Hail to the Chief,' Mr. President?"

"I prefer 'Fanfare for the Common Man.'"

She laughed, but she clearly didn't get it.

"Anyway," said Mark, "who'd you come to the party with?"

"My roommate."

"Where is she now?"

"No clue."

"You know, if we were playing baseball that would be strike three."

She laughed. "Are you hitting on me, or did my father hire you to be my chaperone?"

Mark smiled back, then turned a little more serious. "My sister's a sophomore. Did some dumb things her freshman year. Call it my big-brother instinct."

A Theta brother interrupted them. It was Baine Robinson, house treasurer, and his expression was stone-cold serious. "Cops are outside."

Mark didn't flinch. It was nothing he hadn't handled before, and it was the reason he no longer drank alcohol at frat parties. "Got it. Hey, it was nice meeting you, Lisa."

"Right," she said as Mark started away. "So, like . . . do you want my number?"

Mark glanced over his shoulder, still walking. "I'll bet Baine does."

She shrugged, and Baine stayed behind with her.

Mark continued down the hallway to the foyer. Word of "the badges" outside was starting to spread, and underage drinkers scrambled upstairs to hide. Suddenly the house was filled with students holding only cell phones, as no one was stupid enough to be seen through a window chugging from the telltale red Solo cup. The front door had been wide open all night, but Mark pulled it shut on his way out into the warm night air. He crossed the lawn to the curb, where two squad cars were parked. The police beacons were still flashing, lighting up the front yard with the orange swirl of authority. Four uniformed officers from the Alachua County Sheriff's Department were standing outside the cars, waiting beneath an oak tree.

"Good evening, Officers," he said in his most respectful tone. "I'm Mark Towson, Theta president."

"Towson, huh?" said one of the officers. His name tag identified him as Sergeant Walsh. "You're one of the boys we want to talk to."

That took Mark aback. He'd always been the designated Theta spokesperson when parties got too loud, but never had the police shown up looking for him by name.

"If it's about the party, we're more than happy to—"

"It's not just about the party," the sergeant said.

"Okay. How can I help you, then?"

"I'm sure you heard about Jamal Cousin."

The apparent lynching of the president of the Alpha house had been on the news and social media all day. "Yeah, terrible," said Mark. "Unbelievable something like that could happen."

"Did you know Jamal?"

"I met him. All the fraternity presidents meet as a group a couple times a year. But I wouldn't say I know him. *Knew* him," he said, correcting himself.

"That's part of the problem. For you boys it's party as usual, but that ain't the case over at the black houses."

"Are you asking me to shut it down?"

"Excellent idea," said Walsh.

"No problem. I'll take care of it."

"Put someone else in charge of that. We want you to come down to the station with us."

Mark glanced nervously at the other officers, then back at Walsh. "What's this about?"

"Relax," the sergeant said. "We're not here to arrest anyone. The chief deputy wants to sit down face-to-face with campus leaders like yourself. He's being proactive, so we don't have a full-blown riot on campus tomorrow."

"The chief wants to meet with *me*? *Now?*"

"Yeah. You, Baine Robinson, and Cooper Bartlett."

"Why Baine and Cooper?"

"Because those are the names the chief deputy gave me. You got a problem with it?"

Mark hesitated. Baine and Cooper were definitely not sober. "I don't know."

The sergeant's expression tightened. "Look, son. You college kids live in a bubble, but we're sitting on a powder keg from here to Live Oak. The president of a black fraternity was *lynched*. Jamal Cousin was an honor student and supposed to start medical school next fall."

"I didn't know that."

"Well, the whole world knows it now. Folks are pissed, and they got a right to be. But there's also some badass gangs pouring into town from Miami, Tampa, Atlanta, and God only knows where else. If you give a rat's ass about this university, get your frat brothers to shut down this party right now, grab your two friends, and come with us. It's too late once the buildings are on fire and there's rioting in the streets, which could happen any minute now."

Mark glanced back at the house, still wishing there was a way he could do this alone. "All right," he said finally. "I'll be right back."

CHAPTER 3

Mark Towson and his two fraternity brothers rode shoulder to shoulder in the back seat of a squad car to the Alachua County Sheriff's Department. Mark wasn't worried about Baine. A twenty-minute ride and the seriousness of the situation were enough to sober him up. Cooper looked like he was going to vomit as they entered the station. And he did.

"Aw, man, I feel so much better now," said Cooper, and then he threw up on the tile floor again.

"Dude, you're gonna get us arrested," said Baine.

"Nobody's getting arrested," said Sergeant Walsh. He gave Cooper a towel and sent him off to the bathroom to clean himself up. "You two come with me," he said, and Mark and Baine followed him down the hall.

Mark assumed that they were all headed to the same place, but he was wrong. Walsh stopped at the first door, opened it, and directed Baine inside with another deputy. He then led Mark to a door at the other end of the hall and showed him into the windowless room. Two men were seated at a small rectangular table. They rose and invited Mark to have a seat opposite them, which he did. Sergeant Walsh left the room, closing the door behind him.

The older man spoke first. "Thank you for coming in, Mr. Towson. With your permission I'd like to record this conversation."

The man's finger was already on the RECORD button.

"No problem," said Mark.

With a click, the recording started, and the man's voice took on an official tone. "My name is Oliver Boalt, state attorney and chief legal officer for the Third Judicial District of Florida. With me is Detective Josh Proctor of the Suwannee County Sheriff's Department."

"Suwannee County?" asked Mark.

"That's correct," Boalt answered. He looked like a state attorney, or at least as Mark would have imagined one. His hair was mostly gray and cut short, and even at this hour he wore a suit and tie, as if to announce that he was in control. Boalt continued in a businesslike tone.

"With us on a voluntary basis is Mr. Mark Towson, a twenty-one-year-old student at the University of Florida. It is twelve-fifty-two a.m., Sunday, October the seventh. I will now turn things over to Detective Proctor."

Proctor cleared his throat, then began. "Mr. Towson, have you had any alcoholic beverages this evening?"

"No."

"Are you under the influence of any recreational drugs?"

"No."

"Any prescription or over-the-counter medications?"

"No."

"Would you consider yourself mentally impaired in any way at this time?"

"No. But hold on, okay? I was told that we were going to talk about how to keep the campus safe. These questions make it sound like—like I don't know what."

"Do you have something to hide, Mr. Towson?" the detective asked.

"Well, no. But—"

"But you don't want to answer any questions. Even routine questions. Is that it?"

"I didn't say that. I've just never been in a situation like this."

"Let me be clear about what the *situation* is," said the detective. "You are not under arrest for anything. We are here having a conversation. Can we have a conversation, Mr. Towson?"

The question didn't leave any room to push back. "Yeah. Sure."

Detective Proctor paused for some reason; Mark wasn't sure why. The silence was insufferable. Finally, the detective put the next question. "Do you own a cell phone, Mr. Towson?"

"Yeah, sure."

"Can you confirm the number for me?"

Mark was getting so nervous that he actually had to think for a moment before reciting it.

The detective laid a printed transcript on the table before Mark. "Mr. Towson, this is a verbatim record of a text message that was found on the cell phone of Jamal Cousin. Could you read it, please?"

Mark read it to himself and cringed.

"Out loud, please," said the detective.

His voice quaked as he read it: "'*Watch yo ass on the float nigga. Strange fruit on the river.*'"

"Thank you," said the detective. "Can you flip to the next page, please?"

Mark did.

"This is a call report from Mr. Cousin's cell carrier," said the detective. "It shows the number for every incoming call or text, whether or not that number is on Mr. Cousin's actual cell. Look at the third line from the bottom, Mr. Towson. Do you recognize that number?"

The paper shook in Mark's hand. "I didn't write this text."

"That's your cell number, right?"

"It's my number, but I didn't send that text. I don't even know Jamal's cell number."

"It's in the Inter-Fraternity Council Directory, is it not, Mr. Towson? The cell numbers of all chapter presidents are listed there, correct?"

That was true, and Mark wasn't sure how to respond. "Okay, forget that. Just look at the message. I never use the N-word. And 'strange fruit'? I don't even know what that means. I didn't send this text."

"Then how did it get from your cell to Jamal's?"

"I don't know. When was it sent?"

"The Saturday before Jamal's death. Eleven fifty-one p.m."

Mark didn't have to think long to pinpoint his whereabouts. "I was at a Theta party just like the one we were having tonight. Anybody could have picked up my cell and sent it."

"Let's be real, Mr. Towson. You kids don't ever put down your cell phones."

Mark didn't argue. Instead, he scrolled through his text history, and then with a sigh of relief handed his cell to the detective. "Nothing to Jamal Cousin. See? I didn't send it."

The detective took Mark's phone, but he didn't even look at the screen. "I wouldn't expect you to *keep* this message after sending it. Unfortunately for you, Jamal did."

Mark reached for his cell, expecting it to be returned, but the detective placed it on the law enforcement side of the table, keeping it close at hand. Then he continued.

"Phone records show that Jamal Cousin also received a text message from Cooper Bartlett. And another one from Baine Robinson. Lucky for them, Jamal deleted the message, so we don't know what was said. But those messages were sent just a few minutes after the one you sent."

"*I* didn't send any message!"

The state attorney interjected, his tone much friendlier than the detective's. "Mark, we'd really like to know what your friends texted to Jamal."

"I don't know anything about any text messages to Jamal."

The detective leaned closer, retaking control. "Let's cut to the chase here, Mr. Towson. The critical time period here is roughly eighteen to twenty-six hours ago. Can you tell us where you were late Friday night and after midnight 'til about two a.m. Saturday?"

Mark glanced at the state attorney, who offered a nod of encouragement. "We're just looking for the truth, Mark."

"I went to bed pretty early. Like eleven thirty. I had an accounting midterm Friday morning and was up late Thursday studying."

"What time did you get up on Saturday?"

"Probably around ten."

"Was anyone with you?"

"No. That's one of the perks of being president. I get my own room."

"No girlfriend?"

Mark shook his head.

The detective put an even finer point on it. "So no one but you can tell us where you were from eleven thirty Friday night until ten a.m. Saturday. Is that right?"

Mark froze. The state attorney tried his "good cop" routine again. "You can answer, Mark. We just need your help."

"You don't want my *help*. This is crazy. You're trying to pin this on us."

The men stared back in silence.

Mark took a breath. "Seriously? You think the three of us lynched Jamal Cousin? Is that what this is about?"

"We're just three adults having a conversation," the state attorney said in a matter-of-fact tone. "No one's accusing you of anything. You're not under arrest."

"Yeah, you keep saying that. But—" Mark stopped himself. "Can I have my cell back, please?"

It was inches from the detective's elbow. He slid it across the table, and Mark caught it.

"Another text message you need to delete?" the detective asked.

"Yeah, how'd you know?" said Mark, instantly regretting the sarcasm. Then he pressed entry number one on his contact list, which simply read DAD.

CHAPTER 4

Jack Swyteck woke to a warm face washing—and dog breath.

"Max!" he said, groaning as he nudged his golden retriever away from the bed. The bedroom was dark, not a sliver of sunlight coming through the windows. Jack had just finished a two-week jury trial on Friday afternoon. Saturday had been the first "date" with his wife in a fortnight, and Sunday was his day to sleep in.

"Get up, Daddy!"

It was something Max would have said, if he could talk, but the voice was that of his three-year-old daughter. Jack rolled over and checked the clock on the nightstand: 5:11 a.m.

"Righley, honey. Do you have any idea what time it is?"

"Time to get up."

"Mommy?" he said hopefully. He reached across to Andie's side of the mattress, but she wasn't there. For two months she'd been training for a half marathon. On weekdays she took to the treadmills at the Miami Field Office, which were available to all FBI agents. On weekends she did her roadwork, but rarely before sunrise—too many drunks still driving home. Yet there she was, standing at the foot of the bed, dressed in running clothes and ready to head out.

"Why so early?"

"Your father woke me up."

Harry Swyteck was the former governor of Florida, since retired from politics. "My father?"

"He called your cell at five. You slept through it. I didn't."

"What does he want?"

"He said he'll meet you at the Executive Airport at six-fifteen. It's important. You're going to Gainesville."

The twin-engine prop plane left Miami at 6:35 a.m. with five rows of empty seats separating Jack and his father from the only other passenger on the flight. Jack had seen Saturday's media coverage of "Florida's first lynching in more than fifty years." It was the lead story on the evening news statewide, and national networks had also covered it. By the time Jack had gone to bed, bloggers were abuzz and social media was overheating, though the name "Towson" had not yet been mentioned.

Harry thanked Jack for a third time after takeoff.

"Tucker Towson was a college kid knocking on doors for me when I ran for state legislator. By my second term as governor, he was my deputy chief of staff. I think of him like a little brother."

"I get it," said Jack.

"I should have checked with you before telling him you'd fly up with me," said Harry. "But when an old friend calls at four o'clock in the morning and says his son is in serious trouble, you just get on a plane and—"

"Dad, it's no problem. Really."

Fifteen years of criminal defense work and a string of high-profile trials—mostly capital cases, including one in which his client was finally proven innocent after four years on death row—had earned Jack an impressive reputation. Still, Jack was under no illusion that this gig was strictly about his legal prowess. Although his father had been out of office for more than a decade, the surname Swyteck still carried weight, especially at the University of Florida, Harry's alma mater.

Jack spent the first half of the flight listening as Harry brought him up to speed on his call from Tucker, including what Tucker had told him about the racist text message from Mark Towson's phone. Then Jack took to the Internet. Ten minutes before landing,

Jack looked up from his iPad and said, "There's absolutely no mention anywhere of that text message from Mark to Jamal."

"You sure?"

Jack was. Saturday's coverage had focused on the tragic loss of life, with endless words of praise from relatives, friends, teachers, and virtually anyone who'd ever known Jamal Cousin. The *Sun Sentinel* story about an inner-city kid who stayed out of gangs and became the first in his family to attend college was downright inspirational. The breaking news on Sunday morning was that three white fraternity brothers had been hauled in for questioning and released sometime after midnight, and that one of them was the son of Tucker Towson, former deputy chief of staff to Governor Swyteck. Law enforcement refused to comment further.

"The police must be keeping that part of the investigation confidential," said Jack.

"Maybe they don't want to release it until they can prove for sure that Mark sent it. Which is reasonable. If that text is as bad as Tucker told me, his son will need a bodyguard when it goes public."

The jet landed at Gainesville Regional Airport around eight o'clock. A taxi took them toward campus. Jack was still on his iPad, reviewing the latest coverage, when he looked up and noticed how the business side of University Avenue had changed since his undergraduate days—except for the colors.

"I see Sherwin-Williams is still running a sale on orange and blue," said Jack.

The driver took them past the main campus, then past the law school, and finally to a quiet residential neighborhood west of the university.

Tucker and his wife, Elizabeth, had met as freshmen at UF and moved back to Gainesville in their fifties—not out of nostalgia, but because UF Health Shands Cancer Hospital offered Elizabeth a fighting chance against breast cancer. Both their children attended UF, and the empty-nesters lived alone in a four-bedroom ranch-style house at the end of a cul-de-sac. It wasn't often that Mark spent a Saturday night at home, but last night had been an exception.

"I wasn't expecting this," said Harry, as the taxi turned in to the Towsons' street.

A group of students had already gathered at the end of the street. They were not from the Gator welcome committee. Jack counted about a dozen demonstrators, blacks and whites, their posters sending a message to the neighborhood. JUSTICE FOR JAMAL. END HATRED.

"I figured there would be protests at the Theta house," said Harry. "But not here."

"The article in the *Sun* mentioned that Mark graduated from Gainesville High," said Jack. "They must have guessed he'd go home to deal with this."

A demonstrator stepped toward the taxi and brandished her sign: RACISM IS TAUGHT.

"Or they blame his parents," said Harry.

The taxi continued past the demonstrators, pulled into the driveway, and stopped. Jack reached for the door handle, but Harry stopped him.

"Before we go in, there's something I want to be totally clear about."

"Sure."

"Tucker is a special friend, so I was happy to arrange this meeting. But I made no commitments beyond that."

"We'll see how it goes."

"I'm not finished," said Harry. "I'm all for keeping an innocent college kid from becoming the victim of a witch hunt, which is what Tucker assures me this is. But if the boy actually sent that text message and gets indicted for lynching Jamal Cousin, I have no problem with you walking away from this case."

"Dad, he wouldn't be my first guilty client. And even if he did send that text, it doesn't mean he killed Jamal."

Harry grimaced. "See, you're already doing it."

"Doing what?"

"Your Freedom Institute mind-set."

Jack's first job out of law school at the Freedom Institute—defending death row inmates after Governor Harry Swyteck signed their death warrant—had once divided this father and son. They'd worked past it over the years. Or so Jack had thought.

"Do you want me to help this kid or not?" asked Jack.

Harry breathed out. "If he's being railroaded, I do. But if he's not . . ."

"If he's not, then he *really* needs my help."

"Damn it, Jack. Now I'm sorry I called you."

"Why?"

"Because you're not a hotshot young lawyer fresh out of law school who can do whatever he pleases. You're married to a law enforcement officer."

"Andie would never tell me what cases to take."

"Of course she wouldn't. But have some sense, Jack. I'm speaking now as a former cop. Andie is out there in the field every day. Black agents, white agents—they all got each other's back."

"And you think that's going to change because I defend Mark Towson?"

"If he sent that text, it will. Look, Jack, if you come out of this meeting saying 'I'm in this no matter what,' that's up to you. But if Tucker's son did this, and Andie asks my opinion, I'm not going to pretend that you're doing me any favors for my old friend. I'll be the first to give you a swift kick in the ass for defending the racist son of a bitch. Understood?"

"Yeah," said Jack, his gaze drifting toward the line of demonstrators at the end of the driveway. "Understood."

CHAPTER 5

Jack met alone with his new client in the dining room. Harry waited in the living room with Tucker and Elizabeth Towson. The pocket door was closed for privacy. The furniture was traditional, straight out of an Ethan Allen showroom. A framed portrait hanging on the cabbage-rose wallpaper captured Mark with his parents and younger sister in a much happier time.

"I had nothing to do with this," said Mark.

"That's a good start," said Jack.

They spoke for almost an hour, covering everything from the first time Mark met Jamal to the police interrogation. One new piece of information was that all three boys had left the sheriff's office without their cell phones. By the time the interrogation ended, the police had obtained a warrant to seize the phones.

"The detective kept telling me I wasn't under arrest," said Mark.

"They don't have to arrest you to seize your cell phone."

"But why did he keep saying that? I felt like he was telling me that if I tried to leave, he *would* arrest me."

"Bluffs like that are standard police interrogation tactics," said Jack. "The detective was also making it clear on the recording that he wasn't legally required to tell you that you have the right to remain silent and the right to an attorney. Miranda doesn't kick in until you're arrested."

"Seems slimy to me. Especially after they lied to get me to come to the station. The cop said it was to talk about campus safety."

"That's allowed, as long as the police have a good reason to lie."

"What reason could they have other than to trick me?"

"We can ask. But it doesn't take a genius to think one up."

"That sucks. This whole thing sucks."

Frustration was setting in. It was obvious that Mark hadn't slept all night, like all clients who lie awake and overanalyze their predicament.

There was a knock at the door, and Mark's father entered. "Jack, sorry to interrupt, but it's important. There's something you should see on the TV."

He pronounced "TV" like "Stevie." His son had inherited the Towson height and preppy good looks, but the accent was all Tucker.

"All right, let's break."

Jack and his client rose and followed Tucker into the living room. Harry had stepped out. Elizabeth was seated on the couch. The worry lines Jack had noticed on her face just an hour earlier now seemed carved in wax. A sixty-inch flat screen hung on the wall. Frozen on the screen and cued up to replay was the image of an African American legal giant in Florida. The banner below his face read: "Leroy Highsmith, attorney and spokesperson for the Cousin family." He was standing before a bouquet of microphones from at least a dozen different news organizations.

"Do you know Highsmith?" asked Tucker.

"I've met him," said Jack. "He's not a criminal defense lawyer."

"More like a criminal."

"He's a plaintiff's lawyer."

"Same thing. The man built his practice on 'Have You Been Injured?' billboards posted on all roads *out* of Disney World. His specialty is convincing juries that every bump on the noggin is a life-threatening brain injury."

"He has definitely won some big verdicts," said Jack.

"And he's at it again."

"At what again?" asked Jack.

"One of the boys the police took down to the station last night is Baine Robinson. That family is loaded. Baine's father is a citrus baron from Orange County—probably one of the richest men ever to graduate from UF. The Robinson School of Agriculture was named after Baine's grandfather."

"I'm not sure I follow your point about Leroy Highsmith," said Jack.

"Highsmith practically has his own cottage industry suing companies like Robinson Citrus. Watch," said Tucker, reaching for the television remote. "Listen to what Highsmith just said five minutes ago in this press conference, and you'll see what I mean."

Tucker pressed the remote, rewound the DVR, and the on-screen image came to life. Highsmith was a gifted orator, speaking with the passion of a preacher and the precision of a brilliant lawyer.

"*Strange fruit*," he said, holding a transcript of the text message in his left hand. "Strange fruit hanging from the tree. Chilling words that Billie Holiday sang so powerfully more than seventy-five years ago. But this isn't 1939, you say. The days when just looking at a white man the wrong way could cost a black man his life are over, you say. Lynchings are behind us, you say." He paused for effect, then lowered his voice. "Not so," he said, shaking his head in sadness. "Not so."

Mark grabbed the remote and paused the recording. "Who's Billie Holiday? I never heard of him."

"Her," said Jack.

"I don't know that song! I never heard of strange fruit!"

"We know," his mother said softly. "We believe you."

Tucker took the remote, and with his push of the button, Highsmith continued.

"On behalf of Jamal, his mama and daddy, the entire Cousin family. And on behalf of the nearly five thousand black men who were lynched in this country. I call on State Attorney Oliver Boalt and on all decent folk in Suwannee County to see to it that there is justice for Jamal. Justice without delay!"

Applause followed, and the screen went black.

Tucker tossed the remote onto the couch. "You see, Jack? He's not helping Jamal's family out of the goodness of his heart. He smells money."

"I didn't really get that," said Jack.

"The man *says* he wants justice. To him, justice means a quick guilty verdict against some frat boys at UF, followed by a multimillion-dollar wrongful-death lawsuit against their families—which *I* can't pay, but the Robinson family surely can."

It wasn't unusual for clients to reach for conspiracy theories when facing criminal accusations. This one seemed pretty far afield. "Let's not get too ahead of ourselves," said Jack.

There was a quick knock at the front door, but it was just Harry's way of announcing his return. He let himself in. His expression was noticeably grim as he approached.

"How did it go?" Tucker asked Harry.

"How did *what* go?" asked Jack.

Elizabeth spoke just above a whisper. "Your father went to visit Dick Waterston," she said, meaning the university president.

Harry stepped farther into the living room, facing the others. "I did what I could," said Harry. "The president's office will be issuing a press release at one o'clock."

Tucker put his arm around Mark's shoulder, seeming to know what Harry was going to say next.

"The text message is unacceptable student conduct," said Harry.

Jack watched as Tucker led his son toward the window, where Elizabeth joined them. The family turned away, their backs to the Swytecks as they gazed out the French doors toward the swimming pool. Harry delivered the final blow.

"Mark is being expelled from the University of Florida."

Mark's chin hit his chest. Elizabeth sobbed and hugged her son.

Jack averted his eyes as Harry drew him toward the dining room, allowing the Towsons a moment in private. Harry spoke softly.

"The president isn't buying it that someone took Mark's phone at a frat party and sent that text to Jamal."

"I suspect there's more behind this decision than a text message," said Jack.

"I agree. I think the state attorney showed more evidence to the university than he's sharing with the media." Harry glanced toward the Towson family. "I feel terrible for Tucker and Elizabeth."

Jack nodded slowly, saying nothing, but keenly aware that the expression of sympathy had stopped with Mark's parents.

The Towsons rejoined Jack and his father in the dining room. "Can they really do this, Jack?" asked Elizabeth. "Just expel our son like this?"

"A student has a right to a hearing before being expelled," Jack said. "But Mark needs to steer clear of that circus. In my opinion."

"Why?"

Jack addressed his response to Mark's parents. "I can only imagine what the two of you are going through. But that's a discussion I should have alone with Mark."

"This is a family decision."

"It's really not," said Jack. "Mark is my client. It's important that Mark feels that he can tell his lawyer anything. If he thinks everything he tells me goes straight back to his parents, that's not good. I hope you understand."

Tucker stepped away from his son, perhaps just to create the illusion of respect for the attorney-client relationship. "That's fine, Jack. Take all the time you need. Say all the things that a lawyer has to say. But remember your client is a Towson," he said, his gaze shifting toward his son. "We don't go down without a fight."

He'd clearly intended it as a rallying point—words of encouragement for his son—but it had fallen flat. Mark still looked numb.

"I'll keep that in mind," said Jack.

CHAPTER 6

The midmorning sun burned brightly over Live Oak. Cynthia Porter stepped out onto the covered front porch of her century-old house and settled into a white wicker chair. A paddle fan wobbled out of plumb above her. An orange cat jumped gently into her lap.

"Hello, Mrs. Butterscotch," she said sweetly.

Cynthia had lived in Live Oak since the FDR presidency, married forty-three years to a stubborn man who died on the hottest day of the twentieth century. The front lawn was half-mowed when Bud Porter dropped to the freshly cut grass. Heart attack. Cynthia still owned the house on Pine Avenue where they'd raised a good son. It was a short walk from their church, and for six decades she'd rarely missed a Sunday service. That all changed with one misstep and an eight-inch fall from the curb, which had left her with a broken kneecap. As her arthritis worsened, she got around less. Since Christmas, church on Sunday had been more like once a month.

She stroked Mrs. Butterscotch above her misty-gray eyes and listened to the breeze. Live Oak had grown fivefold since Cynthia was a girl, to a population of seven thousand; but the small-town feel endured and, thanks to preservationists, some parts had changed not at all. The old saying—the more north you go in Florida, the more South you are—defined Live Oak. Workdays passed at the graceful pace of the Suwannee and Santa Fe rivers that bound it, and the inner peace of the Bible Belt filled each Sunday. But this was no ordinary Sabbath. Cynthia could hear crowd noises in the distance. She'd watched Mr. Highsmith's speech on television, and she'd heard him invite the townsfolk to march from their churches to the courthouse. The route from Mission Baptist led right past her house.

The screen door slapped shut, and her hired caretaker stepped onto the porch. "You comfortable, Miz Cynthia?"

"Yes, I'm fine, Virginia."

Cynthia had hired "a Negro"—she still used the word—to move in and help her recuperate from the fall. The two women hit it off, the temporary arrangement was made permanent, and Virginia became her live-in caretaker and full-time companion.

Virginia settled into the rocking chair, and then pulled it a little closer to Cynthia. Somehow Virginia had gotten the idea that Cynthia's left ear was failing, but Cynthia insisted that there was nothing wrong with her hearing, even if the doctor did agree with Virginia.

"Hear the singing?" asked Virginia.

To Cynthia, it had been just noise in the distance. "Is that what that is?"

Cynthia sat up straighter to look out over the porch rail as the crowd came into focus. Peaceful demonstrators, blacks and whites, approached from the south end of Pine Avenue. They marched several rows deep, arms locked in a show of unity that stretched from sidewalk to sidewalk. They walked past the bakery that made the best red velvet cake Cynthia had ever tasted, the salon where Cynthia had her hair done once a week, and the diner that, for the first half of Cynthia's life, was "whites only."

"*We shall overcome*," Virginia sang softly, and only then did Cynthia realize what the demonstrators were singing.

Cynthia drew a breath. "Sad," was all she could say.

Virginia rose from the rocker and stepped to the rail. The crowd was just a block away and closing. "That's Mr. Leroy Highsmith there in the front. That must be Jamal Cousin's parents with him."

"They're here in Live Oak? I thought the boy's family was from Miami."

"Probably come up for the body," said Virginia. "Poor mother. I don't know how she can even stand up, let alone walk. Bless her heart."

Cynthia stared blankly into the middle distance. "Sad. Just makes me so sad."

The singing grew louder. Virginia returned to the rocker and pulled it even closer to Cynthia.

"I can hear ya' just fine," said Cynthia.

Virginia smiled sadly, then joined in song as the demonstrators passed. It seemed prophetic that the verse had just rolled over to the promise of walking hand in hand "someday." Virginia reached over the white wicker armrest and clasped Cynthia's hand. It wasn't the first time the women had held hands, but this felt different. A complicated mix of emotions coursed through her ninety-year-old veins as the chorus of unity marched on toward the Suwannee County Courthouse, as Cynthia's mind clouded with memories.

Cindy hurried inside the house, and the ornaments rattled on the Christmas tree as the front door slammed behind her.

"Cindy?" her mother called from the kitchen.

"I'm home!" she announced, and then she ran upstairs as fast as her fifteen-year-old legs would carry her. She went straight to her room, locked the door, and jumped onto her bed.

School was out 'til January, but Cindy's father had her take a job over the break to help Mrs. Dott at the dime store. Mr. Dott was overseas with the Army for the second consecutive Christmas. Cynthia's younger cousins were counting the days 'til Santa's arrival—just two more—but for most of Live Oak it was a subdued holiday season, tempered by the war effort. The employee gift exchange had been especially understated. "Cards only," Mrs. Dott had insisted. The employees had gathered in the front of the store for about fifteen minutes after closing. Mrs. Dott served cookies and eggnog, and Cindy gave a card to each of her coworkers. All but one had reciprocated at the party; all but one had been welcome at the party.

Willie James was the only black employee at Van Priest's. It would have been a terrible breach of Southern code for him to attend. He would have been equally out of line to give a holiday card to the daughter of a white man of status, a former state legislator who ran the local post office. What surprised her, however, wasn't that he'd been so presumptuous. The surprise was her own feelings when he'd come up to her afterward, away from the others, and slipped the envelope into her hand.

"Merry Christmas," he said in that velvet voice.

She smiled again as she reopened the envelope and read once again—a fifth time—the way he'd signed it.

"With L," was what he'd written.

With love, was what he'd meant.

"Cynthia!"

Her father was in the hallway, right outside her bedroom. To him she was always "Cynthia," especially if she was in trouble. The crystal doorknob jiggled, but the lock kept him out.

"Cynthia, open this door!"

Miz Cynthia?"

She felt Virginia squeeze her hand, which cleared away the memories.

"You was asleep with your eyes open, Miz Cynthia. You okay?"

Cynthia's gaze drifted up Pine Avenue, where the crowd continued on toward the courthouse. "Yes," she said, softly. "I'll be fine."

CHAPTER 7

Jack borrowed Tucker Towson's pickup truck, dropped his father at the Gainesville airport, and continued on to Live Oak alone.

Oliver Boalt had agreed to a 1:30 p.m. meeting with Jack at his office. Jack would have liked to confer with the lawyers for Cooper Bartlett and Baine Robinson beforehand, but neither family had decided on a lawyer. Denial. Jack spoke to Baine's father and Cooper's mother by phone, assured them that this was not going to blow over, and even recommended attorneys to contact. But Mark was already facing expulsion, and Jack couldn't wait for the others to get their acts together. Although the crisis was a little more than twelve hours old, it was impossible to overstate the importance of opening a dialogue with the prosecutor before the high-speed train of public opinion left the station.

The drive was just over an hour, mostly on the interstate, with not much to see. Jack de-stressed by counting billboards. The unofficial tally: LIFE BEGINS AT CONCEPTION, 22; WE BARE ALL, 21. As Jack exited I-75 and crossed the city limits, the billboards gave way to red-white-and-blue yard signs along quiet residential streets, RE-ELECT OLIVER BOALT—YOUR STATE ATTORNEY. A twenty-first-century lynching was explosive by definition. A state attorney up for reelection was like gasoline on the fire.

The office of the state attorney was in a generic bank building on Court Street, directly across from one of the most beautifully restored courthouses in Florida. Built in 1904, the Suwannee County Courthouse was a piece of history and an architectural gem that commanded passersby to stop and admire. Perhaps Jack was just missing his family, or perhaps it was the scourge of one too many "Righley road trips" to Disney World, but Jack couldn't help thinking that the old courthouse would have fit perfectly on the theme park's faux turn-of-the-century Main Street. It was tempting to label Live Oak a time capsule but, walking from his car, Jack immediately noted a sign of change—a law-office marquee that read, ATTORNEYS/ABOGADOS.

"Thank you for coming, Mr. Swyteck," said Boalt. Jack was in the state attorney's corner office. With them was senior trial counsel Marsha Weller. "Marsha will be the lead prosecutor on this case," Boalt added.

Boalt was at least ten years older than he appeared in his campaign posters. His face was fuller, his hair was thinner, the creases in his brow were more pronounced, and his teeth were not as white. Weller was about Jack's age, which meant that this was far from her first murder case, though everyone in the room understood that this was a case like no other.

"How can we help you?" asked Weller.

Jack told them what they already knew—that his client was facing expulsion from the university for sending a racist text message to Jamal Cousin—and then added what they needed to know. "My client didn't send it."

"The university seems to disagree," said Boalt.

"There's been no hearing yet."

"Is your client planning to testify at the hearing?" asked Boalt.

"That depends," said Jack. "I don't know of many lawyers who would advise a client to testify at a school disciplinary proceeding while he is the target of an active homicide investigation."

Boalt paused to measure his response. "No one is saying that your client is a target, Mr. Swyteck."

"And no one is saying that he's not," Weller added.

"Well, pardon my confusion," said Jack. "But I drove up here to look you in the eye and get a direct answer to a direct question: Is Mark Towson a target?"

The prosecutors exchanged glances, and then Boalt answered. "We're not at liberty to discuss the status of an active investigation."

"Let's go at this a different way," said Jack. "Whether you admit it or not, the university is following your lead. So tell me. What do I need to do to convince you that Mark Towson didn't send that text?"

Boalt leaned back in his desk chair, considering his response. "An interview would be a good start."

"You already questioned Mark in Gainesville."

"He terminated the interview before Detective Proctor was finished."

"It was one o'clock in the morning, and he had no lawyer. And even then, Mark told you he didn't send it."

"Well," said Boalt, stretching a single syllable into a deeply southern *weh-eh-ell*. "The boy wasn't under oath."

"If my client swore on a stack of Bibles that he didn't send that text, would it make a difference to you?"

Boalt glanced at his lead prosecutor once more, as if conferring in silence.

Weller took the cue. "There's one thing that might make a difference, Mr. Swyteck," she said. "Would your client sit for a polygraph?"

Boalt followed up, seeming to like his chief prosecutor's suggestion. "We could limit it to one question: 'Did you send the text to Jamal Cousin?'"

Jack wasn't a believer in polygraphs. He'd seen too many guilty men pass and too many innocents fail. But a flat refusal would only raise suspicions.

"Who conducts the examination?" asked Jack.

"The Suwannee County Sheriff's office," said Weller.

"That won't work," said Jack. "It would have to be someone we both agree on."

"How about the Florida Department of Law Enforcement?"

"It can't be anyone currently working in law enforcement," said Jack. "I need some assurance of objectivity. Someone in private security."

"We won't agree to that," said Boalt.

"Why not?"

"Because our examiners are fully qualified and fair. What are you afraid of?"

"Let's not do this dance," said Jack. "Even if we could agree on an examiner, neither one of us will accept the results if they don't go our way."

"That's pretty cynical," said Boalt.

"There's a reason no court in the history of American jurisprudence has ever found the results of a lie detector test to be admissible at trial."

"*We-eh-ell*," Boalt said again, "if your client won't consent to an interview or a polygraph examination, there's not much for us to talk about."

"I said I wouldn't agree to a polygraph on your terms. No lawyer would."

"Baine Robinson's lawyer might."

Last Jack had heard, Baine Robinson had yet to hire a lawyer. "Are you bluffing me, Mr. Boalt? I spoke to Baine's father less than an hour ago, and he said Baine doesn't have a lawyer yet."

"He does now. I just got off the phone with him five minutes ago. Leonard Oden. One of the finest lawyers in all these parts. I'd expect no less. The Robinson family is quite well-to-do."

"So I've heard," said Jack.

The state attorney checked his watch. "Tell you what, Mr. Swyteck. Why don't you and Mr. Oden confer and get back to us. Maybe we can line up both your clients for that lie detector."

"I wouldn't count on that," said Jack.

"Then it's been a pleasure to meet you, Mr. Swyteck," Boalt said. On his lead, they rose and ended the meeting with a handshake.

Weller walked Jack to the lobby and shifted the conversation to Jack's father, whom she claimed to have voted for some twenty years earlier.

"Stressful time around here, I would imagine," said Jack. "Just a few weeks to the election."

"Oliver said it in his press conference this morning, and he meant it. There will be no rush to justice."

The prosecutor wished him well as she unlocked the door and let him out of the building. Jack was walking to his car, cell phone to his ear, when Tucker Towson answered his call.

"How did the meeting with the state attorney go?" asked Tucker.

Jack wished he could say "great." He went with "fine." But he wasn't out of ideas. "I know a retired FBI agent in Miami who works in private security. She specializes in polygraph examinations, and I trust her. Would you be willing to fly her up to Gainesville to test Mark? I could probably get her to do it for around five hundred bucks, plus the plane ticket."

"You want to give Mark a lie detector test?"

"I haven't decided. I might."

"But . . . what if he fails?"

It was a predicament that Jack had faced before. "Then we don't make the results public."

"I guess that makes sense. Go ahead, then. Line her up."

"Thanks."

"And, oh, Jack."

"Yeah?"

"When I asked 'what if Mark fails,' I wasn't implying—well, I just don't want you to get the impression that I have reason to think he wouldn't pass."

"I understand. But let me ask you a question, Tucker. And I want an honest answer."

"Sure."

Jack stopped at his car, standing at the parking meter. "*Do* you have reason to think that Mark won't pass?"

There was brief silence on the line, and Jack wasn't sure if Tucker was simply taken aback by the question, or if he actually needed the time to consider his response. "No," he said finally, adding a little chuckle, as if the answer was obvious. "None whatsoever."

"That's good to hear," said Jack, as he unlocked the car door. "Tell Mark I'll call him from the interstate."

CHAPTER 8

Leroy Highsmith reached across the kitchen table, joined hands with Edith and Lamar Cousin, and led them in prayer. He prayed for their son Jamal. For the family. And for an end to racism. "In Jesus' name, amen."

On the table, beside their clasped hands, lay a copy of the press release from the University of Florida's president, announcing the immediate expulsion of Mark Towson: *The hateful, disgusting text message from Mr. Towson to fellow student Jamal Cousin has no place at our great university. While I am in no way prejudging the criminal investigation into the murder of Jamal Cousin, we must have zero tolerance for blatant bigotry and racism.*

"Amen," Jamal's parents said in unison.

The Cousin family had been in Highsmith's hands since Saturday afternoon. It was Highsmith who'd accompanied Jamal's father to the morgue, and it was Highsmith who'd kept Edith from falling to the floor when Lamar stepped out and told her, "Dear God, honey, it's him." Highsmith had arranged for their overnight stay with his friends in Live Oak, where they'd awakened on Sunday morning to the harsh realization that it wasn't just a terrible nightmare. They were living it.

"Mr. Highsmith, can I speak to you in private for a moment?"

Standing in the doorway was Quinton Press, the brightest star in the cast of talented young lawyers at the Highsmith Firm. Quinton accompanied his boss wherever he went and was the odds-on favorite to become the firm's next partner. Highsmith excused himself from the table and followed Quinton down the hallway and out onto the front porch. If Quinton's plan had been to speak to Highsmith alone, it failed miserably.

"Looks like the media figured out where we're staying," said Quinton.

At the press conference following the church-to-courthouse march, Highsmith had asked the media to give the Cousin family some space. The response was a forest of mobile transmission towers, outside-broadcast vans, and TV crews parked on the street in front of what was supposed to have been an undisclosed place of retreat. They respected the property line, at least, firing questions across the front yard from the edge of the pavement.

"Mr. Highsmith, how's the family doing?"

"Is the expulsion enough?"

Highsmith waved without comment—but no, expulsion was not enough. Sure, the president had also directed the Office of Equal Opportunity to investigate whether Mr. Towson's text message was an "isolated action" or part of systematic racism by a white fraternity. But Highsmith knew what that meant. Damage control. It was the typical university doublespeak when it came to the three Rs—rape, racism, and recruiting violations.

"To the garage," he told Quinton.

The possible involvement of three white college students in a modern-day lynching had pushed the news coverage way beyond facts—even beyond speculation. Since 5:00 a.m., every development and possible future development had been picked apart by pundits, analyzed by trial lawyers, and debated by civil rights activists on television. Only occasionally was it mentioned that the sheriff had yet to announce an arrest.

"They hired Governor Swyteck's son," said Quinton. They were alone in the one-car garage, standing on an oil stain that was as big as an area rug, at least half a century in the making.

"Thank God they picked a lightweight," said Highsmith. "How soon 'til an arrest?"

"Ms. Weller says she doesn't know."

"Bullshit. Quinton, I can't confer with Oliver Boalt every two hours. He doesn't have time, and neither do I. But he promised me that Marsha Weller would keep the family updated. You have to press her."

"I did." Quinton checked his notes on his tablet. "She said that Boalt wants zero lag time between arrest and indictment. So there will be no arrest until they're ready to take the case to the grand jury."

"That's lame. This isn't opening night on Broadway. Any half-assed prosecutor can get an indictment just by asking for it. Really. It doesn't take much more than that."

"They need time to bolster the evidence on motive."

"*Motive?*"

"Technically motive is not an element of the crime of homicide, but in any murder case, motive is important."

Highsmith stepped away, breathing out his anger. "This isn't a fucking murder case."

"Excuse me?"

His anger was turning to energy. He paced from one end of the garage to the other, then looked the young lawyer in the eye. "You don't get it, do you, Quinton?"

"Get what, sir?"

"Millennials," he said, almost spitting out the word. "An entire generation of entitled motherfuckers. You and everyone your age think it's normal that a black superstar athlete gets a seventy-million-dollar shoe contract. You think it's normal that a smart black kid gets into Harvard."

"I really don't know what—"

"Black folk *died* to make that happen, Quinton. There's no *motive* to figure out here. This is *not* a murder case."

Quinton blinked, confused. "Then—what is it?"

"It's—oh, the hell with it. If you don't get it, no way you're gonna make a sixty-year-old white man from Live Oak understand. I'll do it myself. Like everything else around here."

Highsmith checked his reflection in the garage window and exited through the side door. Just the sight of him sent reporters running for their microphones, cameras rolling.

"Mr. Highsmith!"

He crossed the lawn at a deliberate pace and stopped just before the pavement. Questions came from too many directions, so he quickly found a camera from a national news organization and spoke directly to it, ignoring any single reporter.

"I have a quick statement on behalf of the Cousin family," he said, and the crowd hushed to listen.

"Jamal's parents wish to thank everyone across the country for their prayers and love. They are appreciated. Jamal was their only child, their pride and joy, and this is unimaginably painful for them. But it's important for you—I mean the media—to understand how this loose talk about a gruesome murder involving frat boys is adding to their pain. Let me speak clearly about this.

"First, whoever committed this despicable act is not a frat boy, a school boy, a homeboy, or any other kind of boy. They are *men* who enjoy their position of privilege because *men and women* even younger than they are—many of them of color—fight and die for this country.

"Second—and I am speaking to you, Mr. State Attorney—lynching has never been about the murder of one man or one woman. The crime here is terrorism—racial terrorism. The victim is the entire African American community. And the motive is hate. Jamal Cousin was president of the preeminent black Greek-letter organization at Florida's flagship university. Lynching him on the banks of the Suwannee River where he would be found by African American students is an act of terrorism. And no matter how privileged, these terrorists deserve your sympathy no more than the Boston Marathon bombers or the Orlando nightclub shooter.

"That is all," he said, ignoring the cacophony of follow-up questions as he turned and walked back to the house. Quinton met him at the porch steps.

"You get it now, Quinton?"

They continued up the steps and crossed the porch. "I think so."

"You *think so*?"

He opened the front door, allowing his boss to enter first. "I do," he said, following Highsmith inside. "I definitely do."

CHAPTER 9

Jack ignored the speed limit all the way back to Gainesville and headed straight to the Theta house. The latest buzz on social media was that police were headed to the fraternity with a search warrant. The state attorney had yet to return Jack's call to confirm or deny the rumor, which only made Jack believe it was true. It was important that he be there, but he hadn't planned on a street clogged with demonstrators. A traffic cop stopped him eight blocks from Fraternity Row. Jack rolled down his window to plead for passage.

"Campus is closed to vehicles," said the officer.

"I have to get to the Theta house."

"Yeah, you and everyone else."

"I'm the attorney for Mark Towson, Theta president."

"And I'm the Easter Bunny. Move along."

Jack didn't have time to argue. He parked off campus and started down the sidewalk, dialing his client for an update. Mark was still with his parents at home, without a cell phone but available on the landline, and his friends at the fraternity house were keeping him posted.

"Cops just got there and are moving everyone to the dining room," said Mark. "Looks like they want to search upstairs."

Jack broke into a run, speaking urgently into his phone. "Who's your contact in the frat?"

"Cooper Bartlett. Baine's with him. Should I be there, too?"

"No," Jack said, huffing with each footfall. "And tell your friends to say nothing to the police."

Jack tucked away his cell and continued at full speed for another two blocks, flying past groups of students who were on their way to the protest on Fraternity Row. The crowd swelled as he got closer to the Theta house, forcing him to slow down and weave his way through demonstrators. It was a mix of students, half blacks and half other races—which, by Jack's quick estimate, meant that most of UF's fifty thousand students had stayed home but its three thousand African American students had come out in force. The collective mood was somewhere between anger and dissatisfaction with the university's decision to expel just one fraternity member, even if he was the president. Banners and posters made the point, and the message was clearest as Jack pushed his way closer to the house, where hundreds of students, black and white, wore white T-shirts in solidarity, each with the Greek letters of Jamal's fraternity emblazoned on the front and a handwritten message on the back. BLACK LIVES MATTER was a common refrain, along with THETA PI OMEGA HATES ME.

A black student with a handheld loudspeaker was standing atop a redbrick wall that ran adjacent to the crowded sidewalk. Jack recognized him from the news as the fraternity brother on the Ichetucknee tubing trip who had found Jamal's body, Percy Donovan.

"We have a message for you, President Waterston," Percy shouted, the loudspeaker carrying his voice above the crowd. "We will not sit quietly for another investigation into systemic racism that goes nowhere! We will not accept the same old excuse that this is another isolated incident. Racist cowards never act alone. *TPO must go! TPO must go!*"

With fist pumping, he spurred on the crowd, the rhythmic chant beating like the new pulse of Fraternity Row: "*TPO must go!*"

Jack pushed forward, where a line of uniformed police officers kept the crowd from hopping the wall and setting foot on the Theta front lawn. Jack approached the cop with the grayest hair—someone old enough to recognize the unusual name "Swyteck" as that of the former governor. It worked. The officer escorted him around the house to the rear entrance.

Six cars were parked directly behind the house, and a posted sign gave notice that each space was reserved for an elected officer, from president to sergeant at arms. A team of forensic agents from the Florida Department of Law Enforcement had descended on Mark's car—doors, trunk, and hood wide open as the active search of the vehicle was under way.

Jack identified himself and asked to see the warrant, which one of the officers produced. The state attorney had yet to identify Mark Towson as a target of the investigation, but the warrant left little doubt as to the focus. The search was for an "eight-cord nylon rope of any length."

"I assume that's the type of rope used in the murder of Jamal Cousin," said Jack.

The officer was under no obligation to reply, and he didn't. Jack moved to the second item listed in the warrant—fibers from a cotton shirt and denim jeans.

"And I presume the fibers are consistent with the clothing that Jamal was wearing?"

No reply.

"How did you get into the vehicle?" asked Jack. "Break the locks?"

"No. The Theta house mother turned over a set of keys at our request. They are kept inside the house."

"For the record, my client does not consent to a search for any item not listed in the warrant, and he does not consent to the search of any place not described in the warrant."

"Understood. But you should check the other warrants."

"There's more than one?"

"Yep," the officer said, signaling with a jerk of his head. "Inside."

Jack started toward the house, and as he opened the door, a reporter called out his name. Jack stopped and looked. She was on the other side of the wall with her cameraman.

"Is Mark Towson a suspect?" she shouted.

The media had been piecing things together all day, quick to label just about anything "breaking news." A police search of the Theta president's car was the Holy Grail.

Jack stepped inside, closed the door, and called the Towsons' landline. His client answered.

"Just stay where you are until I get back, Mark. This ride is about to get bumpier."

CHAPTER 10

Leroy Highsmith left for the Suwannee County Airport, two miles outside of Live Oak, late Sunday afternoon. Quinton Press drove, and the parents of Jamal Cousin rode with them. The pilot greeted them on the tarmac.

"We're good to go, Mr. Highsmith. I should have you in Miami within the hour."

"Thank you, Jordan."

The *Legal Eagle*, a twin-engine private jet, was the largest aircraft the Suwannee airport could accommodate, and it was perhaps the most obvious symbol of Highsmith's rags-to-riches success. Over his four-decade career, Highsmith had been featured in countless platforms, from the *Wall Street Journal* and *Vanity Fair* to *60 Minutes* and *Lifestyles of the Rich and Famous*. His parents were sharecroppers on white-owned land near Lake Okeechobee, and their nine children grew up in a shantytown of whitewashed shacks with tarpaper roofs. Somehow, their youngest son went on to become the first lawyer ever from Bel Glade, a town so "third world" that the Peace Corps used to train its volunteers there. It was the riches, however, that drew the media's attention. More than a hundred verdicts and settlements in excess of a million dollars paid for a fifty-room mansion in the mostly white enclave of Palm Beach and filled his eight-car garage with a fleet of European-made automobiles, including four Bentleys and two Aston Martins. In addition to the forty-one talented lawyers who worked for him, he had his own manager, publicist, social media consultant, chef and sous chef, relaxation therapist, financial advisers, private investigators, pilots, and aviation mechanics. Some said he traveled to court in a limousine so long that the back end arrived five minutes after the front end; while others wrote more accurately about his $15,000 suits, custom-made crocodile shoes, and a bejeweled Rolex wristwatch.

And there was one nugget that made it into *every* story: the 18-karat-gold fixtures in his Gulfstream G550.

"Is that real gold?" asked Mrs. Cousin.

She hadn't asked on the trip up from Miami, but Highsmith knew that she would, eventually. Black folks always asked. White folks never did—they just sat quietly and assumed it was the typical black man's expression of in-your-face arrogance, harking back to the days of the great Jack Johnson, who capped his front teeth in gold as he knocked out one white fighter after another on his way to becoming the first black heavyweight boxing champion of the world. Highsmith could only imagine what his white guests said about him in the privacy of their automobile on the way home from the airport. And then he just loved their reaction when, days later, he would tell them that he'd purchased his Gulfstream pre-owned from a white businessman, gold fixtures included.

"You'll want to take this call," said Quinton, as he handed Highsmith his cell phone. "It's Oliver Boalt."

Highsmith excused himself from the Cousins, then moved from the main seating area of the cabin to the forward compartment, on the other side of the galley, where he could speak in private. "Hello, Oliver," he said in a pleasant tone.

"I saw your speech on television," said the state attorney. "Those were some very hurtful words."

"You deserved a good kick in the ass. If you're looking for 'motive,' you're dragging your feet."

"*Dragging*—come on, Leroy. It's been two days."

"Which will turn into two weeks, then two months, and then nothing. I can smell it."

"You're not being fair. And I don't just mean the speech. The fact that Jamal's parents came to Live Oak and never met with the state attorney is terrible optics."

"They met with the medical examiner, the lead homicide detective, and the prosecutor you've assigned to the case. That's enough."

"It makes *me* look like an insensitive jackass—or, worse, a racist. I want to meet them."

"Not this trip. They're exhausted."

"That's because you marched them all the way from Mission Baptist to the courthouse. They've met everyone *but me*."

"Let me spell it out for you, Oliver. I will not put these grieving parents through another meeting and more agony just so you can have a photo op to boost your campaign for reelection."

"This has nothing to do with politics," Boalt said, his voice rising. "I've never lost an election in my life, and I'm not worried about this one."

Highsmith paused—not because he was without words, but because he wanted them to have the intended effect. "Maybe you should be worried, Oliver."

There was silence on the line, and then the state attorney spoke, incredulous. "Did I just hear you correctly?"

"It's an observation, not a threat. I have no mind to work against you. You're a decent man, but you are more detached from the black voters of Suwannee County than you know. Maybe that's because in past elections black folk didn't vote. They will this time. If there's no indictment before the first Tuesday in November, you could find yourself out of work on Wednesday."

"This investigation has my full attention. There are things in the works that I can't share with you. I called you for one reason—to meet with Jamal's parents."

"And you will meet them. As soon as there's an indictment. Good night, Oliver."

Highsmith ended the call and tossed the phone onto the leather seat next to him. His associate brought him a scotch on the rocks and placed it on the armrest. Highsmith raised an eyebrow, which sent Quinton running for a napkin.

"So sorry," he said upon his quick return.

Highsmith sipped his scotch, as his associate wiped the beads of condensation from the gold-plated trim on the armrest.

CHAPTER 11

Jack moved quickly through the Theta house. The officer at the bottom of the main staircase produced a second warrant for the search already under way upstairs. Jack read it and immediately called Tucker.

"I need you to make a list of every store between here and the Ichetucknee River that sells eight-cord, three-quarter inch, yellow nylon rope."

"Is that what they're searching the house for?" asked Tucker.

"Just Mark's car. The house warrant is limited to computers—Mark's, Baine's, and Cooper's."

"Why not the rope?"

"Because we're obviously dealing with a savvy prosecutor. If they find rope in Mark's car and it matches the murder weapon, it's a home run. But if they search the entire house and find nothing, that would give the defense something to crow about. It's a calculated risk on the part of the state attorney."

A young man called to him—"Mr Swyteck?"—from the top stair. Jack ended the call with Tucker and headed up. It was Mark's friend Cooper Bartlett.

"They just finished in my room," he told Jack.

"Is your lawyer here?"

"I don't have one."

"You need one."

"I know," said Cooper. "My parents are divorced, and my dad says if I need money for a lawyer, I should sell my car. You don't happen to know an attorney who wants an eight-year-old Miata with eighty thousand miles, do you?"

What kind of father . . . Jack began to wonder, then stopped. He'd seen even bigger deadbeats. "Cooper, you need a lawyer right away."

"My mom's working on it."

"Where is Baine?"

"In his room. With his lawyer."

Jack had called Leonard Oden on the drive back from Live Oak but received no reply. He was eager to meet him—and not just to get some clarity as to his position on Baine's polygraph examination. He continued down the hallway, where another officer was posted outside the open door to Baine's room. Jack introduced himself to the officer, which drew Baine and his attorney out of the room. Jack's mouth opened, but his words were on a several-second delay.

"Leonard Oden," the lawyer said, as he handed Jack a business card. "And yeah, dude: I'm black."

Jack felt a tinge of embarrassment, but Oden seemed to have anticipated his surprise. Jack hoped he had a sense of humor. "Jack Swyteck. And no, dude: I'm not."

That drew a hint of a smile.

A hallway, in the presence of a Gainesville police officer, was no place to talk further. Oden ducked back into his client's room to oversee the search. Fifteen minutes later, Jack did the same in his client's room. By then, Cooper Bartlett's lawyer had shown up. The three attorneys met in the study, which—if cleanliness was any indicator—was the least used room in the fraternity.

Oden struck Jack as more than capable, a former public defender whose practice was entirely criminal defense. Cooper's lawyer, however, gave Jack concern. Edward Post called himself a "trial lawyer," which in the legal lexicon could mean anything from Clarence Darrow to "the parking ticket repairman." Two minutes into the meeting, Jack was leaning toward the latter.

"You need to fight this expulsion," said Post. "The university can't make it stick."

Jack would have liked to focus the discussion on the lynching, but the lawyers were still in the getting-to-know-each-other stage. Talking about the text from Mark's phone was like dipping the big toe into cold river water, testing things out.

"It's a preponderance of the evidence standard," said Jack. "If the conduct committee finds it more likely than not that Mark sent the text, the expulsion stands."

Post looked at Jack as if the guy from Miami just didn't get it. "It's constitutional law one-oh-one."

"I don't think so."

"Let me give you a little history," said Post. "September twenty-six, two thousand thirteen. Around one-thirty a.m., a black female student walks past UF's oldest and biggest fraternity. One of the frat boys sitting on the front porch yells out racial, sexually charged insults. What punishment do you think the university handed down?"

"Something less than expulsion, if I take your drift," said Jack.

"Cultural education," said Post. "The dean of students told the *Gainesville Sun* that as reprehensible as the behavior was, it is protected by the First Amendment as free speech, so it would be illegal to punish him."

"That's different," said Jack. "Threatening to kill someone is never protected speech. Threatening to lynch a man because he's black is even worse. It's a hate crime under Florida law—a first-degree felony. We're talking mandatory prison time. Mark's defense is that he didn't send the text. Not that it was his constitutional right to send it."

Oden agreed. "And Mark also has the football factor working against him."

"The football factor?" asked Jack.

"President Waterston announced the expulsion less than thirty minutes after Devon Claiborne tweeted that his father wants him to de-commit from UF."

"Who's Devon Claiborne?" asked Jack.

"Senior at Booker T. high school. Number one quarterback in the nation."

"What does that have to do with the expulsion hearing?"

"Everything," said Oden. "If you win that hearing, UF loses a future Heisman candidate who can deliver this university its first national championship since Urban Meyer was head coach. I don't care how many constitutional rights you try to wrap around your client. There's only one top recruit in the nation. Only one Devon."

"So, you're saying—"

"I'm saying Mark Towson doesn't have a prayer."

It sounded too cynical, but it had Jack thinking. "I hope you're wrong."

The discussion turned to the search warrants. Seizure of the computers was not unexpected, and they agreed that virtually anybody could have yellow nylon rope in his car or garage—or his fraternity. Still, it wouldn't be a good thing if the search turned up rope that matched the one used in the lynching. The situation was still too fluid for Jack to talk freely, however, and each lawyer was understandably guarded in his remarks, except to say that his client had nothing to do with the murder of Jamal Cousin. Cooper's lawyer checked his watch repeatedly and left the meeting precisely at the top of the hour. Jack surmised that Cooper's deadbeat dad had agreed to pay for one hour of attorney time, not a minute more. The door closed, and Jack turned the conversation to something he'd been waiting since his meeting with the state attorney to discuss alone with Baine's lawyer.

"Oliver Boalt wanted Mark to submit to a polygraph," said Jack. "I told him no, but he said you and Baine were considering it."

Oden burst into laughter.

"What's so funny?" asked Jack.

"Jack, I never said anything to Oliver Boalt about a polygraph. That never even came up."

The chant of demonstrators outside the house grew louder—*TPO must go!* Jack spoke over it. "So Boalt lied to me?"

"Why are you so surprised? This can't be your first rodeo with a country lawyer."

"Far from it."

"Boalt took a big bite out of your big-city attitude, chewed that shit up, and spit in your face. Politely, of course. It's the 'aw-shucks' good ol' boy style. They're all the same."

"No, they're not," said Jack.

Oden removed his eyeglasses, as if Jack needed a better look at his face. "They are if you look like me."

Jack didn't have an immediate response, and Oden didn't wait for one. He rose and shook Jack's hand. "Looking forward to working beside you, Jack. This is gonna be . . . interesting."

"Yeah," said Jack. "Good word for it."

CHAPTER 12

Jack expected a funereal atmosphere inside the Towson home. Instead, he found Mark's father almost bouncing off the walls with renewed energy.

"Jack, so glad you're back," Tucker said, as he took him by the arm and led him inside. "I want you to meet Candace."

"Candace who?" asked Jack.

"Candace Holder," she said, as she emerged from the kitchen. Holder was a tall, well-dressed African American woman who looked like she'd just stepped off a news set. "President and founder of Holder Images and Media Relations."

"You hired a PR firm?" asked Jack.

"Course not," Tucker said with a chuckle. "I could never afford Candace."

"I'm here to give Tucker a few tips," she said. "Tucker and I worked together in the governor's office. I was communications director for your father during his first term."

The first term—when Jack was at the Freedom Institute and Harry Swyteck was signing more death warrants than any governor in Florida history. The dark days when Jack and his father weren't speaking.

Elizabeth stepped out of the master bedroom, then stopped and turned like an awkward runway model. Holder raised an eyebrow in disapproval.

"I'm sorry, honey. That dress and those pearls are way too Paula Deen. Negative association. The last thing we need is for folks to look at you and be reminded of a woman who went down in flames for using the N-word. If there's nothing else in that closet, we're going shopping."

Elizabeth sighed, clearly exasperated. Jack was tired, but Elizabeth looked beyond exhausted, almost ill. "I haven't slept since Mark called and woke Tucker and me up last night," she said. "Can I just go to bed, please?"

"A few more minutes and we're done," said Candace. "We have to get this right. Think of the media as your partner in a Viennese waltz. I'm the choreographer who will make sure that you're the one leading."

Tucker smiled. "Isn't she great, Jack? You know, it was Candace who handled that PR nightmare when the media accused your father of executing an innocent man."

Tucker had apparently forgotten that the "innocent man" was Jack's client.

"Elizabeth, get some sleep," said Jack.

"Thank you, Jack." There was still no color in her face, but her eyes smiled in appreciation as she retreated into the bedroom and closed the door.

Candace looked at Tucker and said, "I was just trying to help."

"You're right," said Jack. "I'm sorry. But let's talk about this. I've seen clients go down the highly choreographed road before. It can backfire."

"Jack, did you not see that pompous ass Leroy Highsmith on TV?" asked Tucker.

"I heard him on the radio on my drive back to Gainesville," said Jack.

"He called my son a terrorist. A *terrorist*!"

"That was a reference to the men who lynched Jamal Cousin. Whoever they are."

"He all but called out Mark and his friends by name. Am I right, Candace?"

"Leroy walked a fine line, but yes, I agree with you, Tucker."

"I'm all for a strong and simple denial of any wrongdoing by

Mark," said Jack. "But Jamal has been dead less than two days. Launching a full-scale PR makeover of the Towson family before the Cousin family has even had a chance to grieve is a serious mistake, in my opinion."

"You underestimate who and what you are up against," said Candace. "Job one is to beat back this perception of a privileged white frat boy."

"Mark *is* a privileged white frat boy," said Jack. "We can't change that, and we're not going to win by trying to change it."

"CNN is back in Live Oak!" Mark shouted from the TV room.

They hurried toward the flat screen. The TV news coverage switched from international to "College Lynching." Jack recognized the beautiful Suwannee County Courthouse behind the reporter. Tucker snatched the remote from the coffee table and raised the audio. The reporter spoke quickly, eager to announce the breaking news ahead of other networks, but the bold, black headline on the white banner said it all.

SOURCE: LYNCHING SUSPECT REFUSES LIE DETECTOR TEST.

"What is she talking about?" asked Tucker. "Jack, that retired FBI examiner you asked me to hire won't even be here for another hour."

The segment ended, and CNN shifted to other news. Jack felt his anger rising but calmly explained the dirty trick that Oliver Boalt had played with the polygraph exam, making an offer that Jack *had* to refuse, then using it against him in the media.

"We need to punch back," said Tucker. "Mark, as soon as the retired FBI agent gets here, you're sitting for a polygraph."

Jack glanced at his client, who looked overwhelmed.

"I need to get outta here," said Mark. He stepped away quickly and went to the living room.

"Mark sits for the examination," said Tucker. "Period."

"Not tonight," said Jack. "Better tomorrow morning, after a good night's sleep. If he passes, Candace gets it out to the media far and wide."

"He'll pass," said Tucker.

"That's step one," said Candace. "Tucker, you should call President Waterston at home right now and demand that Mark's disciplinary hearing be held as soon as possible."

"Slow down," said Jack. "We shouldn't rush into a disciplinary hearing. If it doesn't go well, the student conduct committee could decide that Mark is a racist *and* a liar. Then where will we be?"

"No worse off than we are now," said Candace. "Tucker, it's your call. Let the media drag the family through the mud from now 'til doomsday. Or pick up the phone, tell President Waterston that you want an immediate hearing, and stop playing defense. That's my professional opinion. You two talk it over."

Candace walked away and went to the kitchen. The men stood in silence, and then Tucker spoke. "Jack, I like you."

"That's not important," said Jack. "This is about your son. Mark is *not* going to be ready for a disciplinary hearing tomorrow, the next day, or even next week."

"Then get him ready."

"We have to keep our priorities straight. Mark has not officially been named a suspect in the murder of Jamal Cousin, but those search warrants send a strong message that Mark is at the top of the unofficial list. You're kidding yourself if you don't think the disciplinary hearing will be used in some way to build the criminal case against him."

"So what would you do?"

"I admit I'm not a specialist in college disciplinary hearings. But as a criminal defense lawyer, I do know that Mark has the right to postpone the hearing until after the police investigation has run its course. That's my recommendation. It's what I would do for my son."

Tucker breathed deeply. "What if I go in with him?"

"What?"

"As Mark's father—what if I go into the hearing with him?"

"I know you mean well, but I'm not sure that would help."

"Jack, I love this university. My wife and I met on campus and sent our children here. How can it *not* help?"

How? Jack thought. *Let me count the ways.*

Tucker winked, as if he knew something Jack didn't, and then headed to the kitchen to deliver the "good news" to Candace. Jack went to the living room and, through the front window, spotted his client alone on the front porch. Jack stepped outside and joined him at the rail. The group of demonstrators—RACISM IS TAUGHT—had doubled in size. They were peaceful but still marching in a circle in the quiet cul-de-sac. Jack and Mark watched from thirty yards away, and then Mark broke the silence.

"What did the police take from my car?" he asked.

"There was no rope, thankfully," said Jack. "They collected specimens from the trunk, which they'll compare to Jamal's clothing and hair, and to the nylon rope that was used to kill him."

"This is nuts," Mark said in a hollow voice. "I could hardly believe it when they accused me of sending that text. I sure as hell didn't have anything to do with a lynching. But—"

Jack waited for him to finish, but there was only silence. "But what?" asked Jack.

"How reliable are lie detector tests?"

"Somewhat reliable, if the test is given under ideal circumstances. Not very reliable, I'd say, for someone under your kind of stress. We'll see how you feel in the morning."

"So I could fail, even if I'm telling the truth?"

"Yes. But this is private. No one will know if you fail."

"My parents will know, right?"

"Your father will. I suppose he could tell your mother."

"And then I would have to go to her and say, 'Hey, just forget about that test, Mom. It's totally bogus. I'm not really guilty.'"

"That's between you and your mother, I suppose."

Mark looked away, then drew a breath. "I don't want to take a lie detector test."

Their eyes met, and Jack could see his pain. "Then you don't have to, Mark."

Jack laid a hand on his client's shoulder. Together, and in silence, their gazes drifted back toward the demonstrators, the streetlights blinking on as darkness fell on day one of protest.

CHAPTER 13

On Monday morning, Oliver Boalt drove to Jacksonville, east of Live Oak. Florida's sixty-seven counties were served by twenty-four medical examiner offices, and Suwannee fell under the Jacksonville office. The state attorney and the homicide detective Josh Proctor had a ten o'clock appointment with the chief medical examiner, Elena Ross, M.D., ME.

"VapoRub?" Dr. Ross asked.

She was offering the familiar blue jar. A little dab above the upper lip could be a lifesaver for anyone who wasn't accustomed to the stench of an autopsy. Boalt normally didn't need it, but he remembered the last time a body had been pulled from the river.

"Thanks," said Boalt, and he inhaled the menthol.

Dr. Ross led them to the examination room. Detective Proctor's eyeglasses fogged as they entered, the lenses not yet adjusted to the chilly room. The examiner waited for him to wipe them clean.

"Ready?" asked Dr. Ross.

"Yep," said Proctor, but the state attorney hesitated. Boalt had seen the bodies of dozens of homicide victims and thousands of gruesome photographs. The ability of an evil mind to find perverse ways in which to end another life was limitless. He'd seen shootings, stabbings, burnings, clubbings, and so much worse. But a lynching? Never. Maybe it was Leroy Highsmith's "terrorist" speech. Or maybe it was that, not *really* so long ago, these acts of racial terrorism were not unheard of in Suwannee County—and not once had a coroner affixed an actual cause of death. Boalt was having trouble getting his mind around this one.

"Okay, let's do this," he said.

They moved to the center of the room, where the body of Jamal Cousin was laid faceup on the stainless steel table. Dr. Ross had been at work since 5:00 a.m. Two deep incisions ran laterally from shoulder to shoulder, across the breasts at a downward angle, meeting at the sternum. A long, deeper cut ran from the breastbone to the groin, forming the stem in the coroner's classic "Y" incision. The victim's lungs were set aside on the dissection table.

Dr. Ross aimed her laser pointer at ligature marks around the wrists and ankles. "A hog-tied victim makes it pretty easy to rule out suicide or accident. The manner of death is clearly homicide."

"That's the easy part," said Boalt. "Where are you on cause of death?"

She switched off her pointer. "I've narrowed it down to two possibilities. One: asphyxiation—in this case, hanging. Or, two: death by drowning."

Boalt thought through the implications of the second—drowning. "You realize that, even at high tide, Jamal's head was high enough above the river that his nose and mouth would never have been underwater."

"That's an external fact for you to sort out. I'm looking solely at the body and, forensically speaking, I cannot rule out drowning."

"I need you to explain that to me, doc," said Boalt.

"Happy to," said Ross, and suddenly her inner teacher emerged. "Drowning cannot be proven by autopsy. It is a diagnosis of exclusion, based on the circumstances of death. The first thing I do is determine if the body shows any signs of life-threatening trauma."

"What do you see in Jamal's case?" asked Boalt.

Ross switched on her laser pointer. "The body has bruising at the arms, suggesting that he may not have gone quietly to the river. And you saw the abrasions at his wrists and ankles. None of those injuries are life-threatening. Of course, the compressed airway from the ligature at the neck is in the category of life-threatening, but only if he was still alive when he was hanged."

"Can't you determine that?" asked Boalt.

"I do see classic signs of asphyxiation that are not typically seen in drowning. Petechial hemorrhages, for one," said Ross, pointing her laser at the victim's eye orbits, "the little blood marks on the face and in the eyes from burst blood capillaries. But there are other indicators that the victim may have been dead, or near dead, before he was hanged."

"How can you tell?"

She genuinely seemed happy that he asked. "Sand in the mouth and throat," said Ross. "That's a critically important fact if you think about what happens in a drowning. The normal reaction when the head goes underwater is to hold your breath. Eventually, you can't do it any longer, and your body is forced to gasp for air. That presents a major problem if you can't reach the surface."

"If you're hog-tied, for example," said Boalt.

"Correct. So the victim starts gulping water into the mouth and throat, literally inhaling water into the lungs. This, of course, sends the victim into an even more frenzied panic. If he doesn't break the surface, his lungs continue to fill, struggling and gasping in a vicious cycle that can last several minutes, until breathing stops. In a river, a hog-tied victim would twist and flail, gulping at anything. It's entirely likely that he would have kicked up sand and dirt from the river bottom, and some of it ended up in his mouth and throat."

"And is that what you see in Jamal Cousin?" asked Boalt.

The laser pointed to the surgical incision at Jamal's throat. "That's exactly what I see."

"So you're leaning toward death by drowning as opposed to hanging?"

The laser pointer shifted to organs on the tray. "I'll know more when I've examined the lungs," she said, switching off the laser. "But we may never know with absolute certainty."

"But it's one or the other, right? Drowning or hanging?"

"Or, as I suggested, some combination of the two."

Boalt took a moment, theorizing. "An up-and-down motion, maybe? Like a medieval dunking in the town square?"

"Again, those kinds of mechanics are your department," said Dr. Ross.

Detective Proctor breathed a heavy sigh, as if visualizing the picture that Boalt had just painted. "Not a pleasant way to go."

Boalt stepped away, inhaling the menthol below his lip, but it wasn't the odor that had brought on the sudden nausea. "Nothing pleasant about this case."

CHAPTER 14

Jack's flight landed at Miami International Airport on Monday evening. Andie picked him up on her way home from work, greeting him with a kiss at the curb for arrivals.

Jack held his smile a little longer than usual as he settled into the passenger seat.

"What?" she asked.

"I forgot you were blond these days."

Andie's natural raven-black hair and green eyes made for an exotic beauty. She'd dyed her hair honey-blond and cut it to shoulder length for a "partial" undercover assignment, which had been taking her someplace—Jack didn't know where—three days a week for the past two months.

"Some men have to cheat if they want another woman," she said. "All you have to do is wait for my next assignment."

Jack laughed, but it did kind of make him feel lucky.

Andie maneuvered back into the flow of slow-moving traffic. "Righley can't wait to see you. I told Abuela to let her stay up 'til we get home."

Abuela was Jack's maternal grandmother, but in some ways, Righley was her first grandchild. The Castro dictatorship had kept her from coming to Miami until Jack was in his thirties, more than three decades after the death of Jack's Cuban-born mother. By then, Jack was hopelessly Anglo, raised by his non-Hispanic father and stepmother. It was Abuela's mission to make sure that Righley knew her *ropa vieja* from her *picadillo*.

The sun dipped behind the Miami skyline on the drive home to

Key Biscayne, and night had fallen by the time Andie pulled the car into the garage. Jack had barely set foot in the kitchen when Righley came flying around the corner.

"Daddy, Daddy, there a spidey on the house!"

Jack smiled and gobbled her up into his arms. "A spider?"

"Yeah. Big one! Come see!"

She wiggled out of his grasp, jumped to the floor, and ran to the living room. Jack followed her all the way to the front door.

"Come on, come on! Open it!"

Jack turned the dead bolt. He heard a toilet flush at the other end of the house, followed by the quick shuffle of Abuela's feet in the hallway.

"Righley, no!" she shouted, but Jack had already opened the front door.

He froze.

Abuela hurried into the room, scooped up Righley, and spirited her away. Andie was standing in the living room, as dumbstruck as Jack. It had been too dark outside to notice when they'd pulled up to the house, but there was no mistaking the spray-painted image on the door.

"There's a swastika on our house," said Andie. She approached slowly, in utter disbelief, then led Jack outside and closed the door.

"I'm sorry," was all Jack could say.

"Who would do this?"

"It's a high-charged case. It could be any punk who watches the news."

Andie looked at it again, and it pained Jack to see the expression on her face. "Jack, I have never told you not to take a case."

"I know. And I love you for that."

"When you and the Freedom Institute decided to sue the president of the United States to get a detainee out of Gitmo, I said 'no problem.' You wanted to stop the execution of a man convicted of murdering a seventeen-year-old girl—fine, it's your decision. But this . . ."

"Is the same thing," said Jack.

"No," she said firmly. "It's not."

"How is it different?"

"Because it *is*, Jack. It just *is*."

They stood in silence. A passenger jet rumbled in the night sky above them, on its way to Miami International.

"Are you asking me to quit?"

Andie looked away, clearly struggling. "I don't know."

More silence. "If it helps, I don't believe Mark had anything to do with the lynching."

Their eyes met. "How do you know, Jack?"

"You know I can't get into that. Any more than you can tell me where your next undercover assignment will be."

Andie's head rolled back, as if searching the stars for patience. "Well, isn't that convenient?"

"Would it make you feel better if I told you he was guilty?"

She shot a look of resentment, and Jack quickly regretted his words.

"No, Jack. It wouldn't. But I can tell you what *would*. I'd feel so much better if I didn't have to walk into that house, our *home*—" Andie paused, fought back the tears, and continued in a calmer voice—"and tell our daughter why there's a fucking swastika on our front door."

She yanked open the door, went inside, and slammed it shut before Jack could follow.

He wanted to reassure her, to tell her how rare it was for people to act out against the lawyer in a case, but he let her go. It wasn't as if this was the first time. Eddie Goss came to mind. Defending a man who had confessed to the near decapitation of a high-school cheerleader wasn't a popular move, especially when the victim was white and her accused killer wasn't. It didn't matter that the confession was coerced. Someone had splattered Jack with pig's blood on the courthouse steps. It was the tipping point for Jack—the trial that had brought an end to his four-year stint at the Freedom Institute. Jack had resigned after Goss was acquitted.

Maybe Andie was right. Maybe it was time to hit the reset button again.

Jack went to the garage for a can of paint. All he could find was leftover "princess pink" from Righley's room; not his first choice for a front door, but anything was better than a swastika. He gave it a quick coat and went back inside the house. Andie—the dyed-blond hair almost threw him again—was on the couch in front of the television. Jack washed his hands at the kitchen sink and then took a seat at the other end of the hump in the camelback.

"So, I was thinking about what you—"

"Stop," said Andie. "Before you say anything, I want you to watch this." She aimed the remote at the flat screen, rewound the cable news broadcast, and then let it replay. A reporter was standing on a busy college campus, her shoulder-length hair fluttering in the autumn breeze.

"Is that UF?" asked Jack.

"California, I think. Just watch."

On-screen, the reporter spoke into the camera as students in the background passed by on foot and on bicycles. "The apparent lynching of an African American college student in Florida has been a shock to campuses across the country. But for some students, it has also been an education. At least that's what we discovered when we set out this weekend and asked a simple question: 'Do you know what lynching is?'"

The coverage jumped to a quick sequence of taped interviews in which white college students, each flagged down randomly, attempted to answer the reporter's "simple" question. The first guy was dressed like a rapper and sounded stoned. "Lynching? Uh . . . no, man. I dunno." The segment jumped to two sorority women dressed in their Greek-letter T-shirts. The pretty blonde answered: "It's like those knights in Old England who got on horses and, like, charged at each other with those really long sticks, right?" Her friend laughed and corrected her, getting it almost as wrong. "That's *jesting*, you ditz!"

Andie hit the PAUSE button. The room was silent.

"That's sad," said Jack.

"Beyond sad. I swear, if you asked them what was the 'date which will live in infamy,' they'd probably say the day Miley Cyrus left the Disney Channel."

It wasn't a funny subject matter, but if there was one thing that criminal defense lawyers and FBI agents had in common, it was the struggle to keep a sense of humor in an insane world.

"Are you trying to tell me something?" asked Jack.

Andie looked at him, her eyes two beacons of distress. "What bubble do those kids live in? I don't want Righley to grow up that stupid."

"What are you really saying?"

She didn't answer right away, but her dismay slowly morphed into resignation. "I think you know."

Jack slid across the couch and gave her a kiss. "Thank you."

"You're welcome."

The back of his hand brushed her thigh. "Any shot at makeup sex?"

Andie grabbed the remote and changed the channel. "Don't push your luck."

Jack's cell vibrated in his pocket. He checked the number, stepped away, and took Tucker's call in the kitchen.

"I just heard from the dean of students," said Tucker. "The university has agreed to an expedited hearing. It's at ten o'clock this Friday."

"You know how I feel about rushing into this," said Jack.

"There's no choice. I've laid out the options for Mark. He wants this. The family needs this."

"You don't need to rush."

"Jack, Lizzy's cancer is back."

"I'm sorry. I didn't know."

"We just found out last week."

"Does Mark know?"

"Yes. That's why he doesn't want this dragging out for months and months. We don't have months and months."

Jack thought back to the conversation about the polygraph: Mark's concern that an unreliable test might tell his mother that her son was a liar.

Jack went to the magnetic calendar posted on the refrigerator. Friday had a big red circle around it—parents' day at Righley's preschool. He hoped Andie could make it. He hoped Righley never landed in Mark Towson's shoes.

"I need a full day with Mark before the hearing," said Jack.

"Sure. Oh, and, Jack? The dean told me that there can be only one other person with Mark at the hearing. Those are the university's rules. It's called an 'adviser.'"

"I'm happy to do it. But I also see Candace's point about getting a lawyer who specializes in disciplinary hearings."

"No," said Tucker. "The rules say the adviser can be anybody. Doesn't have to be a lawyer. In fact, I'm told that in most cases it's a parent."

"In most cases, the student isn't looking at a possible indictment for murder."

"If it comes to that, the courthouse is your turf. But this university is *my* turf, Jack. Both Lizzy and I are Gators. We sent our children here. I was dead serious about what I said before you left. I have to fight for my son. If only one person can go into that hearing with Mark, it will be me."

Jack could have pushed back, but nothing in Tucker's voice even hinted that the matter was up for debate. "Then we'll need two days for prep."

"That's fine."

The extra day was to talk him out of it, not to prep. But Jack let it be for now. "All right, then. See you Wednesday morning."

CHAPTER 15

At 10:00 a.m. Friday morning, Mark Towson was seated at the end of a long rectangular table in Peabody Hall. His father was at his side. They were in one of the oldest buildings on campus, a restored redbrick gem in the heart of the university's historic district. Peabody was originally Teacher's College, and it was still home to the College of Education when Mark's great grandparents had met at the University of Florida. It was now the Office of the Dean of Students, including Student Conduct & Conflict Resolution—the site of Mark's disciplinary hearing.

"Just try to relax," his father said.

They were alone in a room that was much smaller than Mark had expected. Lying awake all night, he'd envisioned something on the order of the Supreme Court of the United States or the United Nations General Assembly Hall. It was more like a classroom.

"I can't relax," said Mark.

The door opened. "Team Towson" rose in a show of respect as the seven members of the student conduct hearing committee—four men, three women—entered the room and took their seats at the table. The oldest, about the age of Mark's father, positioned herself dead center as chairwoman. Beside her was a middle-aged man, the committee's faculty representative. The remaining five were students. Each had a personal laptop. The rules stated that a student conduct hearing was not open to the public, but Mark had left his own laptop lying around in so many places that it was hard for him to imagine that anything on a college student's laptop was truly confidential.

"Good morning. I am Dr. JoAnn Pinter, and I will serve as chairwoman of this committee. Mr. Towson, this is not an adversarial hearing. The rules of evidence and procedure that apply in a court proceeding do not apply to student conduct proceedings. Do you understand?"

"Yes, ma'am."

"The charge against you is the creation of a hostile educational environment through a racist threat of violence against a fellow student. Specifically, you are charged with sending the following text message, which was retrieved from the cell phone of Jamal Cousin."

Dr. Pinter took a breath, preparing herself, and then read the message into the record. Mark didn't know whether to make eye contact with the committee members or look away. The latter might make him look guilty, but he didn't want to come across as combative, either.

"Do you accept responsibility for the charge against you?" asked the chairwoman.

Mark had been over this with Jack. Those were the only two choices: *"I accept responsibility,"* or *"I do not accept responsibility."* Words mattered, and in a world that seemed to applaud people who "accept responsibility," Mark wished for a third choice. It had taken Jack an hour to convince him that asserting his innocence was not dishonorable.

"I do not accept responsibility," said Mark.

"Very well," said the chairwoman. "I now call upon Associate Dean Michael Kravitz, Director of Student Conflict, who will present the evidence in support of the charge."

The door again opened, and in walked the associate dean. Aside from Mark and his father, he was the only one dressed in a suit and tie. Tucked under Kravitz's arm was a thick case file, which he laid on the table. He clipped a microphone to his lapel for the recording system, thanked the chairwoman, and began.

"At the outset, I want to make clear that I am not a member of the hearing panel and will play no role in the final decision. The role of director is to serve as liaison and to assist in the presentation of information to the committee."

"Noted," said the chairwoman.

The dean had avoided the word "prosecutor," but to Mark he sure sounded like one.

"Mr. Towson, the evidence against you includes an affidavit from Suwannee County Sheriff's Office Detective Josh Proctor. That affidavit states as follows."

Mark listened, stoical, as Kravitz summarized the evidence, which sounded a lot like the night of interrogation in the Alachua County Sheriff's Department. It lasted only a few minutes, but to Mark it seemed almost as long as the interrogation itself. Then the dean addressed Mark directly, which felt like a knife to the heart.

"Mr. Towson, you admit that the cell phone number referenced in Detective Proctor's affidavit is your number, correct?"

Mark swallowed hard. "Yes, that is my phone number."

"Thank you. That is all I have," the dean said, and then passed the figurative reins back to the chairwoman.

Dr. Pinter said, "Mr. Towson, at this time the committee offers you the opportunity to present your side of the story. Would you like to make a statement?"

Mark glanced at his father, who gave him a nod of encouragement. "Yes, ma'am."

"Proceed."

At the prep sessions with Jack, Mark had been opposed to reading a prepared statement. But now, standing before the actual committee, he was glad to have the typewritten words in front of him. His hand shook as he laid his speech on the table. His voice cracked in the first sentence, but he worked through it. He touched on his family's history at UF, his love for the university, his abhorrence of racism. His voice cracked again as he addressed the substance of the text—the N-word, which he never used, and "strange fruit," a term that he'd never heard. Some of the narrative was written by

Candace Holder; some of it by Jack. The conclusion was in his own words, which he didn't have to read.

"I didn't send that text message. I didn't let anyone use my cell phone to send it. I have no idea how it got on Jamal's phone. That's the truth. Thank you."

Mark returned to his chair, relieved to have finished. "Good job," his father whispered. But it was far from over. The first question came from Chairwoman Pinter.

"Mr. Towson, did you have your cell phone with you on the night of Saturday, September twenty-ninth?"

Mark had expected questions, but the first one startled him nevertheless. "Yes, I did."

"Did you let anyone borrow your phone?"

It was a question that Jack had asked him repeatedly. His answer to the committee was the same. "Not that I remember."

"Were you drinking alcohol that night?"

Jack had prepared him for that one, too. "No. I'm the president and the risk manager for the fraternity. We lose our insurance if I drink at parties."

"Were you doing drugs?"

"No. I don't do drugs."

"Well, if you were not drinking or on drugs, you would probably remember if someone else had taken your phone that night. Right?"

Another question that he and Jack had covered in their prep, but for some reason, Mark was tongue-tied. "I don't—I just don't remember."

The interrogation continued with each committee member taking a turn. Some questions were good. Some were downright stupid. Finally, the room was silent. The chairwoman paused to see if any of the panel members had anything further to ask. They didn't.

"Mr. Towson, apart from your opening statement, do you have any additional information to present?"

"Well, first I have some questions I would like to ask Suwannee County Homicide Detective Proctor about his affidavit." Mark shuffled nervously through his papers, and his father handed him the written list of questions that Jack had prepared.

The dean interjected, "Madam Chairwoman, Detective Proctor will not be appearing at this hearing."

Mark tried not to panic. His father rose and said, "Excuse me, but how are we supposed to challenge—"

"Mr. Towson, please take your seat," said the chairwoman.

"May I speak?"

"No, you may not. The rules are very clear that an adviser may attend the hearing, but he may not speak on behalf of the student."

"But I'm his father."

"Mr. Towson, the rules also state that repeated attempts to speak at the hearing are grounds for removal of the adviser. Please don't make me do that."

"Can I speak to my son?"

"Briefly and quietly. Or you can pass him notes."

Tucker whispered into Mark's ear. Mark rose and parroted his father's words. "The hearing file said that Detective Proctor would be here."

Dean Kravitz responded. "That's true. We were notified just this morning that he can't make it. Detective Proctor is a busy law enforcement officer, and this is not a court. This committee has no subpoena power to compel his attendance."

Mark wasn't sure what to say. "So, I can't ask him any questions?"

"No," said the chairwoman, a tad patronizingly. "Not if he isn't here."

Mark returned to his chair to confer privately with his father. "Should we get Jack?" he whispered.

"No."

"I really think we should get Jack."

"No, I can handle this."

Mark wasn't as sure. He rose and spoke on his own behalf. "Ma'am, I'm pretty sure my lawyer would want me to postpone this hearing to another day when Detective Proctor can be here."

“No!” said his father, springing from his chair. “We don’t want a postponement.”

“Mr. Towson, this is your final warning. If you address the committee one more time, you will be removed from this hearing. To answer your son’s question: the rules are clear that the unavailability of a witness is not grounds for postponement of a hearing. If you want to question a witness, it’s your responsibility to make arrangements for the witness to be here.”

“But we were told he would be here,” said Mark.

“Mr. Towson, you were provided a copy of the rules prior to this hearing. This committee can rely on affidavits or other information, even if it contains hearsay. Live testimony is allowed but not required. Now, do you have any witnesses you wish to present?”

Mark was fumbling, but he collected himself. “Uh, yes. I do. My sister, Shelly Towson.”

Tucker Towson rose, went to the door, and let her in. Shelly was a tall, athletic blonde, handsome in some of the ways that Mark was, and extremely pretty in the way their mother was. Dean Kravitz directed her to the witness chair that faced the panel. She settled into it uneasily.

Mark approached. He couldn’t have felt more awkward. “Um, okay. Thanks for coming, Shelly.”

“No problem.”

“Uh—how long have you known me?”

She chuckled nervously, then got herself together. “Like, all my life.”

The chairwoman interrupted. “You’re a sophomore here at the university?”

“Right,” said Shelly, and then she addressed the rest of the committee. “Mark’s two years older than me.”

Mark checked his notes, not wanting to mess up the next question. “Shelly, in all the time you’ve known me, have you ever heard me use the N-word?”

“Excuse me,” said Dean Kravitz. He approached the panel to

confer in private with the chairwoman, who put the next question to the witness.

"Miss Towson, do you have any personal knowledge of the conduct alleged in the charging documents?"

"I'm sorry, what do you mean?" asked Shelly.

"Were you at the Theta house on the night the text message was sent?"

"No. But Mark is my brother, and I know he would never—"

"I understand," said the chairwoman. "Under the rules, character witnesses are not allowed to testify at student conduct hearings. All character evidence must be presented in advance through a written statement."

"Mark's lawyer explained that to us," said Shelly, "but this is my fault. Our mom has cancer again, and with that on top of everything else, I couldn't focus. We missed the deadline. Could I please have just two minutes to tell you what I need to say?"

"Unfortunately, the time for you to submit a written statement has passed."

Tucker Towson rose, unable to contain himself. "Oh, come on. You're not going to let her talk?"

"Sir, you were warned—repeatedly," said the chairwoman. "I'm sorry, but I'm going to have to ask you to leave."

"What?"

"I'm quite certain that you heard me. Don't make me call UPD," she said, meaning the University Police Department.

Tucker Towson rose, embarrassed, disgusted, and trying not to erupt.

Mark scrambled for a response. "Well, can I bring in another adviser?"

The chairwoman conferred privately with Dean Kravitz, and then she announced the decision: "Yes, you can bring in a replacement adviser. But there will be no delay in this hearing."

Mark looked at his father, his voice a whisper but filled with urgency. "Go get Jack."

CHAPTER 16

Jack entered the hearing room and stood beside his client. "I'm Jack Swyteck, and I will be serving as Mr. Towson's adviser."

Mark was clearly glad to see him. The welcome was a bit cooler from the chairwoman.

"And those will be your last words, Mr. Swyteck. This is an educational process as much as a disciplinary hearing. The system is designed so that students speak on their own behalf. Are we clear?"

Jack nodded. He and Mark took a seat. The next words were from Dean Kravitz.

"At this time, I would like to present the testimony of Brandon Wall." The dean opened the door, invited the young man into the hearing, and led him to the witness chair.

"Who's Brandon?" asked Jack, whispering.

"No idea," Mark replied.

Jack checked the file quickly, then scribbled out a note and passed it to his client.

Mark rose and read it aloud to the panel. "Ma'am, the name 'Brandon Wall' is not on the witness list in the case file. I've had no chance to prepare any questions."

"Brandon is a rebuttal witness," the dean explained. "His testimony bears on Mr. Towson's claim that he was unfamiliar with the term *strange fruit*, which was used in the text message to Jamal Cousin."

"Rebuttal witnesses are allowed," said the chairwoman. "Proceed."

The dean approached the witness, and slowly Jack gathered a

sense of where this was headed. Brandon was wearing a collared shirt of the kind that was typical of Greek letter organizations. A strip of black tape covered the Greek letters on his shirt pocket.

"Mr. Wall, could you please introduce yourself to the committee?"

"Hello, everyone, I'm Brandon. I'm a senior here at UF. Jamal Cousin and I were in the same pledge class together at the Alpha house."

"Let me first express my condolences to you and your fraternity brothers," said the dean.

"Thank you."

"Brandon, do you know Mark Towson?"

He glanced in Mark's direction. "I know who he is. And not just because of what happened with Jamal."

"Tell us how you came to know who Mark Towson is."

His gaze swept the panel of committee members, like a well-coached trial witness who makes eye contact with each juror. "This goes back to last spring," he said. "I was working weekends in the kitchen at the Theta house."

"Was Mr. Towson president at that time?"

"No, just one of the brothers."

"Let me apologize in advance, Brandon, but I need to ask a few questions that I wish I didn't have to ask." Dean Kravitz paused, and unlike many lawyers in academia who weren't very good on their feet, the dean was completely at ease with the silence—the way a skilled trial lawyer would comport himself before going in for pay dirt. It was clear to Jack that Dean Kravitz had done more than earn a law degree. Somewhere along the line, he'd earned his stripes.

"I want you to think hard," he said in just the right tone. "Did you ever hear the term *strange fruit* used at the Theta house?"

"Yes, sir. I did."

"Tell the committee about that."

"There was a party. Last April."

"Why were you at the party?"

"After I turned twenty-one, I started bartending on weekends for extra money. Theta offered me eight bucks an hour to mix drinks at their party. It beats washing dishes, so I said sure."

"Did you tend bar that night?"

"No. I left before the party started."

"Why?"

He drew a breath. "Let's just say I found out why they wanted a black bartender."

"What do you mean by that, Brandon?"

The witness glanced in Mark's direction, then looked back at the director. "There was this special drink that they wanted me to serve that night."

"What was in the drink?"

"Vodka."

"What else?"

Another deep breath. "A watermelon liqueur."

Jack tried not to react, but even the white students on the committee seemed to get it.

"Did the drink have a name?" asked the dean.

"Yeah. It was—" The witness stopped, cleared the emotion from his throat, and then continued. "They called it 'strange fruit.'"

It hit Jack like a swift kick in the gut. In the hours of conversation with his client, not once had the "strange fruit" cocktail come up.

"Just one more question," Dean Kravitz said. "Did you serve the drink?"

"No, sir. I left." An angry glare drifted in the direction of Jack and his client. "Never went back to the Theta house. Not even to pick up my last paycheck."

"Thank you, Brandon. I know how difficult this was, but that's a very important piece of information."

The dean returned to his chair. The room was so still that Jack could hear the breeze from the AC vent overhead. Finally, the chairwoman broke the uneasy silence.

"Mr. Towson, do you have any questions for this witness?"

Mark looked at his lawyer for an answer. Jack whispered it, and Mark delivered it. "Could we have a brief recess?"

The witness raised his hand. "Yes, Mr. Wall?" asked the chairwoman.

"Jamal's funeral is tomorrow. There's a viewing in Miami tonight. I was hoping to be on the road already, so—"

"Say no more," said the chairwoman. "Mr. Towson, do you have any questions for this witness?"

Had the question been directed to Jack, and if the adviser were allowed to speak, Jack's answer would have been yes. As it stood, Mark was digging his own grave. "Live to fight another day," Jack whispered.

Mark leaned closer, panic stricken. "Jack, he's lying. I—"

"Any questions, Mr. Towson?" the chairwoman asked, her tone more assertive.

"No more speaking for yourself," Jack whispered. "I'll handle your father. Stand up, thank the committee, and let's go."

Mark rose slowly. He made no eye contact with the chairwoman, the panel, the dean, or the witness. "Thank you, ma'am," he said in a weak voice. "I don't have any questions."

CHAPTER 17

The unanimous decision of the student hearing committee was affirmed by the dean of students and announced before lunch: expelled. By one o'clock Leroy Highsmith was in Tigert Hall for a meeting with President Waterston.

"It's not enough," said Highsmith.

The president was seated behind his mahogany desk, wearing his signature white oxford-cloth shirt with the button-down collar and a silk orange-and-blue UF necktie. A ceramic alligator stretched across the credenza behind him. Highsmith, the only other person in the room, was seated in the striped armchair. They'd been in regular contact by phone since Jamal's death, but months had passed since Highsmith's last personal visit. Waterston's hair was even more silver than Highsmith remembered. It was probably thinner, too, given the week's events.

"Expulsion is the most severe punishment there is, Leroy."

"I want the death penalty."

"Whoa. The only issue at this hearing was whether Mark Towson sent the text message. This has nothing to do with the criminal investigation."

"I mean the death penalty for the Theta house."

Waterston hesitated. "You want me to pull the fraternity's charter?"

"You bet I do. The president of the University of Oklahoma did it to Sigma Alpha Epsilon when those drunken frat boys got caught on video singing 'hang him from a tree, there will never be an N-word in S-A-E.' I cleaned it up."

"I know you did. But—come on, Leroy. Oklahoma was different."

Highsmith popped from his chair. "Damn it, Dick. I've been hearing that all my life. 'This is an isolated incident.' 'This is just one bad apple.' 'The boy said he was sorry.'"

"You're talking as if I did nothing."

"You did worse than nothing."

"How can you say that? The university expelled Mark Towson."

"And he'll probably enroll in the Ivy League next fall. We're talking about *systemic* racism. Expelling one student changes nothing. The system survives. Worse, the system is told—yet again—that it can't be beat."

"I don't accept your premise, Leroy. There is no systemic racism at this university."

Highsmith replied in an even, assured tone. "There is systemic racism at every predominantly white institution in this country."

The president locked eyes with his visitor. Highsmith didn't blink.

"Well," said Waterston, slapping his leather desktop. "That's a debate for another day." He rose, just in case the slap on the desktop hadn't sent a clear enough message that the meeting was over.

Highsmith started toward the door, then stopped and went to the window. In the distance was the Stephen C. O'Connell Center, the big white dome where the Gator basketball team played its home games. O'Connell was a Florida Supreme Court justice for twelve years before he was named president of the university in 1967.

"You know I've never set foot in that arena," said Highsmith.

"We just finished a major renovation," said Waterston. "You should have a look."

"I would," said Highsmith. "If they changed the name to the Virgil Hawkins Center."

Hawkins was one of eighty-five black students who applied for admission to the University of Florida between 1945 and 1958. All were rejected. Hawkins took his case all the way to the Florida Supreme Court. Seven justices defied the U.S. Supreme Court's ruling in *Brown v. Board of Education* and denied Hawkins' admission to law school. Then Justice O'Connell concurred in the ruling.

"Stephen C. changed," said Waterston. "He became an integrationist."

"I'm sure he did," Highsmith said dryly. "But is that the asterisk you want to follow your legacy?"

The president had no response.

"African American students at predominantly white universities see racism everywhere they look, Mr. President. I'm sorry you don't get that. For a minute there, I thought you did."

Highsmith let himself out, closing the door behind him.

CHAPTER 18

First thing Friday afternoon, Jack called for a joint defense meeting, lawyers and their clients only. Leonard Oden wanted it on his turf. They met at Robinson Tower.

Named for Baine's family, Robinson Tower was a twenty-story private residence directly across the street from the football stadium. The lower fifteen stories were graduate-student housing—a donation from the Robinson family that, reportedly, had greased the bureaucratic wheels for the zoning variance that was required to build the first and only high-rise on University Avenue. The top five floors were for the Robinson family and friends, all "Bull Gators," the highest honor bestowed on any Gator booster.

Jack and his client rode the private elevator up to the penthouse and stepped into a veritable Gator sports museum. Shadow boxes on the wall displayed signed jerseys from Heisman Trophy winners Tim Tebow and Steve Spurrier. On a table, lined up one after the other, were more than a dozen autographed helmets from Emmitt Smith, Percy Harvin, and other Gator greats.

"Baine's dad uses this place at most five weekends a year for football games," said Mark. "Can you believe that?"

Jack would have guessed three, tops. "I can," he said.

A butler led them to the dining room, where the other lawyers and their clients were seated around the rectangular table. The décor was of course in the school colors—tacky, unless you were a Gator, but not cheap, even if you were Bill Gates. Jack and Mark greeted the others and took their seats—Jack's orange, and Mark's blue.

Mark looked devastated. His friends looked worried.

"So, are we next?" asked Baine.

Jack wasn't Baine's lawyer, but Oden seemed equally interested in Jack's take.

"Until the final witness, the hearing was all about Mark," said Jack. "A 'strange fruit' cocktail party could put this in the category of collective responsibility."

"For the *last time*," said Mark, "there was no 'strange fruit' cocktail. I was at every party last spring. I had to be. I was president-elect. That drink didn't exist."

"I sure don't remember it," said Cooper. "I don't even remember having a black bartender."

"Neither do I," said Mark. "I can't understand why, but Brandon Wall is lying."

Someone in the room was conspicuously silent.

"Baine?" asked Jack. "What do you say?"

Baine glanced at his friends, then lowered his eyes. "Brandon's not lying. I pulled the plug on it."

Mark leaned forward, grilling him in lawyer-like fashion from across the conference table. "Pulled the plug on what, Baine?"

"The drink. I was in charge of mixers that night. It wasn't until Brandon got all pissed off that I found out what 'strange fruit' was. He quit. I took three cases of watermelon liqueur back to ABC Liquor and bought what we always buy. Cranberry juice."

The room was silent, as if everyone needed a minute.

"Start at the beginning," said Jack. "Where did you get the idea for the drink?"

"Last fall I visited a girl I know at Boston College," said Baine. "We went to a restaurant in Kendall Square. I don't remember the name of it."

"Oh, come on," said Mark. "Are you going to tell us that a bar in Massachusetts has a drink named for lynching?"

"No," said Baine. "And that's the point. No one ever said it was about lynching. The BC girl I visited is an English-lit major. We went there because the cocktail menu had a 'banned book' theme. There was a flaming drink called Fahrenheit 451—that sort of thing. This one was named for a novel from the 1940s called *Strange Fruit*, by Lillian Smith. It's about a black man and a white woman. The City of Boston banned it. The U.S. Postal Service refused to ship it until Eleanor Roosevelt got her husband to step in."

"I've never heard of that book," said Jack.

"Me neither," said Oden. "Just the Billie Holiday song."

"And I never heard of the song," said Baine. "Until Brandon said, 'Fuck you, I'm not gonna serve drinks and say *yessuh* at a lynching party.'"

Mark could no longer sit, pacing as he spoke. "Jack, this has to be a game changer. Can we go back to the conduct committee?"

"Well, slow down," said Jack. "Good for Theta Pi Omega that there was never a cocktail that celebrated lynching. But what do you want to do? Go back to the committee and say, 'Hey, great news, everyone, it turns out that we were just looking for a black guy to mix watermelon martinis?'"

Mark stopped pacing. He fell back into his chair, glaring at Baine, who fumbled for a response.

"The book's about a white woman with a black man, and we don't have any African American members, so—"

"So you thought we should have a black guy there," Mark said, disgusted. "As what? A human prop?"

"It was a bad idea, okay? But I didn't know it meant *lynching*."

Jack started to say something, but his client reached over and stopped him. "Except that you *did*," said Mark.

"No, I *didn't*," said Baine. "Not until Brandon told me."

"Exactly," said Mark, "that was last spring."

"Yeah, that's what we're talking about," said Baine. "The party last spring."

Jack sensed it—his client was on to something—and he let him run with it.

"No," said Mark. "What we're *really* talking about is the party this fall. The night of September twenty-ninth, when Jamal got the text message. You knew that 'strange fruit down by the river' meant a black man hanging from a tree."

Baine's mouth opened, but words didn't come.

Mark's eyes narrowed. "I didn't know it. Cooper didn't know it. You're the only one, Baine."

"Well, shit, Mark. I'm not the only one in the *world*."

Jack watched, amazed by his client's sudden resurrection from the dead.

"Did you send that text message to Jamal?" Mark asked, his voice shaking.

"*No-o-o*," Baine said, chuckling. "That's crazy."

"Baine," said Mark, his voice rising, "did you send the text from my cell?"

"No!"

Mark launched from his chair, shouting at the top of his voice, "Tell the truth, Baine! *Did you send that fucking message?*"

"No, goddamnit!"

Mark grabbed a water glass and threw it against the wall, smashing it to pieces. "You're a fucking liar!"

Jack restrained his client by the wrists, fearful of what he might do next. Mark shook loose and ran from the dining room. Jack followed. Mark flew past the helmet display and was already in the elevator.

"Mark!" Jack shouted, but the elevator doors closed.

Oden caught up with Jack in the foyer. "I think we have a bit of a situation with this joint defense arrangement."

"Ya *think*?" said Jack, and then he hurried to the emergency stairwell to catch up with his client.

CHAPTER 19

Cynthia turned off the stove, and the kettle stopped whistling. She poured herself a cup of tea and was about to take a seat at the kitchen table when there was a knock at the front door. Virginia was upstairs cleaning, surely unable to hear the knock over the noisy vacuum cleaner. Cynthia left her steaming cup on the table and went to the living room, smiling pleasantly at the familiar face on the other side of the screen door.

"Afternoon, Mr. Boalt," she said.

"Afternoon, Mrs. Porter," the state attorney said in his most southern voice. She was still a "Mrs." in Live Oak, even after so many years alone.

"Come on in," she said, and the door squeaked as she opened it.

Boalt thanked her and introduced the young African American man who was with him. "Reggie is my district campaign manager," said Boalt, and Cynthia took "district" to mean the black neighborhoods. Cynthia was one of the old-timers, one of the few white homeowners left on her street.

Reggie offered her a red-white-and-blue pamphlet. "Would you like some campaign literature, ma'am?"

"Oh, you can keep that," said Cynthia. "Mr. Boalt has already got my vote."

"Thank you, ma'am."

"Would you like a cup of tea?" she asked. "I was just making some."

"That's very kind of you," said Boalt. "But no, thank you."

The vacuuming upstairs stopped, and her caretaker called out from the top of the stairway, "Everything all right down there, Miz Cynthia?"

"Just fine, Virginia," she hollered back.

Boalt glanced up the stairway, then back at Cynthia. "Would it be all right if I spoke with Virginia a minute?"

Cynthia smiled. "Courtin' every vote, are you?"

He smiled back, then turned serious. "Some more than usual."

She knew exactly what he meant, and it explained why he was going door-to-door in her mostly black neighborhood. "I'm sure Virginia would be happy to talk to you."

Cynthia hailed her downstairs and then excused herself, leaving Virginia to talk politics with the state attorney and his "district" manager. Her tea was cold, so she put the kettle back on the stove and waited.

Reggie seemed like a nice young man. Polite. Confident. Handsome.

Cynthia got a clean cup and dropped in a fresh tea bag. She thought she heard Reggie's voice from the living room, but it was just her ears playing tricks on her. The hot water gurgled as she poured, and her mind wandered—back to Reggie for an instant, and then to someone like him. A boy she'd once known. She finished her pour and stared down into the cup.

Steam rose from the clear black liquid like the morning fog on the Suwannee River.

Cynthia!" her father shouted, still outside her room. "Open this door!"

Cindy was in bed, reading. She jumped up, pulled on her robe, and let him in. "Yes, sir?"

Her father entered quickly and closed the door. He towered over her, and she instinctively stepped back. The soft glow of the bedside lamp only seemed to accentuate the anger in his expression. "Did you not tell that boy he owed you a letter of apology?"

"Yes, sir," she said, her voice quaking. "I did."

He pulled the letter from his coat pocket and nearly shoved it in her face. "Is *this* what that boy calls an apology?"

Cindy's eyes widened with fear. "I . . . I don't know. It's what he wrote."

Her father crumpled the letter into a ball and hurled it at the trash can in the corner. It bounced off the rim, rolled across the floor, and came to rest beneath her vanity. Then he grabbed her by the wrist so tightly that her eyes welled with tears.

"I need *the truth*," he said sharply. "You swear you told him? You told him you wanted an apology?"

Cindy wished she'd never taken the job at the dime store, wished that Willie James had never given her that Christmas card, or at least that her father had never found out about it. She'd never seen him so full of hatred, and she'd never been more afraid of him. "Yes, sir. I told him."

He released her, and Cindy slid her hand into her robe, massaging away the pain in her wrist. Then he leaned toward her and kissed her forehead.

"That's all I needed to know, sweetie."

Miz Cynthia?"

Cynthia looked up from her teacup. Virginia was standing in the doorway.

"Did Mr. Boalt and his friend leave?"

"Yes, ma'am. They're gone."

"Could you help me upstairs to my room, Virginia? I'd like to lie down."

They walked slowly from the kitchen to the chairlift in the stairwell. It had been years since Cynthia had walked up a flight of stairs, and the electric motor hummed as it carried her to the second floor. Virginia followed her to the bedroom and fluffed the pillows the way Cynthia liked them. Cynthia walked past the bed, however, and continued to the bureau. There were half a dozen old jewelry boxes lined up from one end of the bureau to the other, only one of which actually contained jewelry. Cynthia opened the one of burled walnut. Inside were faded photographs and other mementos. She removed a single sheet of yellowed stationery, laid it on the bureau top, and smoothed out the wrinkles.

It was dated January 1, 1944, but the rest of the writing was too faded for her aged eyes. She handed it to Virginia and seated herself on the edge of the mattress. "Could you read that to me, please, Virginia?"

Virginia nodded, but her smile turned to bewilderment as she read aloud.

"'Dear Friend. I know you don't think much of our kind but we don't hate you all. We want to be your friends but you won't let us. I wish this was a northern state.'" Virginia's voice trailed off.

"Go on," said Cynthia.

Virginia drew a breath. "'I guess you call me fresh. Write an' tell me what you think of me good or bad. I love your name. I love your voice, for a S.H.—'"

"Sweetheart," said Cynthia.

Virginia swallowed, then continued. "'For a sweetheart you are my choice.'"

Virginia put down the letter and smiled. "It's signed Y.K.W."

"You Know Who," said Cynthia, decoding.

There was silence in the room. Cynthia didn't look at her caretaker. Her gaze remained fixed on the old jewelry box on the bureau. Finally, Virginia sat beside her on the edge of the bed. She laid her hand atop Cynthia's.

"Miz Cynthia, did you have a sweetheart in high school? A colored sweetheart?"

Cynthia was silent. Virginia waited a moment, then tried again. "Does 'You Know Who' still live in Live Oak?"

Cynthia drew a breath and then looked at Virginia, her eyes clouded with memories. "Willie James will always live in Live Oak," she said.

CHAPTER 20

Jack caught up with his client in the parking garage below Robinson Tower. Walking was quicker than driving to campus, and they went straight to the Office of the Dean of Students at Peabody Hall. For Jack, it was like stepping into a time warp, reminiscent of the time he and thirty other undergraduates had marched into the dean's office, barefoot, in protest of a university rule that shoes must be worn to class. Simpler times.

On this occasion, the dean was equally unimpressed.

"The decision of the student conduct committee has been affirmed by this office and is final," said Kravitz. "I'm sorry."

"But I didn't send the text," said Mark.

Kravitz's expression was pleasant but unsympathetic. Jack could only surmise that a mature but impassioned plea from a student like Mark was nothing compared to the tears and outright begging that the dean had endured over the years.

"Unlike a criminal trial," the dean said, "the standard of proof in a student conduct hearing is not evidence beyond a reasonable doubt. It is much lower. The committee found it more likely than not that you sent the text message, or at the very least you knew who sent it and covered for him. Either is sufficient to support the expulsion."

"But there's new evidence," said Mark.

"The time to present evidence has passed. You seem to have forgotten that it was your adviser—your father—who demanded that the hearing be held as soon as possible."

"So, that's your answer? Be careful what you ask for?"

"Let me," said Jack, interjecting. Allowing the client to speak for himself, in accordance with the hearing rules, wasn't moving the ball forward. "Dean, I understand the university has a process. But let's look at the substance. Brandon Wall never mentioned my client's name. There is no evidence to connect Mark to the 'strange fruit' cocktail."

"But the totality of the evidence was sufficient to support the expulsion before Mr. Walls even testified. The 'strange fruit' cocktail bears only on the collective responsibility of the fraternity and the decision to pull the Theta house's charter."

Mark sat bolt upright. "The decision to *what*?"

"President Waterston called the national office of Theta Pi Omega just a few minutes ago to advise them of his decision. It is effective at midnight."

Jack reeled in his client with a tug at the elbow. "The death penalty is a pretty drastic measure for the administration to take without a hearing," said Jack.

"It's a matter of campus safety that requires immediate emergency action. Bigotry and racism have no place at this university. Zero tolerance is our policy."

"I have no problem with the policy," said Jack. "But throwing an entire organization off campus without due process troubles me. If it doesn't bother you, I need to speak to President Waterston."

"Are you the attorney for the fraternity?"

"I represent its president."

"Ex-president. He's been expelled. But even if you or Mr. Towson were authorized to speak on behalf of the organization—which I don't believe is the case—President Waterston is not available. He's traveling to Miami for Jamal Cousin's funeral." The dean checked his watch. "I'm planning to attend as well," he said, rising, as if he were already late. "I hope I have addressed all of your questions and concerns."

Mark glanced at Jack, making it clear that exactly *none* of his concerns had been addressed. Jack thanked the dean, and they shook hands. Side by side, Jack and his client left the office suite, saying nothing until they were outside Peabody Hall.

"What now?" asked Mark.

They followed the brick walkway and stopped in the shade of an old live oak. "Mark, have you ever tried to convince someone that a man is innocent when the whole world '*knows*' he's guilty?"

"No. Have you?"

"Yes."

"Did you succeed?"

"Once."

"How do you win a case like that?"

"You keep at it," said Jack, "until you just can't keep at it anymore. And then you wake up the next morning, and you do it all over again."

In the twisted limbs above them, long clusters of Spanish moss swayed in the breeze.

"This isn't going away anytime soon, is it?"

"No, Mark," Jack said, "it isn't."

They started walking. "Did I push it too far with Baine today at the tower?" asked Mark.

"No. Not at all."

"I think I really pissed him off."

"I think he deserved it," said Jack.

"It did feel kinda good, hitting him with both barrels like that."

"Smashing the glass against the wall was an especially nice punctuation mark."

They exchanged a little smile. Jack laid a hand on his client's shoulder as they continued in silence, away from campus.

CHAPTER 21

Friday supper at the Boalt residence meant a fish fry and coleslaw. Oliver and his three sons used to look forward to the weekly feast, and his wife, Marilyn, never seemed to mind the work or the mess. The boys were grown now, the youngest a sophomore at the University of Georgia. Marilyn continued the Friday family tradition nonetheless, selecting the freshest fish at the market, shredding the cabbage she grew in the backyard, and cooking enough for Oliver and the boys to eat their fill, even if it was just Oliver. Empty-nest syndrome, Oliver called it.

"The moon is full," said Marilyn, as she cleared her husband's empty plate. "What do you say I grab a sweater and we head on over to the Dairy Queen?"

"Not tonight," he said, groaning. "I must have knocked on two hundred doors today. If I walk one more step my feet will explode. Great amberjack, though, honey."

Something was clearly on her mind as she returned to her seat, reached across the table, and laid her hand atop his. "Oliver, you're worrying way too much about this election."

"Come November, it'll be too late to worry."

"Buddy Jenkins isn't even campaigning. I swear his only yard sign in all of Live Oak is the one outside his mother's house. You've had this job for twenty years. He knows he can't beat you."

If Oliver had learned anything from five generations of southerners, it was humility. But he'd also learned a thing or two from his phone conversation with Leroy Highsmith. "Any man can be beat," he said, "if enough folks are voting against him."

"Now you're being paranoid," said Marilyn. "Why would anybody vote against you?"

His campaign polling, though unscientific, put his favorability rating among African Americans down thirty percent since the death of Jamal Cousin. He wasn't in the mood to talk it out with his wife, and the chime of the doorbell answered his wish to change the subject.

"You expecting someone?" she asked.

He was. Oliver pushed away from the table and went to the foyer, moving with a slight limp. Not since his first campaign for state attorney had he walked so many neighborhoods and knocked on so many doors. He had the blisters on his feet to prove it. He opened the front door and greeted Leonard Oden cordially.

"Sorry I'm late," said Oden. "But I wanted to go over the details one more time with my client before driving up."

"That's fine. If Baine Robinson is going to offer up testimony against his own fraternity brother, I want it to be one hundred percent accurate."

"It's accurate," said Oden. "More accurate than Mark Towson would like it to be."

The state attorney smiled, but not too widely. "Come on in, Leonard," he said, leading him toward the den, where they could talk in private. "Let's see if we can come to an understanding."

CHAPTER 22

The time was right for Jack to hold a press conference.

A media alert went out just twenty minutes before the event, allowing demonstrators no time to organize outside the Gainesville Holiday Inn. By 6:00 p.m. the ballroom was packed with members of the local and national media, and they continued to trickle in as Jack stepped to the lectern. Mark Towson, his parents, and his sister stood to Jack's side. The room was silent, and cameras were rolling.

"I'm Jack Swyteck—"

"Can you spell that, please?" a reporter shouted from the front row.

It was a clear sign that media interest had spilled way beyond Florida, where any journalist would know the surname of the former governor. Jack spelled it and continued.

"On behalf of my client, Mark Towson, and his entire family, we express our heartfelt condolences to the family and friends of Jamal Cousin. This is more than tragic. It is an unspeakable atrocity. The Towson family offers its thoughts and prayers to the Cousin family, and we fully support the efforts of law enforcement to find justice."

Jack paused. Photographers moved in for the perfect shot, a few crawling on the floor in front of the first row of seating, their lenses aimed at Jack's client.

"True justice is not a race," Jack continued. "Nor is it *about* race. It takes time. And it is color blind. Over the past thirty-six hours, you have heard some fantastic stories and unhelpful speculation. The facts will only become known as the investigation plays out. Tonight, however, these are the simple facts I would like you to know.

"Mark Towson did not text the hateful message that has been quoted in the media. Mark never in his life sent a text message to Jamal Cousin. Mark had nothing to do with the disappearance or death of Jamal Cousin."

Jack paused again, making sure that the media absorbed the heart of his announcement.

"At a time like this, it's normal for a community to feel everything from sorrow to outrage. It's good to express those feelings. It's not good to express them in a hateful way."

Jack was thinking of his wife, his daughter, and the pink paint over the swastika on his front door. He could have easily spoken longer, but he wasn't sure how long his client and his family could keep this up. Mark's mother had barely been able to pull herself together in time for the press conference. Jack decided to wrap it up.

"There will be an appropriate time to address your questions. Tonight, on the eve of Jamal's funeral, is not that time. In the meantime, I ask you not to prejudge anyone. Please be thoughtful in your words. Please be peaceful in your actions. Thank you."

Jack stepped away from the lectern. Journalists jumped from their seats and jockeyed for position as Jack escorted the Towson family toward the side exit. Reporters called Jack's name and shot questions at his client. The noise ran together, except for one question that caught Jack's ear.

"Is it true that Baine Robinson has agreed to testify against your client?"

Jack didn't respond. He just kept walking, steadily picking up the pace as he directed the Towson family to the exit.

"Mr. Swyteck!" the same reporter shouted.

Jack herded Mark and his family away from the onslaught. Jack was the last one through the doorway and closed the door behind him. Candace Holder was on the other side to meet them.

"It went well enough," she said.

"What about that last question?" asked Mark, his voice laden with concern. "The one about Baine."

"Baine wouldn't turn against you," his mother said. "He's your friend."

Jack hadn't told Mrs. Towson about her son's angry exchange at Robinson Tower, and apparently no one else had, either. "I'll call Leonard," said Jack.

"What if it's true?" asked Mark.

"I think it would only confirm what we already know," said Jack.

"Meaning what?" asked Mark.

"Baine Robinson sent that text to Jamal. And he is not your friend."

CHAPTER 23

Oliver Boalt led Oden through his living room to the den, where the two men could talk in private. They sat on opposite sides of the coffee table in a matching pair of leather armchairs.

"All right, where do we stand?" asked Boalt.

Oden opened his briefcase, removed a legal pad, and checked his handwritten notes. "First, everything Brandon Wall said at this morning's disciplinary hearing about the party at the Theta house and the 'strange fruit' cocktail is true. Baine Robinson will confirm it."

The state attorney shook his head. "Brandon is already a highly credible witness. I don't need anyone to confirm that he's telling the truth. I told you that on the phone."

"Understood," said Oden. "So I went back to Baine. We went over this multiple times. He searched every corner of his memory. Baine now recalls very clearly that he told Theta president Mark Towson about the 'strange fruit' cocktail."

"When?"

"Long before the 'strange fruit' text message was sent to Jamal Cousin. This proves that Towson is lying when he says he couldn't have sent the text because he never heard the term 'strange fruit.'"

As was his style in these negotiations, the state attorney was characteristically underwhelmed. "It's somewhat helpful."

"What more do you want?"

"Jamal Cousin received three text messages on the night of September twenty-ninth. The one from Mark Towson wasn't deleted, so we know exactly what it says. The others, from Baine Robinson and Cooper Bartlett, were deleted. I want to know what was said."

"And if I am able to provide that information to you—then we have a deal?"

"It depends. If Baine's message was just as hateful as Mark Towson's, there's no deal."

"You realize that there is no way to prove what was in Baine's message, other than his own recollection. Text messages don't float around in cyberspace the way e-mails do."

"Understood."

Oden settled back into his chair, thinking. "I'll have to speak to my client."

"You do that."

"But let's not get hyper-focused on the text messages," said Oden. "What I'm looking for is your assurance that Baine will not be blindsided down the road and charged with conspiracy to commit murder."

The state attorney leveled his gaze, making sure that his guest got the message. "Let me be clear, Leonard. I am offering no immunity to *anyone* who planned or carried out the lynching of Jamal Cousin. If your client was part of that, he will be indicted."

"But suppose Baine found out about it after it happened—then what?"

"Then we can talk."

"Fair enough."

Boalt rose to end the meeting, and the defense lawyer took his cue. Boalt led him to the foyer, pushed open the screen door, and escorted him out to the front porch. They shook hands in the annoying yellow glow of a bug light.

"Good luck to you, Leonard. And stay safe."

"Safe? Why wouldn't I be?"

Boalt hesitated, fearful that Oden may have misunderstood his remark. "Didn't mean anything by it. I just assumed you're getting heat for taking this case."

"Since when can't a black lawyer represent a white client?"

"Leonard, your client is from Apopka. Do you know anything about the racial history of Apopka?"

"Should I?"

"Used to be a Klan stronghold. Folks who lived there back in the fifties and early sixties say that probably three-quarters of the white men were members. Even Apopka's chief of police belonged."

"You're talking long before my client was even born."

"Nobody's born a racist, Leonard. It's taught, passed on from one generation to the next. I shouldn't have to tell you that."

"What are you implying? That Baine Robinson comes from a long line of Klansmen?" Oden added a little chuckle, but it came across as forced.

"I have it on good authority that the Robinson family had such ties," the state attorney said in a serious tone. "So don't say I didn't warn you if and when the black community reacts to that news."

Oden bristled. "If that's a threat, you surprise me. I didn't expect you to be so afraid to go up against an African American lawyer in this case."

"I wouldn't call it a threat."

"You're trying to scare me out of representing a white college student."

"A privileged white frat boy with family ties to the Klan. That's the headline, Leonard. I'm giving you a heads-up so that you can do what you will with that information. Call it professional courtesy."

There was no appreciation in Oden's eyes—no sign that he viewed it as a courtesy. "Good night, Mr. Boalt."

"You're welcome," said the state attorney.

Oden stepped down and walked to his car. Boalt remained on the porch, and the screen door opened behind him. His wife handed him a light sweater for their walk to the DQ. Boalt put his arm around her as the defense lawyer's car backed out of the driveway.

"Who was that, sweetie?" Marilyn asked.

Boalt watched as the car pulled away and the taillights faded in the distance. "That, my love, is a damn fool. And my new best friend."

CHAPTER 24

Jack drove himself from the press conference to the Gainesville Regional Airport. His plan was to fly home that night and spend the weekend with his family. A phone call from Tucker Towson changed all that.

"Mark went to the Theta house," said Tucker.

Jack was behind the wheel, just entering the rental car return lane. "I specifically told him not to. This division between him and Baine is real, and not everyone in that house is going to side with Mark. Anything he says will be twisted and used against him."

"The rep from TPO national met with the whole fraternity and announced that the house is being shut down. They've already started moving out. Mark feels like he needs to be there as president."

Ex-president, thought Jack, recalling the dean's clarification. "Where are you?"

"At home. He won't listen to me on this, Jack. Maybe you can get through to him."

"I'm on my way."

Jack steered toward the airport exit and ignored the speed limit all the way back to the university. It was smooth sailing until he hit the crowds of student demonstrators and the police roadblock at the end of Fraternity Row. It was exactly like his last visit, though the procession of demonstrators and crowd noises in the distance seemed a bit more ominous after nightfall. The posters had taken on a sharper edge as well. FRY THE FRAT BOYS caught Jack's attention as he flashed his ID to the traffic cop at the barricade.

"I'm the attorney for Mark—"

"I know who you are," the officer said. The University Police Department had apparently educated its force as to the relevant players since Jack's last visit.

Fraternity Row was closed to traffic, and more than a thousand demonstrators had gathered on the street in front of the Theta house. The police presence was easily double that of Jack's previous visit, while media vans and TV crews had increased by a factor of four or five. Jack avoided the crowd, drove around to the parking lot behind the fraternity houses, and took the first open space. A sandy footpath through a stand of towering pine trees led to the rear entrance of the Theta house. Someone—presumably TPO national—had the foresight to post a security guard at the door. The guy was as big as an oak, and he was stone-cold serious about the "brothers only" entry rule. Jack was pleading his case when the door opened and a young man stepped out carrying a box of his belongings. Jack seized the opportunity, slipped past the guard, and ran inside.

"Hey!" the guard shouted, but the big oak of a man ran like one, too. In just a few quick steps Jack was safely beyond him. As he hurried past two more brothers in the hallway, Jack caught a snippet of their conversation.

"You think Mark sent the text?"

"I don't give a shit. Where the fuck are we supposed to live?"

Jack continued through the house to the big room in front, Theta party central. He spotted Mark standing by the faux fireplace, talking with a group of friends. Through the pair of large windows in front, Jack could see Fraternity Row packed with demonstrators. He heard that chant again, led by the man on the loudspeaker—*TPO must go!* Jack went to his client, but the security guard caught up and grabbed him.

"Gotcha!" he said, huffing and puffing.

"He's my lawyer," Mark told him. "It's okay."

The security guard released Jack, seemingly dismayed to have run all that way for nothing. He was still trying to catch his breath as he walked away.

"I need to talk to you," Jack said. He pulled Mark into the TV room adjacent to the party room, far enough from Mark's friends to talk privately. "Didn't I tell you not to come here?"

"Didn't you know I would?"

Jack had known, on some level. "You don't owe the fraternity an explanation."

"Yeah, I do. Our chapter just got the death penalty. I'm the last president this house will ever have. I fucked it up for everybody."

A loud crash startled both of them. They hurried back into the living room. One of the front windows was shattered, the draperies moving in the light breeze. A rock the size of a baseball was on the floor, surrounded by broken glass.

"Everybody out of here!" said Jack. "Get to the back of the house."

The security guard returned, ready for action.

"Don't draw your weapon!" Jack shouted.

The guard took his hand from his holster and led Mark's friends away. But Mark stayed put, staring through the broken window toward the crowd.

"Let's go, Mark," said Jack.

Mark still didn't move. "This is out of control," he said in a distant voice.

"Which is why I told you to stay away," said Jack. "If this crowd gets word that you're actually here, it's only going to get worse. Now *let's go.*"

"No," Mark said firmly. "I need to fix this."

"Fix it? How?"

"Talk to him."

"Talk to *who*?"

"The guy with the loudspeaker."

TPO must go! TPO must go! The crowd's chant only grew louder.

"Mark, listen—"

"No, *you* listen. Right now every student out there thinks I'm a monster. Maybe if I just go out and talk with this guy, I can stop some of this craziness."

"Mark, that sounds really noble, but it's not at all safe."

"Yeah, well, look at what playing it safe has gotten me. I'm expelled. By tomorrow this house will be empty. The state attorney up in Live Oak thinks I lynched a black student, and one of my best friends is lining up to testify against me."

"The game is still in the first quarter," said Jack. "It's way too soon to throw the Hail Mary pass. If we make a mistake tonight, it won't matter if you're innocent. It will all be about the mistake."

"Fuck that, Jack!"

He started away. Jack grabbed him, but Mark broke free, hurried to the door, and yanked it open. Jack followed him into the night.

"Mark, don't do this."

His client continued up the front walkway, and Jack didn't know whether to make one last appeal to reason or simply tackle him. It was dark in the front lawn beneath the oak limbs, but Mark was just steps away from the intense glow of the television media lighting all along Fraternity Row, where throngs of demonstrators stood shoulder to shoulder in tightly packed unity.

TPO must go!

A police officer stepped toward Jack and his client, the beam of his flashlight blinding them. "Hey, you two! Back in the frat house!"

Jack and his client froze. The bright flashlight had plucked them from the shadows, and getting called out by law enforcement had put them in the public's crosshairs.

"That's him!" someone shouted, and it was quickly repeated over and over again as the news traveled like an electric current.

Another police officer stepped toward Jack with authority. "Sir, back in the house, now!"

Jack sensed that his client was ready to retreat, but just as they turned, a ball of flame streaked so closely overhead that they instinctively ducked. Launched from somewhere in the crowd, soaring above them like a tiny meteor, it went straight at the Theta house and right through the gaping hole that the rock had left in the front window just minutes earlier. A burst of flames erupted inside. Isolated cheers emerged from the crowd, but the pockets of celebration were soon overrun by widespread shrieks of panic and the urgent crackle of police radios.

"Holy shit," said Jack, as the flames quickly roared out of control.

CHAPTER 25

Percy Donovan watched in stunned silence. He was standing atop the brick wall directly across the street from the Theta house, where he'd been working the crowd and leading the "TPO must go" chant.

"What the fuck was that, Kelso?" he shouted down to his friend.

The front of the Theta house was an orange wall of flames. Sirens blared in the distance. Fleeing demonstrators screamed as they scattered in every direction, running into each other, pushing their way to safety, and trampling the fallen. Police scrambled to restore order, and within sixty seconds, a line of sheriff's deputies in full riot gear—helmets, vests, shields—reinforced the uniformed peacekeepers of the university police department. One officer took to the public-address system on his squad car.

"Remain calm! Everyone, please remain calm!"

Percy was close enough to feel the heat from the flames that had overtaken the front of the house. He jumped down from the wall and landed on the sidewalk beside his friend.

"Kelso! What the shit?"

"Molotov cocktail, I think."

"Who's the fucking idiot?"

"I dunno. Wasn't us."

The crowd surged past them, a mix of black and white students, all of them terrified. Percy spotted one of his fraternity brothers amid the confusion. He staggered into another demonstrator, who pushed him away.

"Roland!" shouted Percy.

He looked in Percy's direction but seemed to be in a daze. Percy grabbed him and pulled him toward the wall, out of the flow. His shirt sleeve was sliced open and his arm was covered in blood.

"Fuck! What happened?" asked Percy.

"There's a knife fight over there. 'Cept we didn't bring any knives."

"Who stabbed you?"

"Some alt-right motherfucker."

Percy felt a surge of anger. This wasn't his first march for Black Lives Matter. He was familiar with the tactics of the Traditionalist Worker Party and other white supremacists, and it was a page straight out of their playbook to throw a Molotov cocktail, blame it on the black demonstrators, and then wield their knives in "self-defense" against the perpetrators of "white genocide."

Percy removed his shirt and tied it around the gash in Roland's arm. "Gotta stop this bleeding."

"This is bullshit," said Kelso. "They want a fight, they got one. I'll take it to 'em."

"Don't," said Percy. "We gotta get him out of here. Can you walk, Roland?"

Roland nodded weakly. He was still conscious, but the loss of blood seemed to be draining his awareness.

"Help me lift him," said Percy.

Percy took one arm and Kelso took the other. Just as they got Roland to his feet, something smashed into the brick wall behind them with the force of mortar fire.

"Shit!"

The metal canister ricocheted to the sidewalk and rolled into the street, releasing tear gas and unleashing even greater panic. More canisters were launched in volleys from somewhere behind police lines and landed in the crowd. One hit a demonstrator in the shoulder and knocked her to the pavement. All along Fraternity Row, people were stepping over other people, coughing and wheezing as they ran. Some pulled off their shirts to cover their faces and stop the irritation, but Percy's shirt was the tourniquet on Roland's arm, leaving him without protection. Kelso pulled his jersey up over his mouth and nose, grabbed a smoking canister, and hurled it toward the Theta house. Percy continued forward, but all the pushing and shoving in the crowd made it almost impossible to keep Roland on his feet, let alone make progress.

"Stay with me, Roland," he said, but with his very next step, someone launched from the crowd and broadsided Percy like a runaway truck. The man was huge, and it wasn't the usual bump and jostle of a panicked crowd. He kept coming at Percy, the way a lineman might run all the way through a defenseless quarterback, driving Percy into the brick wall. Percy had barely seen him coming, and his eyes were too irritated to focus on the white face that was suddenly right in front of him. The man's voice, however, was unforgettable.

"Strange fruit, motherfucker. You're next."

The man delivered one last shove, slamming Percy's head against the wall. Percy's eyes rolled up into their sockets. His knees buckled. The crowd noises faded. And then his night went totally black.

CHAPTER 26

Jack caught the Saturday-morning flight to Miami. He couldn't count the number of posters and banners he'd seen over the past few days, so it seemed a tad ironic to be greeted by yet another one as he stepped out of the terminal.

Lov Dada Homm, it read. Righley and Andie were standing behind it.

"Did Mommy make this?" Jack asked playfully.

"No, me!"

"Starting at four a.m.," said Andie, bleary-eyed.

A family lunch in the Brickell restaurant district was a nice escape. They talked about everything but Jack's case. The respite ended when Righley put her head down on the table, closed her eyes, and found the sleep she'd lost while making Daddy's welcome banner.

"I saw the news last night," said Andie. "Three demonstrators stabbed outside Mark Towson's frat house."

Jack didn't mention how close he'd been to it. "Lucky nobody got killed."

"Do they know who burned down the house?"

"Some people say skinheads; others say New Black Panthers. Police are reviewing video from all the media and about five hundred cell phones to sort it out."

Andie checked on Righley before saying more. Still asleep. "How long do you think this will go on?"

"You mean the protests?"

"I mean you, in the middle of it all."

Jack remembered the advice his father had given him a week earlier—the tension between being Mark Towson's lawyer and being married to an FBI agent. "I wish I could say it won't get any worse before it gets better."

The bill came, Righley bounced back, and the direction of the conversation changed by 180 degrees. The rest of Andie's afternoon was planned out. Jack dropped her and Righley at a birthday party for a preschool classmate who, for the next four hours, would be known only as "Ariel." Jack didn't stay. He felt drawn to Coconut Grove, south of downtown Miami, where the funeral procession for Jamal Cousin was under way.

Around 2:00 p.m., police halted all six lanes on busy U.S. 1, South Florida's main north-south artery, as a mile-long trail of sadness flowed westward from the South Grove Baptist Church to Jamal's final resting place. There was blue sky and sunshine for the solemn event. Thousands turned out to line the streets in tribute. Sunglasses were essential, and even though it was a perfect day for shorts and flip-flops, many onlookers wore black, even if they hadn't attended the actual church service. Jack stood among them. He brought his best friend, Theo Knight, who had been planning to pay his respects with or without Jack.

"Not sure how I feel about you bein' Mark Towson's lawyer," said Theo.

Theo was Jack's best friend, bartender, therapist, confidant, and sometime investigator. He was also African American, a onetime gangbanger who easily could have ended up dead on the streets. And he was a former client. After four years on death row for a murder he didn't commit, Theo had Jack and a ragtag team of lawyers at the Freedom Institute—and DNA evidence—to thank for his release. Freedom came with a monetary award from the state, which Theo parlayed into two successful bars: Sparky's, named for the electric chair he'd avoided, and Cy's Place, a jazz bar in the Grove named after his uncle Cy, a sax player who'd been blowing an old Buescher 400 since Miami's Overtown was known as Little Harlem. Theo promised Jack free tequila shots for life. Before Andie came along, on plenty a morning after, Jack had prayed to God that Theo would just stop thanking him.

"Honestly," said Jack, "I'm not sure how I feel about being Mark's lawyer either."

Jack and Theo watched from the intersection of Grand Avenue and Douglas Road, Theo's old neighborhood, where the Knight brothers and their vicious gang, the Grove Lords, had once ruled. It was in the heart of the old Grove ghetto, outside the run-down bars and package stores, that a fifteen-year-old Theo had come upon a crowd gathering around the body of a woman who'd been tossed into the street like worthless trash. His uncle Cy had struggled to keep him away, but Theo was drawn in, as if he needed to see with his own eyes what drug addiction and a string of violent "relationships" had finally done to his mother.

"Justice for Jamal!" a man shouted.

It had been a common refrain all week, but it was jarring in this setting, where virtually everyone in the crowd stood in silent anticipation of the procession. Two escorts on rumbling motorcycles were the first to pass, their blue funeral beacons flashing. The shiny black hearse followed, moving slowly enough for Jamal's fraternity brothers to walk alongside it, about twenty on one side of the street and a roughly equal number on the other. Jack recognized Brandon Wall from the disciplinary hearing. He was in neither line, instead walking alone and directly behind the hearse, closest to Jamal.

An older woman beside Jack dabbed away tears. In complete spontaneity, not choreographed at all, the black men around Jack, including Theo, thrust a black power fist into the air. Jack stood in racial no-man's-land, a white guy who felt like he should be doing *something* to show his support, but he knew he'd look ridiculous if he raised a white fist and pretended to know anything about black power. An awkward gesture like that—doing anything to draw attention and potentially out himself as Mark Towson's lawyer—would have been foolish, though he felt more than safe in the company of Theo, who was often mistaken for Dwayne "The Rock" Johnson.

A black limousine carrying Jamal's parents passed. Jack could barely watch. "I shouldn't be here," he whispered.

Theo seemed to know what he meant. "It's what you people do."

"You people?"

"White people. You need to make yourself feel better."

"You really think that?"

"Yep."

"Why?"

"Because you don't get it."

"Why don't I get it?"

"Because you're white."

"Then why are we friends?"

"Because I decided I can live with it."

"That's fucking depressing."

"Welcome to my world."

Jack's focus returned to the procession. More freshly waxed cars with headlights glowing in the sunshine. More sad faces. The vast majority were black. Jack wasn't sure why, perhaps it was subconscious, but he found himself noticing the white faces. Really noticing them. He wondered what their story was, what had drawn them to the funeral procession of a young black man from Miami who'd been lynched on a river system that was immortalized in Florida's official state song. *Way down upon the Suwannee* . . . Jack wondered if being here made them "feel better."

Jack froze. His gaze fixed on a young woman who was standing across the street from him on the other side of the procession. She was tall, white, and blond, though most of her hair was beneath a broad-brimmed sun hat and her eyes and a good portion of her face were hidden behind dark sunglasses. He tried not to stare, but he couldn't help it, and she didn't seem to notice—until she did.

She quickly looked away. Jack didn't.

Two more cars passed. She glanced back in Jack's direction, as if to see if he was still looking. He was. Even behind sunglasses, Jack could almost feel their eyes meet.

Slowly, she stepped back from the curb, and then suddenly disappeared into the crowd.

Jack was standing elbow to elbow with other onlookers, with virtually no room to maneuver. He tried moving a half step forward, then sideways, to catch another glimpse of the woman. She was gone.

"What's wrong?" asked Theo.

Jack settled back into his unassigned place on the crowded sidewalk. "Thought for sure I saw someone I knew over on the other side."

"Who?"

Jack paused, trying to make sense of it. "Mark Towson's sister."

CHAPTER 27

The funeral procession ended at the City of Miami Cemetery. Leroy Highsmith told his limo driver to keep the air-conditioning running while Edith and Lamar Cousin readied themselves to step out into the hot afternoon sun. Highsmith sat facing Jamal's parents in the rear bench seat.

"Take all the time you need," said Highsmith. "No hurry."

The drive had been straight up Biscayne Boulevard, but the behind-the-scenes route to Jamal's burial in Miami's oldest and most historic cemetery had been more circuitous. City Cemetery sat on ten acres north of downtown near historic Overtown Village, which by law was the only place the black laborers who built and worked the cemetery with shovels and pickaxes were allowed to live in Miami. As the tropical beauty of the site emerged, City Cemetery became the final resting place for pioneers like Julia Tuttle, the "Mother of Miami," and James Jackson, the city's first physician. Deeds to the few remaining plots had long since been issued, and burial was restricted to the deed owner or a family member. It took the active persuasion of a congresswoman, not to mention a generous cash offer from Leroy Highsmith to a ninety-seven-year-old deed holder, to secure an open plot for Jamal.

"God's love is great," said Jamal's mother. It had been her mantra to get through the worst day of a mother's life.

"Yes, He is," said Highsmith.

There had been no "memorial service" for Jamal, but rather a "homegoing celebration." The theme was love. God's love. Love of family. Love from the community. Love from total strangers.

More than two thousand people filled the church, and a thousand others watched by closed-circuit television at the middle-school gymnasium across the street, Jamal's old school. People who didn't even know Jamal traveled from as far away as Houston and Chicago. Florida's governor and U.S. senators stayed away, citing their "respect for the family's privacy"; but dozens of other dignitaries attended, including two members of Congress, state legislators, and a retired Florida supreme court justice. Highsmith's eulogy had been about love, not hate. The message was the same from so many others, from the mayor of Miami to Jamal's football coach in high school. It had been perfect, until the procession rolled past the University of Miami campus, where a group of white students proudly displayed their Greek letters and held posters proclaiming ALL LIVES MATTER—which, as a rejoinder to BLACK LIVES MATTER, was like patting black people on the head and saying, "Sure they do, kid. You keep telling yourself that."

"Are you ready?" asked Highsmith.

Edith sighed deeply. The ceremony had lasted almost three hours, but Highsmith had been in this position before, with mothers of other young black men, and he knew it wasn't exhaustion that kept her from opening the door. It was the thought of placing her twenty-one-year-old son in the ground.

"God's love is great," she said, but this time her voice quaked.

Highsmith climbed out first and held the door open. As if on cue, dozens of car doors opened in the long line of vehicles behind them. Highsmith and Jamal's father escorted Edith toward the black hearse ahead of them. Brandon Wall and five other Alpha brothers, as pallbearers, lifted the metal casket and placed it in a carriage drawn by two white horses.

"Walk on," the driver said with a gentle shake of the reins.

The journey to the burial site began on a wide path of pea gravel, and in the solitude, little more could be heard than the rustling of the breeze and the crunching of stone beneath horse hooves and carriage wheels. They passed countless tombs, many adorned with angels, griffins, or cherubs. A few graves were brightened by fresh-cut flowers, but the most impressive splashes of pink, orange, and other flaming colors came from bougainvillea vines and hibiscus bushes that had been planted many years earlier, probably by mourners who had since found permanent rest here. They passed the large circle in honor of Julia Tuttle, but it was the second circle, a memorial to the Confederate dead erected by the United Daughters of the Confederacy, that drew a few sideways glances from the mostly African American mourners. The walk continued along a shaded path until they reached the west section, which was the designated burial place for blacks in the days of strict segregation.

"Whoa," said the carriage driver, and the horses stopped. In silence, the pallbearers moved into position, lifted the casket, and carried it toward the open grave.

Highsmith felt Edith's hand tighten around his. He and Lamar led her to a seat beneath a canvas canopy at graveside. Uncles, aunts, grandparents, and other family members filled in the remaining seats, while scores of others simply found a place to stand in the sun.

The pallbearers placed the casket on the lift. Jamal's cousin placed two dozen red roses on top. The Reverend Elgin Maynard led them in prayer. "The apostle Paul said in I Corinthians 5:8, 'To be absent from the body is to be present with the Lord.' Today, we know Jamal is present with the Lord."

The plan was to keep the graveside service short, but that could not stop the tears from flowing. The homegoing celebration had brought Jamal back to life, and Highsmith felt the family's pain as Jamal's mother stared down at the hole in the ground and the reality of his death.

Jamal's aunt led the mourners in a final hymn. The Reverend Maynard closed in prayer. Jamal's father thanked everyone for coming. Edith remained seated, seemingly numb, as people started to walk away. They'd reached the end of the program, but Highsmith wasn't finished. He stood beside the coffin and spoke loud enough for everyone to hear.

"Remember his name," he said. "Remember Jamal Cousin."

People stopped. There were a few amens and other affirmations from the gathering.

"The first grave in this cemetery was dug in 1897," said Highsmith. "It was for a black man. We don't know his name. His burial was unrecorded. How many names have been forgotten? How many of our young black men?"

The response was louder and came from all over, the gist of it being "Too many, far too many."

Highsmith plucked a rosebud from the bouquet of flowers on Jamal's casket. More than a dozen bouquets, hundreds of flowers, adorned the setting. "Everyone here loves Jamal," he said. "But we all know somebody else just like him. Somebody special with so much more life to live. A young black man who was supposed to be somebody, but whose life didn't matter to those who hate."

"Yes, sir," the crowd responded.

Highsmith dropped the single rose into the grave. "Trayvon Martin," he said aloud. Then he plucked another flower bud from the bouquet and dropped it into the grave. "Michael Brown," he said. And he continued to drop more flowers into the grave, saying the names of others.

"I want each of you to come forward," said Highsmith. "Drop a flower the way I just did. Say the name of a young man you remember. Jamal will not be forgotten, and we will remember the names of others, too."

A woman dressed in a bright blue skirt suit stepped forward. "Jaden Jones," she said, as she dropped a flower. Others came forward and did the same, saying more names aloud. Fifteen minutes passed. Then twenty. Soon there were more flowers in the open grave than in the standing arrangements around the coffin. Thirty minutes later, most of the crowd had dispersed. Jamal's parents and their closest friends remained seated in the first row of folding chairs in the shade of the canopy. Alone at the end of the row was a very old man in a wheelchair. It was Jamal's great-grandfather. Highsmith went to him and offered to help him forward.

"Is there someone you want to remember?" asked Highsmith.

The old man nodded, his eyes clouded with tears and memories.

Highsmith wheeled him forward. The old man's hand shook as he reached for a red rose on the casket. He plucked it from the stem and squeezed the blossom in his fist. His head wobbled a bit as he prepared to speak.

"The rivers have secrets," he said. "So many secrets. We lost so many of our brothers and sisters in those waters. Nobody said nothin'. No one was ever punished."

Highsmith hesitated, not sure what to think. "Say it now, brother. Say his name."

The old man leaned forward and reached out as far as he could beyond his wheelchair.

"Willie James," he said in a detached voice, one that seemed from long ago.

And then he dropped the flower into his great-grandson's grave.

CHAPTER 28

"Are you sure it was Mark's sister you saw?" asked Andie.

It was Saturday night and Jack was with Andie at Cy's Place. Theo had set them up at a choice table for two, right in front of the small stage where live jazz music would begin at ten o'clock.

"When I got Shelly on the phone, she denied being there," Jack said. "But Mark finally called me back and admitted it was her."

"So what's the story?"

The cocktail waitress brought drinks. They hadn't ordered yet, but Theo knew it was an IPA for Jack and a vodka tonic in a tall glass with lots of ice and extra lemon—not lime—for Andie.

"Mark wanted to be there," said Jack. "He's slept about two hours in the last two days, so Shelly drove. They left Gainesville at four o'clock this morning."

"You mean they were both at the funeral procession?"

Jack shook his head. "It ended up being just Shelly. Mark came to his senses and realized that he could literally start a riot if somebody recognized him."

"So his sister went as his proxy?"

"Yeah," said Jack. "To what end, I don't know."

Andie squeezed the extra lemon into her cocktail. "For some reason Mark felt the need to be there. His sister drove six hours in a car, and then stood on the sidewalk in his place. That's kind of sweet."

"Sweet?"

"Yeah," she said. "Step outside your work for just one minute. I'm talking purely as a family dynamic. Some siblings can't even sit in the same room with each other. Mark and his sister must be close. I think that's pretty great."

"I could see that at the student conduct hearing when Shelly tried to testify. They're two years apart in school, but the difference in age is more like eighteen months."

The musicians climbed onstage to set up for their gig. Uncle Cy wasn't playing tonight, but his spirit could still be felt. Jack signaled their waitress for a food menu.

"Maybe Righley should have a brother," said Andie.

Jack froze, his index finger still in the air. "Really?"

"Maybe an older brother."

It had been a tough pregnancy with Righley. Until that moment, all indications were that she would be an only child. Jack reached across the table and held Andie's hand.

"An *older*—" he started to stay, and then he realized what she was saying. "You want to adopt?"

"Don't you?"

Jack smiled, savoring a moment in a place filled with memories. The grand opening of Cy's Place was where sparks had first started to fly for Jack and an FBI agent who'd sworn she'd never date a criminal defense lawyer. It was at Cy's Place, on what Andie dubbed "the second anniversary of Jack's thirty-ninth birthday," that Jack had put a ring on her finger.

Jack raised his glass. "Here's to one big*ger*, happy family."

Andie smiled back. "I'll let you break the news to Max."

CHAPTER 29

At nine o'clock Monday morning, Oliver Boalt and his senior trial counsel entered the grand jury room in the Live Oak courthouse. Eighteen grand jurors were sworn to secrecy and ready to hear the evidence. It was their job to decide whether "probable cause" existed to elevate a homicide investigation to a criminal prosecution.

"Good morning," said Boalt, greeting his captive audience.

The state attorney's polite smile couldn't hide the pressure he was feeling. Public clamor for "justice" had reached a crescendo over the weekend, starting with the stabbing of three demonstrators on Friday night and continuing through the funeral service on Saturday. By Sunday night media vans and cable news teams had staked out positions around the courthouse in anticipation of an indictment—or a revolt. Boalt and his team worked nonstop with the Suwannee County Sheriff's Department and other agencies. On Monday he was ready to go.

Boalt took the entire morning to explain his theory of the case and the evidence, including the medical examiner's report. Step one in any grand jury proceeding was to give the jurors a reasonable basis to conclude that a crime had been committed—easy enough in this case. Step two was more difficult: connect the would-be defendant to the crime.

Immediately after lunch the star witness was on the stand, sworn and ready to testify. Senior trial counsel Marsha Weller did the honors.

"Your name, sir?"

"Baine Robinson."

The witness shifted nervously. Apart from the prosecutors, jurors, and court reporter, Baine was alone in the room. A grand jury witness has no right to have his attorney present. With just a few quick questions, the prosecutor established him as a fraternity brother and close friend of Mark Towson, someone the jurors could believe. A proper degree of reluctance and hesitation preceded each blow delivered to his "friend."

"Mr. Robinson, are you aware of any text messages between Mark Towson and Jamal Cousin?"

"Yes, I am."

Weller stopped him. With no judge in a grand jury proceeding, a prosecutor could in effect hit "pause" and explain things at her discretion. She presented a copy of the "strange fruit" text to the jurors and allowed them a minute to absorb it. Boalt had referenced the text in his morning presentation, and most jurors had admitted to having seen it earlier in the media and on the Internet. Nonetheless, several jurors winced at the larger-than-life image on the projection screen. Weller continued her examination of the witness.

"Mr. Robinson, have you ever seen *this* text from Mark Towson to Jamal Cousin?"

"Yes, I have."

"When did you first see it?"

"A few minutes after Mark sent it."

"Were you with him when he sent it?"

"No, but I was at the same party. We were both at the Theta house. Mark showed it to me after he sent it."

"Did Mr. Towson tell you that he sent it, or did he tell you that someone else used his phone to send it?"

"He said he sent it."

"What was your reaction, Mr. Robinson?"

"I told Mark that it was a really stupid thing to do and that he should delete it from his cell phone."

"Did he delete it?"

"Yes."

"What happened next?"

"We both went back to the party and talked to our friends—that kind of thing."

"Did you tell anyone about the text from Mr. Towson to Jamal?"

"No. But I kept thinking about it."

"Did you do anything about it?"

"Yes. About thirty minutes later, I texted Jamal."

The prosecutor paused for another explanation to the grand jury. "Ladies and gentlemen, phone records confirm a text message from Baine Robinson to Jamal Cousin. However, the actual text was deleted from Mr. Cousin's phone. So, Mr. Robinson, if you please: Can you tell us what you said in your message?"

"I don't remember the exact words. But it was an apology."

"An apology for what?"

"On behalf of the Theta Pi Omega fraternity, I apologized for the offensive message sent earlier by our president, Mark Towson."

An elderly woman seated in the front row raised her hand. Unlike trial jurors, grand jurors were permitted to ask questions. The prosecutor recognized her.

"Excuse me, but is this witness related to the Baine Robinson whose name is on the College of Agriculture at the University of Florida?"

The prosecutor allowed the witness to answer.

"That's my grandfather," said Baine.

"Well," the old woman said with approval. "Your granddaddy would be right proud of you, young man."

"Thank you, ma'am."

The prosecutor smiled—nothing like a friendly question to move things right along. "Mr. Robinson, let's jump ahead six days on the timeline to the following Friday night. The night that Jamal Cousin went missing."

CHAPTER 30

Jack and Theo were on a midnight ride in an old wooden rowboat, propelled upriver by the quiet hum of an electric trolling motor.

Grand jury proceedings were supposed to be "secret" by law, and while the state attorney wasn't officially talking, the media was already reporting that Baine Robinson had cut a deal and that Mark Towson was the lone target. Jack had no access to the evidence at this stage, so he decided to re-create it, at least in his mind. He wanted to visit the scene of the crime.

Their guide was Owen McFay, a local gator hunter who knew the local rivers after dark better than anyone. He rarely smiled, and when he did, his crooked teeth showed the stains of chewed tobacco. He reminded Jack of the redneck version of Captain Ahab. No peg leg, but his left ring finger was missing, lost to the snap of a bull gator's mammoth jaw and three thousand pounds of pressure per square inch. McFay was the undisputed go-to guy for night trips on the river. Theo went along, in his words, to make sure Jack didn't "end up like the cast in *Deliverance*." Having stood beside him at that funeral procession, Jack knew the reason ran deeper.

"How much farther?" asked Jack.

"Just a bit," said McFay. "Got it full throttle."

Headed upriver, even with a gentle current, "full throttle" on this rig meant throwing a wake that was little more than a V-shaped ripple. They were on the Santa Fe, a true black-water river that received the cooler waters of the spring-fed Ichetucknee. The river was about seventy-five feet wide in these parts, with willow-swept banks that sloped to depths better suited to canoes and kayaks than motorboats. Somewhere in the darkness were egrets and alligators. The tall cypress trees were mere silhouettes, their moss-clad limbs barely visible against the starlit sky.

"There's the boat launch I told y'all about," said McFay, as he steered toward the riverbank. "This is probably where they would've pulled up in their car."

"They must have left tracks in the sand," said Jack. "Crime scene investigators took an impression from Mark's tires."

"Did they get a match?" asked Theo.

"I guess only the grand jury knows for now."

The boat continued its crawl toward a wooden pier that jutted out into the river. A small cottage was visible in the clearing along the bank. "Yonder is where the boat was stole from," said McFay.

Fastened to the pilings at the end of the pier was a fourteen-foot aluminum fishing boat. Beside it was a larger fiberglass flats boat with a small Johnson outboard.

"That little one without the motor is like the one reported stolen on the night Jamal was lynched," said McFay.

Theo glanced back toward the launch and then at the pier. "So they drove here with Jamal in the trunk of the car, stole a rowboat from this pier, and took him upriver on the Santa Fe and then into the Ichetucknee."

"That's the story being leaked to the media," said Jack.

McFay steered back toward the middle of the river. "Wanna see where they took him?"

Theo gazed out over the bow. "That's what we're here for," he said in a tentative voice.

They rode in silence for another mile. Private piers and cottages on the banks disappeared as they entered the state park. The forest thickened, and the perfume-like scent of surrounding water lilies sweetened the night. The boat stopped, the electric motor went quiet, and all was still. Eerily still. The surest signs of life were the chorus of sounds from unseen creatures of the night. The rhythmic belch of bullfrogs. The midnight squawk of egrets and ospreys. At any moment, however, that peaceful pulse of nature could spike into tachycardia. Or so McFay had warned them. He switched on his spotlight, and Jack immediately understood.

Sleek and dark saurian bodies lay perfectly still, concealed in flat water that was black as ink. They looked dead—except for the countless sets of eyes lurking just above the waterline on the flooded banks—primeval red dots caught in the sweep of McFay's handheld spotlight. There was hunger in that eerie, ruby shine.

"Some folks say the Ichetucknee is too cold for gators," said McFay. "I say you need to know where to look. It's the young 'uns, especially, who swim upriver from the Santa Fe, where the big bulls eat anything under six feet. Better to be a chilly little gator on the Ichetucknee than a warm dinner on the Santa Fe, I reckon."

"Six feet is little?" asked Theo.

"Compared to a twelve-foot bull, it is," said McFay. "There's some males in these parts bigger than this boat."

Jack and Theo exchanged uneasy glances.

McFay looked up to the glowing half-moon in the clear night sky. "We're just about high tide. River's up enough for us to float right up next to the tree, if you want."

There was no mistaking what he meant by *the tree*. "Yeah," said Jack. "Closer."

McFay switched on the trolling motor and they eased toward the bank. "I'd never be motorin' like this if we was huntin' gator," he said.

The electric motor was quiet enough not to scare away the wildlife—but only to a point. They were ten feet from the flooded banks when a bull gator spooked. It triggered a chain reaction of splashing and thrashing, which made McFay grumble.

"This is what your amateur hunters do," he said. "Those gators will stay down for hours."

"Hours?"

"Sure. They can stay down all night if they have to."

Jack watched the waters go still, smooth as black ice again, no sign of alligators. “Not to be gruesome, but is it possible that a body could be left hanging here overnight and not be attacked by a gator?”

“Sure, if you spook these gators the way I just did. Now, you leave the body here more than twenty-four hours—well, that wouldn’t be a pretty sight.”

The hull bumped up against the massive trunk of a fallen cypress tree. McFay roped up and steadied the boat. Directly above, through the limbs of trees not fallen, the moon shone down on them.

“This is the spot,” said McFay.

Jack felt chills. It was like a scene out of a horror movie, and he could only imagine what Theo was thinking as the image flashed through his mind. The tying of Jamal’s hands and feet. The placement of the noose. The tossing of the rope up around one of these sturdy limbs. And then—

“How much did Jamal weigh?” asked Theo.

Jack wasn’t sure, but he’d seen photographs of Jamal. “I’d say one-eighty, maybe a little more.”

“Was it high tide, like this, the night this happened?”

That much Jack had confirmed. “Yeah. What are you getting at, Theo?”

“Let’s all three of us stand up in this boat. Come on,” said Theo, rising. “Get up.”

Jack and McFay complied, but the boat immediately started to wobble and Jack felt like he might go overboard. They quickly returned to the safety of their seats.

“Now,” said Theo, “imagine Mark Towson and his fraternity brothers standing up in this boat, trying to string up Jamal, who, I’m guessing, was kicking and fighting.”

“Unless they knocked him out,” said Jack.

“Or drowned him first,” said McFay.

Jack latched onto McFay’s thought. “The charts I saw say it was low tide when the body was found hanging from the tree. What's the difference between high tide and low tide on this river?"

"Three feet," said McFay.

"So Jamal's body could have been at least partly in the water at midnight, but hanging entirely above the water by eleven o'clock the next morning. Is that right?" Jack asked.

"That's possible," said McFay.

"Is that good or bad for you, Jack?" asked Theo.

Jack thought about it. "I don't know. Could be good."

"Or it could be bad," said Theo.

"How?"

"If Jamal was drowned and just left here floating in the water with a rope around his neck, Mark coulda' done this all by himself. Didn't need nobody to help him get Jamal under control. Didn't need another set of hands to hoist him up in the air while standing in a wobbly little rowboat. It's an easy one-man job. That would be bad, right?"

Jack was thinking of the media reports that Mark alone was the target of the grand jury. "Yeah," he said. "That would definitely be bad."

CHAPTER 31

Just after sunrise, Percy Donovan left his fraternity house for Live Oak. Brandon Wall rode with him.

The grand jury had subpoenaed two witnesses from the black fraternities, Percy from Kappa and Brandon from Alpha. They were scheduled to testify back-to-back on Tuesday morning starting at 9:00 a.m. The state attorney and his senior trial counsel wanted to meet with them an hour before the start of the grand jury proceedings. Their testimony would "not take long," he'd promised. The goal was to have them back in Gainesville in time for afternoon classes. Missing class was the least of Percy's worries.

"I'm kind of nervous," said Percy.

They were having breakfast at Denny's just off the Live Oak exit on I-75. With them in the booth was Ted "T.C." Calloway, an attorney retained by the National Pan-Hellenic Council, the body that coordinated activities between and among the many local chapters of the five fraternities and four sororities that made up the "Divine Nine" historically black Greek-letter organizations founded between 1906 and 1963.

"Yeah, I was nervous, too, before Towson's expulsion hearing," said Brandon.

Calloway poured a little sugar into his coffee mug. "Nothing to worry about."

"Then why do we need a lawyer?" asked Percy.

"Nobody should go before a grand jury without talking to a lawyer. When I heard you boys were subpoenaed, I called National and volunteered my time. We're just being smart. Percy, how's the Kappa brother who got stabbed Friday night?"

"He's fine. Took sixteen stitches to sew up his arm."

"I'm not surprised," said Calloway. "I saw the photos that got posted online. His shirt was covered in blood."

"We were scared," said Percy.

Calloway stirred his coffee. "You know what else I noticed on his shirt?"

Percy blinked. It was the lawyer's change in tone more than the question that puzzled him. "No, I don't."

"I noticed that he was wearing Jamal's Greek letters."

"Yeah. Some of the brothers in our house did that to show support."

"You know that's against the rules—to wear the letters of another house."

"We weren't pretending to be from Alpha. Just showing unity."

"I'm sure his intentions were good," said Calloway. "But when someone sees that photo online, they just assume that an Alpha brother got in a knife fight."

"He wasn't in a knife fight. He got attacked by a skinhead."

"Well, let's be fair, Percy. One of the three people stabbed was white. So somewhere in the crowd there was a brotha' with a knife."

"It wasn't us."

"I understand. But unfortunately the caption beneath the photo doesn't say that your fraternity brother wasn't in a knife fight, and it doesn't say that he's not actually a member of the Alpha house. So, going forward, let's all have an agreement that each house wears its own letters. Can you send that message back to your Kappa brothers, Percy?"

Percy glanced at Brandon, who looked away.

"By any chance are you an Alpha, Mr. Calloway?" asked Percy.

"I am. Cornell. Nineteen eighty-one."

Suddenly the business card that Calloway had shared with Percy at the start of the meeting made its impression. Calloway was a partner at the largest law firm in Washington, D.C. Alpha boasted plenty of alumni like him. The most famous alum from Percy's house was Huey P. Newton, cofounder of the Black Panther Party in the 1960s.

"Sure thing," said Percy. "We'll wear our own letters."

The meeting with Oliver Boalt and Marsha Weller was in a conference room at the office of the state attorney. Percy assumed correctly that the focus of his testimony would be on the discovery of Jamal's body while tubing down the Ichetucknee River. The state attorney, however, was working another angle that Percy had not anticipated.

"It's my understanding that you were in charge of organizing the trip down the river," Boalt said. "Is that right, Percy?"

"On the fraternity side I was. There was a sister at Delta Sigma Theta who reached out to sororities."

"Did you invite any white fraternities?" asked Boalt.

"No. This was an event for black Greek-letter organizations at UF and FSU."

"Okay. But it wasn't a secret event, right?"

Percy wasn't sure what he meant. "Secret? No."

"You sent out e-mails, posted the event on Facebook—that sort of thing?"

"Uh-huh. And there were flyers posted in all the black Greek-letter organizations at UF and FSU. I assume they all mentioned it at chapter meetings, too."

"That's what I'm getting at," said Boalt. "The goal was to get the word out far and wide. Right?"

"Right."

"So later this morning, when you testify before the grand jury, if Ms. Weller was to ask you if it was *possible* that Mark Towson knew that dozens of black college students would be floating down the Ichetucknee River on that Saturday morning, what would your answer be, Percy?"

It was obvious what the prosecutor wanted to hear, but Percy gave him the truth. "Honestly, I'd have to say I don't know if he did or didn't."

"I'm just asking if it's possible," said Boalt.

"Anything's possible," said Percy.

"*Exactly*," said Boalt. "It is possible. That's your answer."

"No, like I said. My answer is that I have no idea whether—"

"Percy," said Calloway in a firm voice. "Mr. Boalt is simply trying to be helpful here. It *is* possible."

Percy didn't like anyone putting words in his mouth. "It's also possible that Mark Towson didn't do it."

"Whoa," said the state attorney.

"This is not a time to be flip," said Calloway.

"I'm just saying," said Percy. "Right before that riot started on Friday night, I saw him come walking out of the Theta house. One of the cops—he was black—was interviewed on TV and said that Towson was just coming out to talk with the guy with the loudspeaker, which was me. That doesn't sound like a racist who just lynched the president of the Alpha house."

"Maybe he was coming out to kick your ass," said Brandon.

"I doubt it," said Percy. "That would be suicide. Over the last few days I've been thinking a lot about that night. One thing that sticks out clearly in my mind is the skinhead who shoved me up against the wall—shoved me so hard that it actually knocked me out for about thirty seconds. You know what he said to me? He said, 'Strange fruit, motherfucker. You're next.'"

It was a chilling statement, and neither Calloway nor the prosecutors had an immediate response.

Brandon spoke up. "Hope you got a good look at him before you went out."

"It's what I heard that's important," said Percy. "And I don't mean just the words. It was the *way* he said it. At first I thought he was just a drunk skinhead trying to scare me. But I keep hearing it over and over in my head. It's like he was telling me, 'I got Jamal. I'm coming for you next.'"

The state attorney said, "I'm sorry you had that experience. But your first instinct was probably right. Most likely it was a drunken skinhead trying to scare you."

"But *it's possible* it wasn't," said Percy, turning the state attorney's tactic against him. "Right?"

That drew a look of disapproval from Calloway. "Percy, I don't know what you're trying to accomplish here, but if you really feel threatened, fill out a police report."

"Yes," said the state attorney, "but do it on a confidential basis."

"You want me to keep this quiet?" asked Percy, incredulous.

"I want all of us to act responsibly," said Boalt. "History is our teacher. You're nowhere near old enough to remember when Ted Bundy snuck into the Chi Omega house at FSU one night and bludgeoned two young women to death. Twelve years later Danny Rolling went on a killing spree at the University of Florida and killed five students, decapitating one girl. It was absolute terror. Parents pulled students out of those schools by the hundreds."

"Those were serial killers," said Percy.

"That's my point," said Boalt. "One thing you can be sure of with a serial killer: there will be a next victim. Right now, law enforcement has absolutely no reason to believe that anyone else is in danger. Your story—a threat that 'you're next'—will create panic. Black students will disenroll and head home by the busload."

"People should know what's happening," said Percy.

The state attorney glanced at Calloway. "Can I speak to you in the hallway for a minute?" asked Boalt.

"Absolutely." Calloway rose and the two men stepped out. The state attorney's senior trial counsel went with them, closing the door behind her, leaving Percy and Brandon alone in the conference room.

"Is it just me," said Percy, "or is everyone more concerned about keeping people calm than keeping people safe?"

"Fuck Boalt," said Brandon. "Go public. If you don't, I will."

"Cool."

"And fuck Calloway, too," said Brandon. "If the Kappa brothers want to wear armbands with Alpha letters to show unity with Jamal, you wear 'em."

"Thanks, man."

"We cool, homie?"

They fist-bumped to seal it. "Yeah, man," said Percy. "We cool."

CHAPTER 32

Jack and Theo stopped for breakfast before the trip back to Miami.

The Dixie Grill in the historic section of Live Oak had been family run since Florida's Dixiecrats helped elect Eisenhower president. The chef liked to call the cuisine "new South," but the service was pure "old South"—friendly from the moment you walked through the door, quick to refill your coffee mug, and no rush on your meal. Jack had cheese grits and biscuits. Theo ordered the pork chops 'n' eggs special with a side of hotcakes, bacon, sausage, and potatoes. Jack watched in amazement as the waitress unloaded the line of plates from her arms and laid out the breakfast spread before them.

"Anything else I can bring you?" she asked.

"No, ma'am," said Theo.

"Good thing," she said with a smile. "We're almost outta food."

She stepped away, and Theo dug in. Jack ate slowly, allowing time for the pat of butter to melt into his biscuit, instinctively looking up and taking notice each time a customer entered the restaurant. A truck driver. An elderly couple, probably retirees. A postal worker in uniform. It was a slice of Suwannee County, its makeup as random as the grand jury that had been summoned to the courthouse to weigh the evidence against Jack's client.

"You in the mob or the CIA?" asked Theo. "You're checking out every person who walks through the door."

Busted. It was a trial lawyer's compulsion to get a feel for the jury pool in any town in which he might soon try a case.

The door opened again, but this time it wasn't a stranger. "Hey, there's our river guide," said Jack.

"Am I wrong, or are those the same clothes he had on last night?" asked Theo.

Owen McFay was wearing blue denim coveralls and a flannel shirt. "I think he changed his cap," said Jack. This one was camouflage in color and said *"Duck Dynasty."*

The hostess greeted McFay like a regular, and as she led him toward a small table by the window he spotted Jack and Theo. A smile came to his face, and he walked over to say hello.

"Well, two points for the city boys. Y'all found the best breakfast joint in Live Oak."

"We're learning," said Jack.

"Y'all like catfish?"

The way he'd asked, Jack thought he might actually have one on him.

"I do," said Theo.

"Come back for supper then. Try Chef Robbie's 'Squirrel Fishin',' which is a fancy name for fried catfish in pecan breading. Comes with tomato gravy, grits, and two hush puppies. Man, that's good eatin'."

"Next time for sure," said Jack.

McFay lowered himself into a crouch and rested his sun-leathered forearms on the tabletop, as if he had a secret to share, eye to eye. "Can I tell y'all something?"

"Sure," said Jack.

He checked over his shoulder, making sure no one was listening. "There are certain things folks 'round here don't talk about much. But when we was out on the river last night, talkin' 'bout what happened to Jamal Cousin, it got me to thinkin' about stories I used to hear as a boy."

Jack set his coffee mug aside. "You mean stories—"

"About lynchin'," McFay said. "Some true. Some weren't, I suppose. There's one I'll always remember, and I believe it's true, 'cause my daddy told it to me."

Jack glanced at Theo, who looked on the verge of tearing McFay's face off.

"Your daddy lynched a man?" Theo asked.

"No, no, no," said McFay. "He was a loading-dock foreman at the Bond-Howell Lumber Company. One morning these three white men pulled up in a car. They came looking for this black fella who worked in the sawmill. A man named Howard James. No, James Howard."

"What did they want?"

"They just took him. Put him in the car and drove off. Daddy said he never did come back to work."

"They lynched him?" asked Theo.

"I can't say. But this much is for sure. Four days later, the sheriff pulled the body of a fifteen-year-old black boy from the river. People say it was Mr. Howard's son."

"Were the three white men arrested?"

McFay looked at Jack as if he had three heads. "This is a long time ago. During the Second World War. There's no legal case. But here's the important point. The story goes that the boy was hog-tied. The men tied his hands and feet and threw him in the river."

"Lynched by drowning," said Jack.

"Uh-huh," said McFay. "Maybe like they done to Jamal. Hog-tied him and drowned him in the river."

Jack considered it. "You think there's a connection between the two?"

"I dunno. If there is, it'll take someone a lot smarter than me to figure it out. All I'm tellin' you is that the one made me think of the other. And I thought you should know."

"I appreciate that," said Jack.

"Glad to help." McFay rose and shook their hands. "Y'all try that catfish. I mean it."

"We will," said Jack.

Jack's cell rang as McFay walked away. It was the state attorney, so he took the call.

"Jack, I know your father was a man of his word," said Boalt. "Is it safe for me to assume the same about you?"

"It is," said Jack.

"Good. I need a yes or no answer: Will Mark Towson agree to stay put in Gainesville until I tell you that there is no possibility he will be indicted by a grand jury?"

Jack knew what that meant. The prosecutor already had enough evidence to arrest his client, but he was willing to delay the arrest until the grand jury finished its work, as long as he knew exactly where Mark was.

"You have my word on it," said Jack.

The prosecutor thanked him. Jack hung up, and Theo immediately sensed that it wasn't good news.

"What was that about?" asked Theo.

"Looks like we may get to taste that catfish sooner than I thought," said Jack.

CHAPTER 33

Mark Towson was home for lunch. His mother sat at the kitchen table with him. It was hard to swallow the notion that his next meal might be in a jail cafeteria, sitting across from a drug dealer, a rapist, or worse.

"How do you feel today, Mom?"

His mother had slept almost until noon. Mark had taken the call from Jack while she was asleep. A looming indictment was a significant development, but Mark had decided to tell the family later as a group, when they could support each other. He saw no point in giving his mother more worries. He'd heard her walking the house most of the night—midnight, two o'clock, and again around four Mark was not the only one having trouble sleeping, and she needed the rest more than he did. Her post-mastectomy cancer recurrence was local, but the recommended treatment was systemic. The oncologist wanted her to start chemotherapy before the end of the week.

"I'm doing okay," she said with a weak smile.

Mark swallowed the last of his ham-and-cheese sandwich, chugged the last of his lemonade, and took the dishes to the sink. There was a knock at the front door—more like a pounding.

"I'll get it," said Mark.

He went to the foyer and opened the door. It was his friend Cooper Bartlett. His hair was uncombed, he needed a shave, and his eyes were like falcon slits. His little Mazda Miata was parked in the driveway, but his T-shirt was soaked with sweat, as if he'd just run a 10K.

"I gotta talk to you," said Cooper, breathless.

"Did you just come from the gym?"

"No, man. I just ran for my life. Barely made it to my car."

"What?"

"I was at McDonald's. Some punks recognized me from the pictures of you, me, and Baine that are all over the Internet. They were gonna kick my ass. Dude, we gotta talk."

Mark didn't want his mother to see Cooper in this state. He stepped out onto the front porch and closed the door, but he soon realized that the porch wasn't a good place to talk. The demonstrators in the cul-de-sac had been marching silently all morning, but whenever someone stepped outside the house, the chant resumed.

"What do we want?"

"Justice!"

"When do we want it?"

"Now!"

Cooper's expression tightened. "Mark, we really gotta talk someplace private."

The front door opened, and Mark's mother stood in the doorway. "Oh, hello, Cooper."

"Hello, Mrs. Towson."

The chant from the crowd grew louder.

"Boys, please come inside so the neighbors don't have to hear that."

"We were just leaving, Mrs. Towson."

Apparently, Cooper didn't want to have their conversation within earshot of Mark's mother. Neither did Mark. "That's right," said Mark.

"Where are you going?" she asked.

Thankfully, Cooper had an answer. "I found a place to live. Mark said he'd help me move in. Right, Mark?"

"Right," said Mark, playing along. "We'll be quick about it."

She didn't seem pleased about him going anywhere, but it was hard to say no to relocating a friend after his fraternity house had been burned down. "Okay. Take your new cell phone with you."

Mark's cell was still in police custody, and its replacement had come with a free upgrade. Woohoo. "I will," he said.

"And come straight home when you finish."

Mark promised he would, kissed her good-bye, and followed Cooper to his car.

"What do we want? Justice!"

Mark slammed the passenger door shut, and Cooper got behind the wheel. The keys jingled on the ring, and Mark noticed that his friend's hand was shaking as he turned the ignition on.

"Coop, are you okay?"

"I'm fine," he said, as they backed out of the driveway. The group of demonstrators parted to let the car pass, but apparently not fast enough for Cooper. One had to jump out of the way, shouting angrily as Cooper slammed the transmission into gear and burned rubber on the way out. Only then, in the confined car, did Mark smell the alcohol from Cooper's sweaty T-shirt.

"Have you been drinking, dude?"

"Just listen," he said, as they continued down the street. "You and me are fucked!" At the stop sign he slowed down, but didn't stop, rolling through it in his hurry to get away from Mark's house. "Baine testified to the grand jury."

"I know. It was on the news last night." Although grand jury proceedings were secret, it was standard procedure for reporters to stand outside the grand jury room to see who entered to testify.

"Do you know what he said?" asked Cooper.

"No. Jack told me that all grand jury testimony is under seal until the court releases the transcript."

"I bet he told them."

"Told them what?"

"What I wrote in my text."

Mark froze. "You texted Jamal?"

"You knew that. My phone number was in Jamal's phone records."

"So was mine, Cooper! But I never texted him!"

Cooper punched the steering wheel in anger. As for the text, it clearly had not been his intention to tell Mark something he didn't already know. "Fuck!"

"Cooper, take me back home."

"No, there's more."

"Take me home."

"Oliver Boalt talked to me. He wanted me to testify against you."

Mark was torn, not sure whether to listen or not.

"He's real heavy-handed," said Cooper. "He says to me, 'You know what happens to guys like you and Mark Towson in prison? Two white frat boys accused of lynching a black guy?'"

The thought had kept Mark awake most of the night. He'd been trying very hard not to let his mind go there.

Cooper glanced in the rearview mirror, his eyes widening with fear. "It's them again!"

"Who?"

"The guys from McDonald's. They followed me!" Cooper floored it, and his Mazda seemed to spring to life, lunging forward with so much thrust that Mark's head slammed against the headrest.

"Coop, stop!"

He wasn't listening. The Mazda was gaining speed, flying past every other car in the three westbound lanes on Newberry Road. A slow-moving truck turned in front of them to enter the gas station. Cooper maneuvered around it at seventy miles per hour, tires squealing.

"Cooper!"

"They're still on us!" he said with a quick glance in the mirror.

Mark looked back and saw a Chevy. He pulled his cell from his pocket. "Stop driving crazy. I'm dialing nine-one-one."

"No!" He swung at Mark, knocking the cell from his hand. It disappeared somewhere between the passenger seat and the console.

"Damn it, Coop!"

Cooper steered to the left lane, as if heading for the mall. The

Chevy followed, almost on their bumper. Cooper steered hard right. Horns blasted as the Mazda cut across three lanes and sped onto the interstate on-ramp. Mark's heart was in his throat. The speedometer was pushing ninety. The Chevy was right on them.

"Fuck!" shouted Cooper.

The entry ramp circled around a man-made pond, a typical hole in the ground that fills with spring water after construction crews remove the earth to build an interstate exchange. Cooper was rounding the big, sweeping curve at more than double the speed limit. So was the Chevy behind them. Cooper sped up and then hit the brake, trying to teach the tailgaters a lesson.

"Cooper!"

The stunt was more than Cooper could handle. His Mazda went into a tailspin, and Cooper's overcorrection sent them skidding in circles, completely out of control. In the blur, Mark saw the Chevy speed past them a split second before the Mazda hit the guardrail.

The airbag exploded in Mark's face and then collapsed, but the car kept skidding to the opposite side of the ramp. It was like peering out from the center of a spiraling tornado—spinning, swirling. The front end slammed into the opposite guardrail, but momentum carried the car right over the top. The car nearly rolled over but righted itself and continued down the embankment. Mark's arms flailed and his whole body jerked, his head slamming forward and back against the headrest. The passenger-side window exploded into glass pellets that bloodied Mark's face like buckshot. The skidding stopped with an ominous thud, but the impact seemed cushioned, as if the battered Mazda had somehow made a soft landing, as if they were drifting in slow motion. A wet sensation enveloped his feet and ankles—not the hot, wet feeling of blood on his face, but a cooler, almost cold wetness. Water was suddenly everywhere.

The pond!

Mark splashed his face to clear away the blood. The water was already knee-deep, and still more poured in from every crevice. It had a ghoulish crimson tint of blood—his and his friend's.

"Coop!"

He didn't respond. Mark unbuckled the driver's-side seat belt and shook him. "Cooper, are you okay?"

Mark tried his door handle, but the door was stuck. He reached across and tried the driver's side—no go. The only way out was through the broken passenger-side window. He tried to pull Cooper toward him, but Cooper's leg was pinned below the twisted steering wheel. Mark pulled harder. More blood trickled into his eyes, effectively blinding him. The water was rising. The car was sinking. His mind was a fog, but he fought with every ounce of strength to loosen Cooper's trapped foot. The water inched upward over his waist. He felt weak, almost numb. He called for help—"Somebody, please!"—but it was barely audible. Mark felt himself slipping away, trying to say his friend's name.

Then he slumped over the console.

CHAPTER 34

Jack was in Live Oak for the state attorney's announcement of the criminal indictment.

Shortly after 1:00 p.m., Oliver Boalt appeared on the courthouse steps with his senior trial counsel at his side. Media swarmed around them. Jack and Theo were packed shoulder to shoulder with dozens of other onlookers. Microphones, cameras, and eager reporters captured the state attorney's remarks, which he read from a prepared statement.

"Today, a Suwannee County grand jury has heard sworn testimony relating to the death of Jamal Cousin, and it has returned an indictment against Mark Towson and Cooper Bartlett."

The crowd cheered, with demonstrators thrusting posters and fists triumphantly into the warm afternoon air. Some had been holding vigil outside the courthouse since the start of the grand jury proceedings, most notably the "Dream Defenders," an organization started after the acquittal of private security guard George Zimmerman in the fatal shooting of a seventeen-year-old black teenager. Posters proclaiming I AM TRAYVON MARTIN had been part of a historic twenty-one-day sit-in at the state capitol, and some of those seasoned participants had resurrected the old signs, adding I AM JAMAL COUSIN.

"Count one is against Mr. Towson only," said the prosecutor, looking straight at the cameras. "The charge is murder in the first degree."

The crowd cheered even louder.

"Count two charges Mr. Towson and Mr. Bartlett with conspiracy to commit murder."

Still more cheering, which morphed into a unified chant of *"Justice for Jamal, justice for Jamal!"* It continued for another minute, drowning out the state attorney's reference to the lesser included charges in the indictment. Jack tried to show no reaction. After "murder one," there was only one way to make things worse, and Jack sensed that the state attorney was headed in that direction.

"In today's world I should not have to stand before you and condemn lynching. If we are to stop this backslide to the darkest chapter in our nation's history, we must learn from history. Some say that the death penalty is not a deterrent to crime. History shows, however, that the death penalty is a proven deterrent to lynching."

Here it comes, thought Jack.

"The historical evidence is that lynching stopped only when the use of capital punishment increased," Boalt added. "Therefore, in accordance with the findings of the grand jury, the charge against Mr. Towson is capital murder, for which the State of Florida will seek the death penalty."

It was the proverbial showstopper—the Fourth of July and New Year's Eve on the courthouse steps. The state attorney stepped aside to allow his senior trial counsel a moment in the spotlight, but the crowd wasn't listening, and even the reporters on the front line had trouble hearing. Marsha Weller's remarks were boilerplate anyway, the obligatory promise that "the defendants are cloaked with the presumption of innocence" and have "the right to trial by jury, not by news conference."

Boalt had the final word. "We will not comment further on the process and will certainly not comment on the evidence. Thank you for being here."

The prosecutors turned and walked back toward the courthouse. The crowd gave them an ovation worthy of Super Bowl champs, and the media followed them all the way up the stairs to the courthouse entrance, peppering them with questions that went unanswered.

"Let's go," said Jack.

"You don't want to say anything?" asked Theo.

"Later. I'm not going to hold a press conference with a thousand people booing me."

Jack hurried down the steps, and only then did he notice the pickup truck parked directly across the street. It was wedged between media vans, and in the bed of the pickup was a big red-white-and-blue campaign sign: RE-ELECT OLIVER BOALT—YOUR STATE ATTORNEY.

"No offense," said Theo. "But if I lived here, I'd vote for him."

Jack stopped on the sidewalk at the base of the steps. "That's not cool."

"Neither is lynching."

Jack looked away, then back, but he couldn't quell all the anger in his tone. "Boalt is rewriting history, Theo. Lynching didn't stop in this country because white people feared the death penalty. Lynching disappeared because judges started ordering the swift execution of black men. Capital punishment didn't deter lynch mobs. It replaced them. Why do you think I spent four years of my life trying to get you off death row?"

"Mr. Swyteck!"

Jack turned and saw a reporter running toward him. The media's fixation on the prosecution had ended, and he'd been spotted. Jack started walking toward his car, but the reporter caught up and shoved her microphone toward him. The cameraman jostled with Theo for space on the sidewalk as Jack quickened the pace.

"Is there any news on Mark Towson's accident?" the reporter asked.

"What accident?"

"I just heard that Mark Towson was in a serious car crash. Is it true?"

Jack stopped at his car. "I don't know anything about that. But thank you for telling me."

She continued to fire questions as Jack climbed into the passenger seat and closed the door. Theo drove off. Jack immediately called his client's cell but got no answer. He tried Mark's father and got through.

"I was just about to call you," said Tucker, his voice laden with concern. "I'm at Shands Hospital now."

"So it's true? Mark was in an accident?"

"Yes. Bad one. He's in surgery right now, and we think he'll be okay. He was with Cooper Bartlett."

"Is Cooper there at the same hospital?"

Tucker paused long enough for Jack to know what he was going to say. "Cooper is dead."

Jack swallowed the news. "Okay. Call me as soon as you know more on Mark. Don't speak to the media. I'm on my way."

CHAPTER 35

The door opened, and Mark's father invited Jack into the hospital room.

"Hold it," said the officer. Two guards were posted in the hallway outside Mark's room. He was officially under arrest. A metal-detecting wand was run up and down Jack's body, confirming no weapons.

"You're good," said the officer, allowing Jack entry.

Surgery to remove Mark's ruptured spleen and stop the internal bleeding had lasted almost an hour. He'd spent another hour in recovery before being wheeled on a gurney to a private room. Jack had been waiting in the hallway to give the Towson family time alone. He closed the door behind him, and both Mark's mother and sister gave him a hug when he entered.

"How's he doing?" asked Jack.

"Going to be fine. Doctor said a few days in the hospital, and then he can go—" Tucker stopped himself, clearly wishing he could say "home."

"To jail," said Mark.

Jack stepped toward the hospital bed. Mark was in an elevated position, midway between sitting up and lying flat on his back. A plastic IV tube connected the vein in his forearm to a plastic bag of fluids that hung from the pole. A bedside machine monitored his vitals, a modest beep with each heartbeat. The red marks and abrasions on his face were due to shattered glass, Jack assumed.

"I'd like to speak with Mark alone," Jack told the family.

They obliged and filed out. Jack stood at the bed rail. Mark turned his head and gazed out the window.

"Cooper's dead."

"I know," said Jack. "I'm sorry."

"Are people happy?"

It was the first truly cynical thing Jack had heard Mark say. "I don't think so."

Mark's gaze returned to Jack. "You know how Jamal Cousin's phone records show that he received a text message from Cooper's phone?"

"Yeah."

"Cooper admitted to me that he sent it. Nobody took his phone and pretended to be him."

"So Baine sent the one from your phone," said Jack. "But not the one from Cooper's."

"That's what it comes down to."

"Did Cooper say what he wrote in his text?"

"Nope. And now I guess we'll never know, will we?"

Jack shook his head. "Not unless someone else was there when he sent it."

"Like Baine?" asked Cooper.

"A likely choice."

Mark breathed out his disgust. "Is Baine really going to get away with this?"

"All I can tell you is that he hasn't been indicted," said Jack. "Yet."

Leroy Highsmith did the cable news circuit "live from Miami, Florida."

Highsmith had spent the day in court-ordered mediation for another African American family. That suit was against the North Miami Police Department, filed after an autistic child ignored an officer's command to drop his toy, and the officer for some reason—"I don't know why," he later told investigators—shot the boy's psychiatrist, who was just trying to convince the child to come back inside the treatment facility. Highsmith was wearing his lucky "settlement suit," dark blue with chalk pinstripes, which sent a message to opposing counsel to pay up fast and pay up big. His only adjustment for the television appearance on behalf of the Cousin family was the pancake makeup applied by his publicist to hide a five o'clock shadow. He was seated in front of a green screen that projected Miami's glittering skyline to millions of television viewers. His five-minute gig with CNN was his third of the evening.

"Mr. Highsmith, what does today's indictment mean to the Cousin family?"

"It's only the start," said Highsmith. "And if you read that indictment, you will appreciate how far black people in this country have come just to get to the starting line. The indictment charges that—quote—'Mark Towson, with premeditated design, did intentionally and unlawfully kill Jamal Cousin, a human being.' A *human being.* That's standard language in a homicide indictment. But it's chilling, isn't it, when you consider how long African Americans were just *three-fifths* of a human being? I'm here to tell you that we will not accept three-fifths justice. We intend to see this through to the end, until there is justice in the fullest, most complete sense."

"Mr. Highsmith, sources have told us that Mark Towson in fact knew that the indictment was imminent before the car crash today. Do you believe that he and his fraternity brother, Cooper Bartlett, were fleeing on the interstate in anticipation of their arrest?"

"I can't say for sure," said Highsmith. "But I have been told by someone close to the investigation that two suitcases packed with clothes were found in the trunk of Mr. Bartlett's car."

"That could be very telling."

"You bet it could," said Highsmith.

"Leroy Highsmith, civil rights activist and attorney for the Cousin family, thank you very much for your time."

"You are most welcome."

The video connection ended, and Highsmith's publicist stepped forward to check his makeup. He brushed away her hand, having had enough primping.

"Leroy, come on, now," she said. "We have MSNBC in eleven minutes."

His cell rang, and he was glad for the reprieve. The fact that it was Oliver Boalt confirmed that his intended message had gotten through to the prosecutor.

"Saw you on CNN," said Boalt. "What do you mean by 'three-fifths justice'?"

"I'm sorry," said Highsmith. "I should have been more precise. What I meant to say is that we will not accept *two-thirds* justice."

The state attorney was silent. Highsmith had no doubt that his position was already crystal clear, but he spelled it out anyway. "You got Mark Towson. Cooper Bartlett is in hell, where he belongs. Now I want Baine Robinson."

"Baine Robinson is my star witness."

"That's your problem, Oliver. Not mine."

Highsmith ended the call and returned to his publicist, ready for his next cable news interview.

CHAPTER 36

Wednesday morning marked a career first for Jack: a "court" appearance from a hospital room.

Every person arrested in Florida must be brought before a judicial officer within twenty-four hours of arrest. It wasn't unusual for that first appearance to occur via live video feed from a lockup facility. Jack was willing to postpone his client's initial appearance until Mark's release from the hospital. Oliver Boalt wasn't taking any chances. Or perhaps he wanted another media blast. He arranged for a live video feed from the hospital. On the right side of the split screen was Circuit Judge Kelly Simon. Somewhere in the courtroom but offscreen was the prosecutorial team. On the left side of the screen was defendant Mark Towson, sitting up in bed. Jack had debated whether to dress his client in street clothes and sit him in a chair, but that probably would have unleashed a string of public accusations that Mark was faking or exaggerating a medical condition to stay out of jail. A hospital gown in a hospital bed was the way to go.

Jack stood at the rail and spoke first. "Your Honor, we waive the reading of the Miranda rights," he said.

"Very well. Mr. Towson, the charges against you are as follows."

Mark sat in silence, his head resting on the pillow, as the judge recited all three counts in the indictment. In addition to first degree murder and conspiracy to commit murder, Mark faced an additional charge for threatening serious bodily injury to Jamal via text message—normally a misdemeanor, but because it was racially motivated, a felony under Florida's hate-crime statute.

"Mr. Towson, how do you plead?"

"I'm innocent."

"The plea will be recorded as 'not guilty,'" the judge said. "Count one is a capital offense for which there is no bond. My understanding is that the defendant is currently under armed guard in his hospital room."

"That's correct," said the state attorney.

"Upon release from the hospital, the defendant shall be immediately transported to the Suwannee County Jail, where he shall be detained through trial."

"Your Honor, the defense will be filing a motion for pretrial release," said Jack.

"In a capital case?" asked the state attorney. "Your Honor, I've been doing this a long time, and I can't recall a single case in Suwannee County in which a capital defendant has been released on bail."

Jack knew the odds were against them. "We want a hearing."

Judge Simon checked with his clerk. The duty judge at a first appearance didn't typically stay with the case, and Simon was checking on the assignment. "Chief Judge Calvin Teague will hear the defense's motion in his courtroom immediately upon Mr. Towson's release from the hospital. When will that be, Mr. Swyteck?"

"Monday."

"Got it. Y'all should coordinate with Judge Teague's chambers for a time on Monday. Mr. Boalt, send all grand jury materials to the defense before the end of the day. Is there anything further?"

"Judge, the State of Florida will be issuing a superseding indictment to eliminate the charges against Cooper Bartlett, who is deceased."

"That's fine. Anything else?" A no came from each end of the video feed. "Then we are adjourned," the judge said. "Thank you."

The television screen went black. Mark looked at Jack, his expression sullen.

"So if we don't win the hearing on Monday, I'm stuck in jail even though I haven't been convicted of anything. That's how this works?"

"Getting out of jail before trial on a first-degree murder charge is extremely difficult."

"How long could it be?"

"It will be several months, at least, until we have a trial date."

"At least? How long could it really be—worst case?"

Jack didn't want to dampen his client's spirits further, but he had to be honest. "A year. Possibly longer."

"More than a year," Mark said, shaking his head. "That means even if we go on to win at trial, my mother's last image of her son could be me behind bars in a jail uniform. Did you know that, Jack?"

"Your father told me the cancer was back. No one told me the prognosis."

Mark glanced at the monitor at his bedside, as if checking his own pulse. "Do me a favor, will you?"

"What?"

"If Mom asks for *my* prognosis, lie to her. It could be bad. It might be both good and bad. Maybe you have no idea. No matter how terrible things look, lie to her. And make it believable. You can do that, right?"

Jack had never considered himself a very good liar. But sometimes it was worth the effort. "No problem, Mark. I can do that."

CHAPTER 37

Leroy Highsmith was back on campus at the University of Florida.

That morning he'd received notice from law enforcement that the forensic team no longer needed to restrict access to Jamal Cousin's room. By noon he was aboard the *Legal Eagle*, flying to Gainesville with Jamal's mother. Lamar Cousin was traveling for work, and it fell to the family lawyer to help Edith through a task that she wasn't sure she could summon the emotional strength to finish. It was time to collect her son's belongings.

"Thank you for coming with me," said Edith. She and Highsmith were alone in the TV room of the Alpha house. Most of the twenty-six brothers were in the cafeteria eating lunch. Brandon Wall, the Alpha brother who'd testified at Mark Towson's disciplinary hearing, had stepped away to get the key to Jamal's room.

"It's no trouble at all," Highsmith told her.

Structurally, the Alpha house was modest by Fraternity Row standards. Just one story, the simple stucco-on-frame construction was in the unremarkable architectural style of Florida circa 1975. But nobody pledged Alpha for the building. The Florida chapter was one of the smallest nationwide, but it still logged more community service hours than any other Greek organization on campus.

Brandon entered the room, key in hand. "I can walk you back."

They followed him down the hallway, passing several rooms until they stopped at a door marked "President." On the wall, right outside the door, was a traditional Divine Nine poem that Highsmith had recited at least a hundred times, mostly at funerals; lately, for his aging fraternity brothers. "Success is failure turned inside out /

the silver tint of the clouds of doubt / so stick to the fight when you're hardest hit / It's when things seem worst that you mustn't quit." The author was anonymous—like so many brothers, thought Highsmith, who were taken down to the river and never returned.

"This was my room last year, when I was president," said Brandon. "None of us has been inside since Jamal passed. I made sure of it." He inserted the key and turned the lock, leaving the door closed.

"We can take it from here, Brandon," said Highsmith.

"Okay, I'll be in the dining room if you need anything." Brandon retraced their steps down the hallway, leaving them alone outside Jamal's room.

"Take your time, Edith," said Highsmith. "Go through that door when you're good and ready."

"Can you open it, please?"

Highsmith turned the knob and pushed the door slowly. They stood in the doorway for a moment, and then Edith reached inside and switched on the light. She took a tentative step forward, and then another. Slowly, she made it to the center of the room. Highsmith remained in the doorway, watching in silence as Jamal's mother absorbed every detail of her son's room. She walked to his desk and touched the books he'd been reading. She ran her finger along his chair. She knelt at the footlocker where he kept his basketball shoes, and she laid her hand on the Alpha jersey that was neatly folded on the shelf. The framed photograph on the wall held her attention longest. Jamal was dead center in a team of five black men dressed all in black, from boots to berets, bright stage lights shining down on them.

"Alpha took first place last spring at the soul-steppin' contest," said Edith.

Step dancing has a long-standing tradition among black fraternities, though percussive dance was becoming mainstream enough to find its way into everything from presidential inaugurations to Olympic ceremonies. Teams spent hours rehearsing for annual competitions, perfecting choreographies in which the entire body is an instrument of footsteps, spoken word, and hand claps. Highsmith loved tradition as much as anybody, but his personal preference would have been less steppin' and more of what the Divine Nine were really about.

Edith walked to the bed, peeled back the comforter, and took Jamal's pillow in her arms. She held it the way a mother might embrace a newborn, almost inhaling it. She placed it back on the bed and then did the same with the other pillow. Her eyes brightened with a hint of a smile.

"Flower Bomb," she said in a voice loud enough for Highsmith to hear.

"I'm sorry. What did you say, Edith?"

"It's a perfume. I'm one of those dreaded spritzers at the mall that you run away from during the Christmas shopping season. I do it every year for a little extra money around the holidays."

Her third job, thought Highsmith.

"I can name every perfume on the planet just by scent." Edith inhaled the pillow once again. "Definitely Flower Bomb. Some pretty young thing left her scent on Jamal's pillow. That stinker," she said with a sad smile. "I didn't"—she stopped, her sadness slipping into grief—"I didn't even know my baby had a girlfriend."

She was on the verge of breaking down in a big way, and Highsmith went to her. "Hey, hey, now. It's okay."

Edith sniffed back tears, speaking in a raw voice. "People expect me to be happy, I suppose, now that there's an indictment. I'm not. I'm not at all happy."

"I understand."

She breathed out, collecting herself. "You know, I never had a father growing up. I was just a baby when he got killed in Vietnam. Five years later, when Mama died, people called me an orphan. They have a name for a child who loses her parents."

Highsmith just listened.

"But there's no word for a parent who loses her only child. Not in English. Not in any language. Did you know that?"

"I did not."

"Neither did I," she said. "'Til this happened. But there's a reason, I think, there's no such word."

Highsmith waited, letting her finish the thought.

Her eyes welled as she looked straight at him. "It's too horrible a thing to pack into a single word. That's what I think, Leroy. Too horrible."

He moved closer and held her in his arms, gently trying to stop her from shaking. "I believe you're right, Edith. You are absolutely right."

CHAPTER 38

The Monday morning journey from Gainesville to Live Oak was nothing short of harrowing. It wasn't technically a "first appearance," but it would be Jack's first time in an actual courtroom with the most reviled accused criminal in the state of Florida.

The ordeal started outside the hospital. Mark was able to walk with minimal discomfort, but a wheelchair was required for discharge of a surgery patient. Mark was seated, dressed in the clothes that the state attorney had sent for his court appearance: a Suwannee County Jail uniform. Mark's hands were cuffed behind his back, forcing him to sit awkwardly in the chair in a forward position—"with his head lowered in shame," the media would later observe. Two police officers, one on each side of the wheelchair, escorted them through the main lobby and into the morning sun. The crowd outside the hospital, mostly students, extended well beyond the main entry area and into the parking lot. Jack estimated the turnout to be at least double what he'd seen at the courthouse for the state attorney's announcement of the indictment. The chant was louder, and the message had changed.

"Lock him up! Lock him up! Lock him up!"

Media swarmed and demonstrators howled as the wheelchair stopped at the squad car. The officers put the prisoner in the back seat. Jack assured Mark that they would meet up in the courtroom, and the door slammed shut. Jack ignored the media's requests for comment as the squad car pulled away. He walked quickly to the Towsons' SUV and climbed in the front passenger seat. Mark's father was at the wheel. His mother and sister were in the back seat.

"So here we go," said Tucker. A sea of demonstrators parted for the squad car, and the SUV rolled forward at a snail's pace, traveling in law enforcement's wake.

The chants continued. *"Lock him up!"*

Mark's mother looked out the window. "There's not a single person who believes Mark is innocent. Is there, Jack?"

Jack remembered the promise that he'd made to Mark after the first appearance. "That'll change, Liz. It'll take time. But it will change."

The main courtroom in the Suwannee County Courthouse was packed for the one o'clock hearing. The only empty seats were in the twelve-person box for a jury yet to be selected. The prosecutorial team was at the mahogany table to the judge's left. Directly behind the state attorney, on the other side of the rail, were Jamal's parents. Leroy Highsmith was with them. Jack and his client were at the defense table to the judge's right. Behind them was Mark's family. Members of the media filled the rest of the first row of public seating. The remaining bench seats were for the lucky few who had arrived early enough to snag a spot. Hundreds of demonstrators waited outside the courthouse.

The judge greeted everyone and began without delay. "We are here this afternoon at the request of the defendant, Mark Towson, who seeks pretrial release on bail."

Circuit Judge Calvin Teague was the oldest judge in Suwannee County. Among local criminal defense lawyers he was euphemistically referred to as "Father Time"—partly because he was a gray old man in a black robe, but mainly because anyone unlucky enough to be sentenced by him went away for a long, long time.

"Mr. Boalt, have you prepared an Arthur package?"

"Arthur" referred to the Florida Supreme Court decision *State v. Arthur*, which requires the prosecution to present evidence of the accused's guilt in order to hold him without bail. Typically, much of the evidence was in the form of affidavits, which were part of the "Arthur package."

Boalt rose and buttoned his suit jacket. "We have a partial package, Your Honor."

The judge scowled. "Partial? What are you waiting for? The hearing started two minutes ago. You should have filed it this morning."

"At this time, the State of Florida seeks a continuance of this hearing. We would ask that it be rescheduled two weeks from today."

Jack rose immediately. "Judge, the defense is ready to proceed. Any delay is extremely prejudicial to my client."

"Well, I don't know about that," the judge said. "It's been less than a week since Mr. Towson's arrest. In a homicide case it's not unusual for the accused to sit in jail two or three weeks before he gets an Arthur hearing. Mr. Boalt, what is the reason for the requested continuance?"

"Your Honor, just this morning the sheriff's department obtained new evidence in this investigation. The extra time is needed for forensic analysis."

Jack could almost feel the media breathing down his neck in the public seating behind him. It was possible that the prosecutor was bluffing and merely stalling. There was only one way to find out. "Judge, all I'm hearing is a vague claim of newly discovered evidence. The court should demand more specificity before delaying this hearing."

"That's a fair point, Mr. Swyteck. How 'bout it, Mr. Boalt? What kind of new evidence are we talking about?"

"As the court knows, the evidence of guilt that the prosecution must present at an Arthur hearing has to be convincing. This new evidence could be the most convincing of all. We have uncovered physical evidence that may place Mr. Towson at the scene of the crime."

A chorus of whispers traveled through the courtroom, and Jack could only surmise that the gist of it was, *"See, I told you he did it!"*

Mark leaned closer, speaking softly. "There's no way."

Jack wasn't so certain, but he kept applying the pressure. "Judge, it sounds like this 'new' evidence has already been collected and sent to the lab. If that's the case, the prosecution should just tell us what it is."

"It's a Croc," said Boalt, choosing not to wait for the judge's command.

"I beg your pardon?"

"Those foam shoes that started out as beachwear but now people wear all the time. Croc is the trade name."

"Ah, got it," the judge said. "I thought you meant—well, never mind. Continue, Mr. Boalt."

"The sheriff's department sent its dive team back to the river this past weekend for a second look. Again they searched the area where Jamal's body was found. This time they uncovered a Croc that was buried in the muck."

An ironic refrain crackled in Jack's brain like lightning: *If the Croc doesn't fit, you must acquit.* "This could be good for us," he whispered to his client.

Judge Teague leaned back in his leather chair, thinking. "This seems like a significant development. I don't see it as the end of the world to postpone this hearing as requested."

Jack was back on his feet. "The defense has no problem with a postponement if Mr. Towson is released on bail until the hearing."

"We oppose that," said Boalt.

"On what grounds?" asked the judge.

"Mr. Towson is a serious flight risk. Just a few hours before the grand jury returned its indictment, I called Mr. Swyteck. He gave me his word that his client would surrender if indicted. Two hours later, Mr. Towson and his friend Cooper Bartlett were speeding onto the expressway. The car crashed. Sadly, Mr. Bartlett was killed."

"They were not in flight," said Jack. "They were being chased by a group of young men who had threatened Cooper Bartlett at a fast-food restaurant."

"That's a nice story," said the prosecutor. "But I have an affidavit from the state trooper who arrived on the scene of the accident. He found two duffel bags in the trunk of the car. The bags were packed."

Boalt approached the bench and handed up the affidavit to the judge, providing a copy to Jack on his way back to his seat. Jack read it quickly and then conferred with his client, who had the answer. Jack provided it to the court.

"Judge, the duffel bags were packed with Mr. Bartlett's belongings. The Theta house was burned down in a riot. The bags contained everything that Mr. Bartlett managed to salvage after the fire."

"Now the defense is just making things up," said Boalt. "Mr. Bartlett is obviously unavailable to tell us the real reason why those bags were packed."

Jack was about to respond, but the judge stopped him, raising his hand like a traffic cop. "I've heard enough. The State of Florida's request for a two-week continuance is granted. The request for temporary release before the hearing is denied. Mr. Towson, you are hereby remanded into custody at the Suwannee County Jail in Live Oak. We are adjourned," he said, ending the proceedings with a bang of his gavel.

"All rise!"

The bumps and thuds of a packed gallery filled the courtroom as Judge Teague stepped down from the bench and walked to the side door. Jack glanced at Mark and saw nothing but terror in his eyes.

"I'm going to jail?" Mark whispered, incredulous.

The side door opened and the judge disappeared into his chambers. The media dashed to the rail like sprinters out of the blocks. Others in the crowd applauded as the law enforcement officers approached the defense table and cuffed Mark's hands behind his back.

Mark's family was standing behind the rail. He glanced in their direction, then back at Jack. "I'm going to jail," he said, as the certainty of it finally hit him.

Jack faced him squarely, looking him right in the eye. "I'll push to get you in solitary confinement. You'll feel safer there, but it probably won't happen the first night. It all depends on space available."

"Okay."

"If you talk to anyone in jail, you talk *only* about things like the food, the weather, or Florida football. This is very important. Do you understand me?"

Mark nodded.

"Let's go," said one of the officers.

Mark stopped to get a hug from his mother, which was the shot of the day for at least a dozen photographers and cameramen.

"If you have pain, baby, you ask for a doctor to check your incision," Elizabeth Towson told him. "And call us whenever you can."

Jack watched as the officers led his client away, ignoring the flurry of questions from the media. Then his gaze shifted to the other side of the courtroom, to the rail behind the prosecutor's table, where the state attorney was offering consolation to Jamal's mother. Leroy Highsmith put himself between Jamal's mother and the media, forcing the news gatherers to respect a ring of privacy around Edith Cousin.

"Full and complete justice," Jack heard the family's lawyer tell the reporters. "That's all we seek."

CHAPTER 39

Jack drove the SUV back to Gainesville.

Mark's parents wanted to be near their son in case of an overnight emergency and so took a motel room in Live Oak. Mark's sister needed to get back to UF for classes. Jack agreed to drive her, promising to have the SUV back the next morning for visitation hour at Suwannee County Jail.

"I'm really worried about Mark," said Shelly. Those were her first words of the trip, breaking twenty minutes of pensive silence from the passenger seat.

"There's no reason for anyone to worry," Jack said, trying to sound believable.

"His surgeon said it will take six weeks for him to fully heal."

"I've already arranged for Mark to have regular doctor visits."

"What if someone punches him in the stomach?"

"That won't happen."

"How do you know?"

He didn't. "If something bad happens, Live Oak Regional Medical Center is just five minutes away. It's a surgical hospital." It was the best Jack could do to allay her concerns, but five minutes was an eternity for someone locked in a jail cell with internal bleeding.

They reached the campus around four thirty. On the way to Shelly's class, they passed the Theta house—or what was left of it. The redbrick building hadn't completely burned to the ground. The rear had suffered only smoke damage, but the front was a charred shell. A pair of plantation-style columns had failed in the fire, causing a section of the roof to collapse. The nearby oak trees would survive, but the largest one was scorched and leafless on one side. Blackened debris was scattered across the lawn, including the Greek letters that had once identified the house as Theta Pi Omega. A temporary chain-link fence surrounded the property, and posted signs warned would-be trespassers.

"What are the cops doing there?" asked Shelly.

Jack hadn't noticed any squad cars as they passed. He glanced back through the rear window and spotted three of them behind the house. Shelly had a little time before her class, so Jack turned at the next street and drove around to the back of the house. In addition to the squad cars, a forensics truck from the Florida Department of Law Enforcement was on the scene. Up the hill behind the house were several media vans from local news outlets. Jack parked, and Shelly waited in the SUV as he walked down the pathway to the sheriff's deputy who was posted at the chain-link fence.

"No entry," he told Jack.

Jack identified himself as Mark Towson's lawyer. It was immediately clear that another search was under way. "Do you have a warrant?"

"You own this property?" asked the officer.

"I want to see the warrant," said Jack.

"No can do."

Jack was in no mood for games. He dialed the state attorney, who took his call. "Oliver, I'm at the Theta house. What are you searching for?"

"Nothing—at least not anymore. I just spoke to the search team leader. They found it."

Jack looked beyond the fence. Several investigators were standing at the rear entrance and talking in a group. "Found what?" Jack asked.

"The other Croc," said Boalt.

Jack's pulse quickened. "You found a Croc that matches the one you mentioned in court—is that what you're telling me?"

"I'll let you know about the match just as soon as the lab confirms it."

"Where exactly was it found?"

"Upstairs," said the state attorney. "In Baine Robinson's closet."

Not in Mark's room—Jack could breathe again. "When are you dropping the charges against my client?"

"Ha! Right. Just because Mark Towson had an accomplice doesn't make him any less guilty."

"I've reviewed the grand jury materials," said Jack. "Baine Robinson testified that Mark bragged to him about lynching Jamal. That's a lie, and that's the best evidence you've got against Mark."

"Wrong. That's the best evidence I presented to the grand jury."

"If you have more, I want to see it."

"You will," said Boalt. "I have to be socially responsible. If I backed up the dump truck and unloaded my entire case against Mark Towson in one shot, we'd have a full-blown race riot."

"Bullshit. If you released everything, we'd know you rushed to an indictment."

"You will receive all the materials that the defense is entitled to. I promise you that."

"I want it before the bail hearing."

"Sure," said Boalt. "That won't be a problem."

It was a more reasonable response than expected. Jack would be sure to confirm it in writing. "Are you going back to the grand jury to indict Baine?"

"Do you represent Mr. Robinson?"

"You know the answer to that question."

"Then you know I can't answer."

"Should I ask Leroy Highsmith?"

There was silence on the line, but somehow the state attorney's anger came through. "What kind of question is that, Swyteck?"

"Let me ask it another way," said Jack. "Look at the last twenty-four hours. Highsmith publicly demands 'full and complete justice.' Divers suddenly pull a Croc out of the river muck. The other

Croc rises from the ashes of the Theta house and—*voilà!*—Baine Robinson is Mark's accomplice, even though it's been less than a week since he told a grand jury that Mark acted alone. You tell me, Oliver. What the hell is going on?"

"I never said Baine Robinson is a perfect witness. He's a rat who ratted out another rat. I've been telling jurors this for years: when you look in the sewer, you don't see swans."

"Nice metaphor. Just one problem, Oliver."

"Yeah, what?"

"You're so eager to throw Mark into the sewer, you're willing to ignore the fact that he's never been near the river."

Silence again, but without the anger. "Good night, Swyteck. I'll talk to you soon."

"Yes," said Jack, "you will."

CHAPTER 40

Mark Towson's life behind bars started in a holding pen with seven other inmates, each waiting for assignment to one of 150 beds in shared cells.

Suwannee County Jail was as secure as any maximum-security state prison, suitable for inmates awaiting trial for the most violent crimes—rape, robbery, even capital murder. Cameras and electronic detention operated throughout the facility. Fencing was topped with razor wire. Correctional officers were armed with Mace and trained to use physical force to protect themselves and other inmates from violence.

"Dinnertime," the correctional officer announced.

It was a soggy bologna-and-cheese sandwich that smelled too awful to eat. Mark wished he wasn't so hungry. Over a period of hours, he'd climbed up and down stairs, been shackled, unshackled, and shackled again. The jail nurse applied a waterproof bandage to his incision so that he could take the required delousing shower. A body search by a male correction officer followed, which wasn't pleasant at all. Fingerprinting took another hour. The mug shot was the final indignity—a deer-in-the-headlights classic that was sure to end up all over the Internet. Mark spent the dinner hour watching a cellmate tear his bologna sandwich into pieces, roll them into balls, and one by one pitch them into the community toilet from behind the imaginary three-point line. Around eight o'clock, the guard returned.

"Got a bed for you, Towson."

Mark went to the door of the holding pen, but it didn't open.

The guard's radio crackled and he walked away without explanation. Mark waited. And waited. An hour passed. Ninety minutes. Finally, a different guard returned.

"Let's go, Towson."

The metal door opened, and the guard led Mark down the corridor. Another buzzer sounded, and the iron door slid open. It was 10:00 p.m., and the jail was in lockdown for the night.

"Am I in solitary?" asked Mark.

"Nope."

"My lawyer said I might be. For safety reasons."

"This ain't the Holiday Inn, pal. We're at full capacity."

Another guard joined them, and the pair of correctional officers led Mark down the long corridor, iron bars on either side. A catcall from one of the inmates triggered Mark's darkest fears. The whistler was deep within one of the blackened cells, unidentifiable.

They stopped at the third door from the end of the cellblock. The jail cells that Mark had seen on television usually had solid metal doors, but this one had old-fashioned steel bars. Enough light shone from the corridor to reveal a man in the lower bunk. The top bunk was empty. The guard rattled the bars with his nightstick. The bright-white beam of his flashlight hit the sleeping inmate in the eyes.

"Up against the wall, Bulldog," he said.

Bulldog?

The inmate rolled out of the bunk and did as he was told. The lead guard radioed the door-control booth. A buzzer sounded. The cell door slid open automatically. Mark entered the cell in silence. Another buzz, and the door closed with the clank of metal echoing off concrete floors and walls of painted cinder block.

"Bulldog here is our resident neo-Nazi," the guard said. "You two should get along just fine, Towson."

Mark heard the guards snickering as they walked away. He turned to face his cellmate, who was shirtless. Their eyes locked from opposite ends of a cell. Mark was sharing a cage seven feet wide and twelve feet deep with a man who was built like a football player, and who was covered in enough tattoos for the entire team.

Bulldog stole the clean pillow from the top bunk, tossed the one he'd been using onto the floor, and climbed into the bottom bunk. "You're up top."

Mark debated whether to stand up for himself and say something about the pillow switch. He didn't. He picked up the dirty one from the floor and climbed into the top bunk.

With hands clasped behind his head, he lay staring up at the ceiling. The lights from the corridor were just bright enough for him to discern traces of prison artwork on the wall. Some of it was in black marker, some in pencil. There was a calendar to count down the days, so faded that it could have predated Mark's birth. Someone with a knack for portraits had sketched out a nude Latina from memory or imagination. There were also gang symbols. And a swastika.

"So I hear you lynched a nigger," said Bulldog from below.

Mark didn't respond.

"It's okay," said Bulldog. "That's cool with me."

Mark still didn't answer.

Bulldog pushed up on Mark's mattress, nearly knocking Mark out of the top bunk. "What's wrong with you? Your mama never taught you to speak when spoken to?"

"I didn't kill anyone," said Mark.

"Well, that's too bad," said Bulldog. "Because if you did it, you and me are gonna be good friends."

Mark didn't say a word.

"And if you didn't," he said, sighing loudly enough for Mark to hear him. "Well, if you didn't, then to me you're just another warm fuck-hole."

Mark went cold.

"I'll ask you once again in the morning, frat boy. You sleep on it and lemme know how it's gonna be."

Mark took a breath. He couldn't have responded if he'd wanted to.

"And don't get any bright ideas about changing cellmates. I heard the Malcolm X wannabes talking at lunch today. You end up with one of them, you'll beg to come back to me."

Mark closed his eyes, not to sleep, but in an effort to cope with his living nightmare.

"'Night, frat boy," said Bulldog.

Mark opened his eyes, still unable to believe where he'd ended up.

Bulldog delivered another swift kick to the underside of Mark's mattress, this one even harder than the last. "I said *good night*."

Mark swallowed the lump in his throat. "'Night."

CHAPTER 41

Jack reached Live Oak just after 11:00 p.m. and took a motel room down the hall from Mark's parents. A phone call to the Suwannee County Jail confirmed that Mark was not in solitary confinement. Jack figured his parents could use a little encouragement.

Liz was asleep, but Tucker answered Jack's text and joined him for a nightcap in the lounge—the "Poolside Café," so named even though the motel had been without a swimming pool since 1973.

"I'm feeling better about Mark's defense," said Jack.

Tucker added a spot of honey to his bourbon on the rocks, as Jack told him about the Croc recovered from Baine Robinson's closet at the Theta house.

"Do you think that will help get Mark out of jail?"

"Step one is to get him moved to solitary. I'll know more about his chances on bail once Oliver Boalt turns over the rest of his evidence."

"Does Boalt have to show us what he has against Baine, too?"

"If he charges him he definitely does."

Tucker tasted his bourbon, then shook his head. "I don't understand how the state attorney can go after Baine. Didn't his lawyer cut a deal for him to testify against Mark?"

"There are deals, and there are deals," said Jack.

"What does that mean?"

"My guess is that Boalt agreed not to charge Baine with conspiracy. But he left himself the option to bring a murder charge based on evidence other than Baine's own testimony—like a Croc found at the scene of the crime."

Tucker looked off toward the middle distance, swirling the ice cubes in his glass. "I never liked Baine."

"I'm not surprised."

"Cooper was okay, I guess. I feel bad saying anything against him now that he's dead. But most of those boys at Theta—well, they just weren't like Mark's buddies in high school."

"You can't always choose your son's friends."

His gaze drifted away again. "Or maybe I don't know my son as well as I thought I did."

Jack knew that Mark's parents had to be struggling. "I've been doing this a long time. Wives wonder about their husbands. Children wonder about their parents. It's totally normal to have doubts."

"Not for a second do I think that Mark has murder in his heart. But every now and then, I wonder—did Liz and I do something wrong as parents? Did I miss something that could have prevented this from happening?"

"A little of that can be healthy. But too much is self-destructive."

Tucker set his glass on the bar. "Liz and I had to shut down our e-mail accounts. You wouldn't believe the hate mail we were getting. Now people have started sending us letters the old-fashioned way."

"Don't read that stuff. Just box it up and send it to me. If there's anything to be concerned about I'll let you know."

"Okay. Most of it I just put out of my mind. But one thing has stuck with me. That first day you came by our house, when the demonstrators were outside, did you notice that poster that said 'Racism Is Taught'?"

"I did."

"It's funny where the mind goes. That sign got me to thinking about one morning I drove Mark to school. He was about ten, maybe eleven. It was one of those days where he couldn't find his backpack, the dog peed on the rug, traffic was terrible. You know what I'm talking about."

Jack thought of Righley. "I'm sure I will."

"Anyway, Shelly was one of those kids who couldn't leave the house on time to save her life. But Mark—oh, my God, if he was five minutes late it was a national disaster. So he's watching the clock and telling me 'Dad, hurry up, faster.' I was probably going five miles per hour over the limit, and a motorcycle cop stopped me for speeding. A black guy."

"What happened?"

"Nothing. He wrote me a ticket and drove away. But Mark felt terrible. He thought I should've explained to the cop that it was his fault."

"Kind of admirable for a middle-school kid."

"Except that Mark wouldn't let it go. He couldn't understand why I didn't try to talk the cop out of it. He was inconsolable, and this went on all the way to school. Finally, I lost it. I stopped the car in the drop-off lane and said, 'Damn it, Mark. It wasn't your fault. There is no way on God's green Earth that a black cop on a motorcycle was going to cut a break to a middle-aged white man in a pickup truck.'"

Jack searched for a diplomatic response. "You got mad and blew your top. That happens."

"I did," Tucker said, and then he took another swallow of his bourbon. "But it shouldn't happen in front of your kids."

"I agree," said Jack. "But kids are bombarded with a million different things that shape who they are. I don't think that one slip you had when Mark was ten made him into a racist."

"No," said Tucker. "But that was my chance to push back against all those bad influences. I didn't. I showed him it was *okay* to be racist."

He lowered his eyes, staring down into his drink.

Tucker's expression was truly pained, and Jack wasn't sure how to answer. *Don't worry, Tucker, I'm sure that Mark doesn't even remember it?* Or: *Shake it off, Tucker, it's no worse than some of the things I heard from my old man, and he went on to be governor?*

The bartender returned, and Jack was grateful for the interruption.

"Another round, gentlemen?"

"Nah, I think we're set," said Jack.

The bartender glanced at the television behind the bar. The sports segment was wrapping up on the late edition of the local news. "Some good news for Gator Nation today," said the bartender.

"I didn't hear," said Jack.

"Devon Claiborne recommitted."

Jack recalled his conversation with Leonard Oden about the nation's number one high-school quarterback who'd threatened to take his talents to another university unless the president of Theta Pi Omega was expelled. The bartender obviously had no idea that he was talking to Mark Towson's lawyer and father.

"Devon's coming to UF?" asked Jack.

"Yes, sir," the bartender said with a smile. "That kid is going to be something to watch next fall." He laid the bill in front of Jack, told them "No rush," and checked on the couple at the other end of the bar.

"Beautiful," said Tucker with a dose of sarcasm. "A thousand people demonstrated outside the courthouse today, my son was hauled off to jail two blocks from here, and the most important news of the day to Joe Bartender is that Devon Claiborne recommitted."

Jack wondered how many "Joe Bartenders" might end up on the panel of twelve Suwannee County residents selected as jurors at Mark's trial.

Tucker's cell rang and he checked the number. "It's Shelly," he said, and took the call.

Jack finished his drink, hearing just one side of the short conversation.

"Don't leave your dorm," Tucker said into his cell. "Just stay where you are, sweetie. I love you."

He hung up and laid his phone beside his bourbon. "Major shit in Gainesville tonight."

"What kind of shit?"

"Huge crowd outside Robinson Tower. Baine is under arrest."

CHAPTER 42

It was almost midnight at the Kappa house, and Percy Donovan was alone in his room trying to study. Most of the Kappa brothers were already heading across the UF campus to Robinson Tower. The door flew open, and his friend Kelso rushed inside.

"Let's go, man!"

Percy looked up from his laptop. "I can't. I have a finance midterm first period."

"Fuck that. I got a test, too. Biology."

There was only one honors student in the room, but this was not the time to compare GPAs. "You go without me."

A Kappa pledge burst into the room. He was holding a poster that he'd made for the demonstration. "How's this?" he asked, seeking Kelso's approval.

"'Death Row,'" Kelso read aloud. "'It's for Rich White Frat Boys Too.' Love it! What do you think, Percy?"

Percy shrugged. "I'm not really pro–death penalty."

"Dumb shit," said Kelso. "This is not about the death penalty. It's about equality."

"Then it's perfect," Percy said without enthusiasm.

Kelso gave him a friendly shove. "Come on, man. What's wrong with you?"

"Nothing. I have to study."

"Study," said Kelso, mocking him. "You're afraid to join the crowd over at Robinson Tower, aren't you?"

"I'm not afraid."

"Scared shitless—cuz last time the big, bad skinhead got in your face and knocked you down. Boo-hoo."

"Fuck you, Kelso."

Another Kappa brother appeared in the doorway. "Time's up. The whole house is heading over. You coming or not, Kelso?"

Kelso looked at Percy, but Percy didn't budge. "I'm out. Go."

"Pussy," said Kelso.

The fraternity brothers filed out of the room, leaving Percy alone at his desk. He heard the back door slam on their way out of the house, and the group of voices faded outside his window as they headed toward campus. Percy tried to refocus on his study guide. But his mind was elsewhere.

Scared shitless, cuz the big, bad skinhead knocked you down.

Not really. The Kappa house had a long national tradition of civil rights activism, and the University of Florida chapter was a proud part of it. Percy had been verbally abused, shoved, and knocked to the ground plenty of times in the past. He'd always picked himself up, more determined than before. If there was something different about him of late, as Kelso seemed to think, it had nothing to do with what had happened at the last demonstration. What kept him awake at night, what tormented him when he was alone, were the images in his head.

Percy had never talked it out with a counselor or anyone, but being the first person to lay eyes on Jamal's body was not without a psychological toll. Every night, he could see Jamal's face—the elongated neck, the rope burns at the jaw. He saw Emmett Till's face, too—the chilling photograph that Emmett's mother had allowed at the open-casket memorial service, so that the world never forget the playful fourteen-year-old boy from Chicago who was kidnapped, tortured, mutilated, and shot in the head for whistling at a white woman in Mississippi. And Percy also saw the immortalized but anonymous seven-year-old white girl in Fort Lauderdale, caught by a photographer as she looked up with the bemused curiosity of a child examining a side of beef on display in the butcher shop, her gaze fixated on the strange fruit hanging from the giant oak tree.

Percy looked up from his computer. He heard a noise from behind the house.

The back door?

He checked the clock on his computer. Kelso and the others had been gone for less than a half hour. It was too soon for them to return. Maybe they'd forgotten something. Percy rose from his desk, went to the door, and opened it. The hallway was clear.

"Kelso?"

There was no response, not from Kelso or anyone else. Percy stepped out and started down the hall. The Kappa house had ten rooms on either side, each shared by two upperclassmen or three underclassmen. Most of the doors had been left wide open, but each room Percy passed was unoccupied. Kelso hadn't exaggerated; Percy was the only one left behind. He continued all the way to the end of the hall to the back door. The house rule was to lock the door after midnight. Either Kelso had left at 11:59 p.m. or he'd violated the rule. Percy turned the dead bolt, locking it.

"Hope you took your key with you," he said, as if Kelso could hear him.

Percy started back to his room, but another noise stopped him. It came from the other end of the hallway. His pulse quickened, but he kept perfectly still, listening. He heard nothing. Then a half smile came to his face. This was the classic Kelso-style prank, not unlike the goofball who'd launched underwater sneak attacks on the unsuspecting sorors floating down the river on the tubing trip.

"All right, Kelso. You messing with me?"

Percy continued toward his room, but he didn't get beyond the first open door. In a blur, his attacker launched himself into the hallway and blindsided him. Before Percy could speak he was facedown on the floor, pinned beneath a man who mounted him like a roped steer, yanked his hands behind his back, and cinched up his wrists with plastic handcuffs. Percy wanted to call out for help, but the steel blade at his throat silenced him.

"Not a word!"

The command was from a second man, not the behemoth on top of him. Next was the sound of tearing duct tape, and a silver-gray strip covered his mouth. Then the lights went out, figuratively, as a burlap sack covered his head, and the man tied a cord around his neck just tightly enough to hold the sack in place. Percy's heart pounded, his attacker's breath filtered through the sack to his ear, and Percy heard that voice again. It wasn't the guy who'd just put the knife to his throat and threatened him into silence. It was the earlier voice he'd heard on the street outside the burning Theta house—the skinhead who'd shoved him against the brick wall and gotten right up in his face.

"I warned you, boy," the man whispered through the burlap. "I said you was next."

Percy struggled to breathe as each man grabbed an ankle and dragged him along the carpet to the end of the hall. He heard the dead bolt turn and the door open, and they pulled him into the alley behind the house, where Percy could smell the Dumpster. A vehicle pulled up—it sounded more like a car than a truck. The men grabbed him and lifted him to his feet. Percy heard a hatch pop open—no, a trunk—and they shoved him inside. Percy fell into a fetal position, his head resting on the wheel well and his back pressed against the spare tire. The trunk slammed shut, a car door opened and closed, and Percy could hear his kidnappers in the back seat, less than a body's length in front of him.

"Go, go, go!"

The rear tires squealed, flying gravel pelted the car's underside like machine-gun fire, and Percy prayed to God that he wouldn't be "next."

CHAPTER 43

Jack rode with Mark's parents to the Suwannee County Jail the next morning. They registered with the corrections officer at the window and then waited in the reception area with about a dozen visitors who had come to see other inmates. A small television in the corner was tuned to an ancient episode of *Law & Order*, but there was no sound. At the other end of the room, a man was banging on a vending machine that had stolen his dollar.

"Do you think Mark knows about Percy Donovan?" asked Elizabeth.

The apparent kidnapping from the Kappa house had been the lead story all morning. There had been no mention of a body. A search was under way, however, and the Alachua County Sheriff was planning a news conference at 10:00 a.m. with an update.

"Probably not," said Jack.

"Do you think Percy's still alive?" she asked.

Percy's parents had already taken to the airwaves and expressed the "firm belief" that their son was alive and would return unharmed. The fear of law enforcement, the media, and everyone else, however, was the same—that Percy Donovan was the next Jamal Cousin.

"I'm hoping for the best," said Jack.

The metal door at the end of the room opened, and a corrections officer entered the waiting area. "Mr. Swyteck?"

It was agreed that Jack would meet with Mark first, on an attorney-client basis, separate from his parents. Jack excused himself from the Towsons and went with the guard. A private room at the end of the cell block was for attorney visits. The electronic lock buzzed, the door opened, and the officer directed Jack inside.

Mark was in the center of the room, seated at a small rectangular table, and flanked by a pair of stone-faced guards. He wore the same blue pants that were standard issue at the jail, but his V-neck T-shirt was the bright orange color that distinguished inmates who'd been charged with a capital crime.

"Get up," said the guard.

The chains rattled as the prisoner rose. The correctional officers removed the shackles from his hands and ankles, and Mark returned to his seat.

"I'll be right outside the door," the guard told Jack. "Buzz if you need anything."

"Thanks," said Jack.

The guards left the room, and the door closed behind them. Jack took a seat in the hard wooden chair across the table from his client.

"How you holding up?" asked Jack.

Mark just stared. He looked exhausted. It was clear that he'd slept little, if it all, but his eyes told an even darker story. It had been a night to forget, but one that he would always remember.

"Do you feel unsafe?"

No response.

"I checked out your cellmate," said Jack. "He's no stranger to the prison system. Served eleven years at Raiford for sexual assault. Here now awaiting trial on a robbery charge."

Still, Mark said nothing.

"It's no surprise that your cellmate has a violent past. You're charged with murder, so it wouldn't be protocol to lock you in a cell with someone serving, say, a thirty-day sentence on a misdemeanor charge for trespassing. That's one of the reasons I requested solitary confinement."

Jack waited, but it remained a one-way dialogue. Jack continued.

"The sheriff obviously ignored my request. If he won't move you to solitary, I'll get into court this afternoon on an emergency basis. That is, if you tell me it's an emergency."

Mark lowered his eyes.

"Is it?" Jack asked gently. "An emergency?"

Mark was silent for another minute. Then he slowly nodded his head.

"I'll need facts," said Jack. "I have to explain to the judge why you feel unsafe."

"I don't want to talk about it," he said in a weak voice.

Jack paused. His client was charged with an offense that could land him on death row, but Jack needed no reminder that more Florida inmates died each year by their own hand than by lethal injection.

"Tell me what happened, Mark."

Mark closed his eyes, as if summoning the power to speak. It took a minute. His eyes opened. He drew a deep breath and let it out slowly.

And then he told Jack.

CHAPTER 44

Andie took the Red Line into Washington, D.C., exited the Metro at the Judiciary Square station, and walked three blocks to the J. Edgar Hoover Building. She was alone. Jack would be in Live Oak for at least another day, so Abuela was in charge of Righley until Andie flew back to Miami—hopefully in time to tuck Righley into bed.

Andie was the Miami representative at a team meeting that included agents from field offices in eleven southern states from Texas to Florida. All had been summoned for an emergency update on Operation 777. Andie arrived an hour early for a private meeting with the divisional director, Stan Smith, and the operation's coordinator, Anthony Douglas. Smith was a graduate of Georgetown Law School and had started his legal career in the Civil Rights Division of the Justice Department. To Andie, he still looked and spoke like a lawyer. Douglas was a Gulf War veteran and former Marine officer, the quintessential team leader. Andie had been part of Operation 777 for months. The issue at hand was whether she would remain part of the team.

"What does your husband know about your involvement in the operation?" asked Smith. He was seated behind his desk. Andie and Douglas were in the pair of tufted-leather armchairs, facing him.

"Jack knows nothing," said Andie.

"You didn't say anything to him when he signed on to become Mark Towson's attorney?"

"At first I tried to discourage him. But that had nothing to do with my involvement in this operation. It was simply a personal preference that my husband not be the lawyer for an accused racist." She didn't mention the swastika on their front door.

Smith folded his hands atop his desk. "Operation 777 is the bureau's most important investigation into the growth of hate groups in this country since the Oklahoma City bombing."

"And I'm proud to be part of it," said Andie.

"We can't carve out the lynching of Jamal Cousin and now the disappearance of Percy Donovan from a federal investigation into hate groups."

"I wouldn't expect you to," said Andie.

"Either one or both could impact your husband's case in Live Oak," said Smith.

"Jack and I have an understanding that there are things he can't tell me about his work and vice versa. It's the only way our marriage works, and we take that very seriously."

"No one is suggesting that you would *intentionally* disclose confidential details of an FBI investigation. But as the saying goes, 'Shit happens.'"

"Sir, I've performed more than a dozen successful undercover roles. I infiltrated a cult in Washington's Yakima Valley. I 'worked' on Wall Street to root out one of the biggest financial scams in history. I earned the trust of Turkic-speaking Uighurs from Xinjiang Province in China who targeted the Florida Keys for environmental terrorism. I think I can handle keeping my mouth shut with my husband."

Smith was thinking, silent.

"Let's be practical about this," said Douglas. "Henning is irreplaceable. It would take months for a new agent to reestablish the contacts she's made within the target organizations. Not only would that put the operation way over budget, but it would completely disrupt our timetable."

Smith mulled it over for another minute, though it seemed much longer to Andie.

"There's only one way this can work," he said. "And that's to elevate your status to Level IV."

Andie hesitated. Level IV meant complete immersion and separation—no contact with family or friends. The last time she'd gone Level IV was before Righley was born.

"For how long?"

"At least a month. Perhaps longer."

Andie breathed deeply. She'd known this day would come and in fact wanted the career she'd had before motherhood. But that didn't stop her from considering how much Righley would change while she was away.

"I'd like to fly home first and say good-bye to my daughter."

"That's up to your coordinator," said Smith.

"Sure," said Douglas. "But I need you in Live Oak first thing tomorrow."

Andie agreed and thanked the assistant director. They shook hands, and Smith dismissed them. Andie rode the elevator down with Douglas to the meeting room for the Operation 777 update. They were thirty minutes early, but Douglas' assistant had already queued up the A/V equipment for his presentation. He gave Andie a sneak preview.

"Tech finally made it through the thousand-plus photos we collected from the riot outside the Theta house," he said. "It took some enhancement, but we have a nice shot of the guy who launched the Molotov cocktail from the street."

A click of the remote brought up the first slide. It was a split image. The one on the left was pre-enhancement. The one on the right was a close-up.

"He's white," Andie said.

"I'm ninety-nine-point-nine-percent sure he'd say 'Aryan,'" said Douglas.

Andie studied the images for another moment. The blond hair was hardly a distinguishing feature on this assignment, but the small tattoo of a lightning bolt at the corner of his right eye was a gift to law enforcement.

"Commit it to memory," said Douglas. "You'll be looking for him tomorrow."

CHAPTER 45

Jack and his client were in front of Judge Teague before lunch.

Less than an hour after the jailhouse meeting, Jack had filed an emergency request for a court order directing that Mark be placed in administrative segregation "for his own safety." Judge Simon scheduled an immediate hearing on the motion. In the interest of efficiency, he combined it with Baine Robinson's request for immediate pretrial release.

Jack and Mark were at the defense table with Baine Robinson and his lawyer, Leonard Oden. Oliver Boalt and two assistant state attorneys were at the table for the prosecution. Most of the seats in the gallery behind them were empty, since the general public received virtually no advance notice of the hearing. The media filled the first row, bookended by Mark's parents on one end and Baine's parents on the other. The families were keeping their distance from one another. Jack's opening remarks explained why.

"Your Honor, although the court has scheduled a joint hearing, it's important to understand that there is no joint defense or common interest arrangement between these two defendants. It is my client's position that Mr. Robinson's testimony to the grand jury is false. Mr. Towson never sent a racist text message to Jamal Cousin, and he certainly did not brag to Baine Robinson about the lynching of Jamal Cousin."

Oden rose to speak, but the judge cut him off.

"We're not getting into that today," the judge said. "Let's stick to the issue at hand. Mr. Swyteck, I understand from your written submission that you believe administrative segregation is necessary for your client's personal safety. Let me hear from the state attorney. Mr. Boalt, how do you feel about this court getting into the business of operating a jail?"

It wasn't how Jack would have framed the issue, but it was a pretty clear indicator of which way the judge was leaning. The state attorney ran with it.

"Judge, this request is completely disingenuous. Mr. Towson admitted to his cellmate that he planned and carried out the murder of Jamal Cousin. Mr. Swyteck seeks administrative segregation for only one reason: to create the impression that Mr. Towson feared for his personal safety and that his confession was therefore involuntary."

"Judge, my client was placed in a cell with a convicted sex offender known as Bulldog," said Jack. "He threatened sexual violence against Mr. Towson unless he admitted his involvement in the lynching of Jamal Cousin."

"Was Mr. Towson the victim of sexual assault?" asked the judge.

Jack was all too aware that Mark's parents were seated directly behind him. He'd asked Mark the same question at the jail, and he gave the judge the answer his client had given.

"No, thankfully. But he was able to avoid it only by making false statements to his cellmate."

"We-e-e-ell," said Boalt, turning on his gentlemanly sarcasm. "Judge, if the Suwannee County Jail placed a first-timer into administrative segregation every time another inmate messed with his head, we'd have to double the size of our jail. This request is beyond silly."

"I agree," said the judge. "The request is denied."

"Judge, if I could—"

"I said the request is *denied*, Mr. Swyteck. Next issue. Mr. Boalt, what is the state's position on the pretrial release of the defendant Baine Robinson?"

Baine's lawyer rose and moved to the center of the courtroom, standing physically closer to the prosecution than to Jack. It was clear to Jack where this was headed, and the state attorney made the announcement.

"It is the state's position that Mr. Robinson is not a flight risk," said the prosecutor. "Only Mr. Towson and his now-deceased accomplice, Cooper Bartlett, fled in anticipation of the indictment. In stark contrast, Mr. Robinson cooperated with the prosecution and testified before the grand jury."

"You agree to Mr. Robinson's release?" asked the judge.

"Yes," said Boalt. "We have agreed to his release pending our decision whether to bring formal charges against Mr. Robinson by information or by indictment."

Jack did the translation in his head: whether or not to seek the death penalty. A capital crime could be charged only by a grand jury indictment, not by a simple written "information" prepared by the prosecutor.

"Does the state have a recommended bond in mind?" asked the judge.

"Two hundred fifty thousand dollars."

There wasn't a soul in the courtroom who didn't know that a quarter million was pocket change to the Robinson family.

"So ordered. That concludes our business for today. We are adjourned," said the judge, ending it with the pistol-shot crack of his gavel.

All rose on the bailiff's command, and Judge Teague stepped down from the bench. The silence ended the instant he disappeared behind the door to his chambers. Baine Robinson turned and rushed to the rail to embrace his relieved parents. A group of reporters swamped them, but most of the media attention was directed toward Mark, who remained seated beside Jack, their backs to the gallery.

"I have to stay in a cell with that guy?" he asked, but it wasn't really a question.

"I'm not giving up on this," said Jack.

A pair of armed deputies arrived to escort Mark back to jail.

He rose, struggling to keep his composure as he glanced in the direction of his parents. Their display of emotion could not have contrasted more sharply with the obvious joy of the Robinsons.

"Hey, Towson, did you suck?"

Mark glared, the camera clicked, and Jack cringed. It was a time-honored paparazzi tactic, and with perfect execution a sleazy photographer had captured the image that would lead on the evening news—Mark Towson shooting the angry look of a man who could kill.

Jack stepped between his client and the media, serving as a human shield as the deputies led Mark to the prisoners' exit at the side door of the courtroom.

CHAPTER 46

Percy's eyes blinked open, but the pain made him squint. It hurt too much to open his right eye, so he used only his left. The burlap sack was gone, no longer suffocating him, but the right eye had taken a crushing blow from his attacker. Percy had made the mistake of looking straight into those steely blue dots in the black ski mask. *"Don't look at me, boy!"*

The glowing light above him was annoying, but slowly the strange room came into focus.

Percy was on his back, lying on a floor of cool, unfinished concrete. A bulb hung by a wire from the ceiling. He pushed himself up and wanted to stand, but he could rise only to a seated position. His wrists and ankles were chained to a metal ring set in the exposed studs in the wall. The shackles were in front, which was better than being hog-tied, but there was only enough slack to move a couple of feet in any direction—left, right, or upright. The chains rattled as he lowered himself back to the floor.

Whoa, head rush.

That simple up-and-down motion stirred the fog in his brain, reminding him why his right eye hurt so much. It wasn't just the punch in the face. The punishment after he'd gone down had done the real damage. Percy could almost feel that boot again, the steel-toed battering ram that had rearranged his face. His pleas for mercy—*Stop, stop, I'm begging you!*—had been useless.

The night was coming back to him. The tackle in the hallway, the burlap sack, and the quick binding of his wrists. The men—there were definitely two of them—dragging him out of the Kappa house. A car pulled up—*a third guy?*—and the men shoved him into the trunk. Percy would have offered money, any amount, but he knew in his heart that this was no kidnapping for ransom. The lid slammed shut, and off they went. He was wedged between the spare tire and a container of some sort that smelled like gasoline, which had sent fear racing through his mind: *Are they going to burn me alive?* He'd read enough about Jim Crow to know that "lynching" went far beyond a rope around the neck. Drownings, burnings, mutilations—many of them public events—were all part of the racist legacy.

Percy took a deep breath, which came easy, and he thanked God for that one small improvement in his predicament. It would have been hard enough to breathe in a locked trunk. The sack over his head had made it nearly impossible. He'd almost drowned in his own sweat, and at some point he'd blacked out. The next thing he remembered, he was on the floor with his face pressed against the concrete. A garage? *Yeah, must be.* His kidnappers must have pulled him out of the trunk, dropped him on the floor, and chained him to the stud in the wall.

Percy opened his left eye as wide as he could, and his gaze swept his surroundings in monovision. Four walls with exposed studs, like the interior of an unfinished garage, but it was too small to hold a car, and there was no roll-up door. He spotted the tool bench along the wall—*a toolshed*—and his right thumb and index finger began to throb. The cause of the pain was rushing back to him. His memory was becoming clearer. He remembered the vise-grip pliers, the angry voice of one sadistic bastard, and the laughter from his buddies who were looking on. "Good luck pickin' cotton now, homeboy," one of them had joked.

It made Percy sick to think about it, but he couldn't stop the sound of his own screams from replaying in his mind. He tried to sit up again, then stopped. He heard footsteps outside. Someone was coming. He listened carefully. Just one set of footsteps was all he could discern.

Please, God, not the maniac with the pliers.

The door opened. Percy caught his breath and sat up. A man entered the room, his face covered by a ski mask. Percy smelled food. The man walked toward him and laid a paper plate on the floor in front of him. Then he grabbed the tape that covered Percy's mouth.

"Scream, and I'll give you something to really scream about," the man said. "Understand?"

Percy nodded. The man ripped off the tape, which stung.

"Eat," the man said.

The chains rattled as Percy reached for the sandwich. He was starving, which gave him some indication of how long he'd been unconscious. He chewed off a big bite and swallowed. Some kind of lunch meat on white bread, and it was swimming in Hellmann's—an obvious play on the stereotype that black people hate mayonnaise. "Rapper repellent" was what Percy had once heard a totally hilarious food service attendant call it at the student union on campus. Percy was used to that kind of day-in and day-out bullshit. "Expect it," his high school guidance counselor had told him when he'd turned down Howard and Fisk for a predominantly white university.

A gob of warm mayonnaise dripped onto his pants. *Assholes.* Percy scarfed down the sandwich anyway.

"Happy now?" the man asked.

Percy didn't answer.

"You should be," the man said. "Wouldn't be feeding you if we was going to kill you, now would I?"

The thought had occurred to Percy, but attributing logic to anyone motivated by hate was a leap.

The man opened a bottle of water and handed it to Percy. "But don't get too giddy. You live only if the Theta brothers walk on all charges."

Percy drank his water. He understood the legal system well enough to know that it might be months before the Theta brothers walked—or were convicted.

The guy took away Percy's water bottle, retrieved a metal bucket from the tool bench, and laid it on the floor near Percy. "You know what that's for," he said. "I'm only gonna dump it once a day. You knock it over, you lay in it."

Percy was in need of a bathroom, but the thought of spending the next twenty-four hours alongside a bucket of his own waste took away some of the urgency.

His captor tore a fresh strip of duct tape from the roll and covered Percy's mouth. "Don't cause any trouble, and who knows, black boy? You might not end up like Jamal."

Percy cast his gaze downward. He recognized those steel-toed boots—the ones that had kicked his face so hard that he'd felt whiplash.

"*Might not*," the man added, and then he walked away.

The hinges squeaked as the door swung open. He switched off the light, and the door closed with a thud.

Percy was alone in the darkness.

CHAPTER 47

Jack went from the courthouse to his motel room after the hearing. He was dialing Andie, just to check in and say hello, when his cell rang with an incoming call. He didn't recognize the number, but if Mark was calling collect from jail, Jack didn't want to miss it. He answered.

"Jack, this is Blair Robinson."

Baine's father. Jack recognized the strong and confident voice, even though they'd spoken only once before—by telephone, right before Mark's expulsion hearing at the university, when he'd recommended that Mr. Robinson hire a lawyer for his son.

"How soon can you meet with me?" asked Robinson. The question was loaded with the usual presumptiveness of a successful CEO, most of whom thought that the world would jump at the chance to meet them.

"Mr. Robinson, I've already talked this out with Leonard Oden. As I told Judge Teague, there will be no joint defense arrangement between your son and my client."

"I heard. But you're mistaken if you think there's no benefit to joining forces. What budget has the Towson family given you on this case?"

"That's between my client and me."

"But there *is* a budget, right? My point is this. Leonard Oden has no budget. I will pay whatever it costs to prove that my son is innocent."

"Well, I hope your money is well spent."

"So far, so good. Your client is in jail. My son's not. Your client has been indicted. My son has yet to be formally charged with anything."

If there had been any chance of Jack warming up to him, it had just evaporated. "Pardon the free advice, but you'd be foolish to assume that Baine won't be charged."

"We'll know soon enough. Leonard told me that the state attorney has twenty-one days from the arrest warrant to charge Baine by written information or to get a grand jury indictment."

"That's correct," said Jack. "I expect that Oliver Boalt will use that time to put incredible pressure on your son to double down on his testimony against Mark. If Baine agrees, Boalt will accept a plea of something less than murder in the first degree. If he doesn't, Boalt will go back to the grand jury and ask for the death penalty. The fact that your son hasn't been formally charged yet is purely a negotiation tactic."

"You may be right," said Robinson, and then his voice turned very serious. "But a lot can happen in three weeks."

It came across as anything but a casual remark. "What are you getting at, Mr. Robinson?"

"Look, Jack. I've always liked Mark Towson. A good kid. His parents seem like nice folks."

"He is a good kid. And the good ones don't lynch other students."

"That's for sure," said Robinson. "I know Baine didn't do it. I'd like to believe that Mark had nothing to do with it, either."

"He didn't. But to prove it, I will have to show that your son lied to the grand jury. So I don't see the point of this conversation."

"The point is . . ." Robinson waited a moment, then finished his answer. "Maybe Baine was confused when he said Mark was bragging about what he did to Jamal."

"Confused?"

"Or scared, and pressured to point the finger at Mark Towson by an overzealous prosecutor who's running for reelection."

Jack walked to the window. He could see the courthouse. The jail, too. "Are you telling me that your son is willing to recant his testimony?"

"Let's leave that aside for the moment. What I'm telling you is this: I can prove that the people who kidnapped Percy Donovan from the Kappa house last night are the same people who lynched Jamal Cousin."

"How?"

Robinson laughed arrogantly. "Maybe you didn't hear what I said earlier, Jack. Leonard Oden has no budget."

It wasn't clear if he meant hiring the best private investigators, which was fine, or buying witnesses, which wasn't. The fact that Jack was left wondering told him how to respond.

"I'm not interested."

Another chuckle. "Just like your old man. Harry didn't want to accept my campaign contributions—at first. Eventually he came around. So I'll take your 'no' as a 'maybe.' Think it over. Talk to Mark and his parents if you want. You call me back with the right answer. Soon, I hope."

He hung up without waiting for Jack to say good-bye.

CHAPTER 48

Reporters hounded Oliver Boalt all the way from the courthouse to the office of the state attorney, stretching a three-minute walk across the street into a half-hour trek. The questions ran the gamut, from Mark's jailhouse "confession" and the evidence against Baine Robinson to a possible link between the disappearance of Percy Donovan and the lynching of Jamal Cousin. The prosecutor's answers boiled down to the same message: "We will prosecute everyone involved to the fullest extent of the law."

The state attorney arrived in time for a scheduled meeting with Leroy Highsmith, who was waiting in his office. The men greeted each other cordially. Boalt's secretary brought coffee and closed the door on her way out, leaving them alone in the sitting area by the window. A coffee table, not the power statement of Boalt's antique desk, was between them. Small talk was short. His campaign was in the homestretch, and Boalt got straight to business.

"I've been thinking about timing," said Boalt, "and the endorsement should probably come no later than Monday."

Highsmith crossed one leg over the other, balancing his cup and saucer on one knee. "I'm not going to endorse you, Oliver."

The state attorney smiled, thinking that Highsmith was joking. The expression on Highsmith's face, however, was stone-cold serious.

"What's the problem now?" asked Boalt.

"First of all, you don't need my endorsement. You're an incumbent without a serious challenger."

"Black turnout is going to be double what it normally is. Maybe triple, now that Percy Donovan has gone missing."

"There's no reason to fear the black vote. You've indicted Mark Towson. You're working just as hard to build the case against Baine Robinson. You've done the right thing. Black folk can see it with their own eyes. They don't need me telling them."

That was high praise from a man like Highsmith. Boalt only wished that he'd said it in front of a television camera. "It can't *hurt* for them to hear it from you."

"Jamal's family prefers that I be apolitical. But let's see how it goes. If you run into some tough sledding, I may reconsider."

"I will hold you to that. I may need it."

"I seriously doubt it."

Boalt considered his response. He could have elaborated in a vague way—said that all politicians have skeletons in the closet, and that one never knew what land mine might explode on the political landscape. But such generalities wouldn't likely change Highsmith's mind.

And getting into specifics was definitely not an option.

"Okay," said Boalt. "Let's stay in touch on this."

"There is one more thing," said Highsmith. "I've been told that the FBI is getting involved in both the Donovan and Cousin investigations."

The prosecutor wasn't sure who his sources were, but they sure were reliable. "I can't speak to you about that, Leroy."

"That's fine. I just want to make sure you understand my concern. Years ago, when I was at Berkeley, it was the height of the Oakland Black Panther Party for Self-Defense."

"You were a Black Panther?"

"The party welcomed all brothers and sisters. Which ties in with the point I'm trying to make. The FBI exploited that inclusiveness."

"What do you mean by that?"

"I'll give you a perfect example. About a year after Huey Newton and Bobby Seale founded the party, Huey was convicted of manslaughter. It was later reversed on appeal, I might add, but before that, I was at a 'Free Huey' rally at Bobby Hutton Memorial Park in Oakland. We were called into order and formation, and I was lined up next to this really big brother—six foot eight, three hundred fifty pounds, easy. I didn't remember seeing him at any other rallies, but like I say, we were inclusive, so I figured all was cool. Except that right from the beginning, this dude seemed off. Acting strange. Real aggressive, too. He was out to hurt somebody before the rally even started. Then I noticed what he was wearing under his black leather jacket. It was a hospital gown."

"I'm not sure I see what you're getting at, Leroy."

Highsmith leaned forward, placing his coffee cup and saucer on the table. "He was from a psychiatric ward. And he wasn't the only one. The FBI rounded up psych patients, took them off their meds to make sure they were violent, dressed them in black leather jackets and berets, and turned them loose at our rallies."

Boalt blinked in disbelief. "Come on. That's not true."

"Look it up," said Highsmith. "The reports are public now. CIA Project CHAOS, FBI COINTELPRO. It was the kind of shit they did to discredit the movement, and the Oakland police stood by and let them do it."

Boalt still didn't accept it, but he didn't want to insult the one black civil rights activist who might endorse his candidacy. "Fine. But even if what you're saying is true, it's ancient history. That's not what the FBI involvement is about here."

Highsmith leveled his stare. "That's what they *tell* you, Oliver. The FBI will do it again, if the locals let them."

There was a knock at the door. It opened, and the state attorney's assistant poked her head into the office. "Excuse me, Oliver. There's a woman here to see you."

"I'm in a meeting," he said, sounding more annoyed than he'd intended.

His assistant recoiled slightly. "I know, and I'm so sorry to interrupt.

But she's been waiting, and she's very old. She said you'd know it's really, really important."

"Who is it?"

"Her name is Cynthia," the assistant said. "Cynthia Porter."

Highsmith studied the state attorney's reaction, curious to know who the important old lady was. Boalt didn't explain, but he feared that perhaps his body language did make an allusion, however oblique, to those unspeakable land mines on the political landscape that could upend even a popular incumbent.

Cynthia Porter was definitely one of them.

"I believe we were just about finished," Boalt said, rising. "Leroy, I'll be letting you know if I need that endorsement."

CHAPTER 49

It was time to counterpunch.

Jack liked to land his most devastating blows in a courtroom, but sometimes the opportunity arose outside the ring, so to speak, well after the bell. Jack reminded himself of that as he entered the Suwannee County Jail. He wasn't there to see his client. He'd put in a request to meet with Mark's cellmate. Jack was finishing his lunch when a collect call came from the jail.

"You're on my list," said Bulldog, meaning that he'd added Jack's name to his authorized list of visitors.

It wasn't technically an attorney-client meeting, but the corrections officer took Jack to the same visitation room where he'd met with Mark. It was there, seated at the same table, that Mark had told Jack about his first night in jail.

Jack was no stranger to involuntary confessions. His first win at the Freedom Institute was for a fifteen-year-old boy with an IQ of 70 who'd "confessed" to killing his sister after police lied and told him that his mother had seen him do it and that she never wanted to see him again unless he wrote her a letter of apology. The interrogator provided the pen and paper and helped him craft it. Other cases were less obvious: Was it coercive to appeal to the conscience of a lifelong Catholic by asking him to lead police to a missing body because his victim deserved "a good Christian burial"? The circumstances of Mark's "confession," however, were unlike any Jack had encountered before. Perhaps the closest analogy was a gun to the head. But it was no "gun" that Bulldog had shoved in Mark's face when he'd pushed Mark into the lower bunk in the dark jail cell, pulled the blanket down like a curtain that hung from the top mattress frame, and sat on Mark's chest. What made it especially difficult was that, like many victims, Mark didn't want anyone to know the details. He simply didn't want to talk about the circumstances that led to the words "Yeah, I did it"—not in private with his attorney, and definitely not in a packed public courtroom.

The door opened. Bulldog entered the room and took a seat opposite Jack at the table. Bulldog wasn't charged with a capital crime, so he wasn't shackled, which made it seem even more absurd that Mark had been for his meeting with Jack. Purple tattoos crept up both sides of Bulldog's neck to his earlobes. He was slouching in his chair, as if trying to convey only cool indifference.

"You wanted to talk?"

"I do," said Jack.

"I'm listening, my friend."

Jack had met guys like Bulldog before—total losers with a lengthy criminal record who'd somehow managed to avoid getting caught for their worst offenses and sent away for good. It was a pretty safe bet that half the men on death row had committed less heinous crimes than the ones Bulldog had gotten away with.

"Let me be clear from the get-go, Bulldog. I'm not here to bargain with you. I'm not going to waste my time trying to reason with you. And I am definitely not your 'friend.'"

"Fine by me."

Jack didn't break eye contact. "Mark Towson did not confess to the murder of Jamal Cousin."

"Maybe not to you. But he did to me."

"Did he also confess to kidnapping Percy Donovan? That would be pretty interesting, seeing how he was locked up at the time."

The smug expression remained on Bulldog's face. "No. Just told me that he lynched Jamal Cousin, and, hey, I got no problem with that."

"Did he also confess to the assassination of Martin Luther King Jr.?"

"No."

"How about Malcolm X? Did he confess to shooting him?"

"No."

"Did he tell you he was the guy who pumped three bullets into the back of Huey P. Long's head?"

Bulldog sighed, as if this were getting tiresome. "No."

"Because Mark would have admitted to all those things, if you'd told him it was either that or be your prison bitch."

Bulldog leaned forward, resting his massive forearms on the table and casting his most intimidating gaze at Jack. "Do I look like some kind of fag to you, Swyteck?"

"No," said Jack, glancing at the tattoo on Bulldog's right forearm—a shamrock inscribed with the number 666. "You look like AB to me."

AB—Aryan Brotherhood—was the oldest and best-organized white supremacist organization operating in the American prison system. Born of the intense racial wars of the 1960s and 1970s, AB's racist ideology had taken a back seat to profit, and the modern AB was known to work with Latino gangs and others on everything from drug trafficking to male prostitution inside prison walls.

"Never heard of AB," Bulldog said, smirking.

"It doesn't matter," said Jack. "You spent nine years in Florida State Prison at Raiford, right?"

"Nine years, five months, and twenty-three days."

"That's a long time to be without a woman."

"Yeah, it is."

"So when you go into the courtroom and lie about Mark's confession—when you deny that you threatened Mark Towson with sexual violence—here's what will happen. I'll call to the witness stand every inmate you raped at Raiford. The judge will hear it. The prosecutor will hear it. Everyone in the courtroom will hear it. The whole fucking world will hear it. And then they can decide for themselves what you are."

The cockiness started to drain from Bulldog's expression. "I didn't fuck nobody at Raiford."

This was the reach—the point at which Jack would use a tried-and-true police interrogation tactic that, ironically, the detective had used on his own client after pulling Mark and his friends out of the Theta party. He would lie. "I already know you did, Bulldog. And don't think for one second that I won't find every last victim."

"You're full of shit, Swyteck."

"You're a fool if you think so. See, I've represented probably twenty lifers at Raiford—guys who are never getting out of prison. Some of them are alive today because I got them off death row, which makes them especially grateful. I don't often ask for favors, but they are an amazing source of information."

More of Bulldog's cocky air faded.

"And these guys are good for much more than just information. It's not easy for inmates to come forward and say they were raped. They're afraid of retaliation. That's where my former clients can really help. They may be off death row, but most of them are still serious badasses. All I have to do is ask them to protect the guys you raped, and I'll have no problem finding all the witnesses I need."

Jack let it sink in, then continued. "Of course, that's just the beginning of the shit storm for you, Bulldog. I'm sure Oliver Boalt promised you a sweet deal for testifying against my client. But Raiford is in another county, and your deal with Oliver Boalt won't prevent the Union County state attorney from prosecuting you for rape. It *is* rape, you know. It doesn't matter that the victims are male prison inmates. Oral or anal penetration without the victim's consent is sexual battery."

Jack could almost see the wheels turning inside Bulldog's head.

"Here's the kicker, Bulldog. Sexual battery in Florida carries a minimum sentence of nine years, possibly life. So let's say Boalt gives you no prison time on the robbery charge you're facing right now. When I'm done with you, and it comes out that you raped even just one inmate at Raiford, you're looking at *more* prison time than you would have gotten if you'd just kept your mouth shut and never cut a deal with Oliver Boalt. That's pretty funny, isn't it?"

Jack chuckled insincerely. Bulldog didn't laugh.

Jack rose, went to the door, and knocked on it. The guard opened it.

"Have a great day, Bulldog."

Bulldog sat in silence at the table, staring at the wall. Jack turned and walked out, leaving the inmate alone with his predicament.

CHAPTER 50

Cynthia Porter left the office of the state attorney with a heart full of disappointment.

The meeting with Oliver Boalt had not gone as planned. He'd allowed her just five minutes to share all that she wanted to tell. At this point in her life, it took Cynthia five minutes just to organize her thoughts. She couldn't get the words out. Essentially, she'd managed only to say, "We can't go back to the way things used to be." The state attorney agreed wholeheartedly, but each time Cynthia tried to move beyond platitudes and aspirations, he talked over her. "I'm well aware of Suwannee County's regrettable racial history," he'd assured her, but he didn't seem to want to hear *her* history. He'd thanked her for coming and reminded her to vote.

"The live oaks are dying," said Cynthia. She was back at home, seated at the kitchen table. Virginia was standing at the counter, slicing a Vidalia onion on a cutting board.

"You mean the ones out front of the house?" asked Virginia, flashing concern.

"I mean all of 'em. Here in Live Oak, across Suwannee County, all around these parts."

Virginia smiled the way she always did when Cynthia said something that sounded a bit off the mark. "I don't think that's true, Miz Cynthia."

"Yes, it is," Cynthia said, suddenly animated. "When I was a girl, I'd see a mighty live oak on the savanna. So beautiful. Nothing else around it, limbs spread out so far that it looked like a green mountain on the horizon. The live oak needs that space. We've been taking it away."

"You mean the builders?"

"Partly. It's all this reforestation, too. A live oak can't survive in a forest. Sweet gum, black cherry, and magnolia are some of the culprits. Worst of all is the laurel oak, which looks a lot like a live oak but isn't nearly as sturdy. An impostor, I call it."

"I see."

"All this clutter. We put it there. It looks pretty at first. Who doesn't like a forest? Eventually, though, these impostors smother what was good about the place. The live oak is our soul, Virginia. We named our town after it. Do you understand me?"

Virginia pushed the onion slices from the board into the frying pan. They sizzled in the hot oil. "I—I think I do."

"If you don't clear away all that clutter, your soul withers up and dies. That's all I'm saying."

Virginia smiled. "So you want me to buy you a chain saw?"

They shared a little laugh, and then Cynthia turned serious. "No. I'd like my pen. And a sheet of my fine stationery from Birmingham—the ecru cotton with the pretty magenta border. Could you bring it to me, please?"

"I know just where it is." Virginia lowered the flame on the stove, went to the parlor, and returned with Cynthia's old fountain pen and stationery. She laid them on the table. "Who you writing to?"

Cynthia considered her response. "Someone who I think will listen," she said.

And then she put pen to paper and wrote in her finest script, fighting the tremor in her uncooperative hand.

"Dear Mr. Swyteck," she began.

CHAPTER 51

Jack called home from Live Oak and spoke to Righley before her bedtime. "Where's Mommy?"

"She's going under the covers."

"Beddy-bye?"

Righley laughed. "No, silly! *Under the covers!*"

Jack realized what she was trying to say. Righley's young mind sometimes confused an overnight trip with Andie going undercover, but she had it right this time. She handed the phone to Andie.

"Hey, where you headed?" asked Jack.

"Can't say."

Jack understood what that meant. "How long will you be gone?"

"I don't know. I hired Maria for two weeks."

Maria was their part-time nanny. Abuela was all the help Jack needed when he was home without Andie. But Jack's grandmother was getting on in years, so a part-time nanny was needed when they were both away. Abuela wasn't happy about it, insisting that she could handle "la muñeca" without any help at all from "Maria Poe-pins."

"Two weeks sounds about right," said Jack. That would get him through the *Arthur* hearing, Mark's last shot at getting out of jail before trial.

Jack got a quick reminder of Righley's daily schedule—breakfast, preschool, nap, soccer, afternoon meeting at the White House with the joint chiefs of staff. Andie had thrown in the last one just to make sure he was listening.

"I got it," said Jack.

"Hey, there's something else I want to tell you," she said.

"Okay."

"I was the one who brought up the idea of adoption. We haven't really had a chance to talk more. I didn't want you to think I just dropped it."

"No, I understand. It's been crazy. We can follow up with the agency when your assignment is over."

"Well," she said, hedging, "we may not want to do that."

Jack hesitated. "Did you change your mind?"

"Not exactly," she said. "I'm pregnant."

Leroy Highsmith entered the "Find Percy Donovan" command center and was immediately impressed. Proud, actually. Ask white students what they knew about black fraternities, and they'd probably say something like, "Don't they still brand their pledges?" The Divine Nine were a community, and this was the community in action.

Percy's best friend, Kelso, greeted him at the door. "Mr. Highsmith, thank you, thank you, thank you, sir."

"It's nothing," said Highsmith, and he meant it. He'd merely written the check to rent a ballroom at the University Inn. The hard part was pulling together teams at the grassroots level, both in the virtual world of social media and the real world of old-fashioned legwork. Kelso knew most of Percy's hangouts—restaurants, coffee shops, gym, and so on. With his input, they'd mapped out a search plan on the whiteboard and assigned teams to check each location. Volunteers were out talking to waitresses, librarians, locker-room attendants, and even random people on the street, all in the hope of finding someone who'd heard or seen something—anything. Inside the center, students lined up to distribute flyers, leaflets, and posters with Percy's picture. Sisters from the Delta sorority were busily tying yellow ribbons into bows, which students at another table attached to flashlights for volunteer searchers. A dozen other students tapped away on their laptops, tablets, and other devices, spreading the word in the virtual world of social media.

Kelso had much more to tell him, but Highsmith's assistant interrupted. "Leroy, President Waterston wants you to call him right away."

Highsmith excused himself, stepped out of the ballroom into the hallway, and dialed the university president at his home. After a brief exchange of pleasantries, the president got to the point.

"Leroy, this campus is on the verge of panic. Parents are pulling black students out of Gainesville like we're on the verge of Armageddon."

"Can you blame them?"

"Are you representing the Donovan family?"

"I met with them this morning and offered my assistance. They've accepted."

"How soon are you planning to address the media?"

"Less than an hour from now. I've scheduled a press conference with the Alachua County Sheriff and Percy's parents."

The president sighed, not with relief but apprehension. "I need a voice of calm," said Waterston. "I've issued a press release, but please reinforce the message that this university is doing everything it can to provide for the safety of all students."

All students. It reminded Highsmith of the white establishment's efforts to trump #BlackLivesMatter with #AllLivesMatter. But he let it go. "I'll do what I can," he said.

Highsmith politely ended the call and returned to the ballroom. One of the network affiliates was filming a segment for the local news, showing the command center in action. The reporter nearly tackled Highsmith, begging him to be part of her "on the scene" coverage. He didn't want to undermine the scheduled press conference, but he agreed to provide a quick comment.

The cameraman was ready. The reporter fixed her hair and smiled.

"Not so toothy," the cameraman said. "The kid may have been lynched."

"Sorry," she said, losing the grin. "Better?"

"Try to look more worried—like time is running out."

It was as if Percy were an abstraction. Typical. In Highsmith's experience, the spot-on hashtag for TV journalists was #OnlyMyCareerMatters.

The cameraman raised his fingers—"Three, two, one"—and they were rolling.

"Good evening," said the reporter, taking the cue from the anchorwoman in the local studio. "Tonight the search is on for another African American student gone missing at the University of Florida, where . . ."

The entire spot lasted thirty seconds. The reporter thanked Highsmith and promised to air it on the 11:00 p.m. broadcast.

Highsmith looked around the command center. Kelso was nowhere to be seen, but Jamal's fraternity brother, Brandon Wall, was across the ballroom. Brandon had become the de facto leader at the Alpha house, and he'd called Highsmith earlier in the day about an Alpha-led search for Percy along the Ichetucknee River. It was potentially a grim task, but the entire Alpha fraternity had volunteered, and Highsmith had arranged for a bus to leave Gainesville in the morning. Brandon walked over and, like Kelso, thanked Highsmith for funding the search.

"Do you have everything you need?" asked Highsmith.

"I thought we did," said Brandon.

"What did you forget?"

"I just heard from a friend in Jacksonville," said Brandon. "She says Aryan Brotherhood and some other neo-Nazis are planning to be at the river tomorrow morning when we get there."

Highsmith wasn't surprised. "It's the same old game. They put themselves where they know we're going to be, and then when trouble starts, they blame us."

"I'm not canceling the search," said Brandon. "The Alpha house doesn't back down."

"Good to hear. But let's not be foolish." Highsmith moved a little closer, lowering his voice a bit, as if he had a plan. "I need about a dozen Alpha jerseys or T-shirts by tomorrow morning. Size XXL or bigger. Can you swing that?"

"Sure. Every brother has extras. Why?"

"That's all you need to know," said Highsmith. Then he excused himself, stepped out of the command center, and found the same quiet spot in the hallway from which he had called the president. He dialed his contact at Colson Security Company.

Following Percy's disappearance, Highsmith had taken it upon himself to hire a security guard for each of the black fraternities and sororities on campus. Colson was a full-service operation that provided everything from personal bodyguards to kidnap-and-ransom insurance.

"I need twelve of your best men ASAP," Highsmith told his contact. "African Americans only. Young enough to pass for college students."

"Any special skills?"

"Gotta be able to swim," said Highsmith.

"Anything else?"

"Yeah," said Highsmith. "Vets with combat experience are strongly preferred."

"Wow. With those parameters, I might have to fly in men from twelve different cities. Could be expensive."

"Whatever it costs," said Highsmith. "Have them here in Gainesville before sunrise."

Morning sickness was a misnomer. For Andie it came any time of day.

She emerged from the bathroom in her motel room in time to catch the latest "Find Percy Donovan" news conference on television. Easy viewing it wasn't. Percy's father spoke first, reading from a prepared script, which was the only way to get through it.

"Percy's family and friends are pleading with *anyone* who may know anything about his disappearance, his whereabouts, or"—he paused, his voice quaking—"or his fate. Please call the Alachua County Sheriff's Department at the number on your television screen, or leave information at the 'Find Percy Donovan' website. A reward of one hundred thousand dollars is being offered for information leading to his safe return."

Highsmith was at Mr. Donovan's side, and Andie assumed that the reward was the lawyer's doing.

On-screen, the microphone passed from Percy's father to the Alachua County sheriff, but the camera view was wide enough for Andie to see Mrs. Donovan standing off to the side. The sheriff said exactly the right thing, but Andie hardly processed a word of it. Her entire focus was on that poor mother at the edge of her TV screen. Andie could almost feel the fear, the exhaustion, the worry, the dwindling sense of hope pressing down on her shoulders. Her heart was not merely broken. It was shredded, the pieces falling away live and on camera for the entire world to see, the sadness gathering in pools of despair around her, bottomless pools that could drown the most robust spirit.

Andie had dealt with the families of many victims, but nothing compared with a parent's anguish over a missing child.

Another wave of nausea came over her. She prepared for a second bolt to the bathroom, but the sensation passed. She crawled into bed and set the alarm for 2:00 a.m. In just a few hours, Paulette Stevens—her undercover name—needed to be at the designated gathering spot in the wilderness. The campgrounds at Ichetucknee Springs State Park were open to the public, but she'd have no trouble spotting her friends.

Nearly everyone in the group was blond, like her.

CHAPTER 52

Percy woke to the frightening reality that he was still a prisoner, still chained to a wall. And he was no longer alone.

It wasn't easy to tell. He was no longer blindfolded, but the toolshed was without windows, and the lone lightbulb had remained off since his captor's last visit, when he'd given Percy a soggy sandwich, a few sips of water, and a bucket in which to do his business. *The bucket.* Percy was trying to get used to the stench, but that point had yet to arrive. He blinked, trying to focus. The swelling in his battered eye had improved, and he was slowly adjusting to the darkness. A sliver of moonlight or sunlight—he wasn't sure which—shone through a tiny crack between boards in the wall. It was just bright enough to reveal a set of red, beady eyes at the other end of the shed, beneath the tool bench.

It was staring at him, whatever it was. Percy listened for a growl or hiss but heard nothing. The eyes were fixed, motionless. Surely they were inside the head of a living creature, but it was too dark to see any part of the body. If the frozen gaze was any indication, however, the animal was locked in some unshakable pose. Stiffened with fright, perhaps, or poised for an attack. A primitive thought crossed Percy's mind, as if he were suddenly inside the small brain of his visitor, sizing up his helpless self in the darkness.

Food.

The piercing eyes glowed brighter, and finally they blinked. A chill ran through Percy.

Do pythons have eyelids?

He suddenly heard breathing—his own, as he sucked air through his nostrils. His mouth was still taped shut, so he couldn't speak. But silently he was talking himself out of his worst nightmare, assuring himself that it couldn't possibly be one of those monstrous Burmese pythons that had taken over the Everglades and asserted themselves as the new top of the food chain in South Florida. Surely it was too cold in Suwannee County for pythons.

Unless those racist bastards turned one loose on me.

It would be the ultimate modern lynching—a black man trapped like an animal by men who personified the evil that Malcolm X had labeled the "white devil," forcing Percy to battle an eighteen-foot predator that crawled on its belly like Lucifer. It would be an hour or more of utter terror, as the monster coiled around his body and squeezed the life out of him, its massive jaws locked on to Percy's head in an effort to swallow him the way snakes always swallowed their prey—headfirst.

Percy was shaking, and the predator seemed to sense his fright. Slowly, a fraction of an inch at a time, the red eyes were creeping closer.

It was decision time. If Percy rattled the chains and kicked the wall to make noise, his captors might burst through the door and beat him, shoot him, or worse. But if he remained still, God only knew what was in store for him. Carefully, he sat as upright as the shackles would allow, drew his knees to his chest, and planted the balls of his feet on the rim of the metal bucket. If he could launch it across the shed at those beady eyes, the noise, if not the odor, might scare it away.

On the mental count of three, he summoned all his strength, straightened his legs, and sent the bucket of human waste flying across the shed. The clang of metal on the concrete floor sounded like a car crash, and Percy added to the racket by slapping the chains against the wall. Rather than retreat, the red eyes came straight at him with the speed and glow of a laser-guided missile. Percy kicked blindly in the dark, and the attacker—whatever it was—sank its sharp teeth into his ankle. He screamed, but the duct tape muffled it. He kept kicking at those red eyes but couldn't shake his ankle loose from its jaws.

The door flew open and the light switched on. Percy kicked and rolled in self-defense. Clawing and snapping at his feet was a rat as big as a bulldog.

Then came the clap of a gunshot. The rat was suddenly motionless.

Percy was breathing so heavily that his chest heaved. His captor—pistol in hand—stepped toward him and yanked the duct tape from his mouth.

"What the fuck!" he shouted.

Percy could barely breathe, let alone talk. It should have been pretty obvious that he'd been attacked by a rat. The dead animal lay at his feet, and it was hard to know how much of the blood on his ankle was Percy's and how much was from the rat. *That's WTF!*

He pressed the barrel of the gun to Percy's forehead. "I told you not to make noise."

"It bit me!" said Percy, staring up at his captor.

Only then did it hit him; and simultaneously, the same realization seemed to come over his captor: Blondie wasn't wearing his ski mask. He'd rushed into the shed without it in response to all that noise.

Instinctively, Percy averted his eyes.

"Too late," the man said. "You've seen my face."

"No, no," said Percy. "I was looking right up into the light. I have no idea what you look like."

The man pressed the barrel of the gun even harder to Percy's forehead. Percy closed his eyes and braced himself, certain that this was it—this was how he was going to die, but not before Blondie gave him plenty of time to agonize over it. A minute passed, then another. It seemed like hours.

The man jerked the gun away. Percy could breathe again.

"You fucked up, big-time," the man said.

Percy wanted to talk his way out of it, but for the moment, he was relieved simply to have more than the thickness of his skull between his brain and a pistol.

"You can sit here in your own piss 'til I figure out what to do with you." He pointed with a jerk of his head to the dead rat. "Maybe you'll get lucky and die of rabies."

Percy watched as Blondie walked away, switched off the light, and left through the only door to the shed. The red eyes had been extinguished, but it was another image entirely that stuck in his mind: He would never forget that inch-long tattoo of a lightning bolt that ran from the corner of Blondie's right eye.

Percy yanked the chain that held him to the wall, one thought consuming him: escape was the only answer. Without it, he was as dead as that rat.

CHAPTER 53

Andie heard the gunshot.

She'd been in role since leaving the motel, and by 3:45 a.m. "Paulette Stevens" was deep into the forest, following the footpath through dense undergrowth. She couldn't see the river, but she could smell the swamp in the air, the sulfur-like odor of standing water and rotting flora just off the banks.

Andie stopped and listened carefully. Even for a trained ear it was impossible to tell where a single, unexpected gunshot in the night had come from. The gentle sound of moving water was not far off, the Santa Fe River. Wildlife chimed in, a symphony of nighttime predators and their prey. But that telltale second shot didn't come; no reason it would, if the first had done its job.

Had she been a civilian, Andie would have turned and run back to the park entrance. Had she not been working undercover, she would have drawn her weapon. As it was, she just kept going.

Andie carried a flashlight in her right hand and a hand-drawn map in her left. In the dead of night it was easy to get lost in these woods. The ground was soggy in spots, and after several minutes of hiking through the brush, over fallen logs, and around ant mounds, she came to a clearing and read the sign. Wilderness campsites were filled on a first-come, first-served basis, no reservations. Highly convenient for last-minute planners—and for a bunch of skinheads who wanted to arrive in the middle of the night, raise hell in the morning, and then be gone, leaving no names, no credit cards, and no paper trail.

A fine mist began to fall. It gathered on the green canopy above, hissing like static in Andie's ears. In minutes, enough moisture had collected on the highest leaves to form little droplets that fell to the palmetto scrub and wild grapevines below. Soon, the entire forest glistened in the sweep of Andie's flashlight. She continued down that path, passing a couple of tents in the darkness. She wondered if these unsuspecting campers had any idea that the same thugs who had started a knife fight outside the Theta house were gathering just a few hundred yards from their campsite. These flimsy pockets of shelter were just nylon on sticks, modest protection from wind and rain but not much else. All along this isolated trail, it seemed so easy for anyone with a knife and no conscience to get away with murder, just for the thrill of it.

Just before the footpath began a long curve around a cluster of cypresses, Andie's journey came to an end. Her flashlight bathed the marker to Campsite A-19.

The instructions were to be there no later than 4:00 a.m. Some participants, like Andie, had timed their arrival close to the deadline. Others had pitched tents and spent the night. It surprised Andie to see them pulling up stakes already. The plan, as had been relayed to her, was to hike over to the Ichetucknee River and head off the black-frat search party around 9:00 a.m. By Andie's clock, they didn't need to break camp for another three hours.

Andie approached William, a foot soldier in the organization. He knew her only as Paulette. "Are we leaving already?" she asked.

"You didn't hear?"

"Hear what?"

"The mission is canceled."

"What? When was that decided?"

"Just now."

"What happened?"

"I dunno. Steger says everyone has to pick up and go."

Steger was the supreme commander of the Aryan National Alliance. The Justice Department was building a case against him under federal racketeering laws, which was in part the basis for the

FBI's jurisdiction in Operation 777. Steger ran the Alliance from afar, known best for his hate-filled rants on the Internet against the perpetrators of "white genocide," mostly blacks and Jews who sought the extinction of the white race through mass immigration, integration, miscegenation, homosexuality, abortion, and "forced assimilation." Andie had never met Steger, but that was one of her goals.

"Did he say why?" she asked.

"Nope."

Andie gazed off into the darkness, in the general direction of the river. She wasn't totally disappointed about the cancellation of the mission. If anything was to be learned from the alt-right march on Charlottesville, violence seemed inevitable in a face-to-face standoff between skinheads, who saw the lynching of Jamal Cousin as the end of "white guilt," and the black frats, who were out looking for evidence that Percy was the latest victim of racial terrorism. But she was curious about the reason for the sudden cancellation.

"Do you think it has anything to do with that gunshot I heard on the way over here?"

William shrugged. "Maybe."

"You heard it, too, right?"

"Yeah. Woke me up."

"So it must have been pretty close by. I mean, if it was loud enough to wake you up."

William stopped packing up his tent, looking at her quizzically. "You always ask this many questions at four in the morning?"

Andie hesitated, fearful that she'd stepped too far out of role and revealed her law enforcement core.

"Cuz if you keep it up," said William, "you're gonna blow any chance you had at sucking my cock."

Leaders of the Aryan National Alliance fancied themselves as the new "intellectual" wing of white nationalism, but out in the field, women were still treated like biker chicks. It was Andie's job to pierce the carefully crafted illusion put forth by white nationalists like Steger, and prove their direct linkage to guys like William—violent, criminal thugs who were at least honest about their supremacist ideology.

Andie figuratively bit her lip and stayed in role, smiling. "I'll try to do better, William."

CHAPTER 54

Liz is in the hospital," said Tucker Towson.

It was midmorning, and Jack was still in Live Oak when he got the phone call. Jack was aware that Liz had restarted chemotherapy, and he also knew from his grandfather's battle that chemo didn't normally require hospitalization.

"Is she going to be okay?"

"She's stable."

"Is there anything I can do?" asked Jack.

"Yes, actually. She asked to see you."

Liz wasn't on her deathbed, Tucker assured him, but the request still hit Jack like a dying wish. Without hesitation, he drove to Gainesville, arriving just before lunchtime. Tucker met him in the hospital cafeteria, and over coffee he gave Jack the update.

"They hit her hard with this last treatment," said Tucker.

"Maybe too hard?" asked Jack.

Tucker sighed deeply. "It's her last shot, really. The doctor says her cancer has become resistant."

"Can't they try a different drug?"

"That's what they did. And we switched to what they call a 'dose dense' treatment schedule. The nurse seemed a little nervous about administering it, because the medicine could burn her skin. I was asking myself, 'If you're so freaked out about a drop on your skin, what's it doing to Liz on the inside?'"

"It sounds like the two of you need to huddle with your doctors."

"That's an understatement. She had vomiting with chemo before, but nothing like this. Around two a.m. I had to bring her into the ER. I'm afraid the treatment might kill her before the cancer does. I'm not exaggerating."

"Is she awake now?"

"I think so. You should go up."

"Aren't you coming with?"

"No. She wants to talk to you alone."

Jack got that feeling again—the dying wish.

Tucker remained behind in the cafeteria to make a few phone calls and update Liz's worried friends. Jack rode the elevator to the second floor, checked in with the nurse, and went to Liz's room. The door was open, and he knocked lightly before entering. She was awake, her upper body slightly elevated by the adjustable mattress. She turned her head and said, "Come in, Jack."

It was a double room, but the other bed was empty. Jack stepped inside and stood at the rail. IV tubes fed fluids and painkillers into her veins. A machine on the other side of the bed monitored her vital signs. Lunch—a tray of mashed potatoes, gelatin, and other soft foods on the bedside table—was untouched. It was too early in the treatment schedule for Liz to start losing hair, but the color of her skin and the glaze in her eyes were distinctly medicinal. Her cracked lips shone with a recent application of Vaseline.

"Thanks for coming," Liz said.

"Of course," said Jack.

She looked at him with concern. "I've been thinking a lot about Mark."

It's what mothers do, Jack thought. "You shouldn't worry about anything but getting well."

There was a break in the conversation. She seemed tired and gazed out the window. Jack wasn't sure if he should fill the silence. He waited, and finally she looked back at him.

"The nurse said it's hereditary."

Jack had heard of male breast cancer, but it was rare. He wondered if her worry had suddenly shifted to Shelly.

"Do you think it is, Jack?" she asked. "Hereditary?"

The answer seemed obvious. There wasn't much scientific debate on that subject. "Are we talking about breast cancer?"

"No," said Liz. "Racism."

Jack did a double take. "A nurse told you that racism is *hereditary*?"

"Yes."

It sounded unimaginably cruel—a healthcare professional telling such a thing to a cancer patient who was fighting for her life. "What's that nurse's name?"

"I don't know. It was a man. But listen to me. Do you remember the first day you came to our house? The demonstrators were outside our house. One of them had a sign that said, 'Racism Is Taught.'"

It was déjà vu; Tucker had asked the same question. Of all the things that had been said, that one seemed to hurt the most.

"Yes, I remember. And I suppose racism is passed on from one generation to another. But that doesn't mean it's hereditary in a genetic sense."

"That's what *I* thought," said Liz. "But there've been scientific studies on this. People who are racist are born without chromosome twenty-three."

Jack was still struggling to comprehend. "The nurse told you that racism is a genetic disorder? Seriously?"

"*Yes*," she said. "It's based on genetic mapping. People born with racist tendencies only show twenty-two chromosome pairs, not the normal twenty-three."

"That sounds like bogus science to me."

"I hope you're right. But when I heard about this study, I got so worried for Mark. What if Oliver Boalt makes him take a DNA test? What if the test shows that he's missing chromosome twenty-three? What if the jury hears that it's a scientific fact that my son is a racist?"

Jack paused to unpack what she was saying. He'd heard that chemotherapy could cause depression. Maybe paranoia was another side effect. "I promise you, Liz. That is not going to happen."

"But the nurse showed me the study. It's on the Internet."

The Internet. "Liz, anything and everything is on the Internet."

"Look it up. It's on the website for the Wyoming Institute of Technology."

She seemed dead serious. Jack did a quick Google search on his phone. It came up instantly. The posted comments made it clear that not everyone saw the "study" for what it was, but in thirty seconds Jack had his answer.

"Liz, this is satire. The study concludes that Joe Biden is a racist. This institute is a made-up place that claims to have saved the world from the Y2K virus and only welcomes visitors who consent to a full body cavity search."

"Oh," she said. A smile creased her lips, and then she began to laugh. Jack laughed with her, and it made him feel useful to share in the first laugh she'd had in a long time. But then her laughter turned to tears.

Jack took her hand. "Hey, it's okay," he said.

A tear rolled down her cheek—just one, though surely more would have come if she weren't so dehydrated.

"I don't think I can take this anymore," she said, sobbing.

"We'll get through it," said Jack.

She closed her eyes. Talking, laughing, crying—it had sapped her strength. Jack took a seat in the chair by the window. The chromosome 23 website was a joke, but Jack was still bothered that a nurse had presented the "study" to Liz as fact—obviously just to torment the mother of Mark Towson, accused racist. It made him angry to think about it, but the decision to raise hell with the hospital and staff wasn't his. It was hers.

In a minute, Liz was sound asleep.

Brandon Wall and several dozen young men and women from the Divine Nine gathered on the bank of the Ichetucknee River. With them, dressed in the Alpha colors, were twelve highly trained hires from Colson Security, compliments of Leroy Highsmith. It was Brandon's first time on the river since the tubing trip, when Jamal's body was discovered by Kappa brother Percy Donovan. Brandon wondered if, this morning, one of the Alphas would find Percy.

"Listen up!" said the park ranger. He was standing before the group, along with a deputy sheriff. "Just a few things to note before you head out."

The ranger paused, and the deputy stepped forward. "Simple rule," said the deputy. "If you see anything of interest, don't touch it. Don't try to collect it yourself. You have the phone number we gave you. Call us, and a law enforcement officer will come and check it out."

He yielded to the ranger, who lectured the group on safety in the wilderness. Most of it was common sense. Look out for ant mounds and snakes. If you feel overheated, rest. His final point, however, raised a few eyebrows.

"Most important, stay away from gator holes. Any questions?"

There were none until, finally, a volunteer spoke up. "What's a gator hole?"

The ranger seemed thrilled that someone had asked. "That mist we had last night is the first precipitation this area has had in quite a while. In drought conditions, water drains from normally marshy areas and pools in holes. Some of these holes are burrowed by alligators. The gators hide underwater and wait for a wild turkey, a raccoon, or whatever to come by for a drink. When they do—"

As if on cue, the deputy slapped his hands together in a loud gator chomp.

"That's right," said the ranger. "Dinnertime. I've seen gators hungry enough to eat other gators. Don't let it be you. Is that as clear as Ichetucknee River water?"

Brandon and a fraternity brother exchanged uneasy glances. "Clear," Brandon answered.

"Hey, pardner, I got some news."

The voice on the line was Owen McFay's—the old gator

hunter who'd taken Jack and Theo down the river. Jack found a quiet spot in the hospital hallway outside the diagnostic department. "What's up?"

"I was on the river this morning, like always. I come across a buncha black students from UF. They was out looking for that boy who went missing."

"Percy Donovan," said Jack, his heart sinking. "Did they find him?"

"No, but get this. They found one of those foam shoes along the riverbank."

"You mean a Croc? Like the other one?"

"Well, good question. The police are all hush-hush about it. But nothing happens on the river without me gettin' to the bottom of it. I hear the shoe they found today matches the other one the divers found."

"You mean the one—"

"Yes, sir," said McFay. "The one they pulled outta the muck where Jamal got lynched."

Jack blinked, not quite comprehending. The Croc retrieved from the fire-damaged Theta house was supposed to have been the match.

"That's useful," said Jack. "Thanks, pal."

CHAPTER 55

A long line of motorcycles rumbled across the Florida-Georgia line. By sundown, Andie and a couple dozen other Alliance members entered Stephen C. Foster State Park, eighty acres of wilderness situated at the western entrance to the famous Okefenokee Swamp. The bikers set up camp at the pioneer site. The last directive from Steger had been to clear out of Florida, and the plan was to sit tight and wait for further instructions from their leader.

Of the women making the trip, Andie was one of a handful riding solo. She'd owned a bike in Seattle, before her transfer to the Miami field office—her life before Jack. The Harley-Davidson provided by the FBI for this operation was the fruit of a federal forfeiture proceeding against a criminal gang in South Florida. The Harley Street Glide was bigger than the middle-weight bikes that most women preferred, but Andie's riding skills impressed even the most macho men in the group. Still, she would feel much more comfortable when Paulette's "boyfriend"—Andie's undercover counterpart from the Atlanta field office—caught up with her.

Andie set up her tent next to William's and then joined him by the campfire. The temperature was dropping with the moon's rising, and the fire's warmth felt good. Seated on a fallen cypress log, Andie watched the dance of yellow flames kicking off sparks that drifted up into the night sky.

"So we just sit here?" she asked.

William tossed more wood on the fire and returned to his seat on the log. "Yup. Steger calls the shots."

"I don't understand it."

"I have my own idea."

It had taken Andie weeks to gain William's trust and hear his theories. She was one of the few who seemed to credit his thinking, which he liked. "Tell me," she said.

He glanced over his shoulder, as if checking to make sure no one was listening. "Steger wants the Alliance far away from that whole area, from Ichetucknee to the Santa Fe, cuz something is about to go down."

"That makes no sense. If something is about to go down, doesn't he need us?"

"I don't mean causing a riot outside the Theta house or starting a fight with a search party. I mean Steger, by his lonesome, is up to something. He doesn't want fingers pointed at the Alliance, so he told us to clear out."

"Has that happened before?"

"Sure. About six months ago, he found a traitor inside our group. Steger told us all to clear out. Two days later I saw the pictures of that poor bastard chained to a tree. No hands and no feet. Nobody can ever prove Steger had anything to do with it, and the cops never did figure out who done it. Nearest member of the Alliance was two hundred miles away when it happened."

For strategic reasons, Andie—an infiltrator—chose not to show much interest in the traitor. "What do you think Steger is up to this time?"

"I don't know."

"You have a guess?"

William smiled thinly. "I think he's got something in store for that boy from the frat house."

"Steger has him?"

"Steger or one of his lieutenants. That's what I hear."

Andie gazed into the flames, trying not to show her frustration. She didn't know if William's theory was correct. But she was stuck in the middle of the Okefenokee Swamp with Alliance underlings, while the real work was being done on the other side of the state line. She needed to do something to work her way up—impress one of the team leaders, maybe. The bureau hadn't sent her undercover to take long motorcycle rides.

"Hey, William! You want a beer?"

One of William's friends approached, along with three other members. They walked as if they'd already downed a case of long-neck Buds among them.

"Thanks, Colt." William twisted it open and took a long pull.

Andie didn't recognize Colt and his friends. She watched and listened carefully as they took a seat on the bigger log on the other side of the fire, their images blurred by the heat and rising smoke.

"You missed a good time at UF," said Colt.

"Crack any heads?"

Colt took another long swallow. "It was classic. All these uppity frat boys shouting all their 'justice for Jamal' bullshit. Then the fire starts, and people start freaking out. I go up to one of the Alpha boys, get right up close in his face, and I say, 'Strange fruit, motherfucker. You're next.'"

The men rolled with laughter. Then Colt's gaze cut through the flickering flames and landed on Andie. He seemed to like what he saw.

"So, who's the MILF?" asked Colt.

"Don't call her that," said William.

"It's a compliment," said Colt. He glanced at Andie, flashing a drunk's smile. "Tell him, green eyes. You like being called a MILF."

For guys like Colt, an asshole in his early twenties, any woman over thirty was a "mother I'd like to fuck."

"I don't like it," said Andie. "Not one bit."

"Well that's too fucking bad, MILF. Cuz I'd like to. Right in the ass." Colt rose, towering over the fire, and chugged down the last of his beer. "Stand up for us, bitch. Show us that ass."

William didn't come to her defense. Maybe it was because Colt had more status in the group, or maybe he wanted to see Andie's ass, too. Unless "Paulette's boyfriend" from the Atlanta field office showed up in the next sixty seconds, Andie was on her own.

She rose slowly, locking eyes with Colt.

"That's right," he said, smiling like the pervert he was. "Now turn around."

Andie didn't move. She just stared back at him, studying his face. And then she saw it—the tattooed lightning bolt that ran from the corner of his right eye. Colt was the guy in the photograph she'd seen at FBI headquarters.

"I'm asking like a gentleman," said Colt. "But I'm only gonna *ask* once."

It was the moment of decision. Colt was a big guy, but she was trained to fight bigger. If she backed down, she'd be the lowliest member of the group. "Fuck you, Colt."

Colt chuckled, but it was filled with arrogance, and he wasn't smiling. "I'll see that ass, bitch. Count on it."

Andie studied his expression. Colt wasn't just talking tough to save face in front of his friends. If she didn't defend herself now, he'd be in her tent tonight, and she'd be fighting off a sexual assault. Pregnant or not, her choice was clear.

In a quick motion, she reached for the knife that was strapped to her forearm, pulled it from under her sleeve, and flung it. The tip stuck in a log in the pile of firewood that was beside the fire, equidistant from her and Colt.

Colt smiled again. "You're kidding, right?"

Andie had seen "the Alliance challenge" once before. It was how the members settled internal differences. The challenger threw the knife. It was up to the other guy to go for it. If he didn't, he was a pussy. If he did, the fight was on.

"Uh-uh," said Andie, staring him down. "I'm not kidding."

He made a face. "I'm not gonna fight a girl."

She might not have pushed it, but the options were to fight him now, when Colt was drunk, or fight him later, when he came to rape her. The ace in the hole was that he'd probably never faced a woman who'd trained at Quantico.

"I'm not a girl, Colt. I'm a MILF. And when I'm done kicking your ass, I'll be the mother you wished you'd run from."

"Ooooh," his friends said in unison.

Andie could see that she was getting under his skin. Colt tossed his empty bottle into the fire, glaring at his challenger. Then he lunged toward the knife.

Andie was quicker and grabbed the knife by the handle, but Colt broadsided her like a runaway bus. They tumbled through the pile of firewood, locked in a wrestling match. Andie still had the knife but Colt controlled her wrist as they rolled through the dust. She heard the other men cheering her on, which only seemed to make Colt stronger. When they stopped rolling, Colt was on top, but he was too focused on the knife in Andie's hand to see the split log coming from the other direction. Andie clobbered him across the side of the head.

Colt went down, conscious but dazed. Andie rolled on top, with full control of the knife. She shoved the blade against his throat.

"Not another move," she said.

Colt went still. The night was silent, save for the crackle of the fire.

"Now, repeat after me. The only MILF who would fuck me is my real mama."

He grunted but said nothing. Andie pressed the blade down hard enough to draw blood.

"Say it!"

He did, but Andie could barely hear him.

"Louder! So your friends can hear." She slid the blade a fraction of an inch closer to his jugular, just enough to tell him that he was one second away from a throat slashing.

"THE ONLY MILF WHO WOULD FUCK ME IS MY REAL MAMA!"

It was loud enough for the entire campground to hear. Andie

jumped to her feet. Colt remained flat on his back in the dirt. He brought his hand to his throat, and although it wasn't a serious injury, there was enough blood to scare him stiff.

The other men stared at Andie in amazement.

"The rest of you boys got any bright ideas?" asked Andie.

"Fuck no," was the only answer.

"All right, then. Y'all have a good night."

Andie tossed the log—the one she'd used to club Colt—onto the fire. Then she turned and headed toward her tent, passing another group of men who had been drawn to the campfire by Colt's announcement.

Andie contained her smile, confident that she no longer needed a male undercover partner to keep her safe. But it was still important that he return. And soon.

Someone had to relay William's theory back to headquarters—his guess that Steger was still in north-central Florida, and that he had something planned for Percy Donovan.

CHAPTER 56

The regional crime lab serving Suwannee County was in Jacksonville. Jack made the ninety-mile drive from Live Oak on Thursday morning. He called home from the car to check on Righley before preschool.

"When are you coming home, Daddy?"

The court hearing to determine Mark's pretrial release was scheduled to begin in about twenty-six hours. "A few more days, honey."

"When's Mommy coming?"

When. It was Righley's biggest concern. Jack had lain awake, too, more worried about *what* Andie was doing. "Undercover" could mean anything from working on Wall Street to living on the street. Jack knew that she'd signed on for this assignment—whatever it was—long before she became pregnant. No matter how "maternity friendly" the bureau claimed to be, if Andie withdrew now, the only thing the men in charge would remember when staffing the next operation was that she'd withdrawn the last time. Jack totally got that. He loved that she'd been a Junior Olympic mogul skier while growing up in the Pacific Northwest. That she'd emerged from her FBI training as one of the few female members of the "Possible Club," an informal honorary fraternity for agents who shoot perfect scores on one of the toughest firearms courses in law enforcement. That after moving to Florida, she went cave diving in places like the Devil's Ear at Ginnie Spring, where hundreds of scuba divers have lost their way—and their lives—in the limestone labyrinth of the Florida Aquifer. But after hearing Righley's little voice on the phone, he couldn't help thinking that if he was going to have no clue about what Andie did at work all day, he might have preferred an accountant or a computer programmer.

"Mommy will be back as soon as she can," he said, and it seemed to satisfy Righley enough to head off to school.

Jack entered the lab around nine thirty. Hannah Goldsmith had flown up from Miami and was waiting for him in the lobby.

Jack had known Hannah since she was in middle school, when her father had hired Jack straight out of law school to work at the Freedom Institute. Four years of nothing but "death cases" had proved to be enough for Jack. But a decade later, when Neil passed away, his widow begged Jack to step into Neil's shoes as director. Jack met her halfway: he moved his law practice into Neil's office, kept the institute afloat by paying much higher rent than he should have, and mentored Hannah the way her father had mentored him. Neil would have been proud of the lawyer his daughter had become, and Jack relied on Hannah whenever he needed help in his own cases.

"I think you're going to find this pretty interesting," said Hannah.

Jack had put Hannah in charge of finding an expert to conduct a forensic examination of the Croc that the crime scene investigators had pulled from the Theta house. Official policy required the defense expert to perform his tests at the lab. Dr. Calvin Shad was ready to explain his findings.

An officer led Jack and Hannah to a locked room that was set aside for the testing. Dr. Shad was standing behind the counter with two evidence trays before him, one holding the Croc that had been pulled from the muck at the scene of Jamal Cousin's murder, and the other displaying the charred remains of the foam resin shoe that police had found at the Theta house. The officer left the room so that the defense team could talk in private, but he watched through the window in the door to make sure there was no tampering with the evidence.

"So this is what I can tell you," said Dr. Shad. "There's only one manufacturer of Crocs. All the others are Croc-offs."

There was silence. "Sorry," said Shad. "A little lab humor there. Anyway, Crocs are made of a proprietary closed-cell resin called Croslite. Both foam shoes I examined are made of the proprietary resin, which means they are not imitations."

"Here's what I'm worried about," said Jack. "The Croc found at the crime scene is a half size smaller than Mark's normal shoe size, but that's close enough. Crocs aren't about a perfect fit. So here's the first question: Doctor, is there any way to determine the size of the Croc found in Baine's closet?"

"Unfortunately, no. Look at it. It's burned too badly to ascertain what size it was originally. To be perfectly honest, reasonable minds could differ as to whether these charred and melted remains are from one Croc or a complete pair."

"That's important," said Jack. "Oliver Boalt is very firm in stating that this is *one* Croc, and it's the mate to the one at the crime scene."

"I think he's being very aggressive," said Dr. Shad.

"Second question," said Jack. "Can you collect DNA evidence from either of the Crocs to test for a match to Mark or Baine?"

"Definitely not on the burned one," the doctor said. "To be reduced to this charred and melted condition, that foam resin had to be exposed to extreme temperatures, probably in excess of eight hundred degrees Fahrenheit. DNA found in teeth and bone fragments can survive extremely high heat. But the sources of DNA we're talking about—human sweat, leg hair, flakes of skin—wouldn't survive."

"What about the Croc from the river?" asked Jack. "Any DNA?"

"A different problem, but the same conclusion," said Dr. Shad. "The Ichetucknee is crystal clear and mostly sand bottom, but this Croc was pulled from the muck along the riverbank. The swamp-like conditions surrounding the cypress trees and other flora make for a highly acidic environment. I won't bore you with molecular details, but there are constant chemical reactions occurring to create the tannins that stain swamp water black. Sweat or even fingerprint oils on a Croc buried in that muck won't survive."

Hannah was thinking through the implications. "So this third Croc—the one found yesterday—could be the whole ball game. If it matches the first Croc found in the muck, and if there's DNA on it, we have a killer."

"That's one way to look at it," said Jack.

"But if those two are mates, why was there a third Croc in Baine's closet?" asked Hannah.

"Like the doctor said. The pile of melted foam in Baine's closet could be a pair of Crocs, not just one."

"But that would mean Baine just so happened to own the same color Crocs as the killer," said Hannah. "That would be one heck of a coincidence, wouldn't it?"

"Probably," said Jack. "But if you're not one to accept coincidences, there are a couple of other possibilities."

"What?"

"Either we're looking for a three-legged killer," he said, his gaze drifting toward the charred foam resin on the counter. "Or someone has been planting evidence."

CHAPTER 57

Mark Towson had another visitor.

A corrections officer escorted Mark from his new cell. They'd moved him to administrative segregation that morning, one day before his *Arthur* hearing. The threats from Bulldog had stopped, so when Mark called his lawyer to tell him that jail officials had moved him to solitary anyway, he led Jack to believe that it was simply a protective measure in anticipation of Friday's court hearing, where racially inflammatory evidence would surely surface. That made sense. But it wasn't true. Fearing that Jack might tell his parents, Mark decided not to tell him that they'd put him in solitary after another inmate had tried to grind his "fucking Nazi skull" into the breakfast table with a metal cafeteria tray.

"You got fifteen minutes," the guard told Mark. He unlocked the door, and Mark entered the visitation room.

At Suwannee County Jail, meetings with attorneys were face-to-face, but normal visits were strictly noncontact. Mark took a seat on the stool and peered through the Plexiglas. It was smudged with countless fingerprints of inmates and visitors who'd pressed the glass from opposite sides to create the illusion of contact. The inmate to Mark's immediate left was white, as was the inmate to his right. Farther down the row were black inmates. The segregated seating arrangement was no accident, Mark assumed, given the cafeteria incident.

On the other side of the Plexiglas was his sister, Shelly. Mark picked up the phone and spoke. "How you doing, sis?"

Shelly forced a smile and shrugged.

"How's Mom?" he asked.

"She's still in the hospital. I saw her today. She looks a little better."

"That's good. I tried calling her twice today, but she was asleep."

Shelly took a breath. "It's killing her that she won't be at your hearing tomorrow."

"Tell her not to worry about that."

"I will," she said, and then her gaze focused on his ear. "What's that bruise on the side of your head?"

Mark hadn't looked in a mirror, but he assumed it was from the cafeteria tray. "I fell out of my bunk this morning," he said.

Her eyelashes fluttered. It was a nervous reaction of hers. "You always were a lousy liar," she said.

"I guess that's true."

"Remember that time I cut my own hair? You were the only one who said it looked good."

She was five at the time. Mark was seven. "It *did* look good. Kind of."

"Such a lousy liar."

They shared a smile, but stopped short of laughter. So much history between them, so many laughs. Shelly used to drive him crazy with her knock-knock jokes, until he came up with the perfect knock-knock buster: "Come in," he'd say, which would set her off like a screaming banshee, "Mark, you're supposed to say '*Who's there!*'" He'd been locked up for just a few days, and solitary had been only a matter of hours. But already he was escaping mentally to those happier, innocent times.

"You're biting your nails again," he said, glancing at her hands.

She folded her arms self-consciously. "Yeah. I don't know why I do that."

It was a bad habit she'd started in high school. She'd applied to UF with grades and test scores that put Mark's to shame, but those nails took a beating right up until her acceptance. It only got worse with their mother's first cancer diagnosis.

It suddenly occurred to Mark that the entire focus of the past two weeks had been on him and his mother. But it was Shelly who had to walk on campus, attend class, and dodge reporters. She was *out there* every day. Who was looking after the little sister of the racist murderer?

"Shelly, how are—"

"Cooper's funeral was today," she said, changing the subject.

The words nearly knocked the wind out of him. "Wow."

"Yeah. That's a 'wow,' all right."

"Was there a good turnout from the frat?"

"I assume so. A lot of people said they were going."

Mark hesitated, then asked, "Did Baine go?"

"I don't know. I saw him—"

"Forget it," he said. "Jack said we shouldn't talk about Baine. Jail conversations aren't private. I shouldn't have brought him up."

Silence. Shelly looked down, as if measuring her next words. Finally, she raised her eyes—and her eyebrows. "I have to tell you something."

"About what?"

She did that nervous thing with her eyelashes again, and the way she was looking at him, Mark knew that she wanted to tell him something about Baine.

Mark shifted uneasily, afraid of what she might say—of what the jail officials might hear.

Slowly, she slid her sleeve halfway up to her elbow, exposing what looked like a tattoo. Mark had seen scripted tattoos before, especially on women—a favorite expression or quote. But this was no tattoo. Mark was sure of it. Shelly wouldn't have dared get a tattoo anyplace on her body where their parents could see it.

She'd written him a message.

Mark lowered his gaze, studying, trying not to be too conspicuous. The script was in French. Their mother had insisted that they both take French in middle school and high school. Neither of them was fluent, but when they didn't want others to know what they were saying to each other, mediocre French was like their own code. It worked on most people, and if the guard had searched Shelly before allowing her to visit, a few scripted words in French that looked like a tattoo would have fooled him, too.

Mark translated in his mind, struggling not to show his surprise—shock, really. Then he looked into Shelly's eyes through the glass.

Shelly knew him well enough to interpret what he was thinking solely from his expression—no words necessary. She nodded and then verbalized her response.

"*C'est vrai*," she said, and Mark understood.

It's true.

CHAPTER 58

The line for visitors outside the Suwannee County Courthouse rivaled those for Disney World's most popular attractions.

Spectators had come from as far away as California to vie for the fifty seats available to the general public. Some had camped out all night, and arguments broke out over holding places in line for friends. A near fistfight required police intervention. The media made much of the fact that the altercation had pitted blacks against whites, each having accused the other of cutting in line. More than four hundred press passes had been issued, and every major broadcast network had at least one reporter at the courthouse around the clock. *Time* magazine published an exposé titled "Racial Terrorism Lynchings in America." *The Root* and other leading black media planned daily in-court coverage with hourly updates. Breaking News Network was planning extended coverage and legal analysis from early morning through prime time. Network specials were slated to air over the weekend, including "The Lynching of Jamal Cousin" on *Dateline NBC*, and "Racial Justice in America" on *60 Minutes*.

"Good morning," said Judge Teague. "The purpose of this hearing is to determine whether the defendant, Mark Towson, should be released before trial. The state opposes bail. Bail can be denied only if the prosecution establishes that the proof is evident and the presumption great that Mr. Towson is guilty of the charges against him. This is an extremely high standard to meet."

Jack had heard reference to that "high standard" before—usually right before a judge's denial of bail. Mark sat quietly at Jack's side, having been forewarned by his lawyer that, no matter what the judge said, pretrial release of a defendant charged with first-degree murder was the rare exception to the rule.

"Mr. Boalt, call your first witness, please."

"The state calls Detective Josh Proctor, Suwannee County Sheriff's Department."

It was no surprise to Jack or anyone else in the packed courtroom that the state attorney would begin with the homicide detective who was in charge of the crime scene. Still, there was an uneasy anticipation in the air as Boalt led the detective through the preliminary questions, as if everyone knew that the pivot to more substantive testimony would be powerful.

"Detective Proctor, what did you see when you first arrived on the scene?"

It was the moment that Jamal's parents, seated behind the prosecution, had been dreading. Boalt was about to present the photograph, not previously released to the public, that the media had been waiting for. Jack couldn't think of a legal objection, but as a parent, he knew that if something this horrific had happened to his child, he wouldn't want it displayed on an overhead projection screen in a courtroom.

Jack rose. "Your Honor, even at trial I've seen the projection screen positioned so that only the judge, the witness, and the jury can see the photographs of the victim. I think the same sensitivity should be shown here."

Boalt glared across the courtroom at Jack. "Judge, I frankly resent Mr. Swyteck's implication that it is the defense who respects the victim in this case."

"Let's not make this personal," the judge said. "Mr. Boalt, turn the screen. Members of the media, any photographs accepted into evidence at this hearing will be made available at the conclusion of this hearing. Please exercise good judgment in how you share them."

Boalt complied, and Jack spent the rest of the examination

standing in front of the empty jury box, rather than at the defense table, so that he could see the photographs. "Horrific" did not begin to describe them. Jack couldn't even imagine what had gone through the minds of the two fraternity brothers who'd found Jamal in this position—hog-tied, hovering just above the river, hanging at the end of a rope from a tree limb. Had the image been in black and white, it could have come straight out of the Jim Crow era. Jack glanced out toward the gallery and spotted one of the first witnesses on the scene. Kelso was his name.

Jack wondered what had become of the other young man—Percy Donovan—who was still missing.

The prosecutor's examination continued for another hour. The detective addressed each aspect of the crime. The rowboat that was stolen from a pier upriver. The lynching site a hundred yards downriver. The same rowboat found sunk another quarter mile downriver. And the foam resin shoe that divers had pulled from the muck a week after the lynching.

"What size was that shoe?" asked Boalt.

"Size eleven," said Proctor.

"What size shoe was the defendant, Mark Towson, wearing when he was taken into custody?"

"Size eleven and a half."

"Don't Crocs run big, Detective?"

"Objection," said Jack. "There's no way for this witness to know that."

"Sustained."

The prosecutor moved on, having made his point even if the question was improper.

"Detective, I have just one final exhibit," he said, and it appeared on-screen. "This is a text message that was retrieved from Jamal Cousin's phone. Your Honor, the defense does not dispute that Mr. Cousin received this message one week before the tubing trip down the Ichetucknee River."

"Mr. Swyteck, is that true?" the judge asked.

"We do not dispute that Mr. Cousin received it," said Jack. "We dispute who sent it."

"Understood. Proceed, Mr. Boalt."

"Detective Proctor, can you read it aloud, please?"

"It says, 'Watch yo ass on the float nigga. Strange fruit on the river.'"

The disturbing words hovered in the courtroom. The jury box was empty, but Jack was standing right in front of it, fully able to appreciate the assault on eyes and ears that twelve future jurors would experience at trial.

"Did you ever discuss this text message with Mr. Towson?" the prosecutor asked.

"Yes. I questioned Mr. Towson after the body of Jamal Cousin was found on the river."

"Did you show him the cell phone number from which that message was sent?"

"Yes."

"What was his response?"

"Mr. Towson confirmed that it was his cell phone."

Jack would have liked to object, but the prosecutor had threaded the needle properly: there was no dispute that it was Mark's phone number.

"I have no further questions," said Boalt, and he returned to the seat at his table.

"Mr. Swyteck, cross-examination?" the judge asked.

Jack thanked the judge and approached the witness. Detective Proctor seemed to realize that he'd done little to link Mark Towson to the lynching of Jamal Cousin. Jack had only a couple of points that he needed to make.

"Detective Proctor, your written report states that your investigative team recovered fingerprints from the pier where the owner of the stolen rowboat kept his boat," said Jack.

"Yes."

"None of those fingerprints belonged to Mark Towson, correct?"

"That's correct."

"Your team checked the fallen cypress tree near Jamal Cousin's body for fingerprints, too, right?"

"Yes."

"You found none?"

"No, but in any well-planned homicide, it's not unusual for the killer to wear gloves."

"You didn't find any gloves, did you, Detective?"

"No."

"And you found no fingerprints on the sunken rowboat that you recovered downriver, correct?"

"That's correct."

"What about DNA evidence?" asked Jack. "Did you find any of Mark Towson's DNA at the pier?"

"No."

"At the body recovery site?"

"No."

"In the sunken rowboat?"

"No."

"In fact, there is no *physical* evidence that connects Mr. Towson to the murder of Jamal Cousin, is there?"

"That's *not* correct," Proctor said forcefully. "There's the foam resin shoe that was recovered near Jamal's body."

"That shoe was size eleven, correct?"

"It was."

"You testified that Mr. Towson wears size eleven and a half, correct?"

"I said the shoes he was wearing on the night of his arrest were size eleven and a half."

Jack could have left it at that, but he was concerned about the "Crocs run big" argument that Boalt had snuck in during direct examination. Jack had a decision to make—whether to defend Mark by incriminating Baine. There really was no choice.

"Isn't it true, Detective, that a foam resin shoe was found in Baine Robinson's closet after the fire at the Theta house?"

"Yes, in seriously burned condition."

"Mr. Towson's fingerprints or DNA were not on that burned shoe, correct?"

"Correct."

"The same holds true for the shoe found near Jamal's body—no DNA or fingerprints from Mr. Towson, correct?"

"None that our tests detected."

"You have no evidence that Mr. Towson ever purchased or owned a pair of Crocs like the one found at the crime scene. Isn't that right, sir?"

"Not yet. But we are continuing to investigate."

Jack was satisfied, and that seemed like a good place to end. "Nothing further, Your Honor."

Jack returned to his table. The prosecutor rose. The judge allowed five minutes for redirect examination—Boalt's chance to remedy the damage Jack had done on cross.

"Detective Proctor, when Mr. Swyteck asked about Mr. Towson's ownership of a pair of Crocs, you said, 'We are continuing to investigate.' Where does that investigation stand as of now?"

"The crime lab is in the process of testing a foam resin shoe that was recovered on the bank of the Ichetucknee River two days ago."

"Is that one a mate for the foam resin shoe that was recovered near Jamal Cousin's body?"

"It appears to be. The testing will confirm that."

"Is the lab also testing that shoe for fingerprints and DNA evidence?"

"Yes."

"When will that testing be complete?"

"We should have a report early next week."

It was lame, by legal standards, but Jack knew what the prosecutor was up to. The message—"we are continuing to investigate"—was a play to the crowd and the media. *"Don't worry if the evidence sounds weak at this stage,"* Boalt was telling them, *"we will nail this guy."*

"Detective, are you planning any further testing on the other shoe that Mr. Swyteck mentioned? I'm talking about the burned Croc found in the Theta house."

"Yes," said Proctor.

"What prompted the decision to undertake further testing on that shoe?"

"We met with an expert who was retained by Baine Robinson."

Jack bristled. The state was under no obligation to disclose a meeting with the Robinsons, but the fact that it had occurred without a single media report told Jack that it had been one very secret meeting indeed.

"What was discussed at that meeting?" asked the prosecutor.

"Mr. Robinson's expert did a comparison of the wear patterns on the two Crocs."

Jack smelled a rat. His own expert had told him that the bottom of the shoe was too badly burned to make that comparison.

"What was the conclusion of Mr. Robinson's expert?"

"The shoes do not match."

"Have you accepted that conclusion?"

"Not yet. As I say, that will be in the report issued by the lab next week."

The prosecutor stepped away from the lectern. "I have no further questions, Your Honor."

The witness stepped down, and all eyes followed him as he walked down the aisle and exited through the rear doors.

The judge peered out over his reading glasses and addressed the lawyers. "Here's how I see it, gentlemen. I've reviewed the grand jury materials and other evidence filed with the court before this hearing. If the forensic test on this recently discovered shoe reveals Mr. Towson's DNA or fingerprints, I don't see a need for the two-day hearing I've scheduled. Mr. Boalt, can you have the test results by Monday morning?"

"I can try, Your Honor."

"Try hard," the judge said. "I'm going to adjourn this hearing at this point. We will reconvene at nine a.m. Monday morning."

The crack of his gavel cut through the courtroom.

"All rise!" said the bailiff.

As the defense rose, Mark leaned toward his lawyer and whispered, "How bad is this?"

Jack said nothing. It depended on the answer to one simple question that Jack had yet to ask his client, that another criminal defense lawyer might never have asked Mark, and that Jack still wasn't sure he *should* ask.

Is that other shoe yours?

CHAPTER 59

It's not mine," said Mark.

The Suwannee County Jail was right next door to the courthouse, but nothing happens quickly in any jail system. It was late afternoon before Jack was able to meet face-to-face with his client privately in the attorney-client visitation room.

"I didn't ask you a question," said Jack.

"Yeah, I noticed," said Mark. "It's been the elephant in the room since they found that third Croc. Do you think I'm guilty? Is that why you haven't asked me if that's my shoe?"

Jack paused, taking a figurative step back. "Mark, our relationship can't work if I put you on the defensive. I've seen it happen with other clients. No matter how many times I promise that your guilt or innocence has no bearing on whether I can represent you, it's human nature to fear that I might quit if you give the wrong answer. If I had come right out and asked you if the shoe was yours, you would have given me the answer that you think I want to hear."

"Is that what you think I'm doing now? Telling you what you want to hear?"

"I hope not, but here's the reality. You have no alibi. No one can account for your whereabouts from the time you say you went to bed on Friday night until ten a.m. Saturday. If there are things you want me to know, you can tell me. Just don't lie to me."

Mark leaned closer, looking Jack in the eye. "It's not my shoe."

"Then we will build your defense on that foundation. But do you see how important it is that you not lie to me? If that foundation is no good, your defense will crumble."

"I'm not lying."

"Okay, then. We'll go from there."

Mark looked away. "Do you think the police planted that burned Croc in Baine's closet?"

Jack didn't answer right away. He was no fan of conspiracy theories. "I don't know. But it makes absolutely no sense for Baine to kill Jamal Cousin, lose a shoe in the process, and then go home and put the other shoe in his own closet. That would make Baine the stupidest person in the world."

"So you do think they planted it," said Mark.

Jack leveled his gaze. "I think *someone* planted it, Mark."

Guilty. That's how Andie felt. She'd taken too much risk challenging Colt to a knife fight. More risk than a mother—and an expecting mother—should take. Maybe his words—"I'll see that ass, bitch"—hadn't actually been a threat of sexual assault. Or maybe he never would have followed through, had she just let it go.

That was one way to look at it. Andie's assessment at the time had been simple. The man was drunk, stupid, and had no clue who he was actually up against. Crossing the street in downtown Miami was a riskier proposition than taking down Colt the dolt. Still, Andie had been second-guessing herself, questioning her own judgment—and her line of work.

"You coming to the meeting?" asked William, poking his head into her tent.

Andie was on her knees, sweeping out the sand. She'd grown up camping in the Cascade Mountains, which was nothing like camping in Florida. In the Sunshine State, there was always a nice flat spot to pitch a tent, and there was no end to the dirty sand that got everywhere, from your sleeping bag to your underwear.

"Should I?"

"I hear Steger is going to be there."

The news made Andie's day. "Let's go."

The meeting was a ten-minute walk from Andie's tent, held in a picnic area beneath a tin-roofed shelter that had a concrete floor but no walls. A crowd had already gathered. Alliance members had been arriving from out of state all day. The start of court proceedings against Mark Towson was a rallying point for the organization, and the number of tents, trucks, and motorcycles had at least tripled since Andie's showdown with Colt.

Andie and William squeezed in next to other members at an already crowded picnic table. They sat on the tabletop with their feet on the bench seats. A man holding a wireless microphone entered the shelter, and the crowd erupted in applause.

"That's Steger!" William said, flashing a huge smile.

The ovation continued as Steger took his position before the group. "Hello, hello, my Aryan Nation friends."

It was part of her job to smile and clap her hands, so Andie did. The crowd settled at Steger's beckoning, and then he began.

"Let me see a show of hands, folks. How many white men here own slaves?"

No hands went up.

"I thought so. Now, another show of hands. How many of you are made to feel guilty every day of your life, just for being white?"

Hands went up all around Andie, and she played along. Steger's "white guilt" speech was one that she'd studied in preparation for this undercover role, and she wondered what variation of the theme he would tie to the lynching of Jamal Cousin.

"I just came here from Alabama," said Steger. "You know the liberal establishment has built a monument there. A monument to white guilt."

A chorus of booing and hisses carried through the crowd.

"Of course they don't call it that," said Steger. "They call it a museum. It's in Montgomery. It's a museum about lynching in America."

More than a few in the audience snickered.

"I'm dead serious," said Steger. "It's called the Memorial to Peace and Justice. Now, I wouldn't set foot in that place, but I'm sure they have a prominent tribute to Emmett Till. You heard of Emmett, right? How many of y'all heard of him?"

About half the hands went up.

"Emmett was an innocent little black boy from Chicago," Steger said, the word *innocent* laden with sarcasm. "Emmett got lynched in 1955. The story goes that all poor Emmett did was whistle at a white woman," he added, following up with a whistle into the microphone like a construction worker, just for effect.

"That's the story," said Steger, his voice turning very serious. "But here's the part about Emmett that they leave out of the museums. His daddy was a rapist."

He paused again, then dropped the bomb. "It's true. Emmett Till's black father raped three white women after Emmett was born. And he killed one of those women."

Even the Aryan audience seemed stunned.

"It's a fact," said Steger. "Mr. Till was in the Army, serving in Italy. He was court-martialed and hanged near Pisa in July 1945. The Army suppressed that information until after Emmett Till's murder trial was over. It took two good, hardworking senators from Mississippi to break through the secrecy. Now, why do you think it was so hard for that information to become public? I'll tell you why. Because the liberal establishment didn't want the people of Mississippi to know about Emmett Till's *genetic predisposition* to rape and murder white women."

The crowd applauded.

"If you don't believe me," said Steger, "then listen to what Malcolm X said."

Angry booing came from every corner.

"Now, settle down," said Steger. "Say what you want about Malcolm, but he was spot-on when it came to certain things. Right about the time Emmett Till's daddy was over in Europe raping white women, Malcolm was bedding down with the blond wife of an American serviceman who was overseas fighting for our country. You know what Malcolm had to say about that? It's right here in his autobiography." He thrust the book over his head for all to see. Then he opened it.

"Chapter six," said Steger. "Malcolm X wrote, 'what the white racist said, and still says, was right in those days! All you had to do was put a white girl anywhere close to the average black man, and he would respond.'

"'*Respond*,'" Steger said in disgust, lifting his eyes from the page. "By that, folks, he didn't mean *talk*!"

An empty beer bottle sailed overhead, smashing to pieces against a steel pole.

"Calm down," said Steger, as he laid the book aside. "I feel your anger. But my point is this. Take Malcolm X at his word. We had it right back then. And it's no different today. I'm here to tell you tonight," he said, his voice rising, "and the Aryan National Alliance is uniting to tell the whole world: *White guilt is OVER!*"

He said it again, and then again, until the entire crowd was chanting, *"White guilt is over!"*

Andie reached deep inside herself to stay in role, slapping William a high five as the new voice of "intellectual white nationalism" whipped his followers into a frenzy. And with each pump of the fist, and as the chant grew louder, Andie wondered what Steger might have done had he known that the woman with the green eyes and blond dye job was an FBI agent—born to a Native American mother from the Yakama tribe and a very white father.

CHAPTER 60

Princess Righley was on the evening flight from Miami. Jack picked her up at Tallahassee International Airport, about an hour west of Live Oak. "Uncle" Theo brought the car seat, her pillow, her favorite stuffed animal, her favorite stuffed animal's favorite stuffed animal, and about forty pounds of other stuff that Righley couldn't live without.

As they left the terminal, Theo made sure that Righley was wearing the noise-proof headphones he'd bought her for the trip.

"Fuckin' A, dude," he said for Jack's ears only. "You know what it's like for a black man to fly into this town with a four-year-old white girl? I'd get less suspicious looks if I was carryin' a bazooka."

Even locals disagreed as to whether Tallahassee was part of the Florida Panhandle, but it was indisputably closer to Mobile than to Miami. "Sorry, man," was all Jack could say.

Jack's plan was to spend the weekend in Live Oak, where he could meet with his client and prepare for Monday's hearing. It would be a working weekend, but at least he would have Righley with him. Shelly had agreed to babysit as needed.

"Sit here!" said Righley, as Jack strapped her into the car seat.

She wanted Daddy to ride in back with her from the airport, so Theo drove. He said he didn't mind sitting in front alone, but it took him nearly forty-five minutes to knock off the Morgan Freeman impersonation and stop calling Righley "Miss Daisy."

They reached the motel after nine o'clock, which was past Righley's bedtime. She was barely awake as Jack carried her to the room, dressed her in a pair of Hello Kitty pajamas, and laid her in the bed. Righley was out like a light when Shelly arrived around ten o'clock.

"Oh, she's so cute!" Shelly said, trying to whisper.

Jack smiled proudly. "You sure you don't mind playing nanny?" he asked.

"Not at all," she said, and then she unzipped her bag. "I brought Legos, I have my iPad she can play with—all kinds of toys in my bag of goodies. We'll have a girls' weekend."

"Thank you."

"No problem. Honestly, I'm glad to have someone to help take my mind off things."

Jack understood. He opened the side door that led to the adjoining room. Shelly would sleep there. Jack and Righley had the other room.

There was a knock on the door, and Jack hurried to open it before Righley woke. It was Theo. "Wanna get some dinner?" he asked.

The chances of Righley waking in the next hour were slim, and Shelly was willing to watch her, so Jack and Theo went downstairs. The motel's restaurant was closed, so they went to the lounge and ordered appetizers from the bar menu. Jack didn't necessarily feel like talking shop, but the mystery of three Crocs had been all over the news, and Theo wanted the scoop on the "three-legged killer." Jack told him what he thought—that the shoe in Baine's closet was planted by someone.

"So what?" said Theo, and then he took a bite out of his cheeseburger slider.

"What do you mean 'so what?'"

"Look, Jack. It could have been the police who planted it. It could have been Mark. It could have been that kid who died in the car crash."

"Cooper Bartlett."

"Or it could have been any one of two hundred other frat brothers who can't stand Baine Robinson. Hell, maybe Baine planted it *himself* to make it look like he's being set up. What I'm saying is this: Just because the shoe was planted doesn't mean that Baine didn't lynch Jamal Cousin."

Theo's fresh insight set Jack to thinking. "Back up a second. You just said something smart."

"Sliders *are* brain food," Theo said, reaching for another.

"Earlier this week, Baine's father called me. He was reaching out about a joint defense arrangement between Baine and Mark."

Theo chewed, thinking, then swallowed. "Even an old jailhouse lawyer can see that's a bad idea. Why would *anybody* want to team up with Mark Towson, the one and only guy who is looking at the death penalty if he loses?"

"It only makes sense if Baine's father knows—or strongly believes—that his son is guilty," said Jack. "If Baine's daddy can get me and Leonard Oden on the same team, he knows that I won't try to get Mark acquitted by proving what the prosecutor might not be able to prove: Baine did it. Alone."

The cocktail waitress brought a couple more draft beers, then left.

"So what do you do?" asked Theo.

"I could go hard after Baine. Show that he sent the 'strange fruit' text message. Prove he lied to the grand jury when he said Mark bragged to him about lynching Jamal."

"Is that enough?"

"Maybe. If it's not, I could escalate to nuclear warfare," said Jack, getting caught up in his own excitement. "Hell, I could drop the biggest stink bomb that's ever been dropped in the Suwannee County Courthouse."

"Which is what?"

Jack shook his head. "You'll think it's crazy."

"Better for you to run it by me than have the judge cut your balls off."

"All right, here goes." Jack drank from his beer, then leaned forward. "Percy Donovan was kidnapped to make it look like someone other than Baine Robinson lynched Jamal Cousin."

"Okay," said Theo. "But it also makes it look like someone other than Mark Towson lynched Jamal Cousin. So who's to say it's not your client who's behind the diversion?"

"The Towson family could never pull it off. Baine Robinson's father is a multimillionaire."

Theo made a face. "Sounds far-fetched."

"Baine Robinson's arrest warrant was issued Monday morning. Percy Donovan disappeared Monday night. The media and everyone else immediately asks, 'Is this Jamal Cousin all over again?' That makes both Mark and Baine look innocent. The next morning, Baine's father calls me about Mark and Baine teaming up on a joint defense arrangement. And he tells me that the budget for Baine's defense is unlimited."

Theo didn't answer, but he looked less skeptical than before. "I'm not saying I agree with you, Jack. But how the hell do you prove that?"

Jack sat back in his chair, breathing out. "I don't know."

"You want me to help?"

Jack smiled. "I didn't fly you up here to babysit."

CHAPTER 61

Cynthia Porter woke before dawn, which wasn't unusual. She'd always been an early riser, especially when something important was on her mind.

She switched on the lamp on her nightstand and climbed out of bed. She did her morning routine but spent a little more time in front of the mirror than usual. This was no ordinary day. She wanted her makeup right and her hair just so, but an unsteady hand didn't make it easy. Then she went to the closet. Dark slacks and her pastel blouse would do. A pair of comfortable pumps. Mid-autumn nights were cool in Live Oak, and a sweater would be a good idea until the sun warmed things up. She chose the purple one. People had always said that Cynthia was pretty in purple.

Willie James had always taken notice when she wore purple.

A simple strand of pearls with matching stud earrings was the finishing touch. Then Cynthia stepped into the hallway. Virginia was outside her bedroom, waiting.

"Well, look at you," Virginia said, smiling. "Like a model in a magazine."

Cynthia blushed. "Thank you."

"Would you like me to fix breakfast before we go?"

"No, no. I don't have time."

Virginia guided her toward the lift at the top of the stairs. "You gonna tell me where we're headed, Miz Cynthia?"

Cynthia lowered herself into the chairlift and rested her pocketbook in her lap. "It's a secret," she said coyly.

Andie woke at 5:00 a.m. Her "boyfriend" was scheduled to return to the Okefenokee campsite before sunrise.

Agent Ferguson had made his first appearance the previous night, after Steger's speech. Andie had immediately filled him in—not only about the speech, but also about the gunshot she'd heard along the river, as well as her "friend" William's theory that the Alliance had cleared out of Florida because something was in store for Percy Donovan. Ferguson hadn't planned to come and go, but Andie's intelligence was important enough to put him back on the road to update their Operation 777 contacts in the field. He'd promised to be back by daybreak, before a single member of the Aryan National Alliance had even noticed he was gone.

"Welcome," said Andie, as he climbed off his motorcycle. He'd parked away from the campsite so as not to wake the others. Andie helped carry his gear and provisions back to her—their—tent.

Jack probably wouldn't have liked Special Agent Brian Ferguson. Or at least he wouldn't have liked him playing the role of Andie's boyfriend. Ferguson was probably the most handsome agent in the Atlanta field office, if blond hair and blue eyes were your type. While Andie could have infiltrated the Alliance alone, they worked well as a couple. It was especially useful for one of them to keep a foothold in the group while the other left to relay information to their undercover contacts.

They stored the perishables in the cooler and left everything else in the tent. The rest of the unpacking could wait for daylight. Snoring was all around them, pouring from blackened tents, but it was possible that someone nearby was lying awake in a sleeping bag and able to overhear them. They took a walk down to the lake to talk in private, away from the other campers. They stopped at the shoreline and took a seat on the bright yellow hull of an overturned canoe. Andie gazed up at the stars. Had she been up there in orbit, somewhere in outer space, she could have looked down and seen that the Okefenokee wildlife refuge was a black hole in a sea of light pollution that flooded virtually the entire southeastern United States. It was impossible for any earthling not to be awestruck on a clear night.

"Any follow-up on Percy Donovan?" asked Andie.

"Agents are monitoring both the Ichetucknee and the Santa Fe rivers," said Ferguson.

"What does that mean?"

"Headquarters agrees that the Alliance could have him. But no one believes that they'd hold him anywhere near the site of Jamal Cousin's lynching. It's just too stupid."

"There are some seriously dumb fucks in this group," said Andie, thinking of Colt. "It's worth checking out."

"Agreed. But there's a lot of ground to cover, and the plan is to keep it low-key. The last thing we need is a local SWAT unit going door-to-door, trying to find a needle in a haystack. That's a recipe for a dead hostage."

A splash in the pond startled Andie. A huge bullfrog had narrowly escaped, and a hungry gator slithered through the reeds to find breakfast elsewhere.

"What about the Croc that the black fraternity found on the riverbank?"

"What about it?" asked Ferguson.

"Is it being sent to our lab to see if it matches the Croc found near Jamal Cousin's body?"

"That's between the state attorney and the regional crime lab," said Ferguson. "The forensic team is on it. Not our turf."

"I can confirm that the Alliance was in that general area right before the Croc was found. They could have planted it."

"Why would they do that?"

"To muddy the waters and make it impossible to prosecute anyone for the murder of Jamal Cousin."

"That's not really our focus," said Ferguson.

"Maybe it should be," said Andie. "Manufacturing evidence to disrupt the prosecution of a racially motivated hate crime would be one more piece of evidence that the Aryan National Alliance is nothing but a criminal enterprise. Don't you think?"

His gaze turned toward the lake. The first sign of morning light was just a glimmer on the flat water. "You really want to know what I think?" asked Ferguson.

"I do," said Andie.

"If I were you, I'd take a step back and remind myself what we're really here for. More and more, the way you see things, the way you hear things, is being colored by how it affects your husband's case. That's what I think."

Andie couldn't have disagreed more, but it wasn't the time or the place to have that battle. "Thanks for being honest," she said.

He rose and started back toward the tent. Andie didn't follow.

"You're welcome," said Ferguson.

CHAPTER 62

Cynthia rode in the passenger seat as Virginia drove down the highway at a steady twenty-miles-per-hour below the posted speed limit. Virginia was a careful driver, but it was Cynthia who refused to believe the engineers in Detroit who insisted that it was safe to drive any faster.

Cynthia's mind was a photo album. She could easily recall a time when this part of Live Oak, beyond the old railroad junction that dated back to the Civil War, was the outskirts of town. Much had changed since she was a girl. Where the only sign of civilization had been a clunky old mailbox at the end of a white-sand road there now stood a gas station or a fast-food restaurant. Mobile homes dotted the pastures that had once been covered in slash pines and palmettos. Ranch-style homes—the kind that Cynthia called "concrete shoe boxes"—had replaced horse farms. Live Oak hadn't seen the uncontrolled suburban sprawl of coastal areas, but the life was being choked out of old Florida nonetheless.

Not everything about old Florida, however, was better.

"Turn here," said Cynthia, pointing.

The road didn't have a name, but Cynthia was almost certain that they were going in the right direction. The area had changed a lot, she supposed. She couldn't really say for sure. It was the first time in her life that she'd visited the place where Willie James Howard had grown up—the actual road where his house had stood.

"Stop here," said Cynthia.

Virginia pulled the car onto the shoulder of the road and stopped. "My granddaddy grew up not far from here," she said.

Cynthia wasn't surprised. This entire area had been "colored" during Jim Crow. "Can you help me get out, please?"

Virginia climbed out from behind the wheel, walked around to the passenger side, and helped Cynthia out of the car. Sunrise was just moments away, and the dew-covered greenery glistened in the predawn glow. A cool breeze greeted them as they walked to the edge of the lot and stopped. Before them was a broken gate. It was in terrible disrepair and looked ready to fall over. The walkway beyond the gate was overgrown with weeds. It led to nowhere. The house that had once stood was gone.

"Did you know the folks who lived here?" asked Virginia.

Cynthia held her gaze, trying to imagine what the house might have been like. "Just the boy," she said.

Virginia had no follow-up, as if she knew better than to ask a ninety-year-old white woman how she had known a black boy from this part of town.

Cynthia lowered her eyes and then looked at Virginia. "We can go now," she said.

"Home?"

"No. Take me to the Bond-Howell Lumber Company, please."

Virginia flashed confusion, then concern, as if the old woman's mind were going. "Oh, Miz Cynthia, that old sawmill has been gone for years."

Cynthia's expression turned very serious. "Then take me to where it used to be."

"Yes, ma'am."

She helped Cynthia back into the car, then climbed behind the wheel and closed the door. The ignition fired, their car pulled away, and a trail of dust sparkled in the first burst of sunshine on the horizon.

Percy guessed it was his fifth day of captivity. He couldn't be sure. The passage of time was an elusive concept when living in darkness, chained to a wall. Percy's initial benchmark had been meals, but feeding time seemed random, and it was the same bologna sandwich whether it was breakfast, lunch, or dinner. He wasn't even sure that he was eating more than once or twice a day. Perhaps the confusion was intentional, his captors' effort to throw off his internal clock. His most reliable indicator of a new day had become a bowel movement in the disgusting bucket that was constantly within reach. At least they'd taken away the dead rat.

The door opened, and the light switched on. Percy shielded his eyes from the assault. The longer he remained in the windowless shed, the longer it took his pupils to adjust to the sudden brightness that signaled the return of his captor.

"Bath time," the man said.

Percy was suddenly hit with a blast of ice-cold water from a hose, which was a complete break from the routine. It wasn't exactly a water cannon, but Percy instinctively recoiled against the wall, his mind flashing with the image of civil rights marchers knocked off their feet by firefighters.

"Hold still!" the man shouted, and the streaming water kept coming. It soaked Percy from head to foot and swept away the mess on the floor and around the metal bucket. Then it stopped.

"Better?" the man asked.

Percy looked up, dripping wet. It actually was better, relatively speaking, at least temporarily. But it was hard to think of being hosed down like a dog as an improvement. Percy didn't answer.

His captor stepped toward him. It was a new guy. He'd replaced the man who'd rushed into the shed without his ski mask and shot the rat. Maybe these idiots hoped that if Percy heard another man's voice, studied another man's frame, he would forget the face of his first captor. Percy would never forget that lightning bolt tattoo.

He threw Percy a blanket. "Don't want you to catch cold," he said, and the sarcasm came through.

Percy fumbled with the chains but managed to wrap the blanket around his shoulders.

"Got some good news," the man said. "The FBI is out searching for you."

Percy wasn't sure if he was being messed with. "That is good news."

"Oh, you bet it is." He bent down, getting right in Percy's face, two piercing blue pools staring out through the eyeholes of the ski mask. "It changes everything. With the FBI crawling around, we may need you as a hostage. So we're keeping you alive. For now. How's that sound, Emmett?"

"My name's not Emmett."

"Might as well be." He tossed a wrapped sandwich into Percy's lap, still staring. Then he rose slowly, towering over his hostage. Percy watched as he turned and walked to the door.

"Very, very lucky, *Emmett.*"

The light switched off and his captor left the shed, leaving Percy in the darkness.

CHAPTER 63

The sun was a bright yellow ball between the clouds and treetops as Cynthia and Virginia reached the Suwannee River, just a few miles northeast of Live Oak. Virginia parked the car at Suwannee Springs and helped Cynthia out.

Cynthia hadn't been to the springs since childhood. It was a popular spot for picnicking and swimming on a hot summer day. The main spring—there were at least six in all, by Cynthia's recollection—was within the rock walls of a nineteenth-century bathhouse. Clear, yellow-greenish water pooled behind the wall and spilled out through an opening at the base over limestone boulders into the tannic Suwannee River. Folks used to claim that the spring waters could cure just about any ailment.

Cynthia felt in need of a little healing, but of a different sort.

"This way," said Cynthia.

They followed the path around the wall. The exposed limestone underfoot was smooth where thousands of visitors had walked for more than a century. The path led to a cluster of boulders where spring water flowed from the bathhouse. The rocks formed a ledge, and it was the closest thing in the area to a waterside cliff. Cynthia couldn't count the number of times she and her friends had jumped from these boulders at the river's edge and disappeared into the dark depths of the great Suwannee.

Cynthia gazed out toward the river. The long southwesterly journey to the Gulf of Mexico was a slow one. Sometimes, especially if Cynthia looked way downriver, the water almost seemed motionless. But it was always moving, ebbing and flowing. There was no way to stop it. Definitely no way for Cynthia to stop it—any more than she could erase the horror of what had happened at that very place, nearly a lifetime ago, east of Suwannee Springs.

Cindy was in the living room helping her mother remove the decorations from a dried-out Christmas tree. "Let's Start the New Year Right"—the flip side of Bing Crosby and the Ken Darby Singers' "White Christmas"—was spinning at 78 rpm on the Victrola. The afternoon had seen only one casualty, a glass angel that slipped from Cindy's hand and shattered on the floor.

"Careful, honey," her mother said, as Cindy reached for an ornament on one of the higher branches. "Get the step stool."

Cindy went to the kitchen. Her father entered suddenly through the back door, startling her. Sunday afternoons were usually his time for reading the newspaper in the recliner.

"Where were you, Daddy?"

"Just went over to visit with the Judge."

The Judge had hung up his black robe to enter private practice sometime before the war, but years on the bench made him the most prominent lawyer in Suwannee County, and out of respect everyone still called him "Judge." His daughter was a year behind Cindy at the high school.

"Mama and I are taking down the tree."

He glanced toward the living room. Cindy thought the expression on his face was a bit strange. Before she could ask what was wrong, her mother entered the kitchen.

"Young lady, where's that step stool I asked you to get?"

"Mary, I need a minute with Cindy."

Her mother backed away, and Cindy had the unsettling notion that she was the only person in the room who didn't know what this was about.

"I'll be upstairs," her mother said.

Cindy's father led her to the kitchen table and sat her down. He stood, resting his hands atop the back of his chair, leaning forward just slightly as he spoke.

"I have some sad news," he said.

Cindy braced herself. "Sad?"

"Something terrible happened, honey. We picked up Willie James from his house this morning and drove over to the sawmill, where his father works. Mr. Howard is a decent man. I explained to him what happened—what his son wrote to you."

"Daddy, why?"

"Just listen to me. Mr. Howard fully agreed that Willie James deserved a good whippin'."

Cindy lowered her head, speaking into the table. "You whipped Willie James?"

"No, of course not. I wouldn't lay a hand on another man's child. His daddy and I agreed that he would give his boy some proper discipline."

She looked up at her father. "Did he do it?"

"Well, what we did was drive to the river, where his daddy could find a switch."

"He couldn't find a stick at a sawmill?"

"Don't sass me," her father said in a stern voice. "I wasn't going to make the man whip his own son in front of everybody he worked with."

"Sorry," she said. "So his daddy whipped him down by the river?"

"That was the idea. But see, Willie James got all defiant. He started jumping around and pushing back, sayin' no one could whip him, not even his own father. So we tied his ankles and his hands, just to keep him under control."

Cindy said nothing, but she was starting to shake inside.

"Well, wouldn't you know?" he said. "That boy just got even more defiant. Started cussin' like the devil himself had taken over him. And then . . ."

"What happened?"

"Willie James jumped in the river."

"Is he—"

"He drowned."

"No!" she shrieked.

"I'm sorry, honey."

"What? How?"

"I told you how. I know it might be hard for you to understand, but this is really all for the good."

"*Good?*" she asked, louder than intended. "How is it good that a boy drowned?"

Her father came around from behind his chair and took a seat at the table, looking Cindy straight in the eye. "You're young, honey. You don't know those people the way I do."

"What are you talking about? You don't *know* them."

"Yes, I do. I will tell you something, and I swear it is God's honest truth. When that boy jumped in the river, his father just stood there. Just *stood* there. The man didn't even *try* to help his own son."

Cindy could barely comprehend. "That's . . . terrible."

Her father shook his head. "That's coloreds, honey. They just ain't like us."

Spring water splashed on the limestone boulders at Cynthia's feet. She wiped away a tear from her cheek.

"Are you crying, Miz Cynthia?" Virginia asked.

She dabbed away another tear with her hanky. "I'm all right."

"Let's sit down and rest," said Virginia, gesturing toward the bench near the old bathhouse.

"I'm fine right here," Cynthia said firmly. "I just need another minute."

Virginia took hold at the crook of Cynthia's elbow. "All right, Missy. I got you. But be careful, now. You know I can't swim."

Neither could Willie James.

Cynthia gazed out across the river. "There's no shame in dying. Is there, Virginia?"

"We all have our homegoing sometime," she said.

"It's so unfair, the way some people go out so young. But for others, life goes on. And on. And on. It can be a horrible thing, living long after someone else dies. When you know it was your fault."

"Oh, don't talk like that," said Virginia. "Mr. Porter was a stubborn fool. No sixty-five-year-old man with a heart condition should be out mowing the lawn when it's ninety-eight degrees in the shade. You warned him. It's not your fault he died."

Cynthia sighed. She could have explained, but she didn't have the energy. She had strength enough to do just one more thing.

"Virginia, could you bring me my pocketbook, please? It's on the bench over there."

A check over the shoulder diverted Virginia's attention for a split second. "I think you left it in—"

Cynthia jerked her arm away from Virginia's grasp and threw herself forward—not far, but far enough. Her shins scraped the limestone as she went over the ledge headfirst.

"Miz Cynthia!"

The river was like ice water, but it felt strangely refreshing, cleansing, and exhilarating—the way it had so many years earlier when Cynthia and her childhood friends would swing from a rope, enter with a splash, and buoy back up with screams of delight. This time, Cynthia didn't even try to surface—but she must have for a moment, because she heard Virginia's voice one last time.

"Miz Cynthia, my God!"

The current carried Cynthia along the steep, rocky ledge and around the bend. The last thing she saw was the blur of sunshine in the morning, as she peered up through the clear, black water of the Suwannee River and its secrets.

CHAPTER 64

Jack took Righley to breakfast at the Dixie Grill. Theo had been thinking about the biscuits since their last visit, so he and Shelly joined them. It was almost nine thirty before a table opened and the hostess seated them. By then the restaurant, like all of Live Oak, was abuzz with the news about "poor ol' Mrs. Porter."

It amazed Jack what a child could pick up in the clamor of a crowded restaurant.

"Daddy, what's suey side?"

It was another one of those "boy, do I miss Andie" moments. "We'll talk about that later, sweetie," Jack said.

The waitress filled their coffee mugs and brought menus. Righley's came with crayons and a paper place mat, and she went to work coloring rabbits yellow and raccoons purple. The grown-ups didn't want to discuss the apparent "suey side" in front of her, but it was impossible not to ponder the implications. A lynching, a possible abduction, and now an apparent suicide. Linking the first two was no cause for brain strain. Mrs. Porter was more puzzling.

Shelly looked up from the latest news on her iPad. "This story is going national in a hurry," she said.

The waitress returned and took their orders. Righley was trying to decide between blueberries or bananas in her stack of pancakes when Jack's cell rang. It was from "Jack Swyteck, P.A." A finger to one ear silenced the noisy restaurant as he took the call. His assistant, Bonnie, was on the line.

"Did you hear about the suicide on the Suwannee?" she asked. Bonnie had an urgency in her voice even when there was no urgency, so the question came with all the excitement of "Did you hear that aliens landed on Miami Beach?"

"I did," said Jack. "Why are you in the office on a Saturday morning?"

"I was up early and watching the news at home. When I heard the woman's name on TV, I thought, 'Hmm. That sounds familiar.'"

"You've heard of Cynthia Porter?"

"I was sure I had, but I couldn't remember how. Then it hit me. So I came into the office and went through the stack of letters you've received from people about this case. I'm saving them in a box. More than a hundred already, and most of them—well, you don't want to know what most of them say."

"I can only imagine."

"This one I hadn't read yet. It just came in yesterday's mail. But I remembered it because it was such a nice-quality envelope. Like a wedding invitation, almost. Anyway, I double-checked the return address when I came in this morning, and sure enough: Cynthia Porter, Live Oak, Florida."

Jack felt a chill. "Did you open it?"

"I just did."

"What does it say?"

"A lot, actually. Have you ever heard the name Willie James Howard?"

Jack searched his mind. "No."

"You're about to," said Bonnie.

Leroy Highsmith's jet landed in Gainesville before noon. His meeting with Brandon Wall was at the Alpha house.

After Friday's court hearing in Live Oak, the directive from Oliver Boalt was "be prepared to testify next week." Brandon wasn't sure what that meant. He took up Highsmith on the offer he'd made on his last visit to the Alpha House: "You call me if you need anything, Brandon."

"I'm pretty nervous about this hearing," said Brandon.

They were in the fraternity's study room, seated at the center table. Between them were two cups of coffee and the transcript of Brandon's grand jury testimony.

"Don't be," said Highsmith. "You've already got the grand jury experience under your belt. That's a pretty good blueprint as to how Oliver Boalt will proceed."

"I'm not worried about him. The grand jury was no big deal. Neither was the student conduct hearing in the dean's office. This is different. This time, Mr. Swyteck will be asking me questions."

"It's totally normal to be apprehensive about that. A good criminal defense lawyer can make you look like a liar even when you're telling the truth."

"I'm sure," said Brandon. "And a good lawyer can also bring out the truth."

Brandon was all but wringing his hands, and Highsmith could hear the anxiety in his voice. "Tell me what's bothering you, Brandon."

"Right before Percy Donovan disappeared we met with Mr. Boalt in Live Oak. Percy and I talked afterward. He told me that maybe Mark Towson wasn't the right guy. Maybe Towson didn't kill Jamal Cousin. He thinks it might have been someone else."

"Who?"

"The night the Theta house burned down, Percy was part of the demonstration. You know he got hurt, right?"

"Yes. One of his friends was stabbed."

"Percy ended up with a concussion. Right before one of the skinheads shoved him into the wall, he told Percy, 'You're next.'"

Highsmith sat back, drank some coffee, and considered it. "Have you told Oliver Boalt about that conversation?"

"Yes. He said he's not going to ask me anything I talked to Percy about. The hearing is about Mark Towson and Jamal Cousin."

"He's absolutely right."

"But what if Mr. Swyteck asks me?"

"First of all, how would he even know to ask?"

"I don't know. Maybe he could just ask, 'What did you and Percy talk about the last time you had a conversation?'"

Highsmith looked at him with concern. Obviously Brandon had spent a lot of time worrying about this. A lot.

"If the judge allows the question, you answer it to the best of your ability."

"But won't Mr. Swyteck argue that 'you're next' means that this skinhead lynched Jamal and then did the same thing to Percy Donovan?"

"Swyteck can argue anything he wants. But it's a lousy argument. To me, this whole incident simply demonstrates why people like Mark Towson should be punished severely. They inspire copycat racists. Hate begets hate."

"So, if the question is asked, I tell him what Percy said to me?"

"Brandon, your only job is to answer the question and tell the truth. You can't worry about how it's going to play out. Just be truthful. It's that simple. You think you can do that?"

Brandon swallowed hard. "I do."

Jack read Cynthia Porter's letter in the motel lobby.

Bonnie had scanned and e-mailed him a copy after their phone call. Jack put Righley down for a nap with Shelly, and then he went downstairs to retrieve the letter on his iPhone. It was three pages long, written in the lost art of cursive, albeit in the unsteady hand of an old woman.

Jack read it a second time. And then a third. The letter told the entire tragic story, from the Christmas card Willie James had given to his "sweetheart" at the dime store to the lie Cynthia Porter had lived with since her father sat her down at the kitchen table and explained the disappearance of Willie James.

Theo joined him on the couch in the lobby. He didn't read cursive, so Jack told him the story. He sat in silence for a minute, then finally reacted.

"I can't say I'm shocked," said Theo. "We all know this sort of thing happened."

"Thousands of times."

"I just feel sick."

It was hard to say when Jack had last seen Theo like this. Probably his darkest days on death row.

"I already called the Department of Law Enforcement," said Jack. "They're on the way to my office to pick up the original letter from Bonnie."

"What for? The fucking murderers who did this are dead by now. They gonna dig up their bodies and arrest them?"

"It reads like a suicide note, so it's pertinent to whatever investigation there is into how Cynthia Porter died."

"Is there any doubt she killed herself?"

"Cynthia's caretaker told a reporter that she jumped, so that's the only reason the media has been talking about suicide all morning. This letter is the kind of evidence that law enforcement needs to make it official."

Two black housekeepers walked by on their way to the front desk. The white woman behind the counter told them which rooms to clean. Theo looked at Jack, as if to say, *nothing really changes.*

"Why did this old woman write to you?" asked Theo.

"I don't know. Maybe she wrote to everyone involved in the Jamal Cousin case."

"What does Willie James have to do with Jamal?"

"I don't know that, either."

"Is there anyone you can ask?"

"The letter says there's only one other person alive who hasn't forgotten about Willie James," said Jack. "A man named Kelvin Cousin."

Theo did a double take. "Cousin? He related?"

"According to Cynthia, he's Jamal's great-grandfather."

"Are you going to talk to him?"

Jack looked off to the distance. "The question is, will he talk *to me*?"

CHAPTER 65

On Monday morning the Suwannee County Courthouse was again packed to capacity—plus one. Mark's mother was out of the hospital and in the front row, seated between her husband and their daughter. Jack was beside his client at the defense table. Judge Teague picked up exactly where he'd left off on Friday and went straight at the prosecution.

"Mr. Boalt, what is the status of the forensic tests on this recently discovered shoe?"

The prosecutor rose. "Your Honor, the testing is not yet complete."

The judge was visibly disappointed. It wasn't that he was rooting for either side. But the test results could have truncated the hearing, and he would have rather spent the day on other matters on his docket. Or perhaps fishing.

"Your Honor," said Jack, rising, "just so the record is clear. The state has no evidence to connect Mr. Towson to the shoe that was found near Jamal's body, the burned Croc found at the Theta house, *or* this latest Croc found on the riverbank. Is that correct?"

Boalt was plainly annoyed by the question, but the judge was waiting for an answer.

"As of this time, that is correct," said the prosecutor.

"Noted," said the judge. "Call your next witness, Mr. Boalt."

"The State of Florida calls Dr. Elena Ross."

Jack had read the medical examiner's report and reviewed her grand jury testimony. He listened carefully, jotting down a few notes as the prosecutor elicited the main points through direct examination. Her qualifications were impeccable. Jack noted no inconsistencies between her testimony today and her testimony before the grand jury. It was her conclusion as to the cause of death that Jack would attack on cross. Jack launched straight into it upon the conclusion of Boalt's examination.

"Dr. Ross, your autopsy revealed 'sand and other foreign particles' in the mouth of the victim, correct?"

"That's correct. When a victim drowns in a river, his struggle or the current may stir up debris. That debris ends up in the mouth and throat as he ingests or inhales water."

"And that was one factor that led you to conclude that the cause of death in this case was drowning. Correct?"

"Broadly speaking, the cause of death was asphyxia. The question was whether the mechanism of asphyxiation was drowning or strangulation by hanging. My conclusion was drowning."

"Which means that Jamal Cousin was dead before he was hanged. True?"

"Dead or within moments of death."

"And the basis for that conclusion was the absence of bruising on his neck. Am I correct?"

"Partly," the doctor said. "With strangulation by hanging, there is typically a classic V-shaped bruise running up the neck and behind the ear. The body doesn't bruise after the heart stops beating. The absence of bruising indicates that the hanging was postmortem."

Jack checked his notes, then continued. "Let's take a closer look at death by drowning, Doctor. Generally speaking, when a victim drowns in a river, isn't it true that sand and debris are often found in the lungs in addition to the mouth and throat?"

"That can be the case."

"You didn't find any sand or debris in Jamal Cousin's lungs, did you?"

"No, I did not."

"But you concluded that the cause of death was asphyxiation by drowning. True?"

"Yes," she said, her tone a bit defensive. "Not all drowning victims present with sand in the lungs. Here it was found only in the mouth."

"But sand in the mouth is not always a sign of drowning. Is it, Doctor?"

"I'm not sure I understand the question."

"Let's say a dead body is dumped in a river," said Jack. "Isn't it true that sand can lodge in the mouth as that body scrapes along the bottom, pushed by the current?"

"Yes. It happens. But a trip down the river can be a violent experience, and those bodies typically exhibit postmortem trauma ranging from abrasions to bone fractures. That wasn't the case here."

"Let's consider something a little different," said Jack. "Say a dead body was towed behind a boat to a disposal site, but it wasn't dragged along the riverbed. You wouldn't expect the body to be scraped and beat up in that situation, would you, Doctor?"

"Objection," said Boalt. "Mr. Swyteck is asking questions that simply have nothing to do with what happened in this case."

"Your Honor, we don't know what happened in this case," said Jack.

"Sustained. Ask a different question, Mr. Swyteck."

It wasn't the first time a judge had shut him down incorrectly. Jack regrouped. "True or false, Dr. Ross? Drowning cannot be *proven* by autopsy. It's a conclusion a medical examiner reaches after ruling out other possible causes of death."

"That's essentially true. Drowning is a diagnosis by exclusion."

"Your report does not rule out all possibility that Jamal Cousin was dead before his killers took him to the river. Does it?"

"Objection."

"Overruled. The witness may answer."

"Could you repeat the question, please?"

"I'm asking if it's possible, Doctor. Consistent with your autopsy findings, is it *possible* that someone killed Jamal Cousin on dry land and then took his body to the river?"

The prosecutor leaped from his chair. "Objection. Is Mr. Swyteck suggesting that Jamal Cousin was lynched somewhere else, taken to the river, and then lynched again? The question makes no sense."

"Makes sense to me," the judge said. "Can you answer the question, Dr. Ross? Is that scenario possible, that Mr. Cousin was murdered somewhere else and then brought to the river?"

"Theoretically," said the doctor, "but I want to emphasize that Mr. Cousin wasn't stabbed, shot, poisoned, or beaten over the head. There are numerous indicators of asphyxia noted in my report. If Mr. Cousin was dead before he was brought to the river, the cause of death was still asphyxiation."

"Fair enough," said Jack. "Drowning and strangulation by hanging are not the only forms of asphyxia, are they, Doctor?"

She paused, choosing her words carefully. "There are others. But most can be ruled out in this case. For example, Mr. Cousin's death had nothing to do with carbon monoxide poisoning or choking on a foreign object."

"Let's talk about the forms of asphyxia that are not as easily ruled out, Doctor." Jack paused longer than necessary. Silence could be an effective tool—time to make the witness wait and wonder.

"Is there a question?" asked Boalt.

Jack stepped closer to the witness. "Doctor, asphyxia can be caused by smothering, can it not? By smothering I mean closing or covering the nose and mouth."

"Yes. That is a form of asphyxia."

"In this case, you can't completely rule out smothering, can you?"

"I noted in my report that the nasal and oral orifices were not obstructed."

It was exactly the answer Jack wanted. He retrieved the autopsy report and turned to the flagged page. "You also noted traces of adhesive over the victim's mouth," he said, handing her the report. "Right, Doctor?"

She looked at it, but not for long. She knew it was there. "Yes."

"Which suggests that at some point during the trip to the river, tape covered Mr. Cousin's mouth. Correct?"

"It could have been on the trip to the river," she said. "It also could have been after reaching the river."

Jack exaggerated his confusion. "But if tape covered his mouth while he was *in* the river, sand would not have been present in the victim's mouth. Would it, Doctor?"

Dr. Ross paused, as if debating how hard to push back. "In a drowning, it's possible for sand to enter through the nose and lodge in the mouth."

"Okay. Let's stick with that standard you just articulated: *what's possible*. It's also possible that his mouth was taped before reaching the river. Right?"

Her search for wiggle room was obvious. Then she answered, "I—yes."

Jack retrieved the report and stepped away from the witness. "Let me ask you again, Doctor. Can you completely rule out smothering as the mechanism of asphyxiation?"

Boalt could sit no longer. "Judge, this whole line of questioning is just silly. What's next? Is Mr. Swyteck going to ask if Jamal Cousin was smothered by locking himself in an abandoned refrigerator?"

The judge went pale, and the public's reaction from behind the lawyers was palpable. The toothy grin drained from the prosecutor's face as the realization set in: he'd made a bad joke in a situation that was anything but a laughing matter.

"Overruled," said the judge.

"One more time," Jack said in a serious tone. "Doctor, can you rule out smothering?"

The witness could have jammed him and said, "Yes, to a reasonable degree of medical certainty," relying on the time-honored amorphous standard that allowed doctors to reach virtually any conclusion that cut against the opposing counsel's theory of the case. But Jack had already demonstrated that betraying her own professional integrity could prove to be embarrassing.

"I would have to say no," she answered.

The response didn't trigger the chorus of murmurs across the courtroom that trial lawyers dreamed about, but it was close. Jack could see that Boalt was dying to pop from his chair, but hearing an answer he didn't want to hear was no basis to object.

Jack returned to the defense table and stood beside his client. "Dr. Ross, in some cases a medical examiner is unable to determine a cause of death. Isn't that true?"

"It's rare."

"But it happens?"

"Yes."

"In some cases, what first appears to be the obvious cause of death turns out not to be the cause of death at all. Isn't that right, Doctor?"

"Of course. That's why we have autopsies."

"Exactly. Thank you, Dr. Ross. I have no further questions."

CHAPTER 66

The backlash was immediate.

"Utterly outrageous!" Leroy Highsmith told the crowd.

He'd bolted from the courtroom at the conclusion of Jack's cross-examination. A pack of reporters followed him out the door and surrounded him on the courthouse steps. He was fuming, and his voice boomed even in the open air.

"To suggest that what happened to Jamal Cousin was anything but a racial terror lynching is an insult to the court and an outrage to the community."

A reporter pushed her way to the front, thrusting her microphone in his face. "Sir, isn't Mr. Swyteck doing what all criminal defense lawyers do—raise as many questions as possible about the prosecution's case?"

"I fully understand the concept of reasonable doubt," said Highsmith. "But this crosses the line."

"Why?"

"The very implication—" Highsmith started to say, then stopped himself. He needed to control his anger, or at the very least to express his anger in terms that the white media could understand. "Today, in this courtroom, Mr. Swyteck stooped to the level of a Holocaust revisionist who claims that six million Jews were never actually exterminated. Jamal Cousin was lynched. No clever lawyer can make that fact go away."

"But, sir—"

"That's all I have at this time," said Highsmith. He turned and continued down the courthouse steps, with the media in dogged pursuit.

With Judge Teague's permission, Jack met with his client in the empty jury room. An armed deputy stood right outside the closed door, his torso a blur through the old pane of translucent glass. The hearing was adjourned for one hour, and Jack took the time to strategize.

"Are we winning?" asked Mark.

It was such a simple question, and it reminded Jack to ignore the media, ignore the angry glares from the public, and remain focused on the ultimate objective. "It's a step in the right direction. This opens things up for us going forward."

"Like what?"

"For one, you have no alibi after eleven p.m. Friday night. But the medical examiner just admitted that Jamal could have been killed before he was taken to the river."

"Before eleven o'clock?"

"That's an open question. One thing we have to sort through is that rigor mortis sets in two to four hours after death. Hanging a dead body from a tree after rigor mortis is no easy feat, even if it was already in a hog-tied position."

Mark did the calculation. "So if the hanging was sometime *before* three a.m., the time of death could have been before eleven p.m. I could have an alibi."

"We're not there yet. In fact, we have a long way to go."

"But I might have an alibi after all?"

Jack didn't want to create false hope. Getting a medical examiner to adjust the time of death on a witness stand was no easy feat.

"You might," said Jack.

The state attorney tried not to let it show, but no one leaving the courthouse was angrier than Oliver Boalt. The media pestered him on his hurried descent of the granite steps and followed him across the street all the way to the state attorney's office. He declined to comment, disappeared into the building, and took the elevator upstairs.

The one-hour adjournment gave him time to phone the crime lab and get an update on the testing on the third Croc. He was at his desk, listening by speakerphone.

"We have a match."

Boalt could hardly believe his ears. "The shoe found on the riverbank is the mate to the one that was found at the lynching site. Is that what you're telling me?"

"Yes, sir. Same size, same identification markers from the manufacturer. Even the wear pattern matches."

"Okay," said Boalt. "Now make my day. Is there any DNA to connect it to Mark Towson?"

"Negative."

The prosecutor's heart sank. "Are you sure?"

"Yes. Unlike the other Croc, which was submerged in the acidic muck and had no DNA on it, we did find DNA on this shoe. But it's not Mark Towson's. And it's not Baine Robinson's."

"This can't be right. I want you to retest it."

"There's nothing to retest."

Boalt leaned forward on his desk, getting closer to the speakerphone. "Just listen to what I'm saying. Retest the shoe."

There was silence on the line, but Boalt's tone prevailed.

"Okay," was the response. "We'll retest."

CHAPTER 67

The defense and prosecution were back in court. Judge Teague climbed to the bench and directed all to take a seat. Spectators on both sides of the center aisle squeezed tightly across ten rows of bench seating to make room for everyone who wanted to observe. An elderly African American man with snow-white hair snagged the last available opening in the back row as a deputy closed the double doors at the rear of the courtroom.

The afternoon session started the same way the morning had begun. "Mr. Boalt," the judge asked, "do you have any update from the crime lab on the testing of the shoe?"

The state attorney rose, buttoned his jacket, and spoke in his most forthright tone. "The tests are ongoing, Your Honor."

Judge Teague peered down from the bench, grilling the prosecutor in silence. Jack was the outsider from Miami in this mix, but the relationship between these two fixtures of the Live Oak courthouse dated back decades. Perhaps the judge detected something less than full disclosure, but he didn't have the temerity to call the state attorney on it. It made Jack wonder.

"The prosecution will surely advise the court as soon as that testing is complete," said Boalt.

"Please do," the judge said. "I have to finish early today. There's time for one witness."

The prosecutor turned and faced the back of the courtroom. "The state calls Brandon Wall."

The double doors opened, and all eyes were upon him as Brandon entered the courtroom, walked down the center aisle, and stepped up to the witness stand. The bailiff administered the familiar oath, Brandon said "I do," and the prosecutor approached the witness.

"Good afternoon, Mr. Wall," he said in a cordial tone.

The introductory questions went smoothly. Brandon was a model witness. An honor student. A leader in his fraternity. He worked twenty hours per week to help support his education. He was everything the distinguished Alpha alumni wanted the Divine Nine to be. There was no reason to question his honesty.

A lot like Jamal, Jack thought.

"Mr. Wall, are you aware of certain text messages that Jamal Cousin received approximately one week before his death?"

"I am."

The "strange fruit" text from Mark's phone reappeared on the projection screen. It seemed to have lost none of its impact the second time around. Jack didn't check the crowd's reaction; he didn't have to. All momentum that he'd felt during the cross-examination of Dr. Ross suddenly faded.

"Is this the message?" asked the prosecutor.

Brandon glanced at the screen, in the way a survivor might acknowledge her rapist. "Yes."

"When was the first time you saw this text message?" Boalt asked.

"The night Jamal received it."

"Tell the court how that came about," said Boalt.

"It was Saturday night. We had a party at the Alpha house. Jamal pulled me aside and showed me the text message he just got."

"Was it just the two of you?"

"Yes."

"Did he say anything to you about the message?"

Jack could have objected on grounds of hearsay. He could also have elevated his client from the most hated man in the courtroom to the most hated man in America. He let it go.

"Jamal said that he got two other messages like it. One from Cooper Bartlett. One from Baine Robinson."

"Did Mr. Cousin show those other messages to you?"

"No. He said he already deleted them."

"Did he show the message from Mr. Towson to anyone but you?"

This time Jack did rise. "Objection, Your Honor. The message was sent from Mr. Towson's phone. It was not from Mr. Towson."

The judge seemed to take Jack's point. "Sustained."

"Fine," said the prosecutor. "To your knowledge, Mr. Wall, did Jamal Cousin show the message to anyone but you?"

"I don't believe so."

The prosecutor checked his notes, and Jack couldn't tell if the pause was for dramatic effect or if Boalt was truly searching for the right words.

"Mr. Wall, do you know why Jamal Cousin showed you that text?"

"I have an idea."

Jack had to object. "Your Honor, this is starting to sound like speculation on the part of the witness."

"Agreed. Mr. Boalt, please frame your questions so that they do not invite speculation and conjecture."

"Yes, Your Honor," said Boalt, and he paused to rethink. "Let's approach it this way. Mr. Wall, as of the time you first saw this text message, had you ever met the defendant, Mark Towson?"

"No."

"Had you met anyone in the Towson family?"

"Yes."

"Who?"

"His sister, Shelly."

That was news to Jack, and he shot a subtle glance at his client that asked, *Did you know about this?* But Mark's gaze was fixed on the witness.

"How many times have you met Shelly Towson?" the prosecutor asked.

"Just once."

"When did you meet her?"

"Early this past August. About two weeks before the start of the fall semester."

"Where did you meet her?"

"On the University of Florida campus."

"Where exactly?"

"At the Alpha House."

Again Jack glanced at his client, but Mark made no eye contact, his gaze riveted on Brandon.

"Was there anyone else at the Alpha House?" asked Boalt.

"Jamal."

"Anyone else?"

"No. The summer term was over. It was two weeks before fall semester. Everyone was out of town."

"Why were you there?"

"I was the outgoing Alpha president. The president gets his own special room. I had to move my things out so the incoming president could move in."

"Who was the incoming president?"

"Jamal Cousin."

"What did you do when you arrived at the Alpha house? I'm talking about this day in August."

"I went to the president's room."

"Did you go inside?"

"The door was locked. But I still had my key so I unlocked it and went in."

"What did you find?"

Brandon hesitated, and then answered, "Jamal had already moved my things out and moved his things in."

"Did you find anything else?"

The witness paused, and Jack no longer needed to look to his client or anyone else for what was coming. All he could do was brace himself and show no reaction that might be reported by the media.

"Jamal was in the room."

"Where was he?"

Brandon lowered his eyes, as if not sure where to look. "Jamal was in bed."

"Was he alone?"

"No."

"Who was in bed with him?"

"Shelly Towson."

The prosecutor paused. Even for those who took no issue with interracial relationships, the very existence of an intimate relationship between the victim and the sister of the accused was a completely new development in the case, and the courtroom caught its collective breath. Mark probably wasn't even aware of it, but his leg was so restless that Jack could feel the table shaking.

"What did you do next?" Boalt asked.

"I left," said Brandon. "In a hurry."

Boalt paused briefly and flipped the page in his notepad. "Mr. Wall, was that encounter between Jamal Cousin and Shelly Towson a onetime thing?"

"No."

"Are you aware of another time they were together?"

"I know that Jamal was planning to have her come over the morning of the tubing trip down the Ichetucknee."

"How do you know that?"

"He asked me to make sure every brother in the house went on the tubing trip so he and Shelly would be alone."

"And so that their secret relationship would remain a secret, right?"

"Yes."

Another pause, and another flip of the page. The prosecutor continued. "Mr. Wall, did you ever tell anyone what you saw that day?"

"Never. Well, not until after Jamal was dead, when you and I talked."

"Did you ever discuss it with Jamal?"

"I did."

"What was the gist of that conversation?"

"Jamal didn't want me to tell anyone about him and Shelly."

"Did he tell you why?"

"Objection," said Jack, having let this go far enough. "That's clearly hearsay, Your Honor."

There were a few groans from the gallery, as if Jack should be disbarred. The judge sighed and said, "Technically you may be right, Mr. Swyteck. But there's no jury here. I'll allow the witness to answer and decide later if I should disregard it."

Jack settled into his seat. It was a damned if he did, damned if he didn't situation, and there was nothing more to do.

"You can answer the question," Boalt told the witness.

Brandon leaned closer to the microphone, but his lips didn't move. The prosecutor clearly had an answer in mind. Jack imagined it was a zinger along the lines of *"Jamal feared retaliation by her racist brother, Mark."*

"Mr. Wall," the prosecutor nudged. "Why did Jamal Cousin not want anyone to know?"

Brandon's struggle was on display for the entire courtroom. It was like watching a man getting ready to yank out a fractured tooth. Finally, he answered.

"He said—Jamal said it would kill Shelly's mother if anyone knew."

The answer was perhaps more shocking than anything that came before, hitting Jack like a mule kick. Then, just as suddenly, Jack recalled the way he and Liz had laughed and then cried over the satirical study that the nurse had told her about in the hospital—that racism was "hereditary."

The prosecutor was staring at Brandon, and he appeared less than fully satisfied. It was plain to Jack that "it would kill Shelly's mother" was not the answer that the state attorney had expected—not what they'd rehearsed in witness prep. Finally, Boalt thanked the witness and stepped away, accepting what Brandon was willing to give him.

"Your Honor, I have no further questions," he said, and he returned to his seat.

The judge looked at Jack. "Um, well."

His words of judicial wisdom pretty much summed up Jack's feelings.

Jack rose. "Your Honor—"

"Save your breath," the judge said. "That went longer than anticipated. Let's break for the day."

Jack could not have been more appreciative. "Thank you, Judge."

"We'll start with your cross-examination at nine o'clock tomorrow morning," Judge Teague said. "Mr. Wall, you are still under oath. Do not discuss your testimony with anyone overnight. We are adjourned."

The crack of the judge's gavel cut through the courtroom, and all rose on the bailiff's command. Judge Teague stepped down from the bench, and Jack wished that the walk to his chambers were not so short. Jack didn't want to deal with the rush of the media to the rail. He had no appetite for a gloating state attorney. And he was dreading the expressions he would see when he turned around and looked at Mark's family.

The side door closed, Judge Teague was gone, and all that Jack would have rather lived without immediately came to pass. Jack stayed close to his client, ignoring the flurry of questions from reporters.

"Mrs. Towson, are you a racist?"

"Did you teach hate to your son, Mrs. Towson?"

Mark's parents appeared numb, but Shelly took off like a rocket, running toward the exit. Jack's gaze followed her all the way to the double doors at the rear, where she paused ever so slightly, but long enough for Jack to notice. She looked at the old—*very old*—African American man with the snow-white hair who had entered the courtroom just before Brandon's testimony and taken the last open seat in the last row. It all happened in a flash, but it played in Jack's mind as if in slow motion. And Jack was sure of one thing.

Mark's sister and that old man had met before.

CHAPTER 68

Jack left the courthouse without comment for the media and went straight to the Suwannee County Jail. Mark didn't look him in the eye when he entered the attorney-client conference room. Even after taking a seat at the table, Mark's gaze was still aimed at the floor.

"When did Shelly tell you about her and Jamal?" asked Jack.

Mark took a deep breath. "Last week. When she came to visit me."

"Mark, I told you and Shelly that conversations with any visitor but your attorney are recorded."

"Shelly knew that. That's why she didn't say it out loud."

"Damn it, Mark. They read letters, too."

"She didn't write it in a letter," said Mark. He told Jack about the scripted message on her arm that looked like a tattoo. "It was in French," said Mark.

It would have been somewhat clever, if similar stunts weren't pulled every day in prisons all over the world. "What did it say?" asked Jack.

"'JC was my love. BR knew.'"

JC was clearly Jamal Cousin. "BR—Baine Robinson knew?"

"That's what Shelly said. In fact, right before she showed me the message, she said it was 'about Baine.'"

Jack thought for a moment. "That's why Baine sent the text messages to Jamal. Shit, Mark. Shelly should have told *me* this. This isn't the kind of thing you try to sneak past corrections officers."

"Obviously she was leaving it up to me."

"Leaving what up to you?"

"Whether to let Mom hear it before she dies."

The prognosis didn't surprise Jack. He'd been worried for Liz. The surprise was in the fuller implication of what Mark was saying.

"So what Brandon Wall said is true? It would have killed your mother to know?"

Mark's eyes welled. "I love my mother, Jack. She's a kind, wonderful person. But—"

"It's okay," said Jack. "I get it."

Silence hovered between them. Jack recalled his conversation with Mark's father, who regretted the missed opportunity to show his ten-year-old son the courage to reject all those bad influences that say it's okay to be racist. It had never occurred to Jack that Tucker's own wife was among the bad influences.

"You understand the problem we have now, right?" asked Jack.

"I think I do."

"Where there was once no motive at all for you to taunt and then lynch Jamal Cousin, there is now the oldest and most stereotypical motive in the history of black-white relations."

"I understand."

"I have to call Shelly to the witness stand. She has to explain that you knew nothing about her and Jamal until she visited you in jail. But understand this: Not a single person in that courtroom is going to believe her. Maybe not even your parents. It's going to come across as a sister who loves her brother and will say anything to save his life."

"I'm sorry," said Mark.

"So am I," said Jack, and then a thought occurred to him. "Unless—"

"Unless what?"

"It's possible a surveillance camera captured Shelly showing you the message on her arm."

"How does that help?"

"If the camera caught Shelly telling you about 'JC' after you're in jail, it proves that you didn't know. That negates your motive to send that text message to Jamal and to have anything to do with the lynching."

"Do you think it's on video?"

"My guess is that the jail has a surveillance camera that snaps an image every eight seconds or at some set interval like that. The question is whether the message on her arm will be readable."

"Can you get the images?"

Jack rose, no time to waste. "I'll ask right now."

"Then what?"

"Then I need to have a talk with your sister."

Jack could have walked from the jail to his motel, but driving was the only way to make sure he wouldn't end up on television with a microphone shoved in his face. Theo had flown back to Miami with Righley that morning, but Shelly still had the room next to Jack's. She was alone when she answered Jack's knock. She sat on the ottoman next to the noisy climate control unit built into the wall. Jack pulled up the desk chair.

"Mark told me everything he knows," said Jack.

"Then there's not much to talk about, is there," she said.

"We both know that's not the case."

She looked at Jack, and he could see that she'd been crying. Then she looked away. "Baine Robinson is a pig."

"How did he find out about you and Jamal?"

"I have no idea. He wouldn't tell me who his source was."

"But he told you he knew?"

She chuckled mirthlessly. "Told me is a nice way to put it."

"What do you mean?"

"There's a history with me and Baine. I was a very stupid freshman. I made out with him one night at the Theta house. Terrible mistake. It was the biggest lecture Mark ever gave me. Anyway, I totally blew off Baine. He kept after me, but I was always like, 'See ya, Baine.'" She sighed, her voice filling with regret. "Then he had this over me."

"You and Jamal?"

"Yeah. He wanted me to sleep with him or he would tell my mother. I told you he was a pig."

"How did Baine know that your mother—" Jack stopped himself, searching for the right words. "How did he know that your mother would have such a big problem with Jamal?"

"First of all, Baine is himself a racist. It's like they can sniff each other out. Of all Mark's friends, the only one my mother would make an inappropriate remark in front of was Baine. They kind of had a thing that they shared."

"A thing?"

"It was like their own sense of humor. A private joke between them."

"I'm not sure I understand."

"Here's what I'm saying. One time last year there was a group of Mark's friends over at our house watching a Gator game on television. My parents and I were in the room watching, too. There was a black play-by-play announcer, a former player. To be totally honest, he was really struggling. Most of us were like, 'Okay, it's his first time on television, the poor guy's really nervous,' whatever. But Baine—well, he had a few beers, and he would break into this exaggerated 'yowsa' imitation every time the announcer said anything."

"Yowsa?"

"Yowsa, Mastuh referee. Yowsa, Mastuh alligator mascot."

"Oh."

"It got to the point that we were all telling him to shut the hell up. But Mom—she was noticeably silent. I hate to say this. I love my mom. But I could tell that she thought Baine was funny. Something inside her wanted to burst out laughing. I had to leave the room. Everybody thought it was because of Baine. But that wasn't it. For the first time in my life, I was ashamed of my own mother."

Jack felt her pain. There were things his own father had done—things that had driven them apart when Jack was a young lawyer.

He wished he could have told her that it's possible to work out these differences over time. But time was short in the Towson family.

That made it all the more difficult to ask the question that Jack felt compelled to ask. "Shelly, please don't get mad. But you said earlier that Baine threatened to tell your mother."

"I didn't sleep with him, if that's your question."

"It wasn't. But the fact that you didn't give in to his demand makes the question all the more important. Is it possible that Baine *did tell your mother*?"

Shelly considered it for a moment, but her thoughts quickly turned to resentment. "Seriously? Are you asking me if I think my mother lynched Jamal?"

Or encouraged someone else to do it. "Never mind," said Jack. "I was having one of those 'everyone's a suspect' moments. Forget I said it."

"I will," she said. "And I think you should, too."

There was silence between them. Jack decided not to pursue it any further—at least not with Shelly.

"One last question," said Jack.

"What?"

"Who was the old black man in the back of the courtroom today?"

CHAPTER 69

The sun was setting over southern Georgia, and Andie could hear the sounds of creeping nightfall on the Okefenokee Swamp.

She also heard rumblings among the Aryan National Alliance rank and file.

Since the move to Okefenokee, she'd met Alliance supporters from at least a dozen states, some of whom had traveled hundreds of miles to join the camp, all drawn by the prospect of a showdown with black frat boys. So far, the closest thing to any form of "action" had been Steger's speeches.

"Talk is cheap," said William. "Time to crack some heads."

Tonight's speech was again given in the tin-roofed shelter. Andie was seated beside William, trying to listen to Steger, but there were whispers of discontent around her.

"I agree," said the man behind her and William. "I'm tired of sittin' around."

The sentiment was generally expressed in quiet exchanges between men who knew each other well. If Steger was aware of the growing dissatisfaction, it didn't stop him from talking.

Andie just listened. This speech was of particular interest to her. It was classic Steger—the pseudo-intellectualism that had inspired the naming of FBI "Operation 777."

"On July 7, 2016, a black man opened fire on Dallas police officers," Steger told the group. "His victims were white and black, but make no mistake about his purpose. During the shoot-out, Micah Xavier Johnson told police by phone that he 'wanted to kill white people, especially white officers.'"

Steger paused. He wasn't addressing a crowd of news junkies, but no one would forget the day that bullets rained down on a peaceful #BlackLivesMatter protest in downtown Dallas.

"Johnson was shot and wounded in the exchange of gunfire," said Steger, "but he was determined to fight to the death. Before an explosive robot was sent in to blow him to bits, he used his own blood to write two letters on the wall: RB.

"Now, the liberal media will have you believe Johnson was a lone wolf. No connection to any organization, they say. Let's take a closer look. First, note the significance of the date. The seventh day. The seventh month. The sixteenth year—one-six. How much is one plus six? What three-number combination does that date give us?

"Seven, seven, seven."

Andie discreetly gauged the crowd's reaction. The seven-seven-seven gimmick had caught their attention.

Steger continued. "Interesting, you say. But so what? Could be a meaningless coincidence. Or is it? What about those letters, 'RB,' which Micah Johnson wrote in his own blood? The official investigation concluded that they have no significance. Don't believe it. Rb is the symbol for rubidium, a chemical element. Scientists describe rubidium as "highly reactive." You bet it is. But more important, do you know what the atomic number is for rubidium? Thirty-seven. Or say it another way: Three-seven. It sounds a lot like 'three sevens,' doesn't it?

"Again: seven, seven, seven.

"All this talk of sevens is not just a numbers game. It means something. It tells you what is really afoot."

Andie knew what was coming: for Steger, the hate speech always followed the false intellectual premise.

"Islam describes the numerical miracle of the number seven," said Steger. "On the trip to Mecca, Muslims cast the traditional seven stones at the devil. I don't mean to get silly about this, but this will show you the depth of meaning that this number has for the Muslim-inspired black nationalist movement. Malcolm X was in Miami Beach in 1964 to watch Cassius Clay—later Muhammad Ali—take the heavyweight crown from one of the greatest boxers of all time, Sonny Liston. You know what seat Malcolm X selected to watch that fight? You guessed it: seat seven.

"Do not for a minute believe that Micah Johnson was a lone wolf. Do not underestimate the danger of radical Islam and the influence it has on black nationalism in this country. Again, we can look at the words of Malcolm X himself to prove my point. He was at the height of his career when other black Muslims were turning against him and threatening his life." Steger opened the book again. "Chapter sixteen: 'I knew that no one would kill you quicker than a Muslim if he felt that's what Allah wanted him to do.'"

Steger laid the book aside, and Andie noticed that there were two books Steger carried everywhere: the Bible and *The Autobiography of Malcolm X*. She noted that he never carried the Quran or referenced its text. His understanding of Islam was typical of a hate-monger, based on out-of-context quotes taken from secular writings.

"My friends," said Steger, "Malcolm X's written words foreshadowed his own death. Don't let them foreshadow yours."

Applause followed, but it was not thunderous. It was lukewarm at best.

"Hey, Steger!" a man shouted.

Andie glanced over. It was Colt.

"Do you have something to say?" asked Steger.

"Yeah, I do. When are we actually gonna *do* something? I'm tired of sitting around."

The crowd joined in, some members voicing their agreement and others applauding for Colt—much more applause than Steger's speech had garnered.

Steger raised his hands to quiet the crowd. "That's a fair question."

"Yeah," said Colt. "How about a fair fucking answer?"

Steger glared—long enough and with enough intensity to silence

Colt and those who were egging him on. When the crowd was completely still, he spoke in the dramatic tone of a prophet.

"In twenty-four hours, all the waiting will be over," he said. "It's going to be so big. Huge. And each of you will know what to do. Believe me."

Steger grabbed his books and stepped off the makeshift stage. The crowd broke into small clusters of conversation. The mood among the rank and file had shifted. Andie could feel the energy.

And the urgency.

CHAPTER 70

Jack met with Oliver Boalt at the state attorney's office. The cardboard takeout box was still on the prosecutor's desk, but even without it, Jack would have guessed pizza for dinner. The greasy pepperoni stain was still on the wrinkled white shirt that the state attorney had worn to court that day.

"I have everything you asked for," said Boalt, handing Jack a large manila envelope.

Jack had subpoenaed the Suwannee County Jail to get the surveillance tapes from Shelly's conversation with her brother. He'd scheduled a meeting with Boalt to make it clear that he needed them immediately. He hadn't expected such quick compliance.

Jack peeked inside the envelope and saw a flash drive and a CD. "This is everything?" he asked, still skeptical. "All audio, video, and still images?"

"Yes, sir. And in the spirit of cooperation, I went one step further," Boalt said, as he handed Jack another envelope across his desk.

Jack opened the envelope and removed a photograph. It was a magnified image of the message on Shelly's arm.

Jack looked up. The prosecutor seemed curiously smug.

"You know about this?" asked Jack.

"Before you did," said Boalt. "The audio recorded her saying 'it's about Baine,' and then in the next frame of video surveillance she rolled up her sleeve. Not exactly discreet. We've seen that trick before."

Jack looked again at the magnified image. It was exactly as Mark had described.

"Oliver, you look strangely at peace for a prosecutor who has just handed over irrefutable proof that Mark Towson was completely unaware of the relationship between his sister and Jamal Cousin."

"Irrefutable?" he said, smiling. "I think not."

In a case filled with excess footwear, Jack sensed that yet another shoe was about to drop.

"As you might expect," said Boalt, "I spoke to Baine Robinson and his lawyer about this."

"When?"

"An hour ago. Mr. Robinson admits that he knew."

"Which is exactly what the message from Shelly shows," said Jack. "Baine knew. Mark didn't."

"Not exactly," said Boalt. "When Shelly visited her brother in jail, she was apparently unaware of the fact that her brother already knew about her and 'JC.'"

"That's not true," said Jack.

Boalt slid a third envelope across his desk. Inside was a signed affidavit from Baine Robinson. Boalt explained the highlights as Jack skimmed it.

"Baine Robinson told Mark Towson that his sister was 'doing the president of the Alpha house,' to use Baine's words. As it states in the affidavit, that conversation took place before Mark Towson sent his text message, and well before the lynching of Jamal Cousin."

Jack laid the affidavit on the desk, looked straight at the prosecutor, and said, "Baine's lying."

"Your client's lying to you, Jack. Which is the real point of this meeting."

"You brought me here to gloat to my face. Is that it?"

"Not at all," Boalt said, his expression turning very serious. "I brought you here because this case is doing terrible things to this community. It's not good for Live Oak. Not good for the people of Suwannee County. Not good for anybody."

"Are you offering a deal, Oliver?"

The state attorney leaned forward, his forearms resting on the leather desktop. "Yes."

The two lawyers locked eyes. Then the prosecutor reached inside his suit jacket, pulled a letter-sized envelope from his pocket, and slid it across the desk. He left his hand on the sealed envelope, maintaining his eye contact with Jack.

"This is the only deal I am ever going to offer," Boalt said, and then he slowly retracted his hand and settled back into his chair.

Jack looked at the envelope but didn't open it. A minute passed. Finally, Jack took it, tucked it away in his coat pocket, and then rose. "Good night, Oliver," he said, offering his hand.

The men shook hands, and Jack left the office with much more than he'd expected.

CHAPTER 71

Percy sensed it was time.

It was night. He could tell. It was a new ability he'd developed. Percy was in constant darkness, except when his captor came to feed him or empty his bucket. But over the past few days he'd learned to distinguish between the pitch blackness of night and the slightly less complete darkness of daytime when, from someplace in the shed that was outside his line of sight, a minuscule amount of sunlight seeped through rotting boards or perhaps a crack in the roof. If his figurative clock was correct, it was nearing dinnertime, and his captor would arrive soon.

And then Percy would make his move.

There had been plenty of time to plan. Each time his captor switched on the light Percy stole a glimpse of his surroundings. When the light went out, he replayed the image in his mind. He knew how many steps it was to the door. He knew exactly where the lightbulb was, the length of the exposed wire from the rafters, and how high the bulb dangled above the concrete floor. Most important, he knew where the tool bench was, and which tools might be of greatest use.

Footsteps. They were right outside the shed. *Right on time.*

Percy drew a breath to calm his nerves. He knew what he had to do, and there was no backing down. He'd been told from the outset that he would live only if Jamal's killers went free. Seeing his first captor's face had erased even that small hope. His replacement had given Percy the name "Emmett," and Percy was keenly aware of how the story of Emmett Till had ended.

He heard the lock turn from the outside. The door creaked open, and the blinding beam of a flashlight hit him squarely in the eyes. He heard the door close. The click of the light switch. The flashlight went off, and Percy was in the yellowish glow of the bulb dangling above him.

"Be still," the man said.

Percy sat in silence, waiting for precisely the right moment. The man came toward him. Percy was at the ready. Hours of work were about to pay off. His ankles were still shackled. The only chain binding him to the wall had been the wrist shackles, which his captors had fed through a neatly drilled hole in the exposed stud. Percy had worked tirelessly since his last meal, using the chain like a cable saw to cut through the two-by-four.

With wrists chained together, but no longer tethered to the wall, Percy swung the two-foot length of steel chain with all his arm strength, striking his captor across the side of the head.

"Fuck!" the man shouted, as he fell to the floor.

It was a punishing blow but not enough to knock him out. His captor tried to squirm away from him, and Percy knew that only one of them was going to leave this shed alive. Percy stretched his body, extending his reach as far as possible, and wrapped the chain around the man's neck. And then he squeezed.

The man grunted, clawed, and kicked. But Percy only squeezed with more force. Tighter than he thought possible, as if this were about more than just saving himself.

The man went limp.

Percy maintained the tension on the chain for a moment longer, then released. His captor didn't move. Percy fell back onto the concrete, exhausted. But there was no time to catch his breath. He went to the tool bench, grabbed a hatchet, and sat back down on the floor. He raised the hatchet above his head, took aim at the chain between his ankles, and swung down.

It barely made a dent in the steel link.

His captor groaned. The man didn't move, but he was still alive.

A part of Percy wanted to walk across the shed and bury that hatchet right in that fucking racist's head. Another part told him that there was a difference between fighting off an attacker and crushing the skull of an unconscious human being.

He rummaged through the tools on the bench and found a hacksaw. There was enough slack in the ankle chain for him to shuffle to a safer place where he could stop and cut through the links. He took the hatchet, too. Then he hurried out the door and stepped into the night, realizing that he had no idea where he was—or where he was going.

CHAPTER 72

Jack knew every crack in the sidewalks along Ohio Avenue. Too many times he'd walked the same triangle of downtown Live Oak since breakfast—the courthouse, to the jail, to the state attorney's office. This would be his final visit of the night with his client, but there was so much more to be done before court resumed in the morning.

"Baine's not lying," Mark said softly. "He did tell me about Jamal and Shelly."

It was like having the wind knocked out of him. "So when I asked you when you found out about your sister and Jamal, you lied to me."

"No. The question you asked was, 'When did Shelly tell you about her and Jamal?' I told you: when she came to visit me last week."

Jack did all he could to control his anger. "Don't fuck with me, Mark. You sat there and pretended like you didn't know *a thing* until Shelly told you. You deceived me, and you'd better have a good explanation, or we're done."

Mark slumped even deeper in his chair. "It's—there's no excuse."

"I didn't ask for an excuse. I need to know *why* you did this."

"Okay. The truth is, I—" He drew a breath, as if trying to start again. "I was trying to tell you. But then you got excited and said the surveillance video of Shelly's visit could be the break we're looking for. If we could prove that I didn't know about Shelly and Jamal until after Jamal was dead, all this might go away."

"It can't make anything go away if it's not true. How did you not realize that the truth would come out?"

Mark hung his head, running his fingers through his hair. "Honestly, I never thought Baine would admit that he knew. Doesn't it make him look guilty?"

"It makes *you* look guilty, Mark, because he told *you*. Damn it. The one thing I told you never to do is lie to me."

Mark suddenly seemed much younger than he was, like a schoolboy dressed down by the principal. "It wasn't that big a lie," he muttered.

"You're charged with a racially motivated lynching. If you knew your sister was sleeping with the victim, you had motive."

"This is all so ridiculous. First off, I would have absolutely no problem with Shelly dating Jamal if she wanted to. But even if I was a racist, what Baine told me wouldn't have even mattered."

"How could it not matter?"

"Because I didn't believe him!"

"Why not?"

Mark looked exhausted, physically and emotionally. But he pushed through it. "Do you remember what Baine told us at that first meeting we had with him and his lawyer?"

"Told us about what?"

"That run-in he had with Brandon Wall at the Theta house last spring. Brandon was hired as the bartender for our party. He quit when he found out Baine wanted to serve 'Strange Fruit' cocktails."

"What does that have to do with this?"

"When I first heard about Shelly and Jamal, I thought it was just Brandon tweaking Baine. Baine is not the most enlightened Theta brother when it comes to race. Telling Baine that my sister blew him off to sleep with the black president of the Alpha house is a surefire way to piss him off."

"Hold it," said Jack. "It was *Brandon* who told him? That's how Baine found out?"

"That's what Baine said."

"But Brandon testified today that he never told anyone."

"Then he lied," said Mark.

It wasn't at all clear *why* Brandon would've lied, but Jack's head was spinning. "I don't know the truth anymore. All I can say is that I'm completely disappointed in you."

Mark glowered, and his expression changed from utter embarrassment and remorse to one of pure anger. It was more than he could contain. Mark sprang from his chair and started pacing furiously from one side of the small room to the other.

"Mark, sit down."

"Seriously, that's your reaction?" Mark asked, his anger rising. "You're disappointed in me?"

"Mark, get control of yourself."

Mark stopped and glared, almost shouting. "My mother is dying, okay? I've been expelled from college. My fraternity burned to the ground. One of my closest friends died less than a foot away from me in a car accident, and my own fraternity brother is making shit up about me to save his own ass. I could get the death penalty for lynching the guy my sister couldn't even tell our mother she was in love with. And even if I'm acquitted—which I should be—I'll still be known as the worst racist of the twenty-first century. To top it all off, I'm locked up every day in solitary confinement because my Nazi cellmate, who literally has swastikas tattooed onto his balls, tried to shove his cock down my throat."

"Mark, calm down."

"No, I won't! For a split second in our meeting I saw a way out of this, and I made a mistake. So fuck you, Jack! Fuck you and your 'Oh, Mark, how could you lie to me' bullshit."

Mark went to the exit and buzzed for the guard. The door opened, and the guard entered, but Jack told him to leave. When he was gone, Jack allowed Mark the time he needed to cool down. Then he spoke.

"I have something I want you to look at," said Jack, as he laid the envelope from the state attorney on the table. "Boalt offered us a deal."

"What kind of deal?"

"If you plead guilty to first-degree murder, he'll recommend life in prison with no parole. You avoid the death penalty."

"That's it?" Mark asked, incredulous. "That's his offer?"

"Yes."

"And now you think I should take it, right? I lied to you, so I deserve to spend the rest of my life in solitary confinement? Is that where we are now?"

"No, it's not," said Jack, looking his client in the eye. "I'm sorry, all right? Come sit down. My advice is to tell Oliver Boalt that the answer is no. Hell no, in fact."

Mark took a second to regain his composure. "Okay. Then that's what we'll do."

"Good," Jack said in a warmer tone. "Now try to get some rest tonight. We have a big day tomorrow."

CHAPTER 73

Andie and her undercover boyfriend were alone in their tent. The entry flaps and vents were zipped shut for privacy, and inside it was totally dark. A burning lantern or flashlight would have thrown their shadows against the nylon, enabling passersby to see what they were really up to.

"Can you feel it?" Andie whispered.

After Steger's speech, Agent Ferguson had left the campsite to update his field contact. An hour later he'd returned with new instructions. If "something big" was going to happen in the next twenty-four hours, as Steger had promised, then Ferguson and Andie had until morning to find out what it was. It was Andie's job to wire up and get someone from the Alliance to talk about it.

"No," said Ferguson. His hand was on her back, resting right on the covert body wire transmitter that Andie had planted under her sweater. Andie had worn a wire many times before, and she wasn't the only agent who claimed she could wire up in her sleep. Now she could add "in a dark tent."

"We're good to go," said Andie.

The rumble of motorcycles outside told Andie something was up. She went to see what was going on. About a dozen riders had loaded their gear. Most of them never wore helmets, but in the darkness Andie didn't recognize any of them. Her friend William walked past her, carrying a cooler.

"Where's everybody going?" asked Andie.

William stopped. "You didn't hear?"

Andie's boyfriend emerged from the tent. "No, we were just—you know."

William smiled a little, but it quickly faded. "Somebody tried to kill one of our men in Florida."

"Is he okay?"

"Dunno. But whoever did this won't be. Time to bust some heads. You two coming?"

"Where to?" asked Andie.

"Santa Fe River. South of Ichetucknee."

"Where, exactly?" asked Andie.

William gave her a look, and in the darkness Andie couldn't tell if it was one of annoyance or suspicion. *Shit, Henning, why don't you just ask him to please speak directly into the microphone?*

"Colt knows where," he said. "Just follow."

Andie and her partner exchanged glances. They were on the same page.

"Sure," said Andie. "Count us in."

CHAPTER 74

The viewing for Cynthia Porter was at Carter Funeral Home from 6:00 to 8:00 p.m. Jack double-checked the time in the obituaries and arrived just minutes before it ended.

The parking lot was full, and guests were milling about the lobby, but Jack quickly realized that they were there for the other viewing. People came and went from Parlor A, talking and greeting one another with the obligatory, "Good to see you, old friend, so sorry it's under these sad circumstances." There was none of that at the Cynthia Porter viewing. The double doors to Parlor B were wide open, welcoming guests, but all was quiet. Such was the memorial for an old woman who had outlived her husband, her friends, her siblings, and even her only child.

Jack entered and stopped just inside the doorway. He saw the closed metal casket at the head of the room. A mixed flower arrangement stood on a pedestal beside it. In the first row of chairs was the only visitor, an African American woman somewhere between the age of Jack and the deceased. She noticed his arrival, rose, and welcomed him.

"I'm Virginia. Mrs. Porter's caretaker."

"I'm—"

"I know who you are," she said. "Miz Cynthia and I watched the news together every night."

"I hope you don't mind my coming."

"Would you like to pay your respects?" she said, gesturing toward the casket.

"Um, sure," said Jack.

He hadn't planned his every move in advance, but this seemed like his opportunity. He reached inside his coat pocket and removed a printed copy of his letter from Cynthia.

"I'd be grateful if you would read this," he said, and he placed it in Virginia's hands.

Virginia seemed to recognize it. "I was right there in her kitchen when Ms. Porter wrote this to you."

"Have you read it?"

"No, sir. I put it in the mail for her."

"Read it, please," said Jack.

She didn't say she would, and Jack didn't give her time to say she wouldn't. He went to the casket and waited with his back to Virginia.

The framed photograph atop the closed casket was that of a beautiful young woman. In her sweet smile, however, Jack saw a tortured soul. Her heart had been a vault since childhood, holding the secret of her taboo affection for Willie James and then, for the rest of her life, the horrible secret of his murder. It was such a different world then, Jack would have liked to think, but then he thought of Shelly and Jamal, and it seemed that some differences were merely a matter of degree.

Jack turned, suddenly sensing that Virginia was standing behind him. Her eyes were dark, wet pools. Jack wasn't sure if the tears were for Willie James or Cynthia. Maybe both.

"Have you talked to Kelvin Cousin?" she asked.

Virginia had zeroed in on the issue at hand.

"No," said Jack. "I haven't been able to reach him, and I'm not sure he'd talk to me anyway. I'm the lawyer for the man accused of killing his great-grandson."

"He's in town for the trial, you know. The whole Cousin family is."

"That's what I understand." Jack didn't tell her about the nonverbal exchange between Kelvin and Shelly in the courtroom.

"I'm sure Miz Cynthia would not have mentioned Kelvin by name in her letter if it wasn't important to her."

"That's why I came to you. I was hoping—"

"That I would speak to Kelvin?"

Jack knew it was a lot to ask—to ask anyone to contact a member of the victim's family on his behalf—but he'd run out of viable alternatives. "Yes. Would you?"

Virginia looked toward the casket. "Miz Cynthia didn't really have a last wish. I guess this was it. So yes," she said, her gaze shifting back to Jack. "I will help you. If I can."

CHAPTER 75

Percy was near the river—which river, he had no idea. Moonlight glistened off black water made blacker by cover of night. He was deep in the wilderness, surrounded by scrub pine and cypress trees. No roads in sight. Not even a footpath. The shed in which he'd been held captive was adjacent to a small boathouse, accessible only by boat or off-road vehicle, though he'd seen neither since his escape. He walked as far as he could with his ankles shackled. When he reached what felt like a safe distance from the shed, he stopped along the riverbank to cut through the chain.

This river looked wider than what he remembered of the Ichetucknee, but maybe that was because he was farther downriver. Or maybe it was another river entirely. Maybe he wasn't even in Florida anymore. Who knew? He had to break the chain, or he might well die in the middle of nowhere. He decided that one cut in the middle would be easier than two at each ankle, even if it did mean dragging around a length of rattling chain from each foot. He worked furiously. Cutting through the wood stud in the shed had been easier than this. He worried that the scrape of the hacksaw might carry all the way back to the shed. What if hatchet-head regained consciousness and came looking for him?

Should've killed him. Percy should have just split that fucking head in half when he'd had the chance. But that wasn't who Percy was.

Percy sawed faster. After twenty minutes of constant work, he was only halfway through the steel link. Sweat pasted his shirt to his body, and every muscle in his arm was burning. He fell back in the weeds, exhausted, and then in the moonlight spotted a large rock by the river. He tossed the hacksaw aside and crawled on hands and knees to the rock. Taking the hatchet from the shed had been a good idea. With one well-placed chop—a direct hit to the weakened link—he was free.

Yes!

He was a new man. Chains still dangled from his ankles and wrists, but he could run now, if he had to—had he known where he was going. Heading back in the direction of the shed wasn't an option. He continued downriver along the bank. His eyes were well adjusted to the night, but even so he walked straight into low-hanging branches. Several jabbed him hard enough to break the skin and draw blood. He soldiered on, but he was growing weaker. He'd burned more calories in the last two hours than he'd consumed in the last—how long was it? Five days? More?

Hatchet-head had told him that the FBI was in the area. He was tempted to call out for help, but again he worried that a gang of racists might answer him. What he needed was perspective—a view from above to get the lay of the land. A poplar tree ahead looked suitable. He pulled himself up and climbed until the limbs were no longer big enough to support his weight. The forest was overgrown, so he didn't get much of a view, but he swore he saw a light burning a few hundred yards ahead.

A campsite, maybe?

Percy climbed down from the tree. At ground level he could no longer see the light through the forest, but he had his general bearings. He would approach with caution, but the rattle of his chains would make it hard to go unnoticed. He started through the brush, walking in what he thought was the right direction. Just ahead, he saw the light again, but it wasn't a campsite. It was a shack in a clearing, and the window was aglow. His pulse quickened as he moved toward it. He reached the clearing and stopped about twenty yards from the house. It was made of old, unpainted pine and had a sagging tin roof. There couldn't have been more than two or three rooms inside. The light in the window flickered, which told him that it was probably from a kerosene lamp. There were no power lines connected to the house, so if it had electricity, it was from a generator, which definitely wasn't running at the moment. The night was completely still, quiet enough for Percy to hear the whoosh of the flowing river.

Percy took another step forward and then stopped short, realizing that he was standing amid a plot of grave markers. Eight dead O'Connells, the oldest born in 1909. Someone had lived in this shack a long time.

Someone was still living there.

"Ben!" a woman shouted from inside the house. "There's a nigger in our yard!"

"What?" Ben grumbled.

"And he's wearin' shackles! Must've escaped from a chain gang!"

Percy wanted to shout out in his own defense, *No, no, you've got it all wrong! I need help!*

The front door flew open, and out came big Ben, armed with a shotgun.

"No!" Percy screamed, but the blast of the shotgun followed.

Percy was hit in the leg—how many times, he didn't know, but it was bad enough to knock him to the ground. His thigh burned, and the pain made him dizzy, but he pushed himself from the ground and made one last plea.

"Don't shoot!"

"You got ten seconds to git off my land!"

"Okay, be cool, I—"

He was silenced by the unmistakable sound of a shotgun racking. Percy turned and raced across the clearing toward the river. Arms pumping and chains rattling, he ran through the pain. Another blast of the shotgun cut through the night. Percy was at full speed when he launched himself from the bank, diving headfirst and disappearing into the river as the buckshot flew overhead. He forced himself to stay under as long as he could, swimming in total darkness. It seemed like forever, but he was without air for only a minute. When he surfaced, the light from the shack was a fuzzy little ball way upriver. The current had done most of the work for him, taking him to safety.

Percy rolled over and floated on his back, staring up at the stars. The cold water felt good on his leg wound. Hypothermia was possible, he knew, not to mention shock. He needed to swim ashore. But he let himself have this moment. He didn't know where the river was taking him, but he knew what was behind him. The current was his friend.

His only friend.

CHAPTER 76

"You can come in, Jack," said Virginia.

Jack was standing in the hallway outside Kelvin Cousin's hotel room, and Virginia was inside, holding the door open. The media had reported that Jamal's parents were staying at a private residence with friends of Leroy Highsmith, but the extended family—uncles, aunts, grandparents, and Great-grandfather Kelvin—were at the Hampton Inn. Virginia had contacted him as Cynthia Porter's caretaker and taken him the letter. Jack had been waiting almost thirty minutes.

"He'll talk to me?" asked Jack.

"Yes."

Jack entered and Virginia closed the door. The room was a suite for business travelers, and Kelvin was in the living area beyond the kitchenette, seated in an overstuffed armchair. He reached for his walking cane as Jack approached.

"Don't get up, please," said Jack.

Kelvin Cousin nodded in appreciation of the reprieve from etiquette. The men shook hands, and Jack expressed how grateful he was for the chance to talk to someone who knew something about Willie James Howard.

"What I know is secondhand, you understand," said Kelvin, speaking in a voice that cracked with age.

"Who told you about Willie James?"

"Cynthia Porter. She called the Florida State Conference for the NAACP. I worked there and was the only one in the office that day. I answered the phone."

"When was this?"

"Oh, I'd say nineteen fifty. Fifty-one, maybe. She said there was something she wanted to get off her chest."

"What did she tell you?"

Kelvin reached for the letter Virginia had shared with him. "Everything she wrote right here. It was not a quick phone call. Talked almost an hour, as I recall. She told the whole story."

"What did you do?"

"I listened. Took notes. Then when the call was over, I typed it all up."

"Do you still have those notes?"

"No, sir. I sent them to the governor's office."

"Why there?"

"I knew there'd be no justice in Live Oak. So I wrote to the governor. Bad mistake."

"I presume it went nowhere," said Jack.

Kelvin shook his head. "Worse than that. They must have come down on Cynthia like a ton of bricks."

"Did she withdraw her statement?"

He nodded slowly, an empty expression in his eyes. "I spoke to Cynthia one more time after that. I can't remember if I called her or she called me. But I won't forget her words. She said, 'You and I never talked. Leave it be.' And that was the end of it."

"There was no investigation?"

"No. One of our local NAACP officers in Mims tried to get something going. There was talk of going to the Justice Department, but this was years before the civil rights movement. No federal jurisdiction. Nothing ever came of it."

"Did you ever tell anyone about it?"

"Sure did. Just about everybody I told is dead now. Even Jamal."

"You told Jamal about Willie James?"

"Yes, sir."

Jack wished he would stop calling him "sir." "How did that come about?"

"I was in Gainesville to see him sworn in as Alpha president. Afterward, I sat down with him and Brandon."

"Brandon Wall?"

"That's right. Brandon was the outgoing president, Jamal was the new one. I wanted to tell them how proud I was of both of them, and how important it is for black fraternities to have leaders like them. You know, there's folks who say the Divine Nine are a thing of the past. Used to be that black fraternities produced all our important leaders. Martin Luther King. Thurgood Marshall. That's changing. Barack and Michelle Obama, Obama's attorney general, the last three black men elected to the U.S. Senate—not one of 'em was in a black Greek-letter organization."

"How did that conversation lead to Willie James?"

"At some point Brandon asked me, 'How do you feel about the president of a black fraternity having a white girlfriend?'"

"He meant Jamal?"

"When he asked the question, I didn't know if he meant Jamal or himself. But it wouldn't have changed my answer."

"What did you say?"

"I told them I felt no different than I would about any black man with a white girlfriend. I said be careful. See, when you get to my age, and you realize how fast the years pass, it really isn't *that* long ago that a black man could be lynched over a white woman. So I told them about Willie James."

"You told both Jamal and Brandon?"

"Yes, I did."

"When was that?"

"September. Not but two months ago."

Kelvin's gaze drifted away. Jack couldn't tell if the old man was taking a moment to remember that time "not but two months ago" when his great-grandson was alive with so much to live for, or if he was just getting tired.

"Do you have any more questions, Mr. Swyteck?" asked Virginia.

Her clear implication was that it was time to leave Kelvin alone.

Jack rose and thanked him. Virginia asked if there was anything Kelvin needed before they left, but he assured her that he didn't. He was sharing the suite with his nephew, who would put him to bed upon returning from dinner.

"I don't know what you intend to do about all this," said Kelvin. "But I'm hoping I did the right thing."

Jack shook his hand and said, "You did."

CHAPTER 77

Andie rode past midnight, nonstop, until they reached the river. There were eight in her group, including herself and Agent Ferguson. Andie took comfort in knowing that the GPS chip in her transmitter kept their FBI contact apprised of their exact location.

"We need a boat," said Colt.

Andie hoped that the tech agent monitoring her body wire transmissions caught that remark. Confirmation arrived in less than thirty seconds.

"Let's head this way," Ferguson told the group. "There's private property upriver. We can probably borrow a boat."

Everyone knew what he meant by "borrow." Only Andie knew that his intelligence had come directly from their FBI contact. Agents were in the area, and it made Andie feel safer to know that a team would swoop in if something went wrong. But she also understood that time was running out for her to get one of these Alliance members to say something solid to implicate Steger in the abduction of Percy Donovan.

"What do we do with the bikes?" asked William.

"Paulette can stay here and watch them," said Colt. He meant Andie.

"No," said Ferguson. "She goes with me."

"I'll stay," said one of the old guys. "My back's killing me anyway."

The group of seven set off, heading up the pathway along the river. Ferguson's intelligence had been spot-on. In less than five minutes they came upon a house on private property. A flats boat was moored to a pier that jutted out into the river.

"Bingo," said Colt.

Andie went with the flow. Technically speaking, an undercover agent's participation in a felony—grand larceny—required prior approval. This one had to fall under the "exigent circumstances" exception. They climbed aboard. Colt made short work of the combination lock and pushed away from the pier. The current carried them downriver, and when they were far enough away from the owner's house, Colt started the engine. Soon they were at full throttle, throwing a V-shaped wake against the riverbanks. The tall cypress trees were mere silhouettes, their moss-clad limbs barely visible against the starlit sky. A thin blanket of fog stretched across the river. The speedboat cut through it like a laser through cotton candy.

Suddenly, Colt killed the engine. The boat drifted silently downriver.

"Listen," he said.

There was a hum in the air.

"Is that another boat?" asked William.

"Or a helicopter," said Colt. "Cops must be searching. They must know he escaped."

"Who?" asked Andie.

She was trying to get him to say "Percy," but her question was answered only with a suspicious glare.

"The boogey man," said Colt.

"Should we turn back?" asked William.

"No," said Colt, still looking at Andie. "We keep going. And we find the boogey man. Before they do."

CHAPTER 78

Jack was in the courtroom early, well before the *Arthur* hearing was scheduled to reconvene.

Brandon Wall was shaping up to be the hearing's most important witness. Jack had worked late into the night preparing for his cross-examination. He understood that tone would be as important as substance, and he hoped that his early arrival, while things were relatively quiet, would help his thoughts gel.

Oliver Boalt arrived early as well. He walked straight to Jack's side of the courtroom and laid the crime lab's final report on the table in front of him.

"Testing on the Croc is completed," said Boalt.

"What's the bottom line?" asked Jack.

"No DNA match to Mark Towson or Baine Robinson."

Jack played it cool, as if he'd known all along that no other result was possible. "Whose DNA is it?"

"We don't know. It's obviously someone whose DNA isn't in any available database."

That wasn't bad news, but it wasn't the case-breaking development that Jack had hoped for. "Do you plan to introduce the report into evidence, or shall I?" asked Jack.

"I've already delivered it to Judge Teague's chambers, along with a letter explaining how these findings are consistent with our theory of the case."

"Consistent with *your* theory?"

"Yes," Boalt said with a completely straight face. "It has been my suspicion all along that there was a third conspirator in the lynching of Jamal Cousin."

"There's no allegation of a third conspirator in your indictment," said Jack.

"That will change if and when the third conspirator is identified. Until then, we will proceed against your client on the assumption that there is an unindicted co-conspirator." Boalt turned and walked to his table.

Jack opened the report. The DNA test results were obviously helpful to the defense, no matter how Boalt tried to spin them to Jack, the media, or the judge. But Boalt was right not to panic. It was common for conspiracy cases to proceed against a named defendant and his unidentified, unnamed partners in crime.

Jack opened the written report. The most important matter at hand was the cross-examination of Brandon at 9:00 a.m., but he had time to skim. The results were as the prosecutor had stated. What Jack found almost as interesting, however, was the introductory section of the report. It was standard for an examiner to explain how the Croc had been located, collected, and taken to the lab for testing. Jack had been aware that it was a group of volunteers from the Divine Nine that had found the Croc and alerted the police. Until now, however—until seeing the name in black and white in the forensic report—Jack had been unaware of the exact fraternity brother who had actually found the Croc. It surprised him at first. And then his thoughts, which had been so unsettled all night, finally started to fall into place.

"I'll be damned," he said, reading the name one more time.

It was Brandon Wall.

CHAPTER 79

Percy was deep in chilly river water. It was high tide, or close to it. Percy had found the strength to swim ashore, but the soggy bank that was his refuge had slowly disappeared beneath the rising river. He needed higher land, or he could die of hypothermia.

Percy tried to stand but couldn't. It wasn't just exhaustion. The leg wound from the buckshot was worse than he'd first thought. He'd tied his shirt around his thigh to try to stanch the bleeding, but he was still losing blood, his life draining out of him.

Not gonna die. Not here. Not now.

Percy floated on his belly, moving like an alligator toward a log on the flooded riverbank. His hands stirred up the sediment below, but he couldn't really feel anything. His fingertips had gone numb. He made it to the log and stopped, searching for the strength to pull himself up. It was dark beneath the leafy canopy, but Percy could see patches of sky. The stars were fading. The glow of sunrise was near. If he could slither like a gator, he could sun himself atop a log like one, too. He reached up, grabbed hold of a knot in the fallen cypress, and then stopped. He heard something. A whining in the distance.

A boat?

He listened more intensely. The steady noise was from upriver. Had it been from downriver, his spirits would have soared. Upriver could mean one of two things. Rescue. Or recapture.

First things first—survival.

He pulled with every ounce of strength, and the exertion made his leg throb as if he'd been shot all over again. But he worked through the pain, straining in the darkness, and managed to rest his chest atop the log. He lay there for a moment, legs dangling into the water, his body soaking wet. The night air was colder than the water, but he had faith that the sun would rise again. He had faith.

The whining noise grew louder. His expenditure of energy, just climbing onto the log, had left his mind fuzzy. He struggled to focus. The sound was unmistakable. A motor.

Definitely a boat.

He found the strength to turn his head, his right cheek atop the cypress bark and one eye on the river. He didn't know if the police were looking for him. But if it was a police boat or a park ranger, he would call out to them. If he could find a voice.

Hang on.

Percy lay perfectly still, fighting to keep his eyes and ears open as the boat drew closer.

CHAPTER 80

Mr. Swyteck," said the judge. "You may proceed with cross-examination of the witness. Mr. Wall, you are reminded that you are still under oath."

The courtroom was silent as Jack rose and approached.

Less than twenty-four hours had passed since Brandon's testimony. The courtroom was just as packed, and the tension was equally high. But so much had changed, at least from Jack's perspective—not only about the case, but also the way he saw Brandon Wall. The transformation had started with the prosecutor's final line of questions, when Brandon had identified Mrs. Towson as the reason Shelly and Jamal had kept their relationship a secret. Since Jack's meeting with Kelvin Cousin, little things had been falling into place, and the picture continued to come clear as he stepped toward the witness.

"Good morning, Mr. Wall," he said cordially.

"Morning," said Brandon.

"You were the president of the Alpha house last year, correct?"

"Yes."

"You're very proud of being an Alpha?"

"I am."

"You're proud of the traditions and values of the Alpha fraternity?"

"Of course."

"As a former president, you feel an obligation to uphold those traditions and values?"

"Yes."

"Is it fair to say that you think other Alpha brothers have the same obligation?"

"That's a fair statement."

"That's especially true if we're talking about the president of the fraternity."

"I suppose."

"The president should lead by example. Do you agree?"

"I—yeah, sure."

"You would agree that one of those values is truthfulness. An Alpha president should be truthful?"

The prosecutor rose. "Objection, Your Honor. The witness has already sworn to tell the truth, so I don't see the point of any of this."

Jack looked at the judge and said, "He will see the point, Your Honor."

"Overruled," the judge said. "The witness may answer."

"Yes, an Alpha president should be truthful," said Brandon.

"Yesterday, Mr. Boalt asked you if you had ever told anyone about the relationship between Jamal Cousin and Shelly Towson. You answered, 'Never.' That was your testimony, correct?"

"I believe so."

Jack turned and slowly walked toward the rail. Kelvin Cousin was seated at the end of the first row, behind the prosecutor's table. With his gaze, Jack guided Brandon's line of sight in Kelvin's direction.

"You've met Jamal's great-grandfather, Kelvin Cousin, have you not, Mr. Wall?"

Brandon glanced in the old man's direction, acknowledging him. "I have."

"You met when Jamal was sworn in as new president, correct?"

"Yes."

"He spoke privately to you and Jamal and said how proud he was of you as Alpha presidents. Is that right?"

"Yes, something like that."

"He told you how important it was that young men like you were continuing the traditions and values of the Alpha fraternity?" Jack glanced again at Kelvin, as if sending a message to Brandon.

"He did," said Brandon.

"At some point in that same conversation, you asked him how he would feel about the Alpha president dating a white woman. You asked him that question, right?"

Brandon didn't answer right away. Again Jack cut a glance in Kelvin's direction, sending the message to Brandon.

"I believe I did ask him that question," said Brandon.

"Kelvin expressed some concern about it, did he not?"

"Yes, but his concern was that dating a white woman might not be as safe as we thought it was."

"Let's talk about that a little more," said Jack. "Does the name Willie James Howard mean anything to you, Mr. Wall?"

The prosecutor rose as if shot from a cannon. "Objection, Your Honor. This is going way beyond the scope of direct examination, and I can't see how it has any relevance to this case."

Jack detected a hint of urgency in the prosecutor's voice.

"Judge, I'm not sure how Mr. Boalt would know if it's relevant even before we've established who Willie James Howard is," said Jack.

The prosecutor looked pale. "Judge, may we discuss this in your chambers, please?"

Judge Teague seemed confused by the request, but Boalt's demeanor and tone of voice made it clear that, if the state attorney's years of service to the people of Suwannee County meant anything, Judge Teague would grant him this favor.

"All right," the judge said. "Counsel, in my chambers."

The judge stepped down from the bench, and the courtroom waited in silence as the lawyers followed him into his chambers. Over the next ten minutes, the story of Willie James Howard unfolded. Oliver Boalt denied any awareness of it. It was Jack's impression that he denied it a little too forcefully.

"Judge, we don't even know if this Willie James actually existed," Boalt said finally. "This story could be nothing but a story."

The judge pondered it. "Mr. Swyteck, really, what is the point of dredging up all this history?"

"Your Honor—" Jack started to say, but Boalt cut him off.

"Clearly Mr. Swyteck's point is that just about anybody could have lynched Jamal Cousin because we're all a bunch of racists here in north Florida. I suppose the next thing we'll see from him and his friends in *My-amma* is a warrant to search Your Honor's closet for a white robe and a cross-burning kit."

"That's not my point at all," said Jack.

Judge Teague raised his arms like a boxing referee, silencing the lawyers. "Here's my decision. At this point, I will allow Mr. Swyteck to establish that Kelvin Cousin told Brandon Wall and Jamal Cousin a story about a black teenager who was lynched for sending love letters to a white girl. Beyond that, Mr. Swyteck, I'm keeping you on a short leash. I will not allow you to turn this hearing into a racial indictment of Live Oak in the nineteen forties. Is that clear?"

Jack clung to the fact that the judge had prefaced his ruling with the words "at this point." There was work to do. But if the cross-examination of Brandon Wall proceeded as hoped, Jack was confident that Judge Teague would come around, even if Oliver Boalt did seem to deny the very existence of Willie James Howard.

"It's clear, Judge," said Jack.

CHAPTER 81

The river glistened with the first glint of the morning sun. Percy saw the flats boat approaching. It was white. So were the men on board. Percy felt his pulse quicken. He no longer had the full cover of night. He wondered if they could see him lying atop the log along the riverbank.

The engine ceased. There was silence.

"What the fuck is that?" asked one of the boaters, his voice carrying all the way to Percy.

Percy didn't move. He lay there, motionless, and watched. The boat was in daylight, but Percy was in the forested wetland, still shrouded in predawn semidarkness.

Suddenly, a spotlight hit him straight in the eyes, blinding him. The beam swept his body from head to toe and then back again.

"Well," the man said, "if that ain't the ugliest fucking gator I ever did see."

Percy pushed himself off the log and splashed into the cold swamp below. The spotlight followed him. The engine restarted. Percy could touch bottom, but he couldn't run. He half swam and half walked, trying to escape. The boat drew closer. The spotlight bore down on him like a falling meteor.

"Hard to port!" the skipper shouted.

Percy was getting nowhere—worse than nowhere. He was chest-deep in water, knee-deep in muck. The boat was nearly on him. A rope hit him in the face. A lasso closed around his neck.

"Got him!"

Freeze, FBI!" Andie shouted. She was aboard the boat, her pistol aimed at Colt's chest. Ferguson drew his weapon, too.

"You're surrounded by law enforcement," said Andie.

"That so?" said Colt. "Then where the fuck are they?"

Andie was beginning to wonder the same thing, but she didn't flinch. "Are you Percy Donovan?" she shouted, plenty loud for Percy to hear her.

"Yeah."

"Go ahead and take that rope off your neck. Are you hurt?"

"Yeah," said Percy, as he removed the lasso. "Got shot in the leg. I'm bleeding."

Andie repeated his words to make sure Percy's condition was transmitted by her body wire.

"We'll need medical—" she continued, but suddenly the engine roared, and the boat lunged forward. Ferguson tumbled overboard with the four other men at the bow. Another tackled Andie, her gun discharged, and he went down with a thud. Colt came at her. The fight for her weapon was a rematch of the campsite free-for-all as the boat sped straight down the river with no one behind the wheel.

CHAPTER 82

The courtroom was equal parts media and general public as Judge Teague led the lawyers from his chambers. Jack took his position in front of the witness, and the state attorney returned to his seat at the prosecutor's table. The judge explained his decision from the bench.

"Mr. Wall, you are allowed to answer the following question: Did Kelvin Cousin tell you and Jamal about the alleged lynching of a black teenager named Willie James Howard?"

Brandon leaned closer to the microphone and said, "Yes, he did."

Boalt rose. "Just to clarify the record, Your Honor. Am I correct in saying that the court is not accepting this testimony as proof that a man named Willie James Howard was actually lynched?"

"That's correct," the judge said. "The testimony is admitted only to show that the witness heard the story."

Jack searched the gallery and found Kelvin. He'd struck Jack as an even-tempered man in their meeting, but it had clearly angered him that the judge and the prosecutor had reduced the murder of Willie James Howard to a "story."

Jack continued. "Mr. Wall, what Mr. Cousin told you about Willie James Howard scared you, didn't it?"

"I'd say it opened our eyes," said Brandon.

"But it didn't stop Jamal from seeing Shelly Towson, did it?"

"No."

"You worried about Jamal, didn't you?"

"A little."

"You worried not only because Jamal was black, but also because he was the president of the Alpha house, a black fraternity, right?"

"That was part of it."

"But the biggest reason to worry—and I want you to be totally honest, speaking as a former Alpha president—wasn't your biggest worry of all the fact that Shelly Towson's brother was the president of the Theta house?"

"I don't think that really mattered."

It *had* mattered—Jack was sure of it. He just needed to find a way to get the witness to admit it. Jack retrieved the transcript from Mark's disciplinary hearing.

"Mr. Wall, you were a witness at Mr. Towson's student conduct hearing at the University of Florida, were you not?"

"I was."

"You told the committee about the time that Baine Robinson hired you to serve as bartender at a fraternity party, am I right?"

"I did."

"You quit before the party started, right?"

"Yes."

"You quit because Mr. Robinson wanted you to serve a cocktail made with watermelon liqueur—a drink called 'Strange Fruit'?"

"Yes."

"You quit because you thought it was racist, correct?"

"I think almost anyone would see it as racist," said Brandon.

"Agreed," said Jack. "And still another reference to 'strange fruit' came in the text message we've heard so much about. Can we agree that was a racist message?"

"Absolutely."

"And Jamal told you that he'd received two other messages just like it. One from Theta brother Baine Robinson and the other from Theta brother Cooper Bartlett, correct?"

"Yes."

"Mr. Wall, is it fair to say that, after those messages, you'd heard and seen enough to believe that the brothers of the Theta Pi Omega fraternity were racists?"

"At least some of them, definitely."

"And even though you *believed* the Theta brothers were racists, you *knew* that Jamal Cousin was not going to stop seeing Shelly Towson. Isn't that right, Mr. Wall?"

"I don't think I knew that."

"Well, let's go back to your testimony from yesterday," said Jack. "Jamal asked you to make sure all the Alpha brothers went on the tubing trip down the Ichetucknee so that Jamal could be alone in the house with Shelly Towson. That was your testimony, right?"

Brandon squirmed a little, but it was in the transcript, undeniable. "Right."

"So you *knew* that the president of the Alpha house was going to continue to see Shelly Towson, right?"

"Yeah, I knew."

"And you believed that Shelly's brother had sent a racist text to Jamal."

"Right."

"And you believed that her brother's friends had sent a racist text to Jamal?"

"Right."

"And you had not forgotten that Baine Robinson had asked you to serve 'strange fruit' cocktails at a frat party, had you?"

"No, I didn't forget."

Jack paused, but only for effect. "You had a problem with that. Didn't you, Mr. Wall?"

"I don't know if—"

"Objection."

"I'll rephrase," said Jack. "Jamal Cousin, the president of the most prestigious black Greek-letter organization on campus, was dating a white woman whose brother was the president of a racist fraternity. As a former Alpha president, you had a problem with that. Didn't you, Mr. Wall?"

"I—I didn't like it."

"You wanted the relationship to end, didn't you?"

"I would have preferred it if Jamal stopped seeing her, yeah."

That was good enough. Jack had established the platform he needed to launch the final strike.

"A week after the text messages, Jamal Cousin's body was found on the Ichetucknee River, correct?"

"That's my understanding."

"That's all I'm asking for, Mr. Wall, is your understanding. In fact, I'd like to compare your understanding of what happened to Jamal Cousin to what Kelvin Cousin told you about Willie James Howard."

"Judge," said Boalt, groaning, "I object to this—"

"Overruled."

Judge Teague seemed to understand where Jack was headed. Jack took it as a green light.

"Right before his death," said Jack, "Willie James Howard wrote love letters to a white girl. Correct?"

"That's what Mr. Cousin told us."

"Jamal had a white girlfriend at the time of his death, correct?"

"Yes."

"The men who murdered Willie James took him to the river?"

"Right."

"Jamal was found on the river?"

"Yes."

"The men who murdered Willie James bound his hands and feet. Hog-tied him, right?"

"Yes."

"Jamal was also hog-tied?"

"I don't—"

"You *know* that," said Jack, allowing no wiggle room. "You've seen those awful photographs, have you not?"

"Yes, I've seen them."

"Willie James was thrown in the river and drowned?"

"Yes."

"Jamal Cousin may or may not have drowned."

"I don't know."

"I think you do."

"Objection," said Boalt.

"That one is sustained," the judge said.

Brandon was in desperate need of a break, but Jack forged ahead. He went to his table and retrieved the crime lab report he'd received from the state attorney that morning. He was down to his last round of ammunition.

"Mr. Wall, you were part of a civilian search party that went looking for Percy Donovan after his disappearance, were you not?"

"I was."

"You didn't find Percy, but you did find a foam resin shoe, correct?"

"I did."

Jack handed the report to the witness—not for him to read it, but just to set up his question. "Would it surprise you to hear that a forensic examination confirmed that the shoe you found is the mate to the foam resin shoe that was found near Jamal's body?"

"I don't know how to answer that."

Jack took the report back from him. "Mr. Wall, how big an area did you and the other volunteers search?"

"There were two teams on each side of the river. We walked a couple of miles, I'd say. Maybe more."

"How many volunteers were there?"

"Maybe seventy-five."

"So there were seventy-five volunteers searching four linear miles of riverbank, and it was *you* who happened to find the shoe. Is that right?"

"Yeah."

"You zeroed right in on it, I guess?"

"I found it."

Jack took a step closer, his gaze tightening. "You found it because you knew it was there."

Brandon swallowed hard. "That's not true."

"You found it right where you lost it on the night of Jamal's death."

"That's absurd."

"Objection."

"Sustained."

Jack handed the report to the witness, this time opening it to the appropriate page.

"Look at page five of the report, Mr. Wall. This Croc wasn't found in black water. The environmental conditions that destroyed all DNA on the first Croc didn't exist. This one—the mate you found—has DNA on it. Do you see where it states that in the report?"

Brandon studied the page. The report shook in his hand.

"Brandon," said Jack, deliberately using his first name and a softer tone. "Should I hire a scientist to test that Croc for *your* DNA? Or do you want to tell us the truth here and now?"

Brandon stared at the report, his hand shaking. The prosecutor could have objected, but there was only silence, as if everyone in the courtroom knew that the truth was nigh.

"Brandon," said Jack, nudging a little more. "You 'found' the Croc because if you didn't, one of those seventy-five other volunteers would. Did you think it would look better if you found it? Or did you think you could explain why your DNA was on it by saying that you touched it when you found it?"

Finally, Brandon looked up, his voice quaking. "He suffocated."

"Jamal suffocated?"

He nodded, looking past Jack as he spoke, a vacant expression in his eyes. "We were just trying to scare him. When I opened the trunk, Jamal was dead."

An Alpha brother jumped to his feet in the crowd. "Brandon, don't!"

Judge Teague gaveled down the interruption and then spoke directly to the witness. "Mr. Wall, under the Constitution of the United States you have no further obligation to answer Mr. Swyteck's questions. You have the right to say nothing until you've consulted with legal counsel."

Jack heard what the judge was saying, but he stood dumbfounded, as his own interpretation of a night gone terribly wrong played out like a movie in his mind. A blindfolded Jamal with his mouth taped shut. The Alpha brothers shoving him in a stuffy trunk. The hourlong car ride to the river. The trunk popping open and Brandon's horrified discovery that Jamal had suffocated. The panic over a possible arrest and prison sentence for all the brothers involved, not to mention the disgrace to befall the Alpha house. And someone—Brandon—coming up with a surefire way to divert law enforcement's attention from any involvement of a black fraternity: a staged lynching, inspired by the true story of Willie James Howard.

"I think I need a lawyer," said Brandon.

"Bailiff, please take Mr. Wall into custody," the judge said.

Jack watched in near disbelief as the bailiff cuffed Brandon on the witness stand. A silenced courtroom watched, riveted, as Brandon was escorted to the prisoner's exit—the side door that, an hour earlier, Jack's client had used to enter the courtroom.

"Mr. Towson, please rise," the judge said.

Jack stood beside his trembling client. The judge was looking straight at them, his expression stone-cold serious.

"The defendant's request for pretrial release is granted," Judge Teague said. "The state attorney's office has until five o'clock tomorrow to explain by written memorandum why the indictment should not be dismissed. By order of this court, Mr. Towson is released on his own recognizance without the requirement of bail. We are adjourned," he announced, ending the proceedings with a bang of his gavel.

"All rise!" said the bailiff.

Jack felt his client leaning on him, almost unable to stand.

"I'm out of jail?" Mark whispered.

"Yes," Jack said.

Mark was on the verge of tears. Jack shared his client's relief, but it was hard to feel joy in a situation that remained tragic. On the other side of the courtroom, Jamal's parents looked numb, clinging to each other, struggling to work through the senselessness of it all. The judge retired to his chambers, and the media rushed to the rail.

"Mr. Swyteck, do you admit that your client is a racist?"

Jack didn't respond. Instead, he let his client have a moment with his parents. But that first question from the media, and a slew of others that followed, was a quick reminder that it would take more than the dismissal of a murder indictment to find justice in this case. Jack had more work to do for his client.

And for Willie James.

CHAPTER 83

Andie was locked in battle as the driverless boat sped down the river. The pistol was in her grip, and with her other hand she tried to shove Colt's nose into his skull. Colt twisted free and slammed her forearm against the wheel, but before he could gain control, the boat cut left at nearly ninety degrees, tossing them overboard. The gun flew out of Andie's hand and splashed into the river a split second before she did. The boat slammed into a tree on the riverbank as she popped to the surface and gasped for air.

Andie looked left and right, scanning the surface for any sign of Colt. He grabbed her from below and pulled her under. Andie kicked herself free, resurfaced, and then dived for her weapon. It was too dark in the depths to see anything, and the current had already carried them fifty yards downriver. The gun was gone.

Colt surfaced like a breaching great white and came down on Andie. She clawed his face and kicked with her knees. He was on top, sucking air and water. Andie was below, getting water only. The current was taking them faster and faster downriver. Andie was inhaling water by the mouthful as they slammed into a buoy. Andie grabbed the chain that tethered it to the riverbed and kicked herself free.

Colt continued alone downriver. The current was strong enough to give Andie a fight, but she held on. She saw Colt splashing ahead, his arms flailing. Andie glanced up at the buoy and immediately realized where they were. She'd studied the rivers for this assignment and had been warned about this stretch of the Santa Fe, where the river literally disappeared underground and didn't resurface for another three miles. A few swimmers and canoers had gone down here. None had ever been known to resurface downstream at River Rise Preserve State Park.

Andie caught her breath, clinging tightly to the buoy, fighting through a pain in her kidney that was unlike any she'd felt before. She tried to ignore it, focusing her attention downriver. Colt waved his arms in one last act of desperation. Then he disappeared, sucked down into the dark, watery labyrinth of the Florida Aquifer.

"Good riddance," Andie said, keeping an ear out for an FBI boat or helicopter, gritting out that pain in her lower left back—which wasn't getting any better. It was getting worse. Much worse.

CHAPTER 84

Jack stopped on the courthouse steps, his client at his side as he delivered a very brief statement for a headline-hungry media.

"We're grateful that the truth has come out. Mark Towson is not a murderer, and now the long journey begins to restore his reputation. We express our condolences to the Cousin family and pray for the safe return of Percy Donovan. Thank you very much."

"Percy Donovan is alive and well," a reporter shouted. "Do you have any comment?"

Mark stepped forward. "Thank God," he said.

"Thank you all," said Jack.

He could have said more, but he was content to let the media—every vestige of the media—grill the state attorney. Jack and his client caught a snippet as they struggled to make their way down the crowded courthouse steps.

"Mr. Boalt," a reporter shouted, "does this mean that the third Croc—the burned one found in Baine Robinson's closet—was planted evidence?"

"Not at all," said the state attorney. "It turns out that the UF bookstore has sold over ten thousand pairs of 'Gator Blue' Crocs. So the fact that the charred remains of Mr. Robinson's Crocs were the same color as the ones found on the river is no big coincidence. Funny, I know, but true."

Yeah, funny, thought Jack, as they kept walking. *Fucking hilarious.*

The media followed him all the way to the curb. Mark's parents were in the front seat of the family car, waiting. He and Mark climbed into the back seat and closed the doors without another word. Oliver Boalt was still running his mouth on the courthouse steps, desperately trying to salvage his reelection, as the Towson car pulled away from the curb. No one said anything at first, as if Mark and his parents were still absorbing what had just happened. Then Mark had a question.

"What will happen to Brandon?" he asked.

Jack likened it to a hazing prank gone horribly wrong. "Involuntary manslaughter, I would think. A year in prison, at worst. Probation if he's lucky. Same for any of the Alpha brothers who helped him."

Jack's cell rang as they reached the intersection. It was Virginia.

"Mr. Swyteck? Would you have time to stop by Miz Porter's house today?"

"Sure," said Jack. "What's this about?"

"I've been sorting through Miz Porter's things. I found something you might want to see. It has to do with Willie James."

Pine Avenue was a quiet, tree-lined street right around the corner from the courthouse. The houses were from a bygone era of porch swings and flower-filled window boxes. Boalt had clearly worked the neighborhood, with yard signs aplenty calling for the reelection of the state attorney. The Towson family waited on the porch as Virginia took Jack into the parlor. He took a seat at Cynthia's antique secretary. Virginia laid an old file folder on the desktop in front of him.

"Where did you find this?" asked Jack.

"Upstairs," she said. "It was in a box in Miz Porter's closet with some other legal things."

Jack opened the file. Inside was a one-page document, typewritten. The "e" key bled too much ink, so holes blotted the paper like pips on a die. But the document was plainly legible. It was a sworn statement, including witness attestations. The signatory was A. Philip Goff.

"That's Miz Cynthia's father," said Virginia. "Goff was her maiden name."

Jack noted the date at the top—January 2, 1944—and then read it.

"On this day at eleven o'clock, two of my friends and myself went to the home of James Howard, where we found a colored boy by the name of Willie James Howard."

It read very much like the letter Jack had received from Cynthia. Jack wasn't skimming, but the words seemed to float before his eyes, as if it were the resurrection of a terrible nightmare: . . . *took Willie James in the car with us . . . drove to a place near Suwannee River . . . tied the boy's feet and hands to keep him from running so his father could whip him . . .*

Jack stopped. It wasn't the first time he'd read about it, but seeing it in this format, an old sworn statement, made it almost unbearable: . . . *the boy making the statement that he would die before he would take punishment from his father or anyone else made his way to the river where he jumped in and drowned himself.*

Jack gathered himself, then struggled through the next sentence. *His father stood by and viewed the son without preventing this happening.*

"They made him watch," said Jack, barely able to say it. "They took his father to the river and made him watch them drown his fifteen-year-old son."

Virginia stood in silence.

"This document," said Jack, disgusted, "this despicable lie that Willie James jumped in the river was clearly concocted by a lawyer. I'd like to know who—"

Virginia stopped him by placing another document in front of him. "This was the cover letter that was in the file with the sworn statement."

Jack stared down at cream-colored stationery. It was from the same typewriter, the blotted *e* apparent in almost every other word. The engraved letterhead was in Old English. Jack read the masthead aloud:

"Law Office of Oliver Boalt."

"His daddy," said Virginia.

It was suddenly crystal-clear why Oliver Boalt Jr. wanted Willie James Howard to be no part of Mark Towson's hearing—why he'd even gone so far as to tell the judge that there was "no evidence that a Willie James Howard ever existed, let alone was lynched."

"Did Cynthia show this to the state attorney?"

"I believe she did. I took her to his office. They talked in private."

"How did that go?"

"She was pretty upset when she came out."

"When was this?"

"About a week before she died."

Before she threw herself in the river.

Jack was the last person to hold someone accountable for the sins of the father. But the cover-up—years and years of cover-up—was as bad as the crime.

"Looks like the state attorney has even more explaining to do," said Jack.

Jack told the Towsons to head back to Gainesville without him. The state attorney's office was just a couple of blocks away, and it took Jack less time to walk there than to ride the old Otis elevator from the lobby to the second floor.

"Mr. Boalt is on the telephone," his secretary told Jack. She said it again as Jack blew past her, and she repeated it several more times as she chased him down the hallway, too slow to stop Jack from entering unannounced.

Boalt was at his desk, and he truly was on the phone. Jack dropped the file on his desk and flipped it open to reveal the letter from Oliver Boalt Sr.

"Your father wrote this?" Jack said, more of a statement than a question.

The state attorney stopped talking, still holding the phone as he examined Jack's personal delivery. "I'll call you back," he said, and then he laid the phone in the cradle. His secretary was standing in the doorway, horrified. "It's all right, Janice," said Boalt. "Hold my calls."

"Yes, sir." She closed the door on her way out, leaving the two men alone in the office.

"How long have you known?" Jack asked in a tone that was less than cordial.

Boalt glanced at his father's letter. "Too long."

"This isn't the first lynching to go unpunished," said Jack. "But there have been hundreds of atonement trials in this country. They're not just ceremonial. It's important to recognize the victim as a person and to call out the names of the murderers. Willie James Howard deserves that much."

Boalt didn't respond.

Jack retrieved the file and tucked it under his arm. "I'm taking this to the Southern Poverty Law Center in Montgomery," said Jack, "along with my request that they initiate an atonement trial."

Boalt stared down at his empty desktop a moment longer, then looked up. "Are you planning to do that before or after next Tuesday?"

The question nearly set Jack back on his heels. The election was on Tuesday.

"Rot in hell, Mr. Boalt." Jack headed for the door.

"Swyteck," said the state attorney.

Jack stopped and turned.

"I'm dismissing all charges against your client. Not only murder, but everything, including the text message. But I'm still charging Baine Robinson for sending that text. I think that's the just thing to do."

Jack tapped the file and said, "I'm still taking this to Montgomery before Tuesday. I think that's the just thing to do."

Jack let himself out, leaving as quickly as he arrived. The noisy elevator took him to the lobby, and his cell rang as he exited the building. Jack continued down the sidewalk as he took the call.

"Is this Jack Swyteck?"

"Yes. Who's this?"

"I'm Special Agent Ferguson with the FBI."

Jack stopped. It was something he heard in Ferguson's voice.

"I'm calling about your wife, Agent Henning."

CHAPTER 85

Andie is in surgery."

The words registered, but everything else Jack heard from Agent Ferguson was a blur. Not until he hung up and started breathing again could he begin to think straight.

I need a car.

Andie had been airlifted by helicopter from the river to Shands Hospital in Gainesville, seventy miles from Live Oak. The Towson family was long gone, and renting a vehicle would take precious time, but Jack recalled seeing a Cadillac in Cynthia Porter's driveway. He ran back to Pine Avenue and banged on the front door. Virginia was surprised to see him again so soon, sweating and breathless as he was, but she didn't hesitate.

"I'll pray for her," she said, as she pressed the car keys into his hand.

Jack made the necessary phone calls while speeding south on I-75. First to Theo, who would fly up with Righley. Then to Andie's parents in Seattle.

"Should we get on a plane?" her mother asked.

Jack flashed forward thirty years, imagining Righley in Andie's place. "I would."

Jack made good time to Gainesville, though it seemed to take forever. Another call to Ferguson yielded no further information. Jack left Cynthia's Cadillac with the hospital valet attendant and ran inside. His photo and personal info were already in the system from his previous visits to Mark and Liz, so he breezed through Reception and hurried to the waiting room outside the surgery suite. Agent Ferguson introduced himself—the first time Jack had ever met one of Andie's undercover partners.

"How is she?" asked Jack.

"She's been in surgery for about an hour. We'll know soon."

"What happened?"

"Her weapon discharged in close combat. Contact shot to the perp was fatal, but the bullet passed right through. Andie was hit on the ricochet. I had a chance to talk to her for a couple seconds before the airlift. She didn't even know she was shot until we caught up with her."

"Where was she hit?"

"Left kidney."

The pneumatic doors to the surgical suite opened, a doctor emerged, and a nurse pointed her to Jack.

"Mr. Swyteck?"

"Yes."

"Dr. Coleman. Your wife is one strong woman. She's going to be fine."

Jack wanted to hug her.

"She was sufficiently stable for us to do reconstruction, so we were able to salvage the kidney with pledgeted sutures and wrapping. We'll monitor that over the next few days, but she should have no need for further surgery."

"Thank God. You know she was pregnant, right?"

"Yes. Now, your wife did lose a lot of blood before medics were able to reach her."

"But everything is okay?"

"When a pregnant woman loses that much blood so suddenly, it's a shock to the entire system."

Jack understood what she was saying. "So—"

"I performed a D and C."

Dilation and curettage. It was a term Jack remembered from Andie's first miscarriage, before Righley.

"I'm sorry," the doctor said. "She did lose the baby."

There was suddenly a hole in Jack's heart, but he didn't let himself fall into it. He was more worried about how Andie would handle the loss.

"Does she know yet?"

"No."

Jack took a breath. "How long until the anesthesia wears off?" he asked.

"Another forty-five minutes or so. You can sit with her in Recovery if you like. Be there when she wakes."

"Thank you," said Jack. "I'd like that."

The doctor pointed him in the right direction, and Jack entered the recovery room. It was a large, open area with a nurses' station in the center, surrounded on all four walls by patient bays with privacy curtains. Andie was alone in Bay No. 3. The curtain was peeled back so that the nursing staff could keep an eye on her. She was sound asleep and—Jack had almost forgotten—a dyed blonde.

He went to the rail, squeezed her hand, and gave her a kiss. She didn't stir, and her eyes remained closed, but the warmth from her lips was response enough.

"Hey, beautiful," he whispered, still holding her hand.

Jack stayed there, standing at the rail, watching Andie sleep. He thought about how he would break the sad news to her. There was no easy way. *It's no one's fault? We can try again?*

He watched her for another minute, and then his gaze drifted away. His thoughts went from what had happened to Andie in the last few hours, to what had happened in the last three weeks, to what had happened in Live Oak three-quarters of a century ago. He was thinking, especially, of James Howard coming back from the river. Going home to his wife. Maybe sitting down next to her and holding Lula's hand the way Jack was holding Andie's. And then telling his wife what those men had forced him to watch them do to their only child.

Jack leaned over the rail, slipped his arms gently around Andie's shoulders, and pressed his cheek lightly against hers. Then he did something he hadn't done in a long time—something that he'd almost forgotten he could do.

He let the tears come.

AUTHOR'S NOTE

Although *A Death in Live Oak* is a work of fiction, some scenes are based on the historical record of the lynching of fifteen-year-old Willie James Howard in Live Oak, Florida, on January 2, 1944. The principal documentation I relied on are the written, unsworn statement of Alexander Phillip Goff and the sworn affidavits of Willie James' parents, James and Lula Howard. These documents are part of what historians refer to as the "Lanier Report," prepared by David Lanier, the acting state attorney appointed by Florida governor Spessard Holland in 1944.

Certain facts are undisputed. Cynthia Goff was the daughter of former state legislator Alexander Phillip Goff and a sophomore at the all-white Suwannee High School. Fifteen-year-old Willie James attended the separate Douglass High School and worked at the white-owned dime store where Cynthia also worked. In December 1943, Willie James gave Christmas cards to his coworkers. He signed his card to Cynthia "with L." In a letter of apology dated January 1, he again expressed his affection for Cynthia. On January 2, 1944, Mr. Goff and two other men, Reginald Scott Sr., a local white farmer, and S. B. "Mack" McCullers, a local white salesman, drove to the Howard house. They left with Willie James and took him to the sawmill where James Howard worked. The men then drove Willie James and his father to the Suwannee River, just east of Suwannee Springs. On January 3, 1944, the body of Willie James was found and removed from the river. His wrists and ankles were bound. In a matter of days, James and Lula Howard sold their house and moved to Orlando.

There are conflicting accounts of what happened between Mr. Goff's arrival at the Howard residence and the recovery of Willie James' body the following day. According to Lula and James Howard, the men took their son at gunpoint, picked up James Howard from his place of work at the Bond-Howell Lumber Company, and then forced Mr. Howard to watch as they hog-tied Willie James and then gave him a choice: roll into the river or be shot. He chose the river. According to Goff, he showed Mr. Howard the letter that Willie James had written to his daughter, and Mr. Howard willingly went with them to the river, where the plan was for Mr. Howard to "chastise the boy himself for his misdeed." Goff admitted that he tied Willie James' hands and feet but stated that he did so only "to keep him from running so that his father could whip him" with a switch. Willie James became "defiant," stated Goff, and shouted that "he would die before letting any man dady [*sic*] or white man put a licking on him." Despite Goff's professed efforts to stop him, Willie James jumped into the river and drowned. Willie James' father, Goff stated, "stood by and viewed the son without attempting to prevent this happening."

As news spread, Thurgood Marshall, special counsel to the NAACP and later a Supreme Court justice, demanded that Governor Holland call for a full investigation. In a letter, Governor Holland sent Goff's written statement to Marshall and promised protection for James Howard to come to Live Oak and testify before a grand jury. But the governor cautioned Marshall about the "particular difficulties involved where there will be testimony of three white men and probably the girl against the testimony of one Negro man."

A grand jury was convened in Live Oak in May 1944. James Howard appeared as the only witness. No indictment was returned. Harry T. Moore, a courageous activist who later lost his life in the civil rights movement (Moore and his wife were killed when their home was bombed on Christmas Day in 1951), made it his mission to persuade the U.S. Department of Justice to take up the case. He was unsuccessful.

James Howard died a few years after the death of his son. Lula Howard died in 2004, her last known public statement about the incident having been to the NAACP Board of Directors at their Orlando meeting on March 12, 1944. Goff and his two cohorts are also deceased, buried in a Live Oak cemetery. No one was ever held accountable.

The body of Willie James Howard lay in an unmarked grave for sixty years, until a local funeral director found a log of the death with the notation "lynched." The director, who was also a Suwannee County commissioner, organized a memorial service for Willie James at the Springfield Baptist Church, and on January 2, 2005, exactly sixty-one years after his death, a headstone was laid on the grave. It reads:

WILLIE J. HOWARD
BORN 7-13-28
DIED 1-2-44
MURDERED BY 3 RACIST [*SIC*]

This novel is faithful to the verifiable facts. Certain holes in the historical record were filled by the writer's imagination. My research was inconclusive as to whether Cynthia Goff knew what her father had done and, if so, how she felt about it. Her level of awareness, her true feelings, and all other details of her adult life are unknown to this author, except for the fact that she died in 2011 at the age of eighty-two. The character "Cynthia Porter" is purely fictional.

ACKNOWLEDGMENTS

Rule No. 1 in my creative writing process is "keep it fun," and I'm grateful to the talented group of friends who help me honor that rule. My longtime editor, Carolyn Marino, knows Jack Swyteck better than I do; and my agent, Richard Pine, and I are now officially entering our second quarter century of teamwork—which blows my mind.

You often hear it said that words matter. Well, grammar matters, too. I make plenty of mistakes, to be sure, but I'm grateful to my beta readers, who do their best to clean up the mess. Gloria Villa is like family. Janis Koch has that rare gift of the proverbial favorite teacher—tough when she has to be, but still makes you laugh at your mistakes and learn from them. Every writer should be so lucky.

Finally, to my wife, Tiffany. The publishing world could hardly have changed more since you told me to "go for it"—to follow my dream and be a writer. Your love and support have never wavered. From the bottom of my heart, thank you.

A final note. Jack and Andie have had a daughter since *Gone Again*, and some readers may have noticed that the spelling of her name has changed from Riley to Righley. That's because the parents of Righley Jimenez won the right to name a character in a Jack Swyteck novel at silent auction. Over the years, Jack Swyteck "character auctions" have raised more than $100,000 for a wide range of charitable causes. I'm happy to add the Florida Council Against Domestic Violence Foundation to that list, compliments of Debbie and Frank Jimenez. The foundation was established to ensure the long-term sustainability of lifesaving services for domestic violence survivors and their children by supporting Florida's forty-two certified domestic violence centers.

ABOUT THE AUTHOR

JAMES GRIPPANDO is a *New York Times* bestselling author of suspense. *A Death in Live Oak* is his twenty-sixth novel, and the fourteenth in the Jack Swyteck series. He was a trial lawyer for twelve years before the publication of his first novel, *The Pardon*, in 1994. He now practices law as counsel at Boies Schiller Flexner LLP and is also an adjunct professor of law and modern literature at the University of Miami School of Law. His novels are enjoyed worldwide in twenty-eight languages, and in 2017 he was the winner of the Harper Lee Prize in legal fiction. He lives in South Florida.